A TALE OF THE FIRST CRUSADE

Deus Vult

JAMES LOPEZ

Deus Vult

A Tale of the First Crusade

by James Lopez

ISBN

978-0-578-32542-2 Paperback

978-0-578-32541-5 e-book

Published by Iron Crown Publishing

Interior set in Palatino by Cathy Helms of Avalon Graphics

Interior illustrations by Nic Ferrari of Bramastudios.com

Edited by Aaron Redfern of Historicaleditorial.com

To
My Mom
The strength of your faith has always been an inspiration.

And

In Loving Memory Of
My Dad and Desie

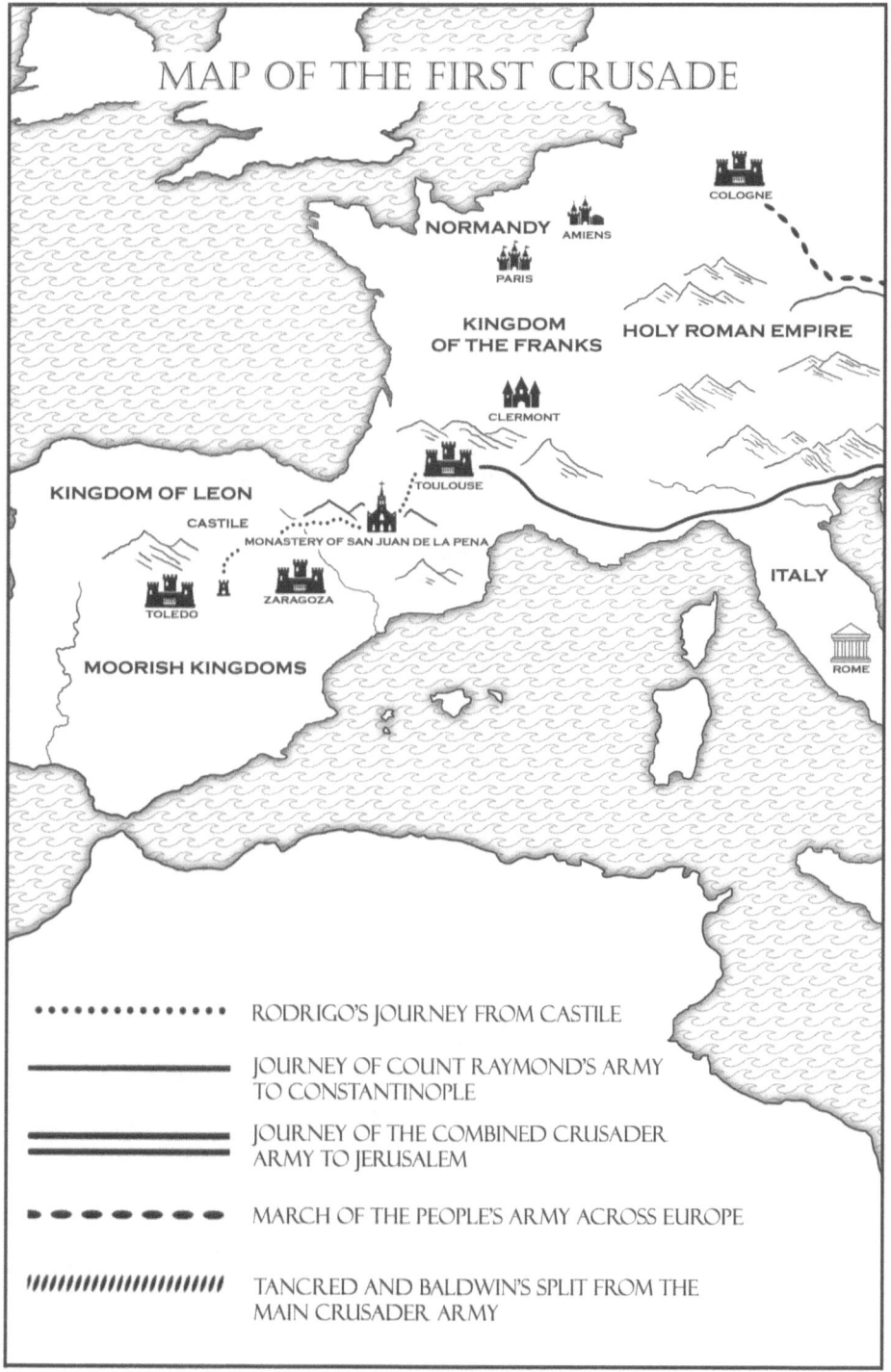

MAP OF THE FIRST CRUSADE

COLOGNE

NORMANDY
AMIENS

PARIS

KINGDOM
OF THE FRANKS

HOLY ROMAN EMPIRE

CLERMONT

TOULOUSE

KINGDOM OF LEON

CASTILE

MONASTERY OF SAN JUAN DE LA PENA

ITALY

TOLEDO

ZARAGOZA

ROME

MOORISH KINGDOMS

• • • • • • • • • • • RODRIGO'S JOURNEY FROM CASTILE

──────────── JOURNEY OF COUNT RAYMOND'S ARMY
TO CONSTANTINOPLE

════════════ JOURNEY OF THE COMBINED CRUSADER
ARMY TO JERUSALEM

▬ ▬ ▬ ▬ ▬ ▬ MARCH OF THE PEOPLE'S ARMY ACROSS EUROPE

//////////////////// TANCRED AND BALDWIN'S SPLIT FROM THE
MAIN CRUSADER ARMY

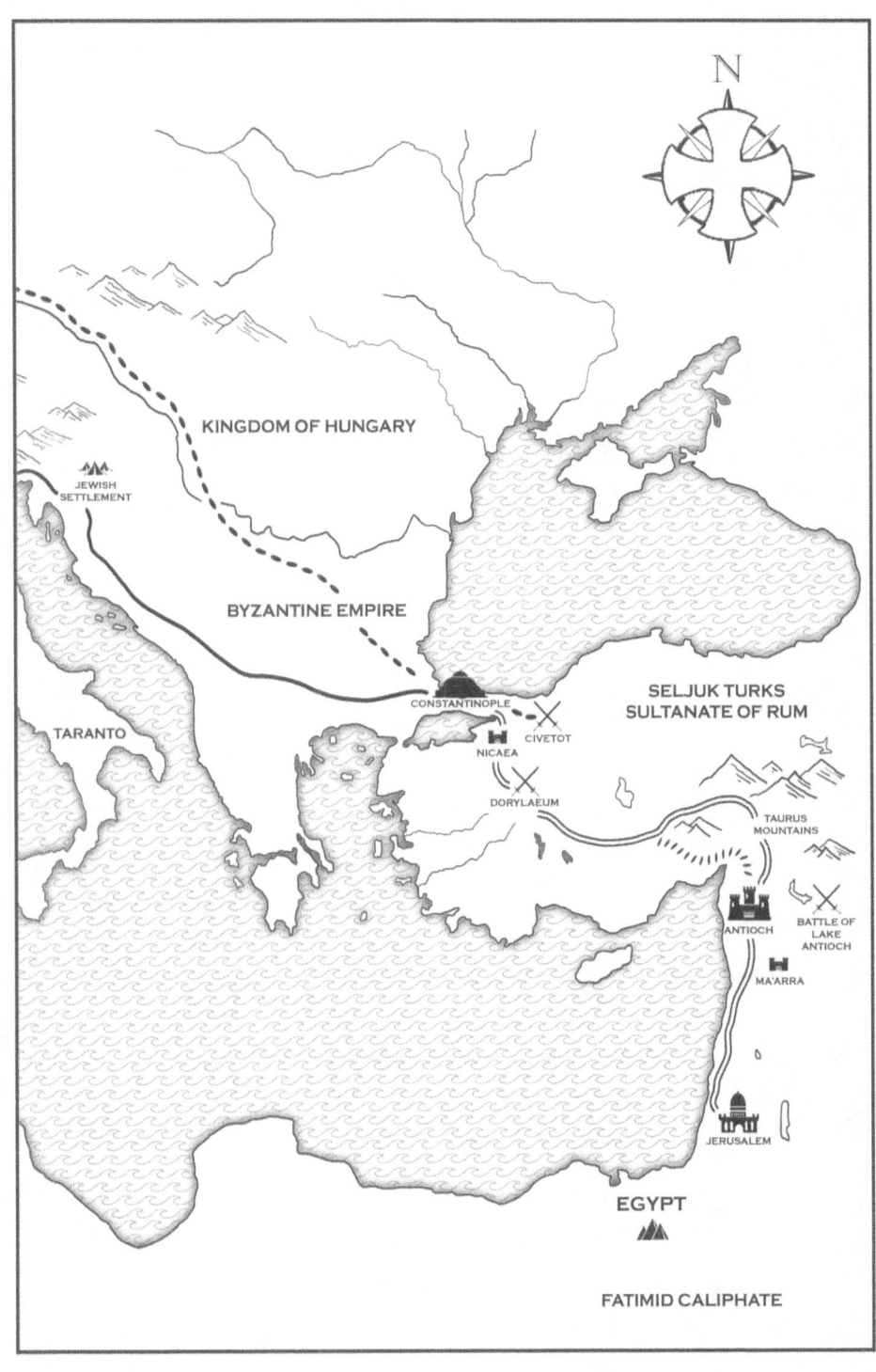

TABLE OF CONTENTS

PROLOGUE

The iridescent light from the stained-glass windows of the cathedral cast a luminescent glow about the figure in white robes as he stood high on the pulpit, looking down upon the huddled masses. Below him, princes, nobles, commoners, and peasants, all were spellbound by His Holiness, Pope Urban II, and all stood in silence, hanging upon his every word. He stood before them like a messenger from God, ready to deliver the final judgment.

The tension in the air was palpable, and the silence in the sanctuary was fraught with anticipation. The Pope's sermon was unlike anything they had ever heard before, and the terrible images conjured by his speech had filled his audience with horror and outrage. The Holy Land and holy city of Jerusalem, the very city where Christ had walked and was crucified, had been overrun by a Saracen horde that had violated everything that was sacred.

The Christians living in the city had been slaughtered like human cattle. None were spared, not even the women and children, whose blood filled the streets and whose corpses were trampled upon by the Saracen invaders. Torn from their homes and dragged from their places of worship, the Christian inhabitants cried out for mercy, but none was given. In the end, the churches were burned, the crosses torn down, and in their place the crescent moon of Islam was raised, casting its shadow across the land.

When the Pope's sermon finally concluded, the hushed crowd was stunned by what they had heard. His fiery words had branded a terrible picture in the minds of all those who came to hear him and had captured their imagination. At last, the Pope spoke again, his thunderous voice shattering the silence. "So let it be known that any man who, for devotion alone, and not to gain honor, money, or lands, journeys to Jerusalem and liberates the holy city from the hands of the Saracens, may substitute this journey for all penance, entering unto heaven upon death, and shall be spared from the fires of hell! *Deus vult!* God wills it!"

A great cheer erupted from the masses in the crowded cathedral that shook its very walls. Men, princes and peasants alike, embraced each other, ecstatic from the proclamation, and began shouting and chanting in unison: "*Deus vult! Deus vult!* God wills it! *God wills it!*"

✠

On November 27, 1095, Pope Urban II had ignited the passions and stirred the hearts and minds of all the nobles throughout Europe with his fiery sermon and promise of a lifetime of penance in return for a holy war against the Saracen Turks.

Europe's most powerful feudal lords had decided to put away their warring and quarrels with each other and unite in a combined effort to retake the Holy Land and the sacred city of Jerusalem from the Turkish invaders. The Pope's proclamation had set into motion a gathering of the princes of Europe as they prepared their armies to answer God's call to avenge the atrocities that had taken place in Jerusalem and restore the rule of the Pope and the holy Catholic Church. An eternity in heaven was promised to all those who took up the cross and the sword and set upon the perilous journey to carry out the will of almighty God.

DARKNESS BEFORE THE DAWN

Dark storm clouds blanketed the sky, and thunder echoed through the valley. The flashes of lightning revealed the silhouette of a lone horseman who struggled down the winding path beneath the pouring rain.

The winds howled, and the darkness of night had descended upon the valley as the rains beat mercilessly down upon the perilous mountainside path. Muddy water flowed down the pass beneath the horse's hooves, causing the beast to slip frequently, and threatened to send both horse and rider tumbling over the cliff and into the valley below.

The young knight dismounted and began leading the beast slowly down a narrow part of the pass that rounded a corner. The water rushing down the pass was now ankle high and cascaded over the cliff on his right like a waterfall. Lowering his head against the violent wind and stinging rain, he squinted and gritted his teeth as he doggedly moved forward in the middle of the raging tempest. A flash of lightning brought him backward in time for a brief moment to when he had lowered his head and knelt, receiving the touch of a sword on his shoulders, bestowing upon him the honor of knighthood. The crackling of thunder that followed brought back the concerned faces of loved ones bidding farewell as he had set out alone from his home in Castile, weeks ago. He knew he had come too far to turn back now or let anything stand in his way.

Amidst the thunder and pouring rain, an even louder noise from above caught his attention and thrust him back into the present. He turned to look up and was struck by a sudden deluge as water swept down the mountainside. His horse whinnied in terror as the force of the flood waters tore them from the path and dragged them both toward the edge of the cliff and the muddy darkness below.

He flailed his arms in a panic, frantically clawing at anything he could find to hold on to as he felt himself careening over the edge. His hands grasped the empty air, and he felt weightless for a moment before his back and head slammed against a steep slope. Pain shot through his body as he began to tumble end over end down the mountainside. Jagged rocks and small trees tore at his sides and limbs as he fell. He desperately tried to slow his descent, but to no avail against the force of the water rushing down the muddy slope.

He continued to tumble out of control down the mountainside until it felt as though he were about to lose consciousness, but at last, his body collided with a large tree, which finally broke his fall. His breath came slowly and in great heaves as he clung to the tree with water flowing all around him. When he was finally able to catch his breath, he opened his eyes, looked around, and realized he had reached the tree line at the bottom of the steep slope. A flash of lightning revealed his horse lying on its side, pinned against some trees not far away.

Battered and bruised, he felt his body and moved his limbs, looking for signs of broken bones, but there were none. He was covered in mud and his tunic was shredded, but his mail armor had saved his flesh from being torn to pieces by the sharp rocks and small trees during the fall. Slowly and cautiously, he stood up and, using the nearby trees to steady himself, he made his way to his horse, wading through the rushing water.

When he reached his horse, its head was under the muddy, flowing water, and there was no movement. Its body was still, twisted and broken. The young knight stood by the once proud steed and leaned over it, placing his hands upon its neck as he lowered his head. The rain fell from his forehead in a steady stream as he stood over the beast and closed his eyes, recalling the fearlessness it had shown when they had charged into battle one year ago. The victory that day had been great, and his actions had earned him the honor of being knighted.

"Thank you . . ." he said, bidding his final farewell beneath the thunder and pouring rain. He stood motionless for a time before lifting his hands and slowly began removing items from the saddle. He had lost his sword, his lance, and most of his belongings, but taking what was left, he packed the items into a saddlebag, which he slung over his shoulder before making his way downward into the forest.

Into the inky blackness, he blindly made his way forward through the forest. After he had staggered through the darkness for what seemed like an eternity, the slope of the forest floor began to level off, and the trees began to thin. The rain had slowed to a drizzle, and the angry sky was now calm and gray as dawn began to break. A light mist arose from the forest floor and curled about his body as he walked, and all was a heavy, dreamy, white silence as he wandered into a clearing.

The young knight's legs felt as though they were about to collapse beneath him, so he sat down to rest upon a large, flat stone that jutted out from the misty forest floor. His head hung low, and his heart felt heavy as he pondered his difficult, near hopeless situation. He clenched his fists and squeezed his eyes shut. It was the same feeling he'd had many years ago as a young boy, the old and faded memories echoing from his past. As a child he stood, shivering and alone with naught but the clothes on his back, when he was brought into the court of his uncle after his father was slain by raiding Saracen Moors. He recalled the men bringing in the lifeless body of his father while he stood by, helpless and alone. His uncle had graciously taken him in and raised him, and even though his uncle had always treated him like one of his own sons, deep inside he had always felt the need to prove himself worthy of

3

the kindness his uncle had shown him and live up to his great name.

Months ago, news of the Pope's proclamation and calls for a holy war had reached the Kingdom of León. He had listened with wide eyes to the incredible news. Eager to test himself and bring honor to his family's name, he had set out alone from his home in hopes of joining the army of Count Raymond of Toulouse who was gathering forces to journey to the Holy Land. The count would be holding a great tournament in the coming days to allow knights and warriors to earn honor and distinguish themselves in combat.

He hung his head with the realization that the tournament was only days away, but with almost no provisions, no horse, and no idea where he was, there was little hope of competing in Count Raymond's tournament. He heard a voice deep inside him as he recalled the words of his uncle: *No matter what situation you find yourself in, be strong in your faith, never lose hope, and always give thanks to God.* His fists loosened, and he opened his eyes and looked to the heavens with a sigh. Though his situation was bleak, he knew he could have easily suffered great injury or even death from the fall, but he had not.

He got up from the rock he was sitting on and knelt on the cold, hard ground. He put his elbows on the rock and folded his hands in prayer as he bowed his head and closed his eyes. *Lord God, thank you for sparing my life and keeping me safe from injury. But I am lost, oh Lord, and need your help. If it is your will that I am to take part in Count Raymond's tournament and join his forces as they journey to the Holy Land, please help me find my way.*

Rising from the ground, he looked around the clearing. He knew that he was at the bottom of a deep ravine with the high cliffs rising up just beyond the forest he had wandered through. He decided to follow along the base of the cliff with the hope of finding a path that would lead him back to the road he had been on before being swept into the ravine.

He walked through the forest along the base of the cliff for a long time, until the trees began to thin again and he came to another clearing. He stopped and stared for a moment, unsure that he could believe what he was seeing. Rising out of the mist like a mythical palace, he beheld a series of buildings in the distance that seemed as though they were carved from the solid stone cliff itself. The magnificent buildings had intricately carved steps that led up to terraces, and some of the buildings had two or three levels. Flowering gardens could be seen on the terraces, and well-manicured trees and bushes lined the front of the buildings. All the structures were so perfectly recessed into the base of the cliff that they were nearly camouflaged from sight. Had he not walked into the clearing, he would have missed them entirely.

He rubbed his eyes, staring in near disbelief. *Is what I am seeing real? Why would there be such a place in the middle of nowhere?*

He continued to walk farther into the clearing, and ahead of him he could make out a path that led to the main building. On the outside of the building, above the large wooden doors at the front, he could see the shape of a cross. It appeared to be a church or possibly a monastery. He followed the path until he came to the double doors at the entrance of the building. He grasped the large iron ring attached the door, then lifted it and let it fall with a thud as he stood and waited. A few moments passed, and he could hear movement from inside. Then one of the large wooden doors creaked open to reveal a young woman who peered at him from inside.

She was dressed in the black robes of a nun and wore a wooden cross about her neck. She had answered the door with a smile, but her smile began to fade and her brow began to crease as her eyes moved up and down, studying him. "What happened to you?" she asked. "Were you robbed and beaten?"

"No," he answered, looking down and picking at a shred of fabric from his torn tunic. "I was on my way to Toulouse when I became caught in the storm and my horse and I were swept over the mountain pass. My horse was killed, and I wandered for a long time before I found this place. Can you help me?" He looked back up at the young woman. "I have some coin, but most of my belongings were lost. I can pay you a little . . ."

The young woman hesitated for a moment, then moved back as she opened the door and motioned for him to enter. Her smile returned. "Please, come in. What is your name, sir?" she asked as he entered.

"My name is Sir Rodrigo Santos. I am a knight from Castile," he answered, looking around. The inside of the building was clean and spacious, but humble. There were no stained-glass windows, ornamentation, or tapestries adorning the plain stone walls. There were only wooden benches, a pulpit, and some wooden tables near the front of the sanctuary. *Strange,* he thought. *This humble interior belies the extraordinary exterior of these buildings.* "What is this place?"

"This is the monastery of San Juan de la Peña, and I am Sister Mary, one of its caretakers," she replied.

Rodrigo saw a cross hanging on a wall at the back of the sanctuary and bowed his head in silence for a moment. *Thank you, Lord, for hearing my prayers and bringing me to this place.* He reached into his saddlebag and withdrew a small bag of coins, which he extended to Sister Mary. "Here. It is all I have."

"Please, sir," she gently replied, "there is no need for you to pay. This monastery welcomes all who come here, and no one in need is turned away. There are some rooms here where you may stay and rest a while. There is not much there, but it is quiet and comfortable. Toulouse is only a few days' journey by horse, but several by foot, I am afraid. I must go, but when I come back, I will bring you some food. There is a bucket of water there to clean yourself and a straw mat to sleep on. You look like you could use some rest."

Rodrigo returned her kind smile and nodded. His eyelids felt heavy, and his limbs ached with every movement. "Thank you, Sister," he said as he followed her to the back of the monastery and entered a room. It was simple, and in the middle of the room was a wooden chair and a table with some drinking water. On the wall there was a cross. A straw mat lay in the corner with a blanket, and next to it was a large bucket of water and a small cloth.

Rodrigo removed his tattered tunic, armor, and boots and washed the mud from his face and body. He splashed some water over his head and placed the cloth against his face as trails of brown water cascaded down his neck and chest. *If I leave on foot tomorrow, I will not be able to compete in the tournament, but, God willing, I may still be able to join Count Raymond's army. I cannot return to my family and uncle a failure. I must find a way to answer the Pope's call to liberate Jerusalem and the Holy Land from the Turks.* He gripped the cloth tightly and twisted it with all his strength, wringing every last drop of water back into the bucket. When he finished cleaning himself, he looked around the room. His clothes were still damp, but there was a monk's robe folded on one of the tables. Donning the robe, he lay down on the straw mat and almost instantly drifted into a deep slumber.

2

WISDOM FROM A STRANGER

The creak of the chair startled Rodrigo from his sleep. He sat up and stared at a strange man sitting at the table, eating from a plate of food. Rodrigo immediately took notice of his garb, for he had not seen its like before. A brown cloak was draped over the back of the chair, faded and worn but with an intricately woven pattern with strange symbols that were foreign in nature. He wore a blue tunic with gold fringe, fastened with a leather belt with a gold buckle, and brown trousers. The worn leather sandals on his feet were in the style of the ancient Romans. *Who is this strange man? His clothes do not look like they are from Europe, nor from any country that I am familiar with.*

The man turned his chair to face Rodrigo, who was sitting up on the mattress. He had a broad smile under a thick black beard and wavy black hair with streaks of gray. The stranger stared at Rodrigo with coal-black eyes that seemed to look right through him.

"You must have been tired. You have been sleeping most of the day," the man said, his deep voice breaking the silence and nearly startling Rodrigo. He held up a piece of bread that he was eating. "Pull up a chair and join me. There is plenty here to eat."

Rodrigo felt his stomach growling. He stood up slowly and

gingerly as he stretched his sore and bruised limbs and stiff back. The last rays of the setting sun illuminated the small room through a window in the corner. "Yes, I will join you. Thank you." He pulled up a chair and sat down. The stranger passed him the drinking water and some bread with a plate of meat and fruit. Rodrigo bowed his head and said a quick prayer before he began hungrily consuming his meal. The stranger ate in silence as Rodrigo devoured his food like a starving wolf. When Rodrigo was finally satisfied and pushed his plate aside, the stranger spoke.

"It seems you have not eaten in weeks," he said with a laugh. He glanced at Rodrigo's armor and tunic lying by the bed. "Though you are wearing a monk's robes, I can clearly see that you are not one. Tell me your name, sir, and what brings you to this place."

Rodrigo introduced himself and recounted his fateful journey from Castile on his way to Count Raymond's tournament in Toulouse. "Although I will not arrive in time to compete in the tournament, I may still be able to join Count Raymond's army. I will not let this misfortune deter me from answering God's call to take back the Holy Land and liberate Jerusalem from the Saracen Turks. The atrocities being committed there against the Christians must be stopped." The stranger said nothing, but stared at Rodrigo with a faint smile as he sat back in his chair. "And what about you?" Rodrigo asked. "Your clothes and your cloak have strange markings. I have not seen their like before. What is your name, and where do you come from?"

"My name is Marcellinus," the man said. "I am a traveler and a wanderer and am new to this part of Europe. I was once a chronicler in the royal Byzantine court in Constantinople, but that was many years ago. I was much younger then, and at that time, I became disillusioned with my work and began traveling extensively. My travels eventually brought me to Jerusalem, where I worked as a scribe for several years, and then later to Alexandria in Egypt. From there I journeyed to Italy, and I have been traveling through Europe for nearly a year now. I work in different places to replenish my purse, and when the wanderlust strikes me, I set off on a new journey and adventure." He smiled.

Rodrigo sat up and leaned forward at the mention of Jerusalem. "You were in Jerusalem for several years? When did you leave, and what did you see while living there?"

"It was nearly three years ago that I left Jerusalem. It is an ancient and magnificent city with a wondrous history. I enjoyed my time there; however, I find myself only able to stay in one place for so long." Marcellinus poured some more water into his cup while Rodrigo stared at him intently. "I guess one could say that I was born with a restless soul."

Rodrigo's eyes narrowed. *Why did he not mention anything about the crimes being committed against the Christians in the city? Is he hiding something?*

"You said you are originally from Constantinople. Are you a Christian?" Rodrigo asked.

"I was raised in the Orthodox Christian Church from the time of my youth, so yes, I am Christian," Marcellinus said before taking a drink of water. "Since then, however, I have grown older, and wiser, and now I choose to worship God in my own way, not in the way of Orthodox Christianity or Roman Catholicism." Marcellinus lowered his cup, and his gaze locked with Rodrigo's. "I know what you are thinking. One can hardly travel through Europe at this time and not hear all that is being said about what is taking place in Jerusalem and the Holy Land." Rodrigo's gaze softened, and he looked down at his plate for a moment as Marcellinus continued. "I *can* tell you this—all the stories of the atrocities being committed against the Christians in the city by the Turks at this time are not true."

"What?" Rodrigo exclaimed, frowning. *He would dare to suggest that the Pope is spreading lies?* "How can they not be true? The Pope himself has spoken about the slaughter of innocent Christians in Jerusalem. You would accuse the Pope of lying to the people of Europe?" he asked, pointing his finger at Marcellinus.

Marcellinus's expression did not change as he sat back and tore a piece of bread from his plate. "I am simply telling you what I have seen and witnessed with my own eyes," he said in a calm voice.

Rodrigo put his hands on the table and leaned toward

Marcellinus. "Tell me then, why would the Pope lie about such things?"

"Why, indeed?" Marcellinus answered. He leaned back in his chair and looked at Rodrigo while he took a bite of bread. There was silence for a tense moment, but Rodrigo stood up from the table and walked to the center of the room as Marcellinus continued. "It is a good question to ask, so let us take a moment and discuss it. Tell me, what effect have the Pope's words about the atrocities in Jerusalem had on all the nobles and princes in Europe?"

Rodrigo paused for moment as he thought. "It has brought them all together, united under one cause, to reclaim the Holy Land and the city of Jerusalem and restore the rule of the Pope and the holy Catholic Church."

"That is correct," Marcellinus replied. "What is more important to understand is that this unification has stopped the constant warring and fighting among those nobles in Christendom. It is true that Jerusalem is now under Turkish control, but they took the city nearly four hundred years ago! In the holy city right now, Christians, Jews, and Muslims all live together in relative peace. Most of the killing being committed by the Turks at this time is against other Turks. They are constantly fighting each other for lands and power, much the same way the Christians do here in Europe."

Rodrigo remained speechless, and he began pacing about the room as he thought. *So, not only is he suggesting the Pope is spreading lies, but it is to further some kind of agenda?* "I cannot believe that our holy Pope would lie outright to the people of Europe for the reasons you have mentioned," Rodrigo said, stopping and folding his arms across his chest.

"The Pope's message is not only for the sake of unity among the European nobility," said Marcellinus. "I believe there are other reasons as well."

"What other reasons?"

"The Turks have been encroaching upon the borders of the Byzantine Empire for some time now," Marcellinus said. "It is fairly well known that Emperor Alexios Komnenos, the Byzantine ruler, has made an appeal to the Pope for aid against the Turks. So, it seems that the Pope has yet another reason to call for a Christian incursion into the Holy Land, none of which has anything to do with atrocities being committed against Christians in Jerusalem." He wiped his hands on a cloth next to his plate.

Rodrigo said nothing, but shook his head and began pacing again. *That may be true, but regardless of the reasons, how could the Pope, the Holy Father, be spreading lies and falsehood to the people?*

"And I have also heard," Marcellinus continued, "that the Pope has offered all who take up this journey penance for all their sins."

Rodrigo stopped pacing and turned to Marcellinus. "Yes, that is true. What of it?"

"Is the Pope God? Does he have the power to absolve the masses of their sins?" Marcellinus asked, his eyes narrowing as he looked at Rodrigo.

"Well, no, but he speaks for God!" Rodrigo answered loudly.

"Does he?" asked Marcellinus, the tone of his voice now matching Rodrigo's. "So, tell me, does God want all the nobles in Europe to wage a holy war against the Turks for reasons that are naught but lies?" Marcellinus's deep voice was loud and commanding and, in that moment, Rodrigo heard the voice of his uncle. Marcellinus's piercing gaze showed an unwavering clarity as they stared at each other. Rodrigo averted his gaze and stared at the ground. He searched for words but could find none.

Marcellinus put his cloth down, calmly pushed his chair back, and stood up. He turned his gaze from Rodrigo and looked around for a moment as he dusted some crumbs off the front of his tunic. "I respect you, Sir Rodrigo, for your passion and conviction of what you believe is the truth. If it is your destiny to travel to the Holy Land, then you will see with your own eyes what is truth and what is not." He replaced his chair back under the table and walked to the door before turning back to Rodrigo. "Wherever fate leads you, always remember this. Place your trust in God and not in man. Men are fallible and may lead you astray, but God will always guide you to truth and salvation." Rodrigo looked up at Marcellinus, who gave him a quick smile and nod before going out the door and closing it behind him.

Outside the room, Rodrigo could hear Marcellinus speaking in the sanctuary with Sister Mary, although he could not hear what they were saying. That evening, Rodrigo sat at the table for a long time, staring at his drinking cup and thinking about all that had been said. *I cannot believe that His Holiness the Pope and the holy Catholic Church are spreading lies and falsehoods for their own political ends. There is only one thing I can do. I must journey to the Holy Land, not only to bring honor to my family's name, but to discover for myself what is truth and what is a lie. If everything the Pope has said is truth, then I will be carrying out the will of God. If everything he said was a lie, then . . .* Rodrigo frowned and lowered his head, and his hands knotted into fists upon the table. He got up to lie back down on the straw mattress. Night had fallen and it was now completely dark in the room, yet he lay awake staring at the ceiling. At last, he fell asleep, tossing and turning in a fitful slumber.

✠

A cock's crow roused Rodrigo from his sleep. Rising from his bed, he gathered his belongings. As he left the room, he saw Sister Mary in the sanctuary carrying some books and approached her. "Sister Mary, my thanks for everything you have done for me. Your kindness and the hospitality and generosity of this monastery will not be forgotten. I will set out for Toulouse and do not want to waste any time, since I travel by foot. Will you help me one last time and tell me what paths I must take to take to get there?"

"Oh!" she exclaimed, her eyes wide and a smile on her face. "Did he not tell you?"

"Who? Tell me what?" Rodrigo asked.

"The man that was here, Marcellinus. He left early this morning, but said he wished to aid you in your travels. He said you were on a journey to the Holy Land and hoped to find something there."

A smile came across Rodrigo's face. "That is true. What did he not tell me?"

"He left one of his horses for you. And a full pack of provisions.

The horse is tied outside the monastery, and the provisions are there as well."

Rodrigo smiled again and bowed his head. *Selfless acts of kindness seem to be rare thing in this world, but since I arrived they have been shown to me twice, by both Sister Mary and Marcellinus.* "I may or may not pass this way again. Thank you for everything, and if the man Marcellinus ever comes back, please give him my humble thanks as well." Then, turning, he walked through the door and exited the monastery.

"I will," said Sister Mary. "Follow the main path from the monastery until you reach the village. The villagers will guide you the rest of the way. God be with you!" she called out as she watched him from the doorway.

Rodrigo walked to the post outside the monastery where the horse and provisions were waiting for him. He took the reins and mounted. The sun was cresting the cliffs above the monastery, flooding the valley with the light of the new day. Rodrigo took a deep breath and filled his lungs with the crisp morning air as he thought about how quickly his fortune had changed and the destiny that lay before him. He spurred the horse into a gallop down the pathway toward the village. Toulouse was only days away, and Count Raymond's tournament awaited.

3

THE TOURNAMENT

The blaring trumpets signaled the beginning of the assault on the castle walls. With their swords, axes, and shields raised high, the attackers let out a thunderous battle cry as they raced toward the walls. Rodrigo felt his heart pounding in a mixture of fear, excitement, and pure adrenaline as the assault began.

The knights and warriors in the tournament were divided into two groups, the attackers and the defenders. A section of Count Raymond's castle was used to conduct the battle. Fifty warriors would assault the wall with ladders, while another fifty would defend the castle walls and protect five flags placed in different areas along the wall. The two most difficult flags were placed in the well-protected flanking towers on either side.

In moments, the attackers had reached the base of the wall. The ladders went up, and metal hooks attached to the top of the ladders came down, biting into the wall. Frantically, the attackers began scrambling up the ladders as others tried to hold them in place to keep them from being pushed off the walls. The clash of steel rang out as axes and swords fell upon those who had reached the top. Their weapons had been blunted, but the dangers they faced were very real. It was not uncommon for men to suffer grave injuries or even be killed in such tournaments.

Rodrigo climbed as fast as he could. One of the grappling hooks on the ladder beside him was pried loose, and the ladder was pushed away from the wall. He watched as several men still hanging onto the ladder fell backward. As the ladder fell back to the ground, some of the men were caught by their fellow warriors below, but others landed hard upon the ground. Reaching the top of the wall, Rodrigo leaped onto the walkway in the midst of the yelling and the chaos. Immediately, he was attacked by two of the defenders, who came at him from both sides. A heavy mace swung downward and was met with Rodrigo's sword as he parried the blow. An axe came crashing down upon his shield on the other side with such force that his arm went numb from the impact.

Bending low at the knees and wheeling around, Rodrigo swung his sword in an arc at the legs of the warrior on his left. The heavy blow buckled the knees of the warrior, who collapsed on the stone walkway. Rodrigo turned quickly again and raised his shield to defend against the blow he knew was coming from the other side. The mace came crashing down onto his shield, just above his head. Lowering his shield and striking quickly before the warrior could recover from the swing, Rodrigo smashed the pommel of his sword into the warrior's face. Blood sprayed from the warrior's shattered nose, knocking him off balance and sending him reeling backward.

Rodrigo hesitated for a moment, staring at the man as he fell to the ground, blood pouring from between the man's fingers as he held them to his face. Rodrigo's heart was pounding, and his mind was racing. He did not wish to seriously injure his opponents, but he felt caught in whirlwind of violence and action with no choice but to push forward. He lowered his head and set his jaw as he swung his sword and fought his way toward the flags. *I must not let fear and concern cause me to lose sight of my goal!*

High above, two men watched the action from a tower overlooking the castle wall. One of the men, Bishop Adhemar of Le Puy, watched the violence and chaos unfolding below with a keen interest, his steady gaze following every action. The permanent scowl etched on his stern face was accentuated by his forked beard. A papal legate and representative of the Pope, Adhemar was no ordinary bishop. Aside from his duties in the Church, he commanded troops, including several ranks of cavalrymen, and had been ordered by the Pope to join with Count Raymond's forces as they prepared to journey to the Holy Land. Upon his arrival at Count Raymond's castle, it was Adhemar who had organized the tournament and spread the word throughout the lands.

Adhemar pointed to one of the warriors below. "Look, this one shows some promise," he said, leaning over to Count Raymond, who watched the battle beside him. "He fights as though his very life depends on victory." Adhemar stared intently as he took a sip of wine from his goblet. *I will need to find out who this man is. He may be one that I can use.*

"He certainly fights like a man who believes in the cause," Raymond said, looking down at the battle. "We will see how long that lasts as the day goes on. Jerusalem will not fall in a single afternoon. The men who take it must be willing to give everything they have, and more. And that, Bishop Adhemar, will be the final test in a long and difficult campaign, if we make it that far." His kindly, bearded countenance was now marred with a frown as he turned away from the wall and sat down on a chair next to a table filled with meats, bread, and fine wine. Count Raymond of Toulouse was one of the wealthiest and most pious of the European nobles who had committed to waging a holy war for the Pope and the Catholic Church.

"If we make it that far? Do you have doubts, my lord?" said Adhemar, raising an eyebrow as he turned to Raymond.

"I have been in enough wars and campaigns to know that this difficult journey will test the mettle of all the men who go with us to the Holy Land," Raymond said, staring into his goblet as he swirled its contents.

"Yes, my lord," Adhemar said, turning his attention back toward the battle taking place below. "All the men shall be tested, and only the strongest, bravest, and most righteous will be there when Jerusalem falls."

"We shall see, Adhemar, we shall see," Raymond replied.

The battle for control of the walls raged below them throughout the morning while Count Raymond and Bishop Adhemar continued their conversation in the tower. All the while, Adhemar had kept a watchful eye on the individual actions of those engaged in combat.

"The tournament fighting has been quite fierce, my lord, as was expected," Adhemar said. Without taking his eyes off of the battle, he motioned for the servant waiting behind them to come and fill his goblet. "There are acts of skill and valor from both sides. I have my eye on a few who have stood out so far."

"Yes. The fighting has been intense," Raymond said as he set his empty goblet aside. "It is a shame that some have already given their lives to prove their honor and bravery. I do not wish to see any more good men throw their lives away needlessly for sport. Should that happen, I may consider calling an end to the tournament."

"What?" Adhemar turned from the battle and stared at Raymond with a frown. "No, my lord, you must not," he said firmly.

"I must not?" Raymond asked, looking back at Adhemar with raised eyebrows. "Need I remind you, Bishop Adhemar, that you are a guest here? I will do as I see fit in my own castle."

Adhemar took a sip of wine from his goblet, but his stern gaze did not break from Raymond's. "And need I remind you, my lord, that no one is above the Pope, and I, as his representative, insist that the tournament continue to its completion. The Pope has requested that five knights be chosen from this tournament for a special purpose. It is my duty to His Holiness to fulfill his request *after* the tournament has completed. You may do with the rest of the men as you please, but you must allow the tournament to continue to the end."

Count Raymond stood up from his chair and walked to the edge of the tower before turning to Adhemar. "Very well, Adhemar. But if any more of these warriors give their lives for this tournament, I will hold you responsible, and you will deliver the last rites yourself."

As Adhemar turned from Raymond back toward the action below, a faint smile curled upon his lips. "Of course, my lord. It would be my honor."

✠

The midday sun beat down upon the attacking force as they huddled in a group below the walls to rest from the fighting and lick their wounds. The fierce battle had raged all morning, and the sun was now high in the sky. The first assault had gone well, and the defenders had yielded two flags. The second assault had been much more difficult, as the defenders had used their experience from the first assault to repel the attackers more effectively and had only yielded one flag. The attackers were preparing for one final assault. The last two flags were in the towers on either side of the wall and would be even more difficult to capture.

Rodrigo wiped beaded sweat from his forehead with the back of his hand as the droplets ran down his face, stinging his eyes. His hair was matted and wet, and he knelt with one knee on the ground and his steel helmet on the other. He looked at the men around him. Most were sitting on the ground, leaning against their shields with their heads hung low. Some were lying flat on their backs, breathing heavily from near exhaustion.

Rodrigo's mail armor was damaged and torn in some areas from the force of the blows he had received, as was the armor of many others. His hand rested on the hilt of his heavily notched sword, and his shield lay by his side, dented and cracked. A heavy silence hung in the air, a stark change from the mood after the first assault, when the group had been buzzing with energy and ideas on how best to assault the walls and capture the flags.

Rodrigo looked down in thought as he replayed the first two assaults in his mind. *What would my uncle do in such a difficult situation?* His uncle, Rodrigo Diaz de Vivar, whom he was named after, was a Castilian warlord and a renowned hero and champion to his people. His uncle had faced overwhelming odds many times in battle and overcame them all with strategy, cunning, and bravery. He was not only a great warrior, but also a scholarly, learned man who had studied the great battles of antiquity. Rodrigo remembered sitting wide-eyed and silent as a young boy, fascinated as his uncle recounted these battles and discussed the strategies that had aided the victorious.

His uncle's words came floating back to him as he pondered their situation. *You see, Rodrigo, all warfare is based on deception. Where we are able to attack, we must appear unable and inactive. We must make the enemy believe we are far away when we are near and strike when they believe we are most vulnerable.*

Rodrigo looked around for a moment, and behind them, he saw the large tent where the wounded men were being treated. His eyes grew large as he stood up and called to the others. "Everyone, listen!" he yelled, waving for his companions to move closer to him. "Come close and listen! I have an idea of how we can capture the flags!"

Though they were exhausted from battle, the men gathered around Rodrigo to hear what his sudden enthusiasm was all about. When he had finished laying out his plans, they quickly dispersed and took their up their positions on the ground, gathering the ladders and their weapons in preparation.

✠

The trumpets blared from the castle, signaling the final assault. A battle cry went up from the attackers as the entire group rushed toward the tower on the far right of the wall. They did not divide their forces as was expected, but instead chose to concentrate their assault on a single target, raising several ladders up against the tower walls. Seeing what was happening, the defenders quickly moved their forces off of the wall and into the tower to repel the assault. The attackers scaled the ladders quickly with shields held high, fending off the terrible blows from axe and sword aimed at sending them down to the ground below.

Rodrigo watched the movement on the walls closely from behind the tent flap while he and others waited in the tents of the wounded. He gave a quick glance behind him at the men inside the tent, then yelled, "Now!" Throwing back the tent flap, he began running, carrying the front of the ladder in one hand and his shield in the other. Four men rushed out of the tent toward the wall, each pair carrying a ladder.

One pair broke off from the small group and headed toward the middle of the wall with their ladder, while Rodrigo and his companion moved closer to the tower on the far left. The ladders went up quickly, and the four men began scrambling to the top as some of the defenders finally noticed what was happening. A cry of alarm went up among the defenders as several left the battle and began moving quickly to the opposite tower. The two knights ascending the ladder in the middle of the wall had just reached the top when they were engaged by the defenders.

Rodrigo reached the top of the ladder unopposed and leaped over the battlement onto the walkway. He glanced at the men in the middle of the wall, holding off the defenders. The walkway was narrow, and the two could hold them back for a time, but not for long.

"Go and help them!" Rodrigo yelled as the man behind him stepped over the battlement onto the walkway. "I will go for the flag!"

The two split up as Rodrigo turned and ran toward the tower, drawing his sword. As he entered the tower, he skidded to a sudden halt. He lowered his sword, and his gaze traveled upward from a pair of large leather boots to the top of a spired helm. A gigantic Norman warrior stood before him, holding an axe in one hand and a sword in the other.

"Ha! Your little ruse may have worked, but did you really believe the flag would be left undefended?" the Norman warrior scoffed as he looked down at Rodrigo. The two stared at each other for a moment, but then the bearded giant roared like a lion and charged at Rodrigo. The fearsome warrior swung his axe as he charged, smashing Rodrigo's shield as it connected. The force of the blow split his damaged shield and spun Rodrigo around, and he landed on the floor. Rodrigo quickly scrambled away, throwing away the useless shield and narrowly avoiding the swing of the warrior's sword, which sent sparks flying as the metal struck the stone floor.

"Get up and face me!" the giant yelled as he pressed his relentless attack.

Rodrigo stood up and desperately swung his sword with both hands to parry the next blow from the warrior's axe. The metallic ring was deafening, and his sword snapped in half, unable to withstand the blow. Rodrigo's eyes went wide. Not knowing what else to do, he rushed the giant warrior as he recovered from the swing and lunged for his legs. The unexpected move caught the Norman off guard, causing him to teeter off balance for a moment before falling to the floor, yelling and cursing as he went.

Rodrigo sprang to his feet and, picking up the hilt of his broken blade, he ran to the base of the flag flying above the tower and struck with all his might. The metal bit into the wooden pole, but it did not break. Prying the broken blade loose, he struck again, but the heavy shaft held firm. Out of the corner of his eye, he saw the giant warrior swinging his sword from behind. Rodrigo ducked, and the sword glanced off the top of his helmet, sending it flying from his head to clatter across the tower floor. A sudden dizziness assailed him, and Rodrigo felt his legs go weak as he crumpled to the floor.

Flashes of light filled his vision, and he turned and looked up just as something fell across his face. Pulling it off, he realized it was the flag. The warrior's sword had glanced off his helmet and into the shaft of the flag, finally bringing it down. Enraged, the giant warrior recovered from his errant swing and roared as he lifted his sword above his head. Rodrigo sat helplessly, knowing there was nothing he could do.

Suddenly, a trumpet blast sounded in the distance, and cheering could be heard from the crowds all around. With a look of anger and defeat, the warrior lowered his weapons. The tournament was over, and the attackers had won.

4

THE CROSS AND THE QUESTION

T he crowded feasting hall was alive with conversation, laughter, eating, and drinking. The glow of light from the candles in the chandeliers above illuminated the great hall as the scent of roasting meats from the firepits nearby filled the room. Mortal enemies mere hours ago, the knights and warriors now gathered to feast together, celebrate the end of the tournament, and recount their personal deeds of valor from the day's combat.

Rodrigo smiled as he joked and laughed with those around him. He basked in the honor and pride he felt as one of the tournament victors, similar to the feeling he had experienced when he knelt on the battlefield among the slain and had been knighted by his uncle for his bravery. *Count Raymond must have noticed the strategy we used to win the battle when all seemed lost. Surely the tournament victors will be offered a place in his great army as they journey to the Holy Land.* Rodrigo looked around the great hall, and his smile disappeared as his gaze fell upon one of the warriors sitting at a table nearby. The warrior gingerly held a tankard to his lips and sipped his ale through cracked teeth under the red stains of his heavily bandaged face. Rodrigo lowered his head and avoided eye contact, staring down at the table, trying to recall the face of the warrior he had smashed with the pommel of his sword. *Our victory has not come without cost, however. Am I the cause of this man's injury? How many other men were injured in the fighting?*

A large hand clasped his shoulder from behind, causing Rodrigo to turn and look up. His smile returned as he saw the bearded face of the giant Norman staring down at him. Rodrigo shook his head and blinked his eyes. "Am I seeing things, or has the giant from the tower returned to menace me once again?" he asked aloud, eliciting laughter from those about him. "In truth, my head is still aching from the blow by your sword." He rubbed the top of his head, grimacing. "It took some time before I fully regained my senses."

The Norman warrior smiled as he looked down at Rodrigo and spoke in a deep voice. "You were extremely lucky today in the tower, my friend. If we were to fight again, I do not think the outcome would be the same."

"It may have been luck," Rodrigo said, taking a sip of ale and setting his tankard down. "Or . . . it may have been fate," he said with a grin. A murmur of laughter and agreement could be heard from those around the table.

"Perhaps it was your fate . . . on this day," the Norman warrior replied. "Should we face each other again, my friend, then we shall see the final outcome of your fate. Enjoy your evening." He removed his hand from Rodrigo's shoulder.

"You as well," Rodrigo said, raising his tankard in salute as the giant Norman turned and continued walking down the long rows of the feasting hall. The sounds of revelry and drinking were now growing louder in the hall as anticipation grew for an announcement by Count Raymond to recognize and honor the tournament victors.

Above the long rows of tables in the feasting hall was another table on a high platform overlooking the revelry. Count Raymond, Bishop Adhemar, and the other nobles sat at the table, looking down upon the crowded hall. A loud banging echoed through the great hall as two guards near the platform began to beat the ends of their spears on the wooden floorboards to silence the crowd. The sounds of carousal and conversation faded as Count Raymond stood up from the table to speak. Rodrigo lowered his head for a quick and silent prayer. *Lord God, I have done all I that can. I leave the rest in your hands.*

"We feast tonight in honor of a historic day of combat. Today we held the largest tournament ever seen in these lands. Joining me this evening is a representative of the Pope, Bishop Adhemar of Le Puy, and together we witnessed some of the fiercest and finest combat we have ever seen. I know that all of you came to this tournament, some traveling from distant kingdoms, to fight for the honor of joining my army on our journey to the Holy Land. This most difficult and dangerous quest calls for warriors who are not only the strongest, but the most determined and most dedicated to their faith in God. The risks of this journey are great, but the rewards are far greater. The Pope has promised us that heaven awaits all who take up the sword and embark on this noble quest, not for glory or for gold, but to deliver the Holy Land and the city of Jerusalem back into the hands of Christians from the grasp of the Saracen invaders. Although those attacking the wall were victorious, after witnessing the combat today, I have decided that *all of you* shall join me as we journey together to retake the Holy Land for God and all of Christendom!"

A raucous cheer went up from the men below, and wine spilled from goblets that were lifted high or tipped over as fists and the pommels of daggers were pounded on the wooden tables. The clamor slowly died away as Count Raymond lifted his hand, preparing to speak again.

"I would ask for a moment of silence to honor four warriors who gave their lives today, as a testament of their will to fight for this holy cause." Lowering their goblets and weapons, all the men in the hall bowed their heads to honor the slain. Rodrigo's brow creased as he lowered his head. *Four men gave their lives today for merely the chance to join Count Raymond's army?* His thoughts drifted back to scenes of devastation he had witnessed after battles with the Saracens. *How many more will be forced to give their lives on this perilous journey? I hope that our leaders will not be so cavalier with the lives of their men as they have been today in this tournament.*

The moment passed, and Count Raymond spoke again. "Bishop Adhemar would now like to recognize five knights who stood out amid today's combat for their strength, skill, and valor. I ask that you stand and come forth as your names are called." Count Raymond moved aside as Bishop Adhemar stood up and unrolled a scroll, looking out among the crowd.

The announcement was unexpected, and Rodrigo sat in tense silence, nearly holding his breath as the names were read from a list. *Such a recognition would bring great honor to my family's name.*

"Sir Richard of Hastings, Normandy; Sir Jean of Saint-Léger, Aquitaine; Sir William of Montrodón, Lorraine; Sir Geoffrey of Charney, Provence; and Sir Rodrigo of Castile, in the Kingdom of León." Rodrigo was the last to stand, and he let out a long exhale as the warriors around them began clapping and pounding the tables in recognition of their honor. Rodrigo looked around at the others who now stood in the feasting hall. Among them was the giant Norman warrior, who was standing a few tables away, towering above those around him. *So the giant now has a name: Sir Richard of Hastings.* "Your deeds in combat today stood out among your fellow warriors," Adhemar continued as he lowered the scroll. "As part of this recognition, I would like to meet with all of you personally. Please follow my servants. I will meet you in the sanctuary."

Rodrigo and the others exited the feasting hall and followed the servants down a long stone corridor, the sounds of revelry disappearing behind them. Rodrigo looked at the knights as they walked to see if he recognized any others from the tournament. Three of the men, Sir Geoffrey, Sir William, and Sir Jean, had been with him on the attacking side. All of them had captured flags during the assaults, and Sir Geoffrey had impressively captured two. Sir Geoffrey had also been with him when they had raced from the tents during the final assault.

The only knight from the defending side was Sir Richard. Besides their battle in the tower, Rodrigo recalled another time during the tournament when he had seen Sir Richard, standing at the top of the wall as Rodrigo scaled a ladder during one of the assaults. He had been barking orders to the other defenders and ruthlessly attacking those who reached the top of the wall, sending many back down to the ground below. *Undoubtedly, Sir Richard is a strong and fearsome warrior and will be a good man to have on our side.*

The servants opened a large door at the end of the hall and motioned for the knights to enter. Rodrigo marveled at the grandeur and opulence of the sanctuary, his mouth slightly agape. Beautiful, ornate tapestries and paintings adorned the walls, depicting Christ and various scenes from the Bible. Intricately carved tables, chairs, and other furniture decorated the sanctuary under stained-glass windows. Pillows, rugs, and brightly colored cloth seemed to flow throughout. Light from the candles in the hanging lamps glinted off of silver goblets on tables.

Never before had he seen such a sanctuary. *Truly, this is a holy place*, he thought. Bishop Adhemar, dressed in a ceremonial white robe, approached the knights, who were now standing in a line facing him in the middle of the sanctuary. A servant stood by his side, holding an ornate wooden box.

Adhemar spoke. "Your actions today have earned you the right to be selected for a special mission by His Holiness, Pope Urban II. Only the strongest, bravest, and most righteous will be there at the end, when Jerusalem falls and is once again in Christian hands. Inside the city lies the Temple Mount, a most holy place built by King Solomon himself." As Adhemar spoke, the tone of his voice changed to one of disgust. "This holy place has been desecrated, stained by the blood of Christians, and converted into a Mosque, called al-Aqsa, by the Saracens. It has been revealed to us by some who have been to this mosque that despite this desecration, several holy Christian relics are still being kept there, safeguarded somewhere within its walls."

Adhemar studied the faces of the knights with a stern gaze as he continued. "These relics are rumored to be: the Holy Chalice, the cup used by Christ during the last supper; the Ark of the Covenant, which held the Ten Commandments; and the remnants of the True Cross, the cross upon which Christ our Lord was crucified. Your mission, decreed by Pope Urban himself, is to recover and protect these holy relics upon capturing the city and entering this holy site."

Rodrigo was completely awestruck by the magnitude of the mission for which he had been selected. *I had only hoped to be part of the army traveling to the Holy Land, but now I am to be among those tasked with this important and noble mission! This is a great honor!* He beamed with pride as he fought to contain his excitement. *I pray that I will have the strength and courage to carry this mission through.*

When Adhemar had finished speaking, the servant opened the lid of the box. Reaching inside, Adhemar withdrew a necklace with a cross made of gold. As he held it up before the knights, the shimmer of the light off the golden cross entranced and captivated all those in the room. "By accepting this cross, you solemnly vow on your knightly honor to return any of the ancient and holy relics recovered from the Temple Mount to its rightful keeper, His Holiness, the Pope. You will also take a vow of secrecy about this mission, telling no one, lest they try to recover the relics for themselves." Adhemar walked to the first knight in line and stood before him with the necklace held high.

"Do you accept these vows?" he asked.

"Yes," said the first knight as he stood before Adhemar and bowed his head. Adhemar placed the cross around his neck and moved to the second knight, with the servant by his side. To each he asked the same question, and from each, he secured their vows. Finished, he stepped back to the center of the line and addressed all the knights.

Adhemar spoke with a loud and forceful tone, his arms outstretched. "Go now, and henceforth, you will be known as the Knights of the Crucem Auream, or Golden Cross. This necklace shall be your symbol and will always remind you of your solemn oath and duty to fulfill your vows. May God protect us and watch over us as we journey to the Holy Land to carry out his will." Adhemar lowered his arms, and his servants walked to the back of the sanctuary and opened the doors as the knights were dismissed.

The five knights turned and walked toward the door, smiling and congratulating each other, each glowing with the honor that had been bestowed upon him. Rodrigo was the last to turn toward the door. Suddenly, his conversation with Marcellinus came floating back to him, and he paused for a moment, looking down at the floor. He felt as if he had awakened from a dream. He turned around and could see Bishop Adhemar standing before him in the sanctuary. Rodrigo felt compelled to ask a question, but found it difficult to speak. He stammered for a brief moment, and then the words came tumbling out.

"Bishop Adhemar . . . I am truly humbled and . . . honored for being chosen from among so many for this extremely important mission, but . . . there is something I want to ask you. It has been troubling me and is something that I wish to know."

Adhemar motioned for him to come closer as the others exited the sanctuary. His stern gaze softened somewhat as Rodrigo approached. "Yes, my son? What is it that you wish to know?"

"Recently, I met a traveler on my journey from my home in Castile to this tournament. This man said he was living in Jerusalem just three years ago. He is a Christian, and told me that for hundreds of years now, since the fall of the city, all the people of different faiths, Christians, Jews, and Saracens, have been living in peace inside the holy city. He said that the stories of recent atrocities against Christians within the city are false, that the only killings being committed by the Saracens at this time are against each other as they vie for power in the Holy Land. I must know: is there any truth to his words?"

"What is your name, my son?" Adhemar asked, looking into Rodrigo's eyes with a sympathetic smile.

"I am Sir Rodrigo."

"Sir Rodrigo, this traveler with whom you spoke . . ." Adhemar placed a hand on Rodrigo's shoulder.

"His name was Marcellinus."

"Yes, this Marcellinus . . . it is obvious that he seeks to deceive you with these falsehoods. Terrible atrocities are being committed every day by the Saracen invaders against innocent Christians in the Holy Land. As a Christian army, it is our duty to protect them and free them from their oppression." Adhemar spoke with a calm assurance, as a father to his son, with his hand upon Rodrigo's shoulder as he looked him directly in the eyes.

Rodrigo silently nodded and broke Adhemar's gaze, looking down at the floor as he thought. *The Pope's words are true, then. But what reason would Marcellinus have for wanting to deceive me? If he were a deceitful person, why would he have gone through the trouble of aiding me, thus allowing me to attend the tournament?* Deep inside, he felt unsatisfied with Adhemar's answer, and he could not let it go.

Rodrigo raised his head again to look at Adhemar as he spoke. "Bishop Adhemar, it is because of this man that I am here and was able to take part in this tournament. I do not understand what reason he would have for trying to deceive me."

Adhemar's hand fell from Rodrigo's shoulder as the sympathetic smile slipped from his face to reveal a frown of displeasure. Rodrigo suddenly felt like he was shrinking under Adhemar's withering gaze, while Adhemar seemed to grow larger until his very presence filled the sanctuary.

"Do you think *I* am lying, then?" Adhemar asked sternly. "Do you believe that the Pope has lied to you and all of Europe?" His booming voice echoed through the sanctuary. Rodrigo stood in stunned silence, unsure of what to make of the bishop's sudden and intimidating transformation.

Adhemar stared at Rodrigo with cold, hard eyes. "Sir Rodrigo, perhaps you are not the man that I and Count Raymond believed you to be. Perhaps you are not meant for this mission, or for the journey to the Holy Land, if you have lost your faith in the Pope and the holy Catholic Church!"

Rodrigo quickly bowed his head and fell to one knee. "No, Your Excellency. I did not mean . . . to accuse you or the Holy Father of lying. Please believe me . . . I humbly beg your forgiveness." He covered his face with his hand as he knelt, feeling embarrassed and foolish. *Will the honor of this important mission now be taken from me simply because of my questions?*

There was silence for a moment, and then Rodrigo felt Adhemar's hand upon his head. "Rise, my son," Adhemar said in a calm voice.

Rodrigo slowly stood up, but kept his eyes lowered, refusing to look up.

"You are forgiven. Understand that there will be many men who will seek to deceive you on your journey, and your faith will surely be tested. Just put your trust in the Pope and the holy Catholic Church, my son, and all will be well. Go now and fulfill your mission with duty and honor."

Rodrigo turned and silently left the sanctuary, closing the doors behind him. In the stone hallway he could hear the sounds of drinking and revelry from the great hall, but he had lost his appetite for celebration. Instead of returning to the great hall, he continued down the hallway. He soon found his way outside and sat down on the stone steps outside the building, alone in the cool night air, thinking about what had just happened.

Though he was relieved to still be part of the mission to recover the holy relics, the feeling he had had when the golden cross was placed around his neck was gone, and he was left with a feeling of disquiet as he stared at the castle walls. *Why the sudden change in Adhemar's demeanor in response to a question? Apparently, even simple questions will not be tolerated.*

A cold gust of wind blew from the south, chilling his skin. *It seems that I will find no answers here. I am on my own if I wish to find the truth.* Rodrigo looked down at the golden cross that hung about his neck and held it in the palm of his hand. *Bishop Adhemar may be a difficult man to deal with, but for now, the importance of the mission for which we were chosen must come before all else. Such difficulties must be endured,* he thought as he let the cross fall back against his chest.

The door to the building creaked open. "There you are!" It was Sir Jean and Sir Geoffrey, two of the knights who had been with him at the ceremony. "We began celebrating after meeting with Bishop Adhemar, but we noticed that someone was missing. Adhemar's servants said you had left the sanctuary, but you did not return to the feasting hall. What are you doing out here alone? You should be inside, celebrating with all of us!" said Geoffrey, enthusiastically raising a tankard of ale into the air.

Rodrigo looked up at Geoffrey and thought for a moment. "You are right," he admitted. "We have a long and difficult journey before us, and we should feast and celebrate while we can. Who knows what tomorrow will hold?" Rising from the steps, Rodrigo, Jean, and Geoffrey left the cold and returned to the warmth and comfort of the feasting hall to celebrate the honor they had received and the beginning of the journey that lay ahead.

5

THE HERMIT

With the tournament now behind them, Rodrigo and the four other knights began the months-long process of assimilation into Count Raymond's army. The long days were filled with weapons and combat training along with cavalry and horsemanship skills. Skills in personal combat were no longer considered a priority. The knights had to learn to fight and maneuver as a cohesive cavalry unit. Although all the Knights of the Crucem Auream were skilled horsemen, Rodrigo was the only one who had experienced real combat as a mounted cavalryman. He had witnessed firsthand the devastating power of an armored cavalry charge against the Saracen Almoravids in battle with his uncle. The havoc it had wreaked upon the enemy lines was unlike anything he had ever seen and had created an immeasurable advantage.

The cavalry unit to which they were assigned would be under the personal command of the papal legate, Bishop Adhemar. They would answer to him and be under his watchful eyes and guidance. Long trains of food and supplies were being brought in from the surrounding farmlands, and the hammering of the village blacksmiths could be heard in the town forges, which ran day and night.

Sunday was the Lord's day and was a day of rest from the constant training and work. Rodrigo had attended Mass that morning in the cathedral and decided to venture out into the ancient city of Toulouse. He was interested in learning more about the history of the city and visiting some of the ancient Roman ruins that still existed after the conquest of the Gauls by Julius Caesar. He had heard many of Caesar's battle strategies recounted by his uncle and was interested in all things from the bygone Roman era.

In midafternoon, Rodrigo was exploring the eastern part of the city when he came upon a large crowd gathered around the steps leading up to the front of a building. Their backs were turned to him, and something ahead of them gripped their full attention. As Rodrigo drew closer, he could hear the voice of someone at the top of the steps. At times, the voice became thunderously loud, at others, as soft as a whisper. Rodrigo turned to look at the faces of the spectators as he walked by. All eyes gazed forward, fixed upon the speaker.

When Rodrigo was close enough to see who was speaking, he stopped for a moment to observe the object of their fascination. At the top of steps was an older, bearded man dressed in a brown hooded robe. The top of his head was shaved bald, like that of a monk. He was noticeably short in stature, but there was a fire in his eyes, and his loud voice was accentuated by his dramatic movements. He would move toward the crowd at times with sweeping gestures and then pull back. He would lift his eyes to the heavens and shout, then lower his head, speaking so softly that the crowd strained to hear him. In one hand he held a cross, which he waved around like a prop that an actor would use in play. Rodrigo watched the spectacle with his arms folded across his chest and his eyebrows raised. *What exactly do the people find interesting about this man?* He thought, looking around. *He seems more like an actor playing the role of a priest than a holy man of God.*

"Who is this man?" Rodrigo leaned over to ask someone standing next to him.

"The priest?" the stranger replied. He continued to stare ahead, keeping his eyes on the speaker. "He is known as Little Peter of Amiens. Some call him Peter the Hermit."

"The hermit? Why do they call him such?" asked Rodrigo.

"He travels from place to place, preaching the gospel and living off the land and the goodwill of others. That is why some call him the hermit. He has been here once before, but now he preaches a new message. I have never before heard anything like it! Listen!" the man said excitedly as Peter the Hermit began to speak again. Rodrigo nodded silently and then continued to move through the crowd to get a better view and to hear Peter the Hermit's message more clearly. When he reached the base of the steps, he went up as far as he could and then stopped to hear the message that had so enthralled the masses.

". . . and so, I ask all of you to join me as I gather all of God's children, and together we shall free the Holy Land and the city of Jerusalem from the Saracens! Are any of you standing here without sin? Do any of you believe you have lived a life worthy of the kingdom of heaven? I tell you now, the Pope has decreed that any man—*any man*—who takes up the cross and the sword to liberate the Holy Land from the Saracens, the Jews, and any non-Christian, shall be awarded direct entry into heaven and be spared from the fires of hell!" Peter yelled, lifting his cross to the heavens as he echoed Pope Urban's proclamation.

A great cheer went up from the crowd when they heard the news, but Rodrigo remained silent. *He parrots the Pope's message to the people but seems to be adding to it. Are we now declaring a holy war on the Jews as well as the Saracens?* He looked around and saw there were a mix of farmers, peasants, and townsfolk. All were cheering enthusiastically, completely spellbound by the sermon. *Why is he recruiting common townsfolk to journey to the Holy Land? What use would they be against the armies of the Turks?*

"We all know Europe's princes are gathering their armies to answer the Pope's call. But do you think the Pope's message was only meant for them?" Peter asked the crowd.

"No!" the crowd shouted in unison.

"Should only princes, nobles, and those with lands and wealth be allowed to enter unto heaven upon death?" he asked.

"No!" the crowd roared again.

"No indeed! The Pope's promise of complete penance to all those who go to the Holy Land to free Jerusalem shall be awarded to any man, woman, or child who goes in the name of God, the Pope, and the holy Catholic Church! *Deus vult!* It is God's will!" Peter yelled, looking up to the heavens.

Another great cheer went up from the masses, and many of those around Rodrigo were excitedly whispering with one another as Peter continued. "This very day, I will begin my journey back to Cologne, where I have been gathering all God's faithful from across the lands for many weeks now. A great Christian army of the people awaits me there, and together we shall descend like a storm from heaven into the Turkish lands to crush the invaders and restore the rule of the Christian Church to the Holy Land! Any of you here who wish to join me are free to do so and will thereby be awarded penance for all sins as decreed by the Pope. God's will be done!" he yelled, sweeping his cross downward to signal a dramatic end to his sermon.

Finished, Peter the Hermit began descending the steps of the building as those in the crowd applauded and began excitedly talking among themselves. Rodrigo frowned and shook his head. *This is madness. I have seen the ferocity and fanaticism of the Saracen warriors in battle. To gather an army of common townsfolk would be like sending sheep to the wolves!* Rodrigo stood out from the enthusiastic crowd as he watched in silence with folded arms while Peter the Hermit descended the stairway.

"You there!" Peter called out as he neared the end of the stairway.

Rodrigo stared silently as Peter approached him. *What does he want with me?*

"What is your name?" Peter asked.

"I am Sir Rodrigo of Castile." Rodrigo looked down at Peter the Hermit, who was now standing in front of him. *He is even smaller up close.*

"So, you are a knight from Castile," Peter said, studying Rodrigo from head to foot. "You look like a strong fighting man. All are welcome to join us, but we could definitely use a warrior like yourself on our journey."

I see. He is trying to recruit me. Perhaps he too realizes an army of townsfolk would not stand a chance against the Turks. Does he even have a plan for travel? "And how will you get to the Holy Land?" Rodrigo asked.

"It is quite simple!" Peter answered loudly with a smile as others around them began to listen in. "Our army, some say nearly thirty thousand strong and growing, will travel east until we reach the Rhine and then follow it south to the Danube River. Then we shall follow the river through the Kingdom of Hungary until we reach the great city of Constantinople. It has been said that Emperor Alexios of the Byzantine Empire has been calling upon Europe to aid in the fight against the Turks. Once we are there, he will no doubt welcome us with open arms and outfit our army with supplies. From there it is but short distance to the Holy Land." He flashed a broad, confident smile to all those around them.

I do not think it is quite as simple as he believes. "Is your army already supplied to make the journey to Constantinople?" asked Rodrigo.

"Those who have joined the People's Army are not men of means and great wealth, Sir Rodrigo," Peter said. "Most have come with only the clothes on their backs and all their belongings in tow. But all who have joined are people of great faith, and we place our faith in God that he will keep us fed and supplied throughout our journey to Constantinople. Did God let the tribes of Israel starve as they wandered through the desert? No! They were fed with mana from heaven! God will watch over his flock," Peter asserted to all those listening in. "Do you not have faith in God, Sir Rodrigo?" Peter asked and his smile began to fade.

Now he questions my faith in God because I question his plan? Rodrigo was silent for a moment as Adhemar's face flashed in his memory. "I do have faith . . . *in God*," Rodrigo answered. "Speaking of the tribes of Israel, you had mentioned something about the Jews in your sermon."

"Yes, yes, the Jews," Peter said disdainfully. "Of course, they were the original children of God. But after they put Christ our Lord to death on the cross, and with the rise of the holy Catholic Church, we are now the chosen ones to rule the kingdom of heaven! Not the Jews, nor the Saracens, nor any other faith or religion. The Holy Land belongs in Christian hands! What say you, Sir Rodrigo? Will you join us?" Peter asked loudly with a smile, lifting and opening his arms in a welcoming gesture.

Foolishness! I would not join this man and his People's Army even if I had no other way of getting to the Holy Land. "I am already part of Count Raymond's army," Rodrigo answered flatly.

"Bah!" said Peter, frowning in disgust as he turned from Rodrigo and continued to make his way down the stairs. "You will be sorry!" he yelled to Rodrigo as he reached the bottom. A man had brought up a donkey from the crowd and helped Peter mount it. He turned to look back at Rodrigo from atop the donkey. "You will be sorry when you reach the Holy Land and discover it to be liberated from the Turks by the People's Army, and your opportunity to answer the Pope's call will be gone!"

Unlikely, but I suppose we shall see. It is doubtful that the People's Army will even reach the Holy Land. God help them if they do. Rodrigo stood silently and watched Peter the Hermit ride away toward the gates of Toulouse with a great multitude of people following him.

The crowd by the steps slowly began to disperse, but there was still a buzz of excitement in the air when Rodrigo left the area to continue his exploration of the city. He thought about Peter the Hermit's method of preaching as he walked and the impact it had on those that heard it. *The power that this man wields over the masses with his words is incredible. What he is choosing to do with that power, however, is reckless and dangerous.* Rodrigo frowned and felt his stomach turn at the thought of what might happen if the People's Army was able to reach the Holy Land and face the Turks. *Will the Church put an end to this man's reckless ambitions before something terrible happens? Do they even care?*

Large stone pillars and columns rose from the ground before him as he reached the Roman ruins. They held up nothing but empty sky and were surrounded by crumbling walls that had fallen to ruin. *Vestiges of the once mighty Roman Empire that now lie forgotten,* Rodrigo thought as he entered the ruins. He held out his arm as he walked to feel the cold stone of the pillars on the palm of his hand. *I wonder what our legacy will be as we begin our journey to the Holy Land. Will we be remembered as liberators of the Holy Land, or conquerors like the Romans?*

Rodrigo sat down on the steps at the edge of the ruins. He picked up a small piece of the ancient concrete that lay on the steps beside him. He closed his hand and squeezed the concrete, which instantly crumbled into dust, falling between his fingers. *Or perhaps if we fail in our mission to retake Jerusalem and are defeated by the Turks, then just like these ancient ruins, we too shall be forgotten in the sands of time.*

A TALE OF SORROW

It was the fall of 1096, and Count Raymond's army was at last ready to depart for the Holy Land. A Holy Mass was held that morning with several priests blessing the knights, warriors, and camp followers as they exited the gates of Toulouse on the first leg of their journey to Constantinople. The armies of the princes of Europe were to rendezvous at the great Byzantine capital, where they would pay homage to Emperor Alexios, resupply their units, and formulate their plans to invade the Turkish-held lands.

At great personal expense, Count Raymond had outfitted his entire army with tunics emblazoned with the cross to signify them as *cruce signatus*, those who wear the sign of the cross, or Crusaders, as they had begun to be known. At the head of the army, Count Raymond rode out on a great white stallion, with Bishop Adhemar by his side, into the Frankish countryside. His vassals, the peasant farmers, lined the roads for many miles, waving their adieu and wanting to catch a glimpse of Count Raymond and the great Crusader army as they embarked upon their historic journey. Rodrigo smiled and felt a great sense of pride as he waved to the peasant children who ran near the column, throwing flowers at his horse's feet. Silently, he gave thanks to God for allowing him the opportunity to be part of such a great and noble quest and prayed for the success and safety of all.

The next few weeks passed without incident as the Crusader army journeyed along the southern coast of the Kingdom of the Franks, heading east below the Alps through the Holy Roman Empire. Once they reached the Kingdom of Hungary, they would begin to head south toward the Byzantine Empire and rendezvous with the other Crusader armies at Constantinople.

Rodrigo soon began to get used to the camp life of a soldier. Each man had a job, whether it was tending to the horses, cleaning weapons, setting up camp, or foraging for food. The knights, who made up the cavalry units, would take turns being part of hunting expeditions and scouting units. The scouting units would ride ahead several miles from the main body of the army and report back to their leaders. Their reports were invaluable and contained information on potential routes for travel, villages or towns that harbored food and supplies, or signs of the enemy when traveling through enemy territory.

Rodrigo was excited to be part of a scouting unit, since it was his first time in such a role. Lightly armored to increase speed and carrying only swords for protection, the scouting party rode out, leaving the camp where the army had chosen to stop for the evening. The scouts that rode with him were his fellow Knights of the Crucem Auream, as they were frequently assigned duties together. Adhemar had arranged for this, as well as having them bunk together in the same tent. He wanted them to form a close-knit group, to rely on each other and never lose sight of their mission. Having them together all the time also made it easier to keep them under his ever-watchful eyes.

The five knights had ridden for several miles when they decided to ride to the top of a nearby hill to get a view of the surrounding area. Rodrigo held his hand above his eyes to shield his gaze from the late afternoon sun. The smoke from several small campfires caught his eye by the mouth of a river below. "Look there!" he said, pointing toward the campfires.

"Yes, I see it," Jean said as the others pulled their mounts up next to Rodrigo. "What do you think it is?"

"There are no farms or towns near here. Nomads or gypsies, perhaps?" Richard suggested.

"If the river below is the one on the map, then we are approaching the Kingdom of Hungary," William said, looking up from a map that he had pulled from his saddlebag. "Maybe part of their army is camped there."

"The camp is quite large, but it doesn't seem to be organized or set up like a military camp," Rodrigo said. "Why don't we go down and see for ourselves who camps there?"

"Do you feel that is wise, Rodrigo?" Richard asked with a frown. "Our job as scouts is only to observe and report. What if they spot us and attack?"

"We are not in hostile territory, so the chance of them attacking if they spot us is low," Rodrigo said. "I think our leaders would want to know who is camped here, so we should do our best to inform them. What do the rest of you think?"

Richard dissented, but the other knights agreed with Rodrigo, and together they rode down the opposite side of the hill toward the mysterious camp beside the river. Richard was the last to leave the hilltop, cursing as he rode. When they reached the bottom of the hill, they dismounted, and four of them crept quietly through the forest to spy on the camp while William stayed with the mounts. When they were close, they stopped and knelt behind a grove of trees not far from the river's edge. They could see some women and children at the river gathering water in buckets.

"What do we do now?" Geoffrey whispered.

"This is foolish," Richard asserted in a harsh whisper. "We still have no idea who these people are, and at any moment they may spot us. The sun will be down in an hour, and here we are, putting ourselves at risk. For what?"

"These are naught but women and children," Rodrigo said. "They pose no threat to us. Why don't we approach them and simply ask them who they are and what they are doing here?" *Richard always seems to be in opposition to everyone unless he is in charge.*

"If you like, Richard, you can stay here or go and wait with William and the horses."

"Are you implying that I lack courage?" Richard asked, raising his voice slightly as he narrowed his eyes.

"No. It was only a suggestion," Rodrigo said in a hushed voice.

"I will go with you," Geoffrey offered. "Richard and Jean can stay hidden here, so in case we need them, they will not be far away."

Rodrigo nodded. *Thank God that Geoffrey will listen to reason.* Rising from the forest floor, Rodrigo and Geoffrey walked out of the grove and approached the women. One of the women looked up and screamed in terror when she saw them. All the women quickly abandoned what they were doing, grabbed the hands of their children, and fled into the forest.

Geoffrey, startled by their actions, began to draw his sword. "Wait!" said Rodrigo, holding out his hand. "I do not think we should draw our weapons and frighten them any further."

"I understand," Geoffrey said as he shoved his sword back into its scabbard, "but now they know we are here, and I do not think we should wait around to find out if they are friend or foe."

"You are right," Rodrigo admitted. "Let's head back to camp and report what we saw here." The two backed away from the river and turned toward the grove where Richard and Jean were waiting.

"Please!" a voice suddenly called out from behind them. Rodrigo and Geoffrey stopped and turned to see who it was.

An elderly man dressed in torn black sackcloth stood barefoot at the water's edge where the women and children had been. He had shoulder-length white hair and a long white beard. His skin was pale and seemed to hang upon the bones of his emaciated frame. "Please, good sirs," he said again, nearly shaking as he spoke. He looked at them with hollow eyes, and his face was full of fear. Rodrigo and Geoffrey stood on guard, ready to draw their weapons as he continued in a trembling voice. "I humbly beg you, please leave us alone. I have come to speak on behalf of the others. You have already taken everything, and there is no more to take. We have nothing. I am telling you the truth."

Relaxing their guard, Rodrigo and Geoffrey walked closer to the man. "We are not here to harm you," Rodrigo assured him, holding his hands up, away from his weapons. "We are Crusader knights from Count Raymond's army, on our way to Constantinople."

Upon hearing the words, the man fell to his knees and immediately began to beg for his life. "Please, please do not kill us!" he pleaded with his head down and his hands clasped together and held out before him.

Geoffrey shrugged in bewilderment as he and Rodrigo looked at each other. Not knowing what else to do, Rodrigo knelt in front of the trembling man and gently helped him to his feet. He could see a deep fear in the man's scarred face as he looked into his eyes. *What happened to him, and why does he fear us so?*

"We will not harm you or rob you, as God is my witness," Rodrigo told the man. "We only want to know who you are and how you came to be here. Then we shall leave you in peace. You have my word." A flood of relief washed over the man as he put his hands to his face and wiped away tears.

The old man breathed several deep sighs of relief, and when he finally removed his hands from his face, he spoke. "Thank you . . . thank you," he murmured. "My name is Samuel. Our camp is but a short distance from here." He pointed toward the forest, away from the river. "If you will follow me, I can take you there and you may warm yourself by our fire. I shall gather the others and tell you what happened to us and how we came to be here."

Rodrigo looked where Samuel pointed, then back at the grove from where they had come. *This man, Samuel, seems sincere, but perhaps it is best if the others remain hidden in case something happens.* "We will go with you; however, we cannot stay long," he answered as Geoffrey nodded in agreement.

Samuel led the way as the three walked into the forest. The sun was sinking behind the trees as they entered the camp, and its last rays through the treetops revealed the barren and shoddy accommodations of its inhabitants. The crudely fashioned tents seemed barely able to stand and looked like they had been pieced together with scraps of cloth. The tools and pottery by the fire in the middle of the camp were old and worn, and the inhabitants were nowhere to be seen.

Rodrigo and Geoffrey went to stand by the fire as Samuel disappeared into the rows of tents. Soon, like silent shadows emerging from the forest around them, people slowly began to appear. Mostly women, along with some older men and children, stared at them as they stood, the firelight dancing upon their haggard, melancholy faces. Most were barefoot, and their garments were old and torn, scant comfort in the chilly evening air. At last, Samuel returned to Rodrigo and Geoffrey, who stood speechless, stunned at what they saw.

"Tell us, Samuel, who are you, and what happened to all of you?" Geoffrey asked, breaking the silence.

Samuel walked to a stump by the fire and sat down. With a sullen face, he stared at the fire, his thoughts disappearing into the flames as he began to recount their tale of sorrow. "We are Jews who traveled here from our homes in the Rhineland. Many months ago, a great army came from the west. They marched into our towns and villages, and at first, they just demanded food and supplies. We gave them what we could, but when they discovered we were Jews, they began attacking us, taking everything, and killing everyone, including our women and children. When they finished, they burned our villages to the ground. We are those who were fortunate enough to escape the slaughter. We left the Rhineland and came here, hoping to start a new settlement. We have nothing, as you can see. Winter is coming, and we will be lucky to survive. When we first saw you, we thought the great army had returned . . ." Tears welled up in his eyes as he spoke.

A frown was etched upon Rodrigo's face as he listened to the harrowing tale. *I believe I know who committed these atrocities.* "This great army, who were they led by?"

"I did not see their leader," Samuel said, "but some of the survivors who fled the slaughter swear they were being led by a priest riding a donkey. I did not believe them."

Rodrigo's jaw clenched and his fists tightened upon hearing the man's words. *Peter the Hermit and his People's Army! So this is how he will keep his army supplied on their journey to Constantinople—through pillage, plunder, and murder. The blood of all those people is on his hands.*

"A priest on a donkey?" Geoffrey asked Rodrigo with raised eyebrows. "What do you make of that?"

"I believe I know who it was—a man named Peter the Hermit," Rodrigo said. "I will explain how I know him when we get back to camp."

Rodrigo walked next to Samuel and put his hand on his shoulder. "Thank you, Samuel, for telling us your story." He looked around at the others in the camp and raised his voice so everyone could hear him. "You have endured much, and my heart feels heavy knowing what you have been through. Count Raymond's army is camped several miles from here, but we are well supplied, and you have nothing to fear from us. Our army will pass by here tomorrow, but we will direct them around your camp, so as not to disturb you. If I am able, I will try to bring you some extra supplies from our camp, to help you through the winter months. We must go now and return to our camp." With tears of gratitude, Samuel and the other members of the camp thanked Rodrigo and Geoffrey as they left the camp and returned to the grove by the river's edge. The first stars of the evening had begun to appear in the darkened sky.

"At last!" Richard exclaimed angrily when Rodrigo and Geoffrey walked into the grove. He scowled as he quickly stood up and walked directly in front of Rodrigo. "We waited here in the cold and dark, not knowing if you were alive or dead! What happened to you? Who are those people?" he demanded.

Rodrigo said nothing but took a step back and returned Richard's stare. The feelings of outrage and anger from hearing the survivors' story were still fresh in his mind, and he could feel his heart beating faster, but he held his tongue and remained silent. *I will not take out my anger on Richard.*

"It is a Jewish settlement, and they pose no threat to us," Geoffrey said, stepping in between Rodrigo and Richard, who continued to stare at each other. "They took us into their camp and told us the tale of how they came to be here." The mist of their breath was beginning to show in the cold night air. "It is cold and dark now. Let's head back to our own camp, and we will tell you the rest when we get there."

The tension diffused as Richard took a step back, still staring at Rodrigo. "You put us through all of this so we could report the discovery of a camp full of Jews?" he asked with a smirk, shaking his head. "In that case, Rodrigo, you can have the *honor* of reporting this to Adhemar." Saying no more, the four began to walk through the forest toward William, who was waiting with the horses.

☩

The furs and skins that lined the tent shut out the cold, and the warm glow of the many lamps inside and the comfort of the furniture within was a stark contrast to the meager accommodations of the average solider. Adhemar relaxed upon his couch, sipping wine, when a guard came through the tent entrance. "Bishop Adhemar, I am sorry for this disturbance, but one of the knights from the scouting party has returned to give his report."

"Let him in," Adhemar replied, sitting up on the couch. The guard left, and Rodrigo entered the tent. Adhemar looked at Rodrigo for a moment, recalling their meeting in the sanctuary. *The one who dared to question the Pope's proclamation.* "Sir Rodrigo, what do you wish to report?" he asked with a stern voice.

Rodrigo cleared his throat. "We came upon an encampment of Jewish settlers near a river just beyond the hills to the east."

"So, you discovered a camp of settlers to the east," Adhemar said as stood up to get a bottle of wine from a table. "Are you sure they are Jews? What would they be doing there? There are no Jewish settlements in these lands."

"I am sure, Bishop Adhemar," Rodrigo said. "Sir Geoffrey and I spoke to them. They have traveled from their home in the Rhineland to start a new settlement. They left because they were attacked and pillaged by the People's Army led by Peter the Hermit. The survivors fled south and are hoping to start a new settlement near the river."

Adhemar poured the wine, refilling his goblet. "That is an

interesting tale, Sir Rodrigo. Assuming this is what they told you, how do you know it is true?" *Even if it is, why would it concern us?*

"The survivors said the army that attacked them was led by a priest riding a donkey." Rodrigo paused for a moment, looking down at the floor. "They have nothing, Bishop Adhemar. They are weak, weary, and without any supplies for the winter."

Adhemar stared at Rodrigo as he sipped his wine, then lowered his goblet. *Again, this is no concern of ours.* "What do you know of Little Peter?"

"I met him while he was preaching in Toulouse many months ago," Rodrigo said. "He tried to recruit me to join his People's Army."

Adhemar silently nodded as he reflected on his memories of Little Peter. "I am not surprised. He is quite an ambitious little man. I have known him to be a wandering priest for many years, traveling from city to city, but I suppose now he has found a different calling." He sat back down on the couch. *It shall be interesting to see what becomes of Little Peter's ambitions.* "Was there anything else?"

"Bishop Adhemar, the People's Army is looting and pillaging their way through Europe to Constantinople," Rodrigo said. "Will the Church do nothing to stop these terrible acts?"

The tension rose in the room as Adhemar stared at Rodrigo and his brow began to crease. *Again, he questions the will of the Church?* "The army Little Peter gathered was not sanctioned by the Pope and therefore has no affiliation with the holy Catholic Church. Whatever was done to the Jews by the People's Army is *not* our concern. Thank you for your report, Sir Rodrigo. You may go."

Rodrigo stood for a moment in silence, looking at the floor. "Forgive me, Bishop Adhemar, but those people are without food or provisions." He looked back up. "Without supplies, they may not survive the winter. We may not be responsible for what happened, but if we do not help them, then we too are contributing to their deaths. Are we not better than those who committed these atrocities?"

Adhemar stared at Rodrigo for a tense moment. *Why would he care so much for these Jews? If I allow this, then how many more pointless requests will I receive? Perhaps he shall not be so quick to offer charity if he must pay for it out his own pockets!* "Very well, Sir Rodrigo," he replied. "You may deliver some supplies to them in the morning, but you may only take from the reserves, not the main supplies. And *anything* you take will be deducted from your soldier's pay and your share of any plunder you receive when we reach the Holy Land." *That should give him pause before he comes to me with any more frivolous requests,* he thought as he studied Rodrigo and waited for his reaction.

A calm, contented smile came over Rodrigo's face as he heard the answer. "Thank you, Bishop Adhemar. I will gladly pay for the supplies, and the relief it will bring will be well worth it." Rodrigo bowed with humility, then quietly left the tent. Adhemar continued to frown as he watched Rodrigo exit the tent; it was not the reaction he had anticipated.

Adhemar swirled the contents of his wine goblet as he leaned back against the couch, thinking about Rodrigo's request. *I will need to keep a closer eye on this one. If all of them begin to question the actions of the Church, then I will begin losing control, and our mission will be in jeopardy. I will not let that happen!*

7

THE GREAT CITY

I t was December when Count Raymond's army crossed the borders of the Byzantine Empire and finally approached the great city of Constantinople. The passage through Hungary had gone without incident; however, various scouting parties reported hostile and tense encounters in all the villages and towns that they ventured into. Emissaries from King Koloman, the Hungarian ruler, had also visited the Crusader camp and issued stern warnings not to enter the towns or cities that were now being guarded by the Hungarian army.

Word had come that Peter the Hermit and his People's Army had ravaged the surrounding countryside on their way through Hungary. Lacking any sort of discipline, organization, and the leadership of a professional army, the nearly forty thousand members of the poorly outfitted People's Army had resorted to taking food and supplies wherever they could find them. Many Hungarian farmers' crops and livestock had been devastated, and the grain storehouses of local villages had been plundered.

The final straw for King Koloman came when the People's Army had assaulted a Hungarian town after a dispute with some locals, which had ended with the massacre of thousands of the local populace. This had led to several skirmishes with the Hungarian army and made them wary and distrustful of any other foreign armies passing through their lands. Other stories that had come down from the Rhineland said that the number of Jews massacred there by the People's Army was in the tens of thousands.

For several days after their encounter with the Jewish settlement, Rodrigo was haunted by the gaunt faces of Jewish survivors. His feelings of anger and revulsion would return whenever he heard stories of the many atrocities committed by the People's Army. In the last few weeks, however, those feelings had subsided, replaced by wonder and great anticipation as they drew closer to Constantinople, the fabled city of the Eastern Roman Empire and the last Christian stronghold before venturing into Turkish-held lands.

The long columns of soldiers and cavalry wound down the dusty road until they disappeared in the distance as they marched toward the city in the early afternoon. Rodrigo and Geoffrey were engaged in conversation as they rode together in the columns. The two had become good friends along their journey, and all the Knights of the Crucem Auream had become a closely bonded brotherhood as Adhemar had intended.

"I have heard that no words can describe the beauty of the Hagia Sophia in Constantinople. It has been said that a vision of heaven has been truly captured in its architecture," Rodrigo said, looking down the road ahead of them.

"I have heard the same," Geoffrey said. "There is so much in the city to see, I cannot wait to explore all that it has to offer."

Without warning, William galloped up from behind and flanked Rodrigo on the right, pinning him in the middle. He had a broad grin on his face as he spoke. "Rodrigo, Geoffrey, a fine day, is it not? I am sorry, did I interrupt you two? Was Rodrigo recounting how he won Count Raymond's tournament? Or perhaps he is explaining his plan to deliver all the holy relics to the Pope once we return?" he asked with a smirk.

"You had best quiet your tongue, William," Geoffrey said with a smile. "Adhemar instructed us not to speak of those things. His eyes and ears are everywhere. Perhaps he is listening." He pretended to look around.

"No, William, I was telling Geoffrey about how you will turn and run with your tail between your legs at the first sight of the Turks," Rodrigo said, causing Geoffrey to laugh as they trotted along the road.

As they were speaking, Richard and Jean rode up from behind to join the three. "What is this, a secret meeting? Why were we not invited?" Richard called out.

"Richard, Jean, how good of you to join us!" William said. "Rodrigo was just entertaining us with his grand plan to take the city of Jerusalem. You know he won Count Raymond's tournament with his masterful strategy, do you not? Has Rodrigo not told you?"

"Only 324 times, by my last count!" Jean replied. "By all means, Rodrigo, please make it 325." The others laughed as Rodrigo tossed a piece of bread he was eating at Jean.

Suddenly a cry came from the head of the long column in the distance. "There they are! The city walls!"

Without warning, Rodrigo spurred his horse and broke away from the center of the group, galloping along the side of the road toward the head of the column. The other four knights hesitated for a moment, then spurred their horses and chased after him.

"Get back in formation!" a cavalry commander yelled as the knights rode past the other soldiers. Not heeding the command, the four galloped to the head of the column and stopped alongside Rodrigo, who was staring into the distance. Ahead of the knights, framed against the clear blue sky, were the walls of Constantinople. They had reached the great city at last.

8

THE CONFRONTATION

The setting sun painted streaks of red and orange across the sky as Rodrigo and Geoffrey leaned on the battlements of the massive walls surrounding the city and peered out over the horizon. Across the grassy plains and rolling hills, long columns of marching soldiers and cavalrymen could be seen approaching Constantinople for nearly as far as the eye could see. A steady stream of knights and warriors had been flooding in for weeks as the princes and lords of Europe descended upon the city with their armies, the banners of their various kingdoms fluttering in the wind.

One of the nobles who stood out from the rest was the Norman lord, Bohemond of Taranto, from southern Italy. A giant in stature, he stood a head taller than even the tallest of the knights and warriors around him. With a permanent scowl etched upon his face, he barked commands at his officers that were quickly followed. It was rumored that not only was he fearsome in combat, he was also highly educated and spoke fluent Greek and Arabic, a rarity among Europeans, even among nobles who were often fluent in multiple languages. The Byzantine locals spoke of him with a hushed, fearful tone, since it was also widely known that he had spent much of his military career attacking the Byzantines on the Greek peninsula and had engaged in several battles with Emperor Alexios and his forces there.

Only recently had Bohemond offered terms of peace with the emperor, in order to join the Crusade to the Holy Land. Despite all his talent and leadership, however, he was a prince without land or a kingdom to his name. He had spent his life in the shadow of his older brother's more legitimate claims to the lands and kingdom of his father while unsuccessfully trying to carve out a kingdom for himself.

Geoffrey leaned against the battlement and turned toward Rodrigo. "I had hoped to spend our days exploring the various sites within the city. Instead, we have been imprisoned upon its walls. I wonder how much longer Adhemar will have us suffer this pointless guard duty."

Rodrigo rested with his back against the battlement and shrugged. "As long as he deems fit, I suppose, although I fear it may be a while. He was not too pleased with us for breaking ranks and disobeying the cavalry commander's orders. At least he doesn't know about us speaking in jest of the holy relics." He laughed.

"Yes, that is true," said Geoffrey, smiling. "If he did, we would all be hanging from these walls, not guarding them." He peered down at the soldiers entering the gates below them. "How many more soldiers can this city hold? There has been a steady flow into the city for weeks. The city must be nigh to bursting."

"That is true, but I think the last should be here in a matter of days," Rodrigo said, glancing over the edge of the wall. "I have heard that on Sunday after Mass, there is to be a grand ceremony where all the lords and princes will swear fealty to Emperor Alexios."

Geoffrey thought for a moment. "Why would they offer him fealty? It is the emperor who has called for aid against the Turks. We are the ones who have answered that call, so he should be indebted to us."

Rodrigo pointed toward the walls on the opposite side of the city, beyond which they could see blue waters. "Emperor Alexios controls those waters and all who pass through them. Not far beyond them lie unknown lands controlled by the Turks. I am sure our leaders will need to rely heavily on the emperor for supplies and guides as we make our way to Jerusalem. In return, I am told that they must swear fealty and return any lands or kingdoms they conquer to the Byzantines."

"I suppose we will have to see if that happens," Geoffrey replied with a smirk. "The emperor asks much, as we are the ones who will be taking all the risk and doing all the work. I hope, at least, that our leaders come up with a better plan of invasion than that of the People's Army. I do not wish to share the same fate."

Several months had passed since Peter the Hermit and his People's Army had arrived at the gates of Constantinople. Fearing such an unruly and undisciplined mob within his city walls, the emperor had outfitted them with food and supplies and ferried them across the Bosporus Strait as quickly as he could to be rid of them. They had been forewarned to await the arrival of the Crusader army before venturing into Turkish-held lands, but the advice had fallen upon the deaf ears of those hungry for plunder and conquest.

Early reports had told of their successful bid to capture a small Turkish stronghold called Xerigordon, which they had used as a base to attack surrounding towns and villages, both Turkish and Christian. It was also reported that there had been disputes among the leadership of the People's Army, and while some had journeyed west to lay siege to the city of Nicaea, the main body of the army had ventured eastward.

The capture of Xerigordon and the activity of the invading force had driven a sultan named Kilij Arslan into action, and he led an army of Turkish warriors to oppose the invaders. He was able to recapture Xerigordon with ease and had quickly destroyed the forces laying siege to Nicaea. Those who were captured had been put to the sword or sold into slavery. He then laid an ambush to trap the main body of the People's Army at a place called Civetot.

The bloody massacre that ensued had been swift and brutal. The several hundred survivors, from a force of nearly twenty thousand, said that the Turks were like howling, mad demons as they attacked, raining arrows and spears upon them before cutting them down with curved sabers on horseback. Those that survived did so by feigning death or fleeing like cowards. The news of the massacre of the People's Army had reached the city shortly after Count Raymond's arrival.

Rodrigo folded his arms across his chest and frowned. "Their massacre was unfortunate, but I cannot say they did not deserve their fate after what happened to the Jews and Hungarians. A fitting end to Peter the Hermit, as I see it. I trust that our leaders will come up with a better plan."

"Perhaps you are correct, but I would not voice that opinion in front of Adhemar, or he will excommunicate you!" Geoffrey laughed. "Come, let's go. The sun is down, and our guard duty is over." He picked up a water skin along with his spear on the walkway. "Unfortunately for Jean, Richard, and William, their duty is just beginning!"

Rodrigo and Geoffrey came down from the walls of the city and returned to their camp as the long columns of soldiers, now traveling by torchlight, continued to stream into the city gates throughout the night.

✠

That Sunday, Rodrigo and the other knights attended Mass in the Hagia Sophia. They stood in awe and wonder at its magnificent architecture. Never before had any of them seen its equal. *The largest cathedral in Europe would easily fit inside this room,* Rodrigo thought.

Beautiful chandeliers hung throughout the huge cathedral, and rays of sunlight poured in from the windows surrounding the massive domed ceiling above, illuminating the interior. The soft light shimmered off the gold leaf that was embedded into the ornate décor of the cathedral. Frescos adorned the interior and spoke of the rich and majestic history of the Eastern Roman Empire. Rodrigo marveled as his eyes traveled upward to the center of the domed ceiling where the figure of Christ was looking down upon them, and it felt as though he was ascending into heaven.

The height of the arched pillars on multiple levels within the cathedral created a sense of grandeur that was furthered by the spectacle of the emperor accepting oaths of fealty from the European lords as they were called forth to stand before him, one by one. In return, they received his promise to aid them in taking back the Holy Land and recapturing the city of Jerusalem.

The pomp and ceremony of the event reminded Rodrigo of when Adhemar had bestowed upon him and the other Knights of the Crucem Auream their golden crosses. He remembered having the same feelings of awe and wonder at that ceremony and how the feeling had suddenly vanished the moment Adhemar became displeased with his questions. *Is our mission to reclaim the Holy Land truly blessed by God, or is this all for show? Will the emperor behave the same way as Adhemar if our leaders question his authority?* When it was finally over, Adhemar summoned the five knights to his quarters near the palace gardens, not far from the Hagia Sophia.

The five stood outside the building where the servant had instructed them to wait. Adhemar exited the doorway and walked down a few steps beneath the entrance of the building but stopped before reaching level ground. Standing above the knights, Adhemar began to speak. "I trust you are all well rested and eager to begin our journey to the Holy Land. I have decided that your duty atop the walls of the city is over. However, it is of utmost importance that you follow the commands of the cavalry officers at all times. Remember, you are no longer lone knights, but are now part of a cavalry unit and must act and fight as a single entity. There *will* be order and discipline." He looked down at the faces of the knights below him, stopping at Rodrigo's.

"Yes, Bishop Adhemar," the knights answered together.

"In the next few days, you will begin your preparations to make the journey. Each of you will be responsible for the maintenance of his own weapons, equipment, and mount. In your spare time you may help with loading supplies aboard the ferries at the city docks. I am sure it will take a few days to get everything loaded." Adhemar paused for a moment before speaking again. "If there are no questions, you are free to return to camp."

Rodrigo shook his head in frustration. *Why are we constantly kept in the dark about everything? If there is a plan of invasion, I believe we have the right to know.* He stood still as the others were turning to leave. "Bishop Adhemar."

"Yes, Sir Rodrigo?" Adhemar asked, his eyes narrowing as he stared at Rodrigo. The other knights stopped and turned to listen. "I think I speak for all of us when I ask: what is the plan for invading the land of the Turks? We have all heard what happened to the People's Army. With no clear plan of invasion, Peter the Hermit led his followers straight to their deaths like lambs to a slaughter. I would hope that our leaders do not wish to repeat that mistake."

Adhemar remained silent for a moment before answering. "Yes, it is true that the People's Army was utterly destroyed by the Turks in battle. But this is what happens when an army's leadership breaks down and the people stop following a man of God."

Rodrigo looked back at Adhemar with a furrowed brow. *Peter the Hermit, a man of God? When they were slaughtering Jews in Europe, the Church denied affiliation with him and his People's Army.* "What do you mean, they stopped following a man of God? Were they not being led by Peter the Hermit?" he asked as the others looked on in silence.

Adhemar continued to stare down at Rodrigo. "Little Peter of Amiens was not leading the People's Army when they encountered the Turkish forces at Civetot. After they began their invasion of the Turkish lands, there were disagreements among the leaders in the army, and they ultimately decided to abandon Little Peter's authority and instead chose to follow a Frank named Burel and an Italian named Rainald. They were in command when their army was defeated by the Turks."

Rodrigo paused for a moment and frowned while the other four began to whisper to one another. "So what happened to Peter the Hermit?" he asked.

"He is here, in Constantinople!" Adhemar answered. A rare smile curled upon his lips, and he lifted his arms as he proclaimed the news. "You see, when the people rejected the authority of a man of God, they were effectively abandoned by him and became a godless mob, hence their fate. God saw fit to spare Little Peter, who came back to Constantinople after the other men took over, and he began to preach here in the city. Apparently, the emperor has become quite fond of his teachings, and now he will accompany us on our journey to the Holy Land."

The whispers ceased as the other four knights began openly talking among themselves. Rodrigo remained silent as his gaze broke from Adhemar's and sank toward the ground. *God did not spare Peter the Hermit! His followers simply replaced him after growing weary of his ill planning and poor leadership. Little did they know he had already led them into the lion's den, and it was only a matter of time before they were devoured by the beast.*

Adhemar continued to smile as he watched Rodrigo. "You see, the plans of an army come second to the will of the holy Catholic Church. For without its divine leadership, no Christian army can be successful despite the best-laid plans. Fear not, Sir Rodrigo, for our army has both divine leadership and the excellent planning of our leaders. You and the others shall be privy to those plans in due time." Adhemar paused as he looked around at the other knights. "I must go now, for I have work to do. Enjoy the rest of this holy Sabbath. I shall send you my instructions tomorrow." He turned and began walking back up the steps.

Rodrigo continued to stare at the ground as he thought. *First the Catholic Church stood by idly while Peter the Hermit and his People's Army looted, pillaged, and murdered civilians on their way to Constantinople. Then, after he led all his followers to their deaths, the Church is going to accept him back with open arms as he joins us on our journey to Jerusalem?* Rodrigo suddenly looked up and called out to Adhemar. "Bishop Adhemar! Forgive me, but I was . . . momentarily stunned by the news. Please tell us, where is Peter the Hermit right now in the city?"

Adhemar stopped and turned around. "I believe he is at the Church of Saint Andrew near the western gates. Why do you ask?"

"You said he is to be joining us as we journey to the Holy Land. Perhaps we should hear the teachings of this man of God before we depart Constantinople," Rodrigo said before he abruptly turned and began walking away with the others. *And now that I know where he is,*

I think I shall pay him a visit. Adhemar stared for a moment before disappearing inside his quarters as the five walked toward the exit of the palace gardens.

"Clearly you speak in jest. What is the real reason you seek his whereabouts?" asked Geoffrey as they walked out into the city streets, which were crowded with soldiers and locals ready to begin their day after Sunday worship.

"Now that we know where he is, we can avoid the Church of Saint Andrew," Rodrigo said, looking around. "I think I will explore the city on my own for a while. I will meet you back at camp."

"Are you sure?" Geoffrey asked with raised eyebrows, studying Rodrigo's face. Rodrigo's frown had not changed, and inside he felt like a seething cauldron, ready to explode. Geoffrey's brow creased with concern as he and Rodrigo stood on the corner. "We are going to a tavern to get something to eat. You should come with us," he said, putting his hand on Rodrigo's shoulder. "You can vent your frustrations to us about the man over a tankard of ale or two." He grinned.

"I will meet with you later," Rodrigo said, looking down at the ground. "I do not feel hungry." He turned and walked away, quickly disappearing into the crowds that lined the city streets, leaving the four behind.

✠

The afternoon sun cast long shadows from the buildings that lined the bustling streets of Constantinople. Rodrigo walked with purpose through the crowded streets, and although they were alive with activity, it seemed as though he walked in a dead city, through throngs of dim ghosts, while lost in the thoughts and memories that haunted him.

The arrogance on Peter the Hermit's face and in his voice echoed in Rodrigo's ears as he walked. *We place our faith in God that he will keep us fed and supplied throughout our journey to Constantinople!* It stood in stark contrast to the fear in the face of Samuel which could be heard in the trembling of his voice: . . . *when they discovered we were*

Jews, they began attacking us, taking everything, and killing everyone, including our women and children. Rodrigo clenched his teeth as the dark eyes and despondent faces of the women and children emerging from the forest flashed back in his memory.

The sun was retreating behind the walls of Constantinople when Rodrigo finally reached the western part of the city. His shirt was stained with sweat, and his lips were parched. "Where is the Church of Saint Andrew?" he asked some the locals, who pointed him to a church nearby. Rodrigo felt his heart beating faster as he walked toward the building.

When he reached the large double doors, he paused for a moment, putting his head down with his hands against the doors, the sweat running down his face and his pulse racing. He knew that he was being driven by his anger and hatred for the man, and although he was not sure how it would end, he was not willing to turn back. Pushing the doors open forcefully, he entered the sanctuary and looked around. The sanctuary was empty except for a church deacon who was carrying some scrolls down the center of the pews.

"Where is he? Where is Peter the Hermit?" Rodrigo demanded menacingly as he approached the deacon.

Backing away, with the scrolls slipping out of his arms, the trembling deacon answered, "He is in the priest's quarters, in the back of the sanctuary."

Silenced by the look in Rodrigo's face, the deacon stared at him as he walked by. When he reached the door in the back of the sanctuary, Rodrigo kicked the door, which flew open from the force, slamming against the back wall. A priest in a brown robe in the back of the room turned around, surprised by the noise and sudden intrusion. It was Peter the Hermit.

"How dare you enter my quarters in such a manner!" Peter yelled. "Do you know who I am?" Rodrigo could clearly see that he was used to his submissive, loyal followers and expected a swift apology.

"I know exactly who you are," Rodrigo said, nearly growling the words. "You are Little Peter, the liar . . ." With malice in his eyes, he began to walk toward Peter. ". . . the trickster, the pillager, the murderer of thousands of innocent Jews, and the snake whose silver tongue led forty thousand men, women, and children straight to their deaths!" The scowl on Peter's face quickly faded, and his eyes widened as he shrank back in fear from Rodrigo, who was now standing over him. Grabbing Peter by the front of his robes, Rodrigo pulled the cowering priest close to him as he spoke. "The blood of all those people is on your hands! You claim to be a man of God? You hide behind the cross and the robes of a priest! You're not a man of God! You're not even a man!" Rodrigo pulled Peter's face even closer, lifting him off his feet as he stared into his eyes and whispered through clenched teeth. "You are a serpent, a reptile who poisons the hearts and minds of people with his vile tongue. There is nothing I would like more than to carve out that which has caused the destruction of so many."

Without warning, Rodrigo released Peter from his grasp, and the priest fell to the floor with a thud, cowering and whimpering in fear. He looked down at the cringing figure as he spoke. "But it is not my place to make final judgment upon you. When your time comes, you will have to stand before God and answer to him for all the evil that has been done at your hands." Rodrigo turned and walked back toward the door. The deacon was watching in the doorway and hurried past Rodrigo to assist Peter the Hermit, who lay on the floor where Rodrigo had dropped him.

Rodrigo continued through the sanctuary and walked outside of the church. He paused and turned his head toward the heavens, closing his eyes and breathing out a long sigh, before lowering his head back down. Although it felt as though a large weight had been removed from his shoulders, inside he felt exhausted, weak, and weary. *Forgive me, Lord, for allowing myself to be consumed by anger and hatred for so many days. I have spoken my piece, and now it is done. If this man is to be punished for his actions, it will be by your hands, not mine.* With a final glance toward the twilit sky, Rodrigo left the church and headed back to camp.

✠

Rodrigo hopped off the back of the horse-drawn wagon and walked around the front to drop some coins into the palm of the driver. "My thanks for the ride and for the food," he said as the driver nodded and gave the reins a shake to get the wagon moving again. He had been dropped off at the front of Count Raymond's camp in the southern area of the city. The moon was now high in the evening sky as Rodrigo walked through the torchlit camp. When he reached their tent, he was met by Geoffrey coming out through the tent flap.

"There you are! Where have you been all afternoon?" Geoffrey asked as the two stood outside the tent.

"I went to seek out Peter the Hermit," Rodrigo said.

"What?" Geoffrey exclaimed with wide eyes. "Did you find him? What happened?"

"I found him at the Church of Saint Andrew. Nothing happened. I spoke my piece, and that is the end of it," Rodrigo answered calmly.

"You only spoke to him? That is all?" Geoffrey asked skeptically.

"That is all, I swear," Rodrigo said, placing his hand over his heart.

Geoffrey looked at Rodrigo for a moment, studying his face. "With the look that you had in your eyes after meeting with Adhemar this afternoon, I thought you would have hurt or even killed him. I can see that you look different now."

Rodrigo nodded as he lowered his eyes. "Believe me, brother, I wanted to," he admitted. "I have been letting my anger and hatred build toward that man for quite some time. I truly did not know what I would do to him when I found him. But when I saw the trembling and fear in his eyes, I understood something."

"What was that?"

"That we cannot let our anger and hatred bring us down to the level of those we despise. If I had hurt or killed him, then I would be no better than he is. God will be our final judge, and no one else."

"That is true," said Geoffrey, thinking about what Rodrigo had said. "God willing, perhaps someday he will change."

"I don't know about that, but I am fairly certain he will need to change his priest's robes after the scare I gave him," Rodrigo said with a smirk.

Geoffrey laughed. "That also may be true. I just hope that Adhemar does not find out. You risk much by going there just to speak your mind."

"I know," Rodrigo said, slowly shaking his head. "It would give Adhemar yet another reason to dislike me," he said with a smile.

"Come, let's join the others," said Geoffrey. "They are still at the tavern, drinking ale and flirting with the local women even though none of them speak a word of Greek." He laughed.

"Agreed, but I will change my clothes first," said Rodrigo, opening the tent flap. "If this is to be our last night of freedom before we leave the city, then I must look presentable!" When he emerged, the two left camp to meet the others and enjoy their last night in Constantinople.

9

INTO THE GREAT UNKNOWN

I t was the spring of 1097 when the massive Crusader army, nearly sixty thousand soldiers, cavalry, and camp followers, were ferried across the Bosporus to the Anatolian peninsula and established their camp near the city of Nicomedia. The largest army ever assembled since the fall of the Roman Empire now sat camped on the border of Turkish-held lands. The mood among the soldiers was one of excitement and anticipation, but an ever-growing frustration over the army's leadership began to emerge after one week had passed and still no word was given as to how they would proceed.

Rather than a unified force under a central command, the massive Crusader army was made up of a loosely allied confederation of smaller armies, each with its own leader who was accustomed to autonomy and not used to sharing command with others. A great tent in the middle of the camp served as the headquarters where the leaders would meet, but it scarcely held enough room for everyone, as each leader felt it necessary to bring his own entourage with him.

The Norman princes, Count Robert of Flanders and Duke Robert of Normandy, seemed to be at odds with the French nobility, Duke

Godfrey of Bouillon and his brother Baldwin. Men of great wealth, Count Stephen of Blois and Count Hugh of Vermandois, not only brought their entourages to the meetings but their courtesans as well. Count Raymond had Bishop Adhemar at his side, and both insisted that the divine leadership of the Church take precedence over all, but this did not sit well with the fearsome Bohemond of Taranto and his nephew Tancred, who ruled by the might of their swords.

The differences in personalities and leadership styles, and the clash of egos, were evident in the shouting matches that could frequently be heard emanating from the great tent whenever the leaders convened to discuss the plans for the Crusader army. On the morning of the seventh day, Rodrigo and Geoffrey were tending to some of the more mundane camp duties when they passed the great tent in the middle of the camp. The shouting was louder and more aggressive than usual. Apparently, even the leaders were growing frustrated over their inability to agree on anything. The two stopped to watch as the flap of the great tent was thrown back and a scowling giant in a fur cloak stormed out, followed by several others.

Rodrigo nudged Geoffrey with his elbow. "Look, there goes Prince Bohemond of Taranto, judging by his height. If I were one of the leaders, I am not sure how quick I would be to disagree with him and risk drawing his ire," Rodrigo said with a grin.

"I am sure he believes that he should be the leader of this army," said Geoffrey, arms folded as he watched. "As do they all, I suppose. The problem is, if they do not come to a consensus and agree on a plan of invasion, we may be stuck here for quite some time."

"And the longer we wait, the more time the Turks will have to assemble their forces against us," Rodrigo replied. "Count Raymond must also be caught up in the power struggle. Adhemar has not called us to meet with him since we set up camp, and he is always by Raymond's side."

"Come then, let's head back to the tent and tell the others the good news—that we are still no closer to a plan of action then we were one week ago," Geoffrey said with a laugh as he and Rodrigo continued the walk to their tent.

✠

On the morning of the tenth day, unexpected and exciting news began spreading all over the camp that the incessant infighting among the leaders had finally come to an end, and they had agreed to split the leadership of the Crusader army between Duke Godfrey, Duke Robert, Prince Bohemond, and Count Raymond. It was also agreed that the city of Nicaea to the southwest would be their first objective. The anticipation and waiting were over at last, and the orders soon came to begin breaking down camp as they prepared to move forward across the border and venture into the great unknown.

THE SIEGE OF NICAEA

Like a storm from the east, the Crusader army descended upon the city of Nicaea without warning and surrounded the city save for the western side, which bordered on Lake Ascanius. Not willing to give up without a fight, the garrison within the city put up a rugged defense against the attacking Crusaders, who tried to smash the city gates with battering rams, breach the walls with catapults, and storm them with ladders. The Crusader army had been well supplied by Emperor Alexios with troops, siege engineers, and equipment, but the gates and walls were holding strong. Multiple storming attempts by the Crusaders over the last few days had failed, and the number of tents containing the wounded began to increase.

Rodrigo, Geoffrey, and Jean stood by their mounts and watched the battle from afar. They were not allowed to be part of the storming attempts, since the possibility of a counterattack from the south remained high. The cavalry was ordered to stand by, battle ready in full armor, and guard their southern flank should a Turkish army arrive and attempt to break the siege. Dark gray storm clouds blanketed most of the sky that afternoon, with rays of sunlight trying to break through in some areas. As the battle atop the city walls raged on, Rodrigo frowned and shook his head. *Why do they continue with the same failed strategy over and over?*

Rodrigo continued to stare at the walls in silence as Geoffrey turned to speak to Jean, who was leaning on his lance as he watched. "This is the third time they have tried storming the walls, without success. The battering rams cannot breach the gates, and the catapults have failed to topple the city walls. What is happening? I thought you said we would take the city easily?"

"I don't know. I thought it would be. Perhaps we should send Rodrigo to advise the soldiers in their storming attempts?" Jean said with a smirk.

"I wish I could," Rodrigo answered in frustration. "I certainly would not continue storming the walls with ladders over and over like they have been doing. If our leaders would take the time to build siege towers, we would have a much better chance. Employing sappers to fell a section of the wall would also be a better strategy than this. If they continue to try and take the walls by attrition with only ladders, it will not happen anytime soon. Also, did either of you notice the ships that sailed to the western edge of the city last night?"

"No," Jean said. He looked at Geoffrey, who also shook his head.

"They were Turkish ships. That means the city is being resupplied from across the lake. If they are feeding in fresh troops and supplies unhindered, this siege could drag on for weeks or maybe even months!" He raised his hands in exasperation.

A voice cried out suddenly among the cavalry soldiers behind them, causing the three to turn around. "A rider! A rider approaches from the south!"

Without speaking, Rodrigo, Geoffrey, and Jean quickly mounted their horses and turned them to get a better view. A cloud of dust could be seen trailing a lightly armored rider bearing a Crusader flag who was galloping full speed toward them from the south. Earlier that morning, scouting parties had been deployed to the south and to the east, but neither had been seen or heard from since.

"What do you think it is?" Geoffrey asked.

"Whatever it is, it must be urgent," Rodrigo replied, sitting up as high as he could to get a better look.

"Come, let's move up closer to get a better view," Jean suggested. "The cavalry commander has just left the group to meet the rider."

The three rode to the front of the cavalry line facing south and watched as the commander spoke to the rider, who had come to a halt and was now giving his report. Although they were too far away to hear what was being said, the rider could be seen frantically pointing to the south and waving his arms. Their meeting ended abruptly with the rider galloping away toward the city and the commander quickly returning to the front of the cavalry lines to meet with the other officers.

The meeting was soon followed by a shrill trumpet blast ordering battle formations. Rodrigo felt his pulse quickening, and his mind began to race. "Where are Richard and William?"

The movement and noise of the cavalry around them were disorienting as they looked about for their missing comrades. "William told me they were headed back to camp to get food and water. They should have been back by now!" Geoffrey said.

"It is too late! We must get into formation with the others!" Jean yelled as he moved his horse forward toward the cavalry line that was beginning to form. Rodrigo and Geoffrey looked at one another for a moment and then rode to join him.

Giant clouds of dust began rising from the south as thousands of Turkish horsemen came into view, riding up from the plains under the stormy skies. The rows of mounted warriors grew larger as they approached, their pointed helms and rows of spears gleaming in the rays of sunlight that managed to break through the clouds. The memory of his charge at the Saracen warriors in his first battle flashed through Rodrigo's mind as he scanned row upon row of the advancing enemy cavalry. *Our cavalry is vastly outnumbered again, just as we were when we battled the Almoravids near Valencia.*

"Why are we waiting here? Why don't we charge them?" asked Geoffrey. He was rocking back and forth, unable to stay still in his saddle as they watched the Turkish army grow closer.

Rodrigo adjusted his lance. "Patience, brother. They outnumber us nearly three to one. Charging them now would be disastrous, as they would quickly outflank and surround us. Look, they have turned and are heading toward the soldiers attacking the wall!"

The Crusaders on the ground had abandoned their assault on the city walls and turned to face the Turkish cavalry. Resting the base of their large shields upon the ground and interlocking them, they began to create a long wall of shields, a defensive formation against the coming charge. Without warning, the Turkish cavalry let loose a hail of arrows, followed by a ferocious yell as they sped toward the shield wall with lances and sabers, aiming to crush the Crusaders and break through to the city defenders.

Rodrigo watched in tense silence as the first wave of the massive cavalry charge smashed into the Crusaders' shield wall. His heart was in his throat as he watched, but to his surprise, most areas of the shield wall held strong, and the charge was shattered like a wave hitting a rock. The subsequent waves of cavalry behind them immediately had to slow to a stop or risk running into and riding over their own troops. The Turkish cavalry, now at a standstill, began hacking and slashing at the warriors on the ground with their sabers from atop their horses as the shield wall disassembled and the melee fighting began.

Rodrigo's heart was racing, and he knew the right moment had arrived. The trumpet blast signaled the charge as the six-thousand-strong Crusader cavalry set their lances and spurred their horses into a full gallop, attacking the side and rear formations of the Turkish cavalry while they were still engaged with the Crusader infantry. With adrenaline flowing and blood pounding in his ears, Rodrigo braced for the impact as the knights rode full speed at the horses and riders ahead of them.

With a deafening battle cry moments before impact, the mounted knights crashed headlong into the Turkish cavalry. Rodrigo could see stark fear in the faces of the Turkish warriors as they turned to defend themselves, only to be violently struck down by the Crusaders' steel-tipped lances, backed by the weight of a thousand pounds of horseflesh and heavily armored riders. The sound of splintering wood from the lances, screams of the dying, and horses whinnying in fear and pain filled the air. Rodrigo's lance impaled one of the Turks from the side with such force that the tip burst out the other side and pierced another rider behind him. The force of the charge carried the knights deep into the center of the Turkish cavalry, trampling the fallen men and mounts beneath them.

Surrounded on all sides by both friend and foe, Rodrigo quickly drew his sword and began swinging it at the Turkish warriors around him, parrying saber slashes and knocking enemies off their mounts. The Turks were not as well armored as the Crusaders, but their sabers were light, fast, and sharp. Rodrigo felt several glancing blows from the sabers on his armor and helmet, but he knew at any moment one might deal significant damage. He gritted his teeth as he desperately struck back, slicing off the forearm of a Turk who swung at his head, sending arm and saber flying through the air. The fighting was becoming confusing, and Rodrigo quickly scanned those around him to avoid being struck from behind or accidentally killing one of his own. He suddenly realized he was surrounded on all sides as the Turks came into range with their sabers, ready to cut him down. He knew he would not be able to defend against all of them.

"Rodrigo!" a voice called to him from one side. Rodrigo turned to see Geoffrey swinging his sword as he caught one of the Turks off guard, tearing open his side and knocking him off his horse. Rodrigo parried the slash of a saber on his right and returned the blow, striking the Turk in the face. The Turk dropped his saber as he grabbed his bloodied face and howled in pain. The ring from the clash of swords behind him let Rodrigo know that one Turk was now engaged with Geoffrey, while the one in front of Rodrigo wheeled his mount and began to flee.

The Turks were desperately trying to regroup, but they faced an insurmountable wall of Crusaders to their front, and having their lines broken and penetrated deeply by the mounted knights, they were beginning to fall apart. Horns sounded in the distance as the rest of the Turkish cavalry began to turn and flee. Rodrigo and the others lifted their swords and shouted in victory and defiance as the broken Turkish cavalry fled to the south, leaving the ground littered with the bodies of their dead.

Rodrigo was breathing heavily and bleeding from several wounds as he rode up beside Geoffrey, who also looked exhausted from the brief but intense battle. "Thank you, brother," Rodrigo said between breaths. "They had me surrounded. You came at just the right moment."

Geoffrey unbuckled his chin strap, and sweat ran down his brow as he took off his helmet. "I noticed you were in trouble," he said with a smile. "I am glad that I could help out. Where is Jean? Did you see him?"

Rodrigo saw a rider waving his arm at them as he approached. Geoffrey turned and saw Jean trotting toward them.

"Rodrigo! Geoffrey!" Jean called out with a smile, beaming as he stopped his mount beside them. "I lost track of you after our initial charge. How did you fare in the battle? Did you kill many Turks?"

"We did! Probably many more than you!" Geoffrey said with a laugh.

"We are victorious and survived the battle," Rodrigo said, loosening and removing his helmet. "I think that is all that matters." He remembered that this was Geoffrey and Jean's first battle and recalled the thrill and excitement he had felt after his first. "Come, let's regroup with the other cavalry and then return to camp and find out what happened to Richard and William." The rays of sunlight had disappeared, and the gray sky was growing dim as the three rode off the battlefield together, leaving the carnage and devastation behind.

✠

The next few days passed uneventfully as the fervor and excitement from their first battle with the Turks began to wane. The siege of the city had resumed, and the assault on the city walls continued, but with little progress. The cavalry again stood guard some distance from the city, but the threat of another attack remained low, and they stood by idly watching and waiting.

Richard and William had not been part of the cavalry charge that had crushed the Turkish attempt to break the siege. Instead, they had been forced to stay and help prepare camp defenses in case the Turks had broken through the Crusader lines. Much to their chagrin, they had missed the battle completely. Meanwhile, Rodrigo felt his frustration continue to grow as he watched the Crusaders assault the walls of the city again and again only to be repelled each time. Then, on the morning of the third day since the cavalry charge, the five emerged from their tent to see a bewildering sight.

"Look at the battlements!" Rodrigo exclaimed as he stared at the city, shielding his eyes from the morning sun. Several yellow flags showing a black double-headed eagle with a crown fluttered in the wind from the battlements around the city. It was the imperial Byzantine standard.

"The city has surrendered?" asked Geoffrey. "How can this be?"

"Then why are the city gates still closed?" Richard said. "Why are all our warriors gathered around the base of the walls by the gates? Come, let's go and see what is happening there."

The five knights left the camp and walked to the base of the walls by the gates where they could see the crowds of Crusader warriors gathered around, waiting to be let inside. Rodrigo walked over to one of the warriors who was standing about. "What is going on here?" he asked. "If the siege has ended and the city has surrendered, why are the gates still closed?"

The warrior had bloodstains on his ragged tunic, and he looked and smelled as if he had not washed in days. A deep scowl masked his bearded face, and the axe he held still had blood on it. "Byzantine ships blockaded the western walls of the city late yesterday evening. It is being said that the city surrendered to the Byzantines in the night, but now they refuse to open the gates to us! They want to keep all the loot inside the city for themselves!" He spat on the ground.

Rodrigo listened intently. *The fighting atop the walls has been long and brutal, while we simply stood by and watched. I understand his frustration and anger, but why such concern over loot? Did they intend to loot and pillage the city upon entering?*

"They want to keep the loot for themselves?" Rodrigo asked. "Did our leaders not agree to return all conquered lands and strongholds back to the Byzantines anyway?"

"They can keep the damned city!" The warrior growled through clenched teeth. "We lost nearly two hundred men trying to take these walls! And now we get nothing?" The warrior stared at Rodrigo, looking at him up and down. "Maybe a share of the city loot means nothing to a wealthy knight like yourself, but to us it means everything!" he yelled, placing his hand upon Rodrigo's chest and shoving him backward.

Taken back by the force of the warrior's words and surprised by his actions, Rodrigo instinctively placed his hand on the hilt of his sword as the warrior lifted his bloody axe into the air, and the two squared off against each other. The yelling had attracted the attention of others around them, and seeing what was happening, William and Geoffrey jumped in to intervene. They quickly placed their hands on Rodrigo's shoulders and pulled him back, away from the warrior.

"Calm yourself, brother," Geoffrey said as the three backed away from the scene. "No need to spill any blood over an argument, especially against our fellow Crusaders. Let's return to the tents." Geoffrey called for the others, and together they began to walk back to camp.

"I was not going to fight the man," Rodrigo said. "He was the one that wanted to fight me when I simply questioned him about looting the city. Perhaps it was best that the city surrendered to the Byzantines. Had the assault of the walls been successful, the city would have been sacked and plundered, and likely many innocent civilians would have been killed."

"What does that matter?" Richard asked. "The city is full of Saracens who have the blood of innocent Christians on their hands. And now none of us will see any plunder from the city."

Rodrigo stopped and turned to Richard with a furrowed brow. "It is the Turkish warriors that are our enemies, not the civilians that live in the cities and villages. And did you embark upon this journey to liberate the Holy Land and the city of Jerusalem, or to fill your coffers with loot and plunder?"

Richard stared back at Rodrigo as he spoke. "Spare us the self-righteous talk, Rodrigo," he shot back. "All of us began this journey with more expectations than to simply liberate the Holy Land from the Turks. As for the Saracen warriors and civilians, they are one and the same, as I see it."

Rodrigo frowned. *More expectations such as earning honor and seeking truth, yes. But we are not here to loot and plunder cities! As for Saracen civilians and warriors being one and the same . . .* Rodrigo was about to speak his mind when a man on horseback approached the five knights and stopped in front of them. "Are you the Knights of the Crucem Auream?" he asked.

"We are," Geoffrey replied.

"You are summoned by Bishop Adhemar," the messenger announced before turning his mount and riding away.

"Let's go and see what he wants," Geoffrey said. Deciding to hold his tongue for the time being, Rodrigo walked with the others in silence as they entered the camp and proceeded toward Adhemar's tent.

When they arrived, the five knights gathered outside the tent as a guard went in to inform Adhemar. The guard returned and held the tent flap as Adhemar emerged and stood in front of them. "Greetings, my Knights of the Crucem Auream," he began. "In three days, we break camp. The city has surrendered to the Byzantines and will remain under their control, but the city gates will not be open to us. However, to compensate us for our losses and for our aid in retaking the city, Emperor Alexios has graciously offered us a generous share of the city's treasury." The knights murmured in surprise and excitement, save for Rodrigo, who remained silent. "Your share of the treasure will be delivered to your commanders, who will distribute it evenly among the men." Adhemar paused and turned toward Rodrigo. "Sir Rodrigo, your share will be forfeited as per our previous arrangement." Rodrigo said nothing but bowed his head in agreement as Adhemar continued. "I will inform all of you of the plans to move forward in two days. In the meantime, begin your preparations to move out. If there are no questions, you may return to your tent." Hearing none, Adhemar turned and walked back into his tent as the five began talking among themselves.

"Why will you be forfeiting your share of the treasure?" Geoffrey asked.

"I will take your share if you do not want it," Jean offered with a grin.

"It is not that," Rodrigo said. "I told Adhemar I would pay for all the supplies that were delivered to the Jewish settlement to help them through the winter."

Richard's eyes widened. "That is why you gave up your share?" he asked in near disbelief.

"Perhaps you were wrong, Richard," Geoffrey said, patting Rodrigo on the back. "It is not just self-righteous talk. I will split my share with you, Rodrigo."

"Do as you please, but I will keep mine!" Richard said with a laugh as the five began walking back to their tent.

11

THE SPLIT

The month-long siege had finally come to an end, and having successfully accomplished their first objective, the Crusader army prepared to continue their march south in the month of June. An unexpected development had occurred within the ranks of their leadership, and they prepared to split into two groups, traveling one day apart from each other.

One-third of the Crusader forces, nearly twenty thousand men, would form a vanguard and depart one day early under the leadership of Prince Bohemond and Duke Robert. The rest of the army, led by Count Raymond and Duke Godfrey, would depart one day later. The official reason given for the split was to conserve supplies, as the winding road south was reported to be over rocky and hilly terrain with few villages and scant resources along the way. Unofficially, there was speculation that the four leaders simply could not get along and wanted to split up. Whatever their reasoning, the decision had been made.

The weather was beginning to warm rapidly as they entered into the summer months, and Rodrigo stopped to rest and mop the beaded sweat from his brow with a cloth as he, Geoffrey, and Jean worked to take down their tent and pack their belongings for travel.

The other two knights, however, had been suspiciously absent that morning. "Do either of you know where Richard and William have gone? Why have they disappeared when there is still work to be done?" Rodrigo asked as they stopped for a break to drink.

"I don't know," said Geoffrey, handing a water skin to Jean. "They left earlier this morning, and I have not seen them since. Perhaps we should look for them after we finish here."

Later that afternoon, the three went to look for their missing brothers. When they approached the stables, Rodrigo could see Richard and William leading their saddled mounts away. Both men were dressed in full armor. "Richard! William! Wait!" he called out, jogging after them as the others followed. Rodrigo could see that Richard had stopped and was speaking to William as the three caught up to them.

"What are you doing?" Geoffrey demanded. "Are you leaving?"

"Yes," Richard answered flatly, his expression matching the tone of his voice.

"Why?" asked Rodrigo, wide-eyed. "Without telling us? Give us a reason, at least. Have we done something to offend you?"

William's eyes lowered to the ground for a few moments as he held his horse's reins. "No. None of you have done anything to offend us," he answered meekly. "Last night, Richard and I came to feed and water our mounts when we heard that Prince Bohemond was asking for volunteers as he seeks to strengthen the cavalry units of the vanguard. We volunteered, so we shall be going with them." He continued to avoid their gaze, while Richard remained silent with folded arms.

"Is this wise, brothers?" Jean asked. "Adhemar will be extremely displeased when he finds out. He ordered us to stay together in *his* cavalry units."

"We know what his orders are," Richard replied sharply. "I will deal with Adhemar when we next regroup."

"I do not understand this decision," Rodrigo said, searching their faces for an answer. "What have you to gain by defying the will of Adhemar and joining a group that will surely come under attack? The Turkish cavalry we defeated was but a fraction of their army.

With time to regroup and plan an ambush, they will be out there, somewhere, just waiting for an opportunity to strike back." He pointed to the hills outside the camp.

The five stood in silence for a moment as William continued to stare at the ground. Richard's brow creased as he concentrated his gaze on Rodrigo. "It is true that we are likely to be attacked, but I believe Prince Bohemond to be the strongest of our leaders. With a force of twenty thousand Crusaders, I am confident we will be able to defend ourselves against any attack by the Turks. During the last battle, William and I were left out, while all of you were able to earn honor in combat with the enemy. Now it shall be our turn to do the same as we lead this army into the Holy Land." Richard unfolded his arms and took the reins of his mount. "Come, William. We do not want to be late for the cavalry muster."

"Wait a moment!" Rodrigo shouted as he moved in front of Richard. He looked into Richard's eyes and knew his mind would not be changed. "God be with you, brother," Rodrigo said, and he suddenly moved forward, catching Richard off guard with a farewell embrace. For a moment, Richard stood still, surprised by Rodrigo's actions, before returning the embrace.

Releasing Richard, Rodrigo walked over to William and placed his hand upon his shoulder, causing William to look up. With a smile, Rodrigo embraced William as he bid him farewell. "God be with you as well, brother. May we meet again soon." Following Rodrigo, Jean and Geoffrey did the same, embracing their two brothers while wishing them luck and saying their goodbyes.

The afternoon sun shone brightly in the sky as Richard and William left the group and mounted their horses, riding away from the camp toward the columns that were forming to the south. Rodrigo, Jean, and Geoffrey watched in silence until the two had disappeared into the crowds of soldiers and cavalry that were gathering in the distance.

12

REBELLION IN THE RANKS

The sky was growing dark in the evening hours as stars began to appear, but the activity in the camp remained high as the Crusaders prepared to move out at dawn, following Prince Bohemond's vanguard. Adhemar had summoned his Knights of the Crucem Auream to his tent that evening to give them their orders, but only three had arrived, the other two conspicuously absent. The news of Richard and William's departure was met with an angry and withering reprimand by Adhemar as he stared with disgust at Rodrigo, Jean, and Geoffrey, who stood outside his tent. A foul mood gripped Adhemar, and he felt his temper rising as he considered the punishment for their rebellious behavior. He would not dismiss the prospect of having all the men lashed until the flesh peeled from their backs for having disobeyed a direct order.

The burning intensity of Adhemar's anger and his searing gaze whipped the three into a silent submission as they stared at the ground. His gaze came to rest upon Rodrigo, who seemed to squirm with discomfort. *Perhaps Sir Rodrigo's unruly attitude is beginning to influence the others. The threat of taking their wealth is apparently not enough. While having them lashed is certainly warranted, it would be unwise to physically weaken the men while the possibility of battle with the enemy remains high. I shall need to think of something else.* An idea came to Adhemar as he observed their discomfort becoming increasingly noticeable. *I wonder how they will try to justify their actions?*

"And you just let them go and did nothing to stop them?" Adhemar asked loudly, his voice laced with anger and disgust. The three remained silent for a moment, but then Rodrigo raised his head and at last spoke up. "We *tried*, Bishop Adhemar. We spoke to them, but William and Richard would not be dissuaded from their intentions to join Prince Bohemond's vanguard."

"Why did you not come and tell me of their intentions at once?" Adhemar demanded loudly as he stared at Rodrigo. Rodrigo frowned and stammered for a moment as he seemed to struggle to hold back what he wanted to say, but then he lowered his head in silence along with the others.

At least he is learning to control his tongue. Perhaps these feelings of discomfort will give them pause in the future if they again consider defying my orders. "I see," Adhemar continued, lowering his voice. "The three of you chose not to tell me because *you knew* that I would stop them," he said with disdain. "Therefore, all of you will be held responsible for their disobedience and shall be punished accordingly. What reason did Sir William and Sir Richard give for this reckless act of defiance?"

Geoffrey raised his head and spoke. "They were unhappy, Bishop Adhemar, that they were not able to take part in the battle with the Turks when they attempted to break our siege. As knights, it is important to distinguish ourselves and gain honor through combat. They simply wanted an opportunity to do the same."

"Distinguish yourselves and gain honor through combat?" Adhemar yelled, feeling his temper rising again. "I have told you all before that the will of the holy Catholic Church comes first! Your vows to fulfill the Pope's mission and to obey my orders come before all else! Do you understand?" he shouted, nearly trembling with anger.

"Yes, Bishop Adhemar," the three humbly replied.

"Bishop Adhemar . . ." Rodrigo began as he raised his head to speak.

"Enough!" Adhemar yelled, cutting him off. "We are to rendezvous with the advance party near a town two days' march to the south, called Dorylaeum. There I shall decide your punishment for disobeying my orders and decide whether or not you five are worthy of continuing the mission to which you have been assigned. You are dismissed," he said with a wave of his hand. Silently, the three turned and left as Adhemar entered his tent and sat on a couch near the entrance, deep in thought. *Sir Richard and Sir William must be made an example of, and their punishment for this behavior will be severe. I may also need to take their crosses and remove them from the Pope's mission, depending on how they respond to their punishment. If this happens, then I must leverage the others' guilt to my advantage.*

✠

Dawn was breaking on the eastern horizon as the trumpet blasts cut through the morning air, ordering the Crusader army to fall into columns as they prepared to move. The camp followers were loading the last of the tents and supplies onto wagons in the now empty camp while Rodrigo, Geoffrey, and Jean waited in the long columns for the marching orders atop their mounts.

"I think we made a mistake, brothers, letting William and Richard go," Geoffrey said at last.

"So you think we should have betrayed them by telling Adhemar their intentions?" asked Rodrigo.

"They would have been very angry," Jean said, offering his opinion. "At least, Richard would have been angry. I do not think William really wanted to leave."

Rodrigo nodded in agreement.

"I think we could have done more to talk them out of it," Geoffrey said. "If not, then perhaps we *should* have notified Adhemar. Is our mission to recover the holy relics not more important than seeking honor in battle?"

"Perhaps William would have stayed had we done more, but I do not think Richard would have changed his mind. He is very stubborn in his thinking and his beliefs," Rodrigo answered. "I agree with you, however, about our mission to recover the holy relics. That should come before all else, including personal glory and honor."

Three short trumpet blasts sounded in the distance. The marching orders had been given, and the long columns of soldiers, cavalry, and supply wagons began slowly moving down the road to the south.

13

DORYLAEUM

All day and into the evening, the Crusader army marched down the winding, dusty road toward Dorylaeum. At last, they stopped along the road to camp. The full moon had risen, framing the three against the darkened sky as they stood guard, following Adhemar's orders, on a hill beside the road where the army had camped. Rodrigo sat in quiet contemplation by the fire, staring into the distance. *Somewhere out there, among those moonlit hills, the enemy is waiting for us.* He bowed his head in silent prayer. *Lord, please watch over our brothers and all of the men in the vanguard and keep them safe.*

The moon slowly made its journey across the sky, and after they had been relieved of their duty, the three laid down to catch a few hours of sleep before the break of dawn when the army would prepare to move again. The Crusader army had broken camp by midmorning and was on the move again when a trumpet blast sounded and the long columns abruptly came to a halt.

"What do you think it is?" Jean asked.

"We will have to wait and see," Rodrigo said with a furrowed brow.

"I can see clouds of dust from the road toward the south at the head of the column, but I cannot see who or what it is," said Geoffrey, sitting as tall as he could in his saddle to get a better view. "Maybe it is someone from the vanguard with a message."

A feeling of unease came over Rodrigo as they waited. *Any news from the vanguard before we reach Dorylaeum cannot be good news.* Time seemed to slow to a crawl as the three anxiously awaited an answer as to why the column had halted and if indeed a rider had come from the south. Suddenly, a series of short trumpet blasts signaled a formation. Moving with the cavalry, the three broke off from the main column and rode to a nearby field with their unit, awaiting orders. They were soon met by a cavalry officer who rode to the front of the formation.

The officer had a look of deadly seriousness upon his face as he reined his horse to a halt. "The vanguard is under attack!" he shouted. A hushed silence fell over the cavalry group. A lump began to form in Rodrigo's throat as he listened. "Their camp was ambushed at dawn on the plains near Dorylaeum by a large Turkish force. They are about a half day away from us if we move at a swift pace. All cavalry units and three infantry units will move ahead to join the battle. The rest will stay behind with the camp followers. Prepare to move out!" He reined his horse around and left to prepare for the march south.

The infantry and cavalry units of Godfrey and Raymond were quickly organized into groups, and plans of attack were hastily drawn up. The cavalry of Duke Godfrey would ride out first and lead the counterattack against the Turks. Count Raymond's cavalry would be mixed with Byzantine troops and Crusader infantry. They would take an alternate route to Dorylaeum that rounded the hills and would surprise the Turks as they emerged from behind. Their route would take longer, but the element of surprise would give them a heavy advantage.

"We should never have let them go," Geoffrey said as the three waited on the fields for further orders.

Rodrigo shook his head. "They made their decision. All we can do is pray that they will be safe until we get there."

"We should be going with Duke Godfrey's cavalry!" Jean said in frustration. "They will reach the battle ahead of us!"

"I agree, brother," Rodrigo said. "I want to get there as quickly as possible too, but the strategy is sound. If we surprise the Turks from behind, we may have a chance to wipe out their entire army."

The trumpet blasts sounded the marching orders as the two groups began to move out on separate paths to aid the besieged Crusaders. Godfrey's troops continued south, while Count Raymond's headed east. The hours seemed to pass like days as their group moved over the winding road around the hills. The cavalry had to move at a slow trot to allow the infantry to keep up behind them at a forced march. The sun was casting long shadows on the ground when at last the hilly terrain began to lessen and they could see a broad plain before them. The sounds of battle could be heard in the distance. Straining to see what was happening, Rodrigo could see dust rising from the plain ahead of them from the movement of men and horses. Every so often, a hail of arrows, like a swiftly moving black cloud, would arc into the air above the clouds of dust on the ground.

As they moved farther onto the plain, the group quickly began to organize from marching into attack formations while continuing to move forward. Soon they were close enough to clearly see both sides in the conflict. It appeared that the Turks had the Crusader camp completely surrounded and continued to shower them with volleys of arrows from horseback as they moved in and out from the battle lines.

Farther to the west, Rodrigo could see tents in the distance, but the flags flown there were Saracen, not Crusader. They had come up behind the enemy camp and were poised to strike a deadly blow. The thought of how the Crusader camp could still be holding on after sustaining such attacks for nearly half the day was both astounding and gut-wrenching at the same time. As they drew closer and closer to the battle, Rodrigo and the others were nearly bursting with anticipation to get into the fray, knowing that the Crusader camp could be overrun at any moment. The trumpet blast behind them signaling the charge could not have come soon enough.

A battle cry went up from the infantry units as they rushed toward the Turkish camp while the cavalry raced toward the Turkish forces attacking the Crusaders. The Turkish horse archers continued to loose their volleys into the Crusader camp, while the Turkish cavalry and infantry continued to charge at the Crusader lines, trying to break them. A Crusader shield wall encircled the entire camp as they doggedly held on. Suddenly, horns within the Turkish ranks sounded, as they turned to face the surprise attack from behind.

With a furious roar, the Crusader cavalry set their lances and charged into the Turkish forces, who were caught completely off guard. Rodrigo could see the look of utter surprise and fear in the faces of the enemy as they smashed into the ranks of Turkish infantry and cavalry. Buckling from the shock of the heavy cavalry charge, the Turkish lines immediately fell into disarray.

Rodrigo's lance struck a Turkish warrior, catapulting him from his saddle, taking the lance with him as Rodrigo felt the shaft being torn from his grasp. Immediately, Rodrigo drew his sword as their momentum ground to a halt and the melee combat began. The impact had carried them deep into the enemy lines, and men and horses were nearly on top of each other.

Blocked by a fallen horse and rider in front of him, Rodrigo clung to his reins as he spurred his mount to vault over the downed animal, crushing a Turkish warrior as it landed on the other side. Immediately after he landed, a mounted Turk beside him thrust his lance at Rodrigo. Rodrigo turned his shield just in time and managed to deflect the lance, which became stuck and immobilized in his shield. Rodrigo quickly took advantage of the situation and slashed downward with his sword, breaking the lance at the tip.

Recovering from the slash, Rodrigo raised his sword and struck downward at the mounted Turk, hitting him in the shoulder. The force of the strike carried the blade down into his chest. The Turkish warrior fell from his horse as Rodrigo turned his mount to face the Turkish cavalry and horse archers around him. The horse archers were lightly armored, and not used to close-quarters fighting. Most had dropped their bows, useless at such close distance, and were fighting with their sabers as the Crusader knights began cutting them down with their swords and axes.

Rodrigo swung his sword ferociously from side to side, hacking off limbs and inflicting terrible wounds on the Turks. The number of Turkish warriors had begun to thin, but clouds of dust from all the movement began to obscure his vision. The sounds of clashing metal and the screams of dying men and frightened horses were deafening. The fog of war was descending as Rodrigo looked around and struggled to get his bearings. Suddenly, he spied the Crusader camp in the distance. The shield wall was opening, and through it charged Crusader cavalry led by Prince Bohemond, attacking the Turks from the opposite side. Seeing an unbroken lance impaled in the body of Turk nearby, Rodrigo wheeled his horse and quickly snatched it up.

"Follow me!" Rodrigo yelled to those around him. When they saw what was happening, other Crusader cavalry joined him and rode toward the besieged camp. Leading the charge, Rodrigo set his lance and galloped full speed toward the Turkish forces that Bohemond was charging from the other side. The Turkish infantry attacking the camp began to panic as the Crusader cavalry closed in on them from both sides. Not knowing which way to turn and having nowhere to run, many froze in fear as the Crusader cavalry smashed into the front and rear of their ranks. Like metal being struck between a hammer and anvil, the stunned Turkish forces broke almost instantly.

Those that survived immediately dropped their weapons and began to flee. His second lance now broken, Rodrigo drew his sword, but hesitated for a moment as he watched the other Crusaders begin to pursue the Turks. Never before had he attacked a defenseless enemy fleeing the field of battle. *What honor is there in killing a foe that is retreating?* Sweat streamed down his brow under his helmet, and he was breathing heavily as his mind raced. *But if we do not decimate their numbers now, they will regroup and attack us again.* Rodrigo frowned as he drew his sword and spurred his horse to a gallop to join the other cavalry who gave chase as the Turks retreated.

Rodrigo rode up behind a Turk fleeing on foot and swung his sword. The chopping blow struck the Turk on the back of his neck, sending him tumbling, dead before he hit the ground. Two, three, then four Turks went down, one by one, with a blow nearly splitting the skull of a fleeing Turk who had lost his helmet. The momentum of the swiftly moving horse combined with the swing of the blade made the killing blows brutally effective.

At last, he reined his horse to stop, and the sounds of battle began to fade away as he watched the last of the Turkish forces retreat to the south, bloodied and broken. The Turkish camp was in flames, and the Crusader infantry had either captured or killed many of them in their retreat.

The adrenaline from the battle was finally wearing off, and Rodrigo was exhausted and winded as he paused to catch his breath. He lowered his sword and stared at the blood and gore dripping from the blade, shaking his head. *There is no honor in killing a retreating, defenseless foe. I will never again engage the enemy in this manner.*

He sheathed his sword and turned his mount back toward the Crusader camp. With the battle over, his thoughts once again turned toward William and Richard. It was truly fortunate that Count Raymond's forces had arrived when they did, for had they been delayed for any length of time, the Crusader camp would have been completely overrun. With the casualties the camp had sustained, however, Rodrigo began to worry for the well-being of his brothers as he spurred his horse to a gallop and headed toward the camp. Riding past the dead bodies of both Turks and Crusaders, he slowed to a trot, and then a walk, as he approached the camp. He was stunned by the carnage.

Thousands of dead Crusaders lay about the camp, and shields that resembled giant pincushions with arrows protruding from them littered the ground. Never in his life had he seen or imagined such a sight. He dismounted and looked around. Soldiers who could still stand were making their way through the bodies. Some tended to wounded warriors, while others searched for those still alive. Rodrigo felt his heart sinking at the sight. Silently, he said a prayer for William and Richard that they would not be among the dead. Arrows were everywhere: in the tents, the shields, the ground, and the bodies of the dead Crusaders. *The hail of arrows must have continued nonstop for hours while they waited for us,* he thought as he looked around at the devastation.

"Help . . . help me," a wounded warrior on the ground called out to him.

Although his thoughts remained fixed on finding William and Richard, Rodrigo knew he could not ignore the needs of the wounded around him. He tethered his horse to one of the tents and returned to the man. The injured warrior was in pain and had arrows in his shoulder, arm, and thigh. Helping him to his feet, Rodrigo steadied him by placing the man's arm over his shoulder, and slowly the two moved to a tent nearby. Inside the tent were dozens of others with similar grievous wounds. Blankets were being laid upon the floor, and strips of cloth were being torn for bandages. Gently, Rodrigo laid the man on the floor of the tent and went back outside. The ground was becoming muddy with pools of blood, and the sounds of men groaning in agony could be heard all over the camp. *There is no glory in this victory,* Rodrigo thought.

The next few hours Rodrigo spent walking up and down the edge of the camp where the warriors had heroically held on for hours against swarms of arrows and wave after wave of attack from the Turks. The wounded and dead numbered in the thousands, and a great number of bodies were being laid on the ground outside of the camp, separating them from the wounded. Helping injured Crusaders wherever he could, Rodrigo kept his eyes open for any sign of William or Richard.

"Rodrigo!" a voice called out to him from a nearby tent. It was Jean, waving at Rodrigo to come inside. Hurriedly, Rodrigo followed him. The tent was full of the wounded, and he saw Jean and Geoffrey standing over William, who was lying on the ground, his body covered in blood-soaked bandages. Two broken arrows were still embedded in his leg and chest. It was clear that he was dying.

Rodrigo knelt and took William's hand in his own. "Rodrigo . . ." William said, gasping for breath. "I am paying the price . . ." His voice was shaky and unsteady. ". . . for my pride and my envy of you and the others." He looked up at Rodrigo. Tears were running down the sides of his face, and his eyes were full of sorrow and remorse.

"No. No, brother. You fought with courage and valor," Rodrigo assured him, holding William's hand tightly. "You will go with honor. Your penance has been paid in full. This day, you will rejoice in the kingdom of heaven."

Rodrigo felt a hand on his shoulder as someone spoke. "There is nothing more you can do. His time has come." Letting go of William's hand, Rodrigo stood as a priest moved forward to stand over William and delivered the last rites as William exhaled his final breath. Finished, the priest walked away as another man approached the three.

"Take this one out. We need to make room for the wounded," he said unsympathetically. The three said nothing as they lifted William's lifeless body and carried it to the edge of the camp, where thousands of dead were being laid in long rows.

"What of Richard? Is he dead also?" asked Rodrigo, at last breaking the silence.

"We asked William about Richard when we found him," Geoffrey replied.

"What did he say?"

"He said Richard left with a scouting party when they first arrived and set up camp," Geoffrey said, looking down at William. "He said the scouting party never returned, and the camp was attacked at dawn."

Rodrigo felt a sinking in the pit of his stomach. "And what will happen to the dead? Will we just leave them here?"

"No," said Jean. "They will be given a Christian burial once the last of the dead have been separated from the wounded. The bodies of the Saracens will be piled high and burned."

Kneeling by William's lifeless body, Rodrigo reached under William's tunic and withdrew the bloody, golden cross still attached to the chain around William's neck. With a slight tug, Rodrigo broke the chain and stood up. "We will return this to Adhemar when we see him." Silently, the others nodded in agreement.

"Farewell, brother," Rodrigo said. When the three had said their final goodbyes, they walked back toward the camp. The last rays of the sun faded as it slowly sank behind the hills, and a new moon was rising in its place.

THE BURDEN OF THE CROSS

The Crusader dead were buried and given a mass funeral service in the morning, led by Bishop Adhemar with several priests at his side, aiding him during the service. One of the priests was noticeably shorter than the others and held a wooden cross in one hand, which he waved around with animated gestures during his speech. Rodrigo watched with disgust. *Peter the Hermit! Why is he creating such a spectacle during a funeral service? He obviously does not care about the deceased or their sacrifice. He is just using this opportunity to garner attention from Bishop Adhemar and the nobles.*

Farther away from the camp, the bodies of the slain Turks were cremated to reduce the likelihood of vermin and disease. Nearly four thousand Crusaders had perished in the battle, and the Turkish losses numbered around three thousand. Immediately following the funeral procession, Adhemar called a meeting with the three remaining Knights of the Crucem Auream in his tent.

The three entered the tent and stood in somber silence in front of Adhemar. His stern gaze held no emotion as the three hung their heads and looked at the ground while he spoke. "In two days, we will break camp and continue our journey south to the Holy Land. Scout reports indicate that the Saracen army no longer poses a significant threat, and we may advance without any major threat of attack, at least for some time. I have given some thought to the matter, and I decided that the three of you will continue the mission for which you were originally chosen. This mission set forth by the Pope is too important to be entrusted to those unproven and unworthy." He raised his voice. "However, I will not tolerate any more of this rebellious behavior! If you wish to continue this mission, you will put aside all personal interests and completely submit to my authority! Is this understood?"

"Yes, Bishop Adhemar," the three answered.

Adhemar stared at the three for a moment before continuing. "This has been a difficult lesson for you to learn, but understand that all of you are at fault for what happened to Sir William and Sir Richard. This is the result of your rebellious attitude and willingness to disobey my orders and the will of the holy Catholic Church," he said unsympathetically.

Rodrigo's jaw tightened as he stared at the ground. *He twists the knife of guilt into our backs as we mourn the loss of our brothers. Is losing them not punishment enough?*

"Furthermore," Adhemar continued, "you will forfeit your share of any plunder recovered from the enemy camp and, in order to humble your pride, you will be assigned to menial camp duties until I deem otherwise. At the end of every day, I will expect a full report regarding your daily activities. Now, are there any questions before you are dismissed?"

"Bishop Adhemar," said Rodrigo, raising his head.

"Yes, Sir Rodrigo?" Adhemar asked with irritation.

"We recovered this from William when we laid him to rest outside the camp," Rodrigo said. He held out his hand to Adhemar, revealing the golden cross, stained brown with William's blood. "We wanted to return this to you."

"Keep it!" Adhemar snapped, turning his head and refusing to look at the cross in Rodrigo's hand. "May it remind all of you what happens when you disobey my orders and the will of the Church! You must pray fervently for his soul and for the safe return of Sir Richard."

"Richard is alive?" asked Geoffrey, eyes widening at the news.

"He may yet be," Adhemar replied. "We captured many Saracen warriors during their retreat. If Sir Richard is still alive, we may be able to trade some of the prisoners for some of our own who have been captured. Go now and pray."

A flood of mixed emotions came over Rodrigo as the three left Adhemar's tent. He felt saddened by William's death and upset over the blame and guilt laid on them by Adhemar, but elated that Richard might be alive and relieved that they would be allowed to continue the Pope's mission. "I can only speak for myself, but I am not sure what to feel right now," he said to the others. "I am glad to hear that Richard may still be alive, but I do not accept the guilt and responsibility Adhemar lays upon us for what happened to him and William. Do you?" he asked, stopping for a moment as they all studied each other's faces.

"As I said before, I think we could have done more to keep them from going, but I do not think it is fair to blame us for what happened," Geoffrey answered.

"Nor do I," said Jean. "At least Richard may yet be alive. We must pray for his safe return."

"I agree," said Geoffrey. "What will you do with William's cross?" he asked Rodrigo.

Rodrigo held up his hand and opened his palm, revealing the cross. "If Adhemar insists that I bear the burden of William's cross, then so be it. I will keep it along with my own."

"We all bear that burden," said Geoffrey. "He was our brother, as is Richard. I only hope that it is just one cross we must bear and not two."

"As do I," said Rodrigo.

TWO PATHS

T he heat of the midsummer sun beat down upon the long column of soldiers as they slowly made their way south down the Anatolian peninsula. The blistering heat made wearing the heavy coats of mail and padding beneath nearly unbearable for many of the Crusader knights.

"Have you ever felt heat like this?" Geoffrey asked Rodrigo, who rode beside him. The sweat from his brow left brown trails down his face as the three rode in formation behind clouds of dust kicked up by the columns of horses and men ahead of them.

"Never," said Rodrigo. "Here." He reached down into a saddlebag and withdrew a white cloth, which he handed to Geoffrey. Rodrigo had removed his mailed hood and coat, which lay behind him on the saddle. On his head he had wrapped layers of white cloth, creating a makeshift turban, which also covered his neck from the sun and his mouth from the dust.

"You look like one of the local Saracen villagers," Jean said with a grin. "What will you do if we are attacked?"

"If I need to, I can don my armor quickly, but I do not think it is necessary to wear it while we travel," said Rodrigo.

"Perhaps we can fool the Turks into thinking we are a Saracen army," Jean said with a laugh.

"You are right, it does feel much better," Geoffrey remarked after removing his coat of mail and wrapping the white cloth about his head. He and Rodrigo turned to look at Jean, who was wiping the beaded sweat from his red forehead. The three rode in silence for a time before Jean finally turned to Rodrigo.

"Rodrigo, do you have another white cloth that I might use?" he asked.

"Are you sure you want one? You may be mistaken for a Saracen villager," Rodrigo answered with a smirk as Geoffrey laughed. "Here," Rodrigo said, tossing Jean a white cloth that he had pulled from another saddlebag. "I do not want to see any of us fall victim to this heat."

✠

All day and into the evening the army marched. Far to the southeast, Rodrigo could see a large mountain range rising from the dusty plain. At last, the trumpets sounded, bringing the long columns to a halt, and soon they began to set up camp.

Rodrigo and the others huddled around a small fire at the edge of camp, knowing their guard duty would last well into the night. Jean held his hands close to the fire as he spoke. "Unbearably hot during the day and uncomfortably cold at night. What kind of godforsaken land is this?"

"Indeed, this is strange land, but at least we are making good progress toward our goal," said Geoffrey, pulling his cloak more tightly about him. "If we continue to move at this pace, without any major obstacles, we should be close to Jerusalem in perhaps a month's time."

Rodrigo remained quiet for a moment, deep in thought. *The Turks have been beaten for now, but they will be back. The mountain range to the south may also present a major challenge should our leaders choose to cross it.* "That is assuming there are no obstacles. I have a feeling that things will not continue to go so smoothly," Rodrigo said at last, staring into the campfire. "If we get held up somewhere for a length of time along the way, it will give the Turks the chance to regroup and strike again."

"Thank you, Rodrigo," Jean said sarcastically. "We can always count on you to boost morale."

Rodrigo picked a stick off of the ground and poked the fire, sending embers floating up into the air. "I am just thinking realistically. The Turks will not just hand over Jerusalem and other cities along the way without a fight. They are waiting for the chance to strike again, and it will come at a time when we are at our most vulnerable—of that I am sure." As he put the stick down, his thoughts began to turn to Richard. "Have either of you heard any news about our leaders trading the Saracen prisoners we captured during the battle?"

Geoffrey and Jean were silent for a moment before Geoffrey answered. "I have seen many of the Saracen prisoners performing camp labor and marching under heavy guard, but I have not heard anything yet about a trade. I think all we can do is continue to pray for Richard, that he will return to us alive and unharmed."

"Yes, you are right. We must continue to pray for his safe return," Rodrigo said. The campfire crackled in the cold desert air as the three kept watch throughout the night.

✠

The long, hot days and frigid nights passed slowly as the Crusader army marched farther and farther south. The practice of stripping their chain armor to the waist and wearing white cloth upon their heads as protection from the sun and dust had caught on among many of the knights and soldiers. However, the heat and the lack of supplies and fresh water were beginning to take their toll on the army. Many men, horses, and pack animals began to fall victim to the difficult conditions along the way.

Water was now being rationed, and the men were ordered to drink sparingly or go without. Occasionally, Rodrigo would look to the side of the column and see horses and pack animals that had fallen and been stripped of their loads, their carcasses left to rot in the sun. Several times, he saw a soldier collapse while marching or a rider fall off his horse, dizzy and exhausted from the relentless heat of the afternoon sun. When this happened, they would be lifted onto a wagon and usually received little care until late into the day when the army stopped to set up camp. In the evenings, at almost every camp, funeral services were being given by the priests and fresh graves were being dug by the men.

Scouting parties had not reported any enemy activity, but the foraging parties had returned to camp with scant supplies. Reports indicated that the surrounding villages had been empty of all inhabitants, all the grain stores were depleted, and all the wells with fresh water had been either filled up or poisoned. The water rations were becoming smaller and smaller each day. It was rumored that Kilij Arslan, the sultan who had defeated the People's Army and attacked the Crusaders at Dorylaeum, had ordered these things to weaken the Crusader army by denying them supplies and fresh water. It was also rumored that he was gathering an army and preparing another attack.

Several more days had passed when at last the great Crusader army reached the base of the Taurus Mountains, where they set up camp. Two paths now lay before them. One path led southwest toward the cities that lined the coast and the other to the southeast, across the vast mountain range. Rodrigo stared at the foreboding mountains, recalling the history lessons with his uncle about the famous Carthaginian general, Hannibal Barca. Vividly, he remembered listening to and imagining the stories of Hannibal's perilous journey through the Alps with his army on his quest to invade the Italian Peninsula and attack the Romans. *The similarities to our own situation cannot be overlooked. Especially the dangers of crossing such difficult mountainous terrain with an army nearly the same size.*

The scorching heat of the midsummer sun beat down upon the Crusaders as their leaders pondered which path to take. Rodrigo sensed that trouble among the leadership was brewing again when the army sat idle and had not moved in three days. When he passed by the tents of the leaders, he could hear the familiar sounds of raised voices and heated conversations. Which path the army would take was becoming highly contentious.

✠

On the fourth night camped in the shadow of the Taurus Mountains, Rodrigo, Jean, and Geoffrey passed the long hours of guard duty in conversation. "I have been praying that our leaders do not take us through the mountains and that we continue along the coast," Rodrigo said as they sat around the campfire.

"Why is that?" asked Geoffrey. "It would be impossible for the Turks to stage a major attack in the mountains, so the threat of ambush would be less likely."

"Are you afraid of a little mountain climbing, Rodrigo?" Jean asked.

"Afraid of mountain climbing, no. Afraid of history repeating itself, yes," Rodrigo said, looking up at the looming silhouette of the mountains against the starry sky.

"What history? What are you talking about?" Jean asked.

"Do you know the story of Hannibal crossing the Alps?" Rodrigo said.

"I have heard the story," Geoffrey answered, glancing at the mountain range before them. "He tried to take elephants across the Alps, did he not?"

"Elephants? He took elephants across the Alps?" Jean said skeptically. "I have not heard this story before. I do not care much for history lessons." He folded his arms as he leaned back against the wooden log by the fire.

"You should study more history, Jean," Rodrigo said. "It can teach you much."

"Why study when I have you?" Jean asked with a grin. "So, please teach me, Rodrigo—who is Hannibal, and why did he take elephants across the Alps?"

Rodrigo stared into the fire for a moment as he recalled the lessons with his uncle. "Hannibal was a Carthaginian general in ancient times who waged war against the Roman Republic. He invaded the Roman lands with his army by crossing over the Alps into the Italian Peninsula. His army was about the size of ours, fifty thousand soldiers with cavalry, baggage trains, and war elephants."

"So what happened to them?" Jean asked.

"The mountainous passes and terrain in the Alps were so difficult and treacherous, and the freezing cold from the high mountains so deadly, that it took weeks to navigate through it all and cross into Italy. He lost nearly half his men and animals in doing so." Rodrigo frowned. *If we were to lose half our men to such hardships, it would cripple our army severely.*

"Half of his men and animals?" asked Jean, raising his eyebrows.

"Yes," Rodrigo answered. "Twenty-five thousand men perished in those mountains, along with half of his war elephants and baggage animals." *And that was after weeks of unimaginable hardship and suffering.*

"It is almost difficult to comprehend such a feat. Can you imagine such a thing?" asked Jean in near disbelief. "I am surprised he had any elephants left at all. So what happened then? Was his army destroyed by the Romans?"

"No, he went on to defeat a major Roman army in a great battle and nearly conquered Rome itself," Rodrigo said, staring into the flames as he thought. *If only our army were united and led by a single strong and brilliant general like Hannibal instead of being divided by several bickering leaders, each with their own agenda.*

"Well, hopefully history does repeat itself then," Jean said with a laugh. "Except for losing half his army in the mountains, of course."

"Do you really think this mountain range will be as difficult to cross as the Alps?" asked Geoffrey.

Rodrigo let out a sigh and looked up from the fire at last. "I cannot say for certain, but if you look at the tallest peaks of these mountains in the morning, you will see that they are covered with snow. That means those peaks are extremely high and cold. Moving an army of this size through that range will be quite difficult and dangerous, in my opinion." *Not only must we pray for Richard's safety, but for our own as well if it is our leaders' decision to cross them.*

✠

The night had passed quietly, and the three lay down to rest after being relieved of their duty only to be awaked shortly after and summoned to Adhemar's tent. When they arrived, they found Adhemar standing and waiting to receive them.

"Your prayers have been answered, for I have good news," said Adhemar. "Our camp was approached by Turkish emissaries early yesterday evening. They wanted to discuss exchanging prisoners of war. We were able to negotiate an exchange with them, and twenty of our Crusaders were returned to us. Sir Richard was among them."

"God be praised!" Geoffrey said as the other two stared at Adhemar with wide eyes.

"Where is he?" Rodrigo asked with a smile. A mixture of joy and relief washed over him. *Thank the Lord! Our brother has been returned to us!*

"He and the others are being kept in tents not far away," Adhemar replied. "Do not worry. They are being well cared for, but we must allow them time to recover." He paused. "Also, we need to know what information they can provide to us about the Turkish army, and what information they may have been . . . *forced* to give about our own. In a day or two, I will allow them to reunite with the other men."

Rodrigo's smile began to fade. *Forced to give* . . . the words lingered in Rodrigo's mind. *I cannot even imagine what those men must have gone through. At least they are safe now—but why must we wait days before we see him? And what about our path moving forward?* "Thank you for giving us this most welcome news about Richard, Bishop Adhemar. But what about our path into the Holy Land? Have any decisions been made yet by the leaders?"

"It is still being discussed," Adhemar said. "We must consider that the threat of attack is now more likely than ever." Adhemar narrowed his gaze at Rodrigo. "Trust in the wisdom of our leaders, Sir Rodrigo. They are men of God, and he will guide their decisions. I will give you more information when necessary. You are dismissed," Adhemar said with a wave of his hand.

Silently, the three turned to exit Adhemar's tent. *Will our leaders even be able to hear the Lord's guidance above the clamor of their own personal squabbles?* Rodrigo thought as he and the others began to walk back to their tent.

"This is great news, brothers! Our prayers have been answered!" Geoffrey said excitedly as they walked.

"It is extremely good news," Rodrigo agreed, "and I hope that he is able to swiftly recover from his ordeal. I am a bit troubled, however, that no decision has yet been made by our leaders."

"Yes, that is true," said Jean. "No matter. We must celebrate good news when we receive it and prepare for Richard's return."

1 6

A LOST SOUL

The next few days passed, yet still no word came as to which path the army would take or when Richard would rejoin them. The sound of metal striking metal rang out among the tents that afternoon as Rodrigo and Geoffrey faced each other with their swords in a sparring circle nearby. "Rodrigo! Geoffrey!" Jean called out to them, interrupting their match. Lowering his sword, Rodrigo saw Jean standing by a tent nearby. Beside him was Richard, who was leaning on wooden staff that he was using for a crutch.

"Richard!" Rodrigo exclaimed. Rodrigo sheathed his sword and smiled broadly as he and Geoffrey hopped the wooden fence that formed the sparring circle and walked toward Richard and Jean. As they approached, Rodrigo's smile began to fade, and he was struck by the dramatic change of Richard's appearance. Richard was extremely tall with a powerful build and had always been a pillar of strength and vitality in the past.

Now, however, Rodrigo could scarcely believe that the frail man who stood by Jean was the same Richard as the one he knew before. He appeared thin and weak as he leaned on the crutch, and his gaunt cheeks and hollow eyes made him nearly unrecognizable, a mere shadow of the man he had been. Richard's arm and leg were bandaged, and visible scars could be seen on the parts of his body that were exposed by his loose-fitting clothing.

Richard managed a faint smile as they drew near, but the scars on his face and the pain in his eyes told a different story. *My God, what has happened to him? Clearly, whatever he has been through has taken a heavy toll,* Rodrigo thought as he became conscious of his shocked expression and quickly averted his eyes.

"God be praised, brother!" Geoffrey proclaimed with open arms. "The Lord has answered our prayers, and you have returned to us!" He placed his hands on Richard's shoulders.

"Richard . . ." Rodrigo said as he forced an awkward smile and looked back up. ". . . Welcome back, brother." Richard remained silent and nodded in acknowledgement. Rodrigo composed himself. "Come, let's go to our tent, so that you may sit down and rest while we talk." The others agreed, and they walked through several rows of tents while Jean helped Richard, who hobbled slowly on his crutch.

When they reached their tent, Geoffrey held the flap while Richard entered with help from Jean. Gingerly, Richard sat down upon a wooden stool as the four pulled up stools and cots to sit down around him.

"I was helping to load the supply wagons when one of Adhemar's men told me to come and fetch Richard and return him to our tents," Jean said with a smile. "We came straight here."

Rodrigo held up a flask of water to Richard. "Are you thirsty or hungry? Can we get you something to eat?" Richard shook his head as Rodrigo lowered the flask and continued. "Thank God you are alive, brother, and have returned to us safely. We have been praying every day for your return." He paused for a moment as the others sat silently. All eyes were on Richard. "Can you tell us what has happened since you left us?" he asked Richard. "We are all eager to hear your story."

The four were met with silence as Richard stared back at them from the stool. The muscles of his jaw tightened, and his brow was knitted deeply. Though no words escaped from his mouth, the anguish in his eyes began to tell of his suffering and sorrow. Richard's gaze turned toward the ground as he began to run his hand over the scars on his arm next to his bandage. Jean rose from his stool and knelt by Richard as he gently put his hand on his shoulder. "If you are not ready to talk about it yet, we understand."

"What happened to me . . . is difficult for me to talk about," Richard said at last, breaking his silence. "I will tell you my tale, so that you may know, but after I do, I shall never speak of it again. I want you all to understand that because of what happened, my heart has changed, and along with it, my faith," he said as Jean returned to his seat. When they heard his words, the mood of the group began to change, and a darker one descended upon them as Richard recounted his ordeal.

"We had begun to set up camp that evening when I left with a scouting party to survey the valley ahead of us. At the southern end of the valley, we came upon a massive Turkish army camped near Dorylaeum. We believed our presence had gone unseen as we spied on their camp, and we were about to leave, when we were met with a hail of arrows that wounded and killed many and felled our steeds from beneath us. Those of us that could fled on foot, but the Turks gave chase and quickly ran us down with their mounts.

"We were bound, gagged, tethered to their horses, and then dragged back to the Turkish camp. Those that were too wounded to be moved were slain where they lay. Out of the twelve from the scouting party, only six of us were taken back to camp. Once we were there, they stripped us of our armor and beat us until I lost consciousness. When I awoke, I was in a tent being questioned by a Turk who spoke our language. In that tent were instruments of the worst kinds of torture, which I will not describe. They were intent upon getting information about the size of our army, our capabilities, and our plans moving forward.

"Under pain of torture, the six of us gave up what little information we had, but none of us divulged any information about the rear party a day behind us. We knew that doing so might doom us all. The Turks came up with a plan to attack the next morning, but because of our silence, they were completely surprised when the rear guard caught up and attacked them from behind. They lost nearly half of their army in that surprise attack, and we were taken from their camp just before it was overrun by Crusaders.

"We went south with the fleeing Turkish forces, and when the sultan Kilij Arslan found out that we had withheld information about the rear forces, he was furious. We were tortured even more, beaten and humiliated daily by the Turkish troops, and barely given enough food and water to survive. I prayed to God fervently every day to give me the strength to persevere, but eventually I lost hope. Then I began to pray for death, just so the misery would end, but neither prayer was answered. They demanded that we renounce our faith and embrace Islam to make it stop. I resisted as long as I could." Richard's voice began to crack as tears welled in his eyes.

Moved by his words, the others rose from their seats and gathered around Richard, and they began to place their hands upon him in sympathy.

"No!" Richard shouted suddenly. In shock, the others stepped back and withdrew their hands. As Richard looked up at them, Rodrigo could see that behind the tears in Richard's eyes was a fomenting rage that began to seep out as he continued.

"No. Let me finish my tale. I do not want your sympathy," Richard said, lowering his head again. "While others were strong enough to die with their faith intact, I was *not*. I had given up all hope and did as they demanded. I renounced my faith in God and embraced their religion of Islam as my own. Only then did the daily torture, beatings, and humiliation cease. Nearly a month had gone by since my capture, and I had begun my new life as a Saracen, when suddenly I was brought to this camp, and now here I am." Finished with his tale, Richard looked around at the group, who stared at him, stunned into silence.

At last Geoffrey spoke. "Perhaps it seemed as though God had abandoned you, Richard. But we did not give up hope. You have come back to us, and our prayers have been answered," he said with a sympathetic smile.

Richard returned Geoffrey's smile with a glare. "Mine have *not*," he replied with contempt in his eyes. "I tell you truthfully, I cared not whether I ever returned."

"But you still wear the necklace of the Crucem Auream," said Jean, pointing to the cross dangling from Richard's neck. "You are here with us now. Surely you will return to the Christian faith and our mission?"

Looking down at the cross upon his neck, Richard held it with an open palm for a few moments in thought before he began to speak. "This cross was torn from my neck the day I was captured and brought to the Turkish camp. I watched as it was thrown on the ground and spat upon, and that was the last I saw of it. When I was brought to the Crusader camp, I met with Bishop Adhemar. Apparently, he demanded that the Turks return my cross as part of the prisoner exchange. He returned it to me only after I swore to him that I did not divulge the secret mission to recover the holy relics in Jerusalem." Richard's hand tightened into a fist, gripping the cross as the lines of anguish on his scarred face began twisting into snarl of hate and rage. "Adhemar does not care about me, nor any of you!" Richard shouted in anger.

"Calm yourself, brother," said Geoffrey, moving forward with open hands.

Richard speaks with raw emotion, but it is true what he says about Adhemar's callous and controlling ways, Rodrigo thought as he looked on in silence.

"He only cares about the Pope's mission and his precious holy relics!" Richard yelled as he tore the cross from his neck, snapping the chain, and threw it to the ground. "I am no longer one of you! You are *not* my brothers," he said, turning his head away. "I have no faith, and I have no God."

"Blasphemy!" Jean yelled, standing over Richard. Rodrigo moved forward and extended his arm in between them. Jean stood still momentarily as he glared down at Richard, then turned and left the tent, hurling the flap open as he exited.

Rodrigo looked down at Richard and spoke. "Richard, what you have experienced, none of us can even imagine. Therefore, I do not believe any of us can sit in judgment of your words and actions. We can only hope and pray that in time, your wounds and faith will heal, and you can return to us as a Christian and our brother."

"Rodrigo," Richard replied, struggling to his feet using his crutch, "I believe you are a good and honorable knight. But I will never return . . . *to this*," he said with disdain as he stood up. The sorrow in his eyes was gone, and in its place was a smoldering, hate-filled rage. "My only mission now is to kill as many Turks as possible before going to my grave and take revenge for what was done to me and the others at their vile hands. I will not stay here with you. I will take up quarters with the regular cavalry soldiers." He turned and began to make his way to exit the tent.

"Richard!" Rodrigo called out. "A moment, please. Hear me out."

Richard stopped at the tent flap with his back to the others and turned his head to speak, but would not face Rodrigo. "Do not waste your time. Nothing you can say will cause me to change my mind." He began to open the tent flap.

"I do not wish to try and change your mind," Rodrigo began. "I can see that your choice has been made. I only want to say that I agree with your feelings toward Adhemar, and I understand the pain that you feel and your hatred toward the Saracens." Richard paused and stood still at the exit. He released the tent flap and slowly turned around to face Rodrigo while Geoffrey looked on in silence.

A deep scowl was etched upon Richard's scarred face as he stared at Rodrigo. "How can you possibly understand the pain that I have felt?" he asked through clenched teeth. "And if you feel the same about Adhemar, why do you choose to stay here, bowing to his every demand?"

Rodrigo sighed as he nodded in agreement. "You are right— Adhemar is a difficult man to serve, and he does not care about us, only that we serve his will and the Pope's mission," he admitted as he took a step closer to Richard. "But it is for that very purpose that I am willing to humble myself and bow to his demands. I believe in the mission for which we were chosen and want to believe that we are doing God's will in liberating Jerusalem."

Richard's eyes narrowed as he stared at Rodrigo. "I no longer care about any useless holy relics, nor the liberation of Jerusalem. Those things mean nothing to me. And what about my pain you claim to understand? I am aware that William died at the hands of the Turks. Was his death so painful for you?" he asked with a mocking tone. "Of the two of us, he was the fortunate one."

"I felt deep sorrow at William's death," Rodrigo said, his brow creasing as he looked down and recalled the final moments of William's life. He looked back up at Richard. "But the greater pain that I experienced was as a young boy, when my father was slain by the Saracen Moors. I have never spoken of these feelings to anyone until now."

The three stood in silence, looking at one another. Richard's scowl began to lessen somewhat as he searched for a reply. "Then you too must share my anger and hatred of the Saracens and harbor a desire to see them all destroyed," Richard said at last, staring at Rodrigo, waiting for his reaction.

Old and faded memories began to flood into Rodrigo's mind, and his eyes became pools of glass as he looked at Richard and began to pour out his heart. "For many years after my father's death, I felt as you do now. I was full of hatred and bitterness toward the Saracens for what they had done. My uncle took me in and raised me, and as I grew older, I lived in both Christian and Saracen kingdoms because my uncle fought for both sides in order to survive after being exiled by the king of León. For a time in my youth, I lived in the Saracen kingdom of Zaragoza, where I experienced their way of life, learning their language and their culture. It was then that I began to understand that the Saracens are not evil, nor the monsters I had made them out to be in my mind. When I finally came to that realization, my hatred began to melt and slowly faded away." Rodrigo paused for a moment as he looked into Richard's eyes. "I know your heart and your spirit can heal; it just takes time."

Richard's voice began to rise as he spoke, and his scowl of hatred and rage returned. "It just takes time? Does it not matter to you that the Saracen Turks continue to murder and commit atrocities against Christians every day, even now as we speak?"

Rodrigo lowered his head as he thought about Richard's question. "I want to believe that the Pope speaks the truth about the atrocities taking place against Christians in the Holy Land, but . . . I will only believe it when I see it with my own eyes," Rodrigo said as he looked up at Richard. "The only murder and atrocities that I have witnessed since beginning this journey have been done by Peter the Hermit and his People's Army. Everything else is just . . ." Rodrigo shook his head and raised his hands in frustration. ". . . the reality of war."

A burning hatred took hold in Richard's eyes as he glared at Rodrigo. "So, all the unspeakable horrors that I and others have been through . . . are just the reality of war?" The muscles of his jaw tightened, and his words came through clenched teeth. "Living with the Saracen filth has obviously polluted your mind and corrupted your soul," he growled in a low voice, dripping with bitterness and vitriol, as he continued to glare at Rodrigo. "You mock William's death and dishonor the memory of your father. My mind is clear, for I see the Saracens for what they are. Do not ever speak to me again," he said as he slowly turned and exited the tent.

Rodrigo and Geoffrey stared at one another for a moment before Geoffrey spoke. "I will try talking to him."

"I think we should let him go . . . for now," Rodrigo replied. "It is clear that he has been broken, and I believe his soul has wandered and is lost. Perhaps it is best if we leave him alone and allow him time before speaking with him again about this path he has chosen."

Geoffrey stood and pondered Rodrigo's words for a moment, then silently turned and exited the tent.

Alone in the tent, Rodrigo knelt and picked up Richard's cross from the ground and looked at it as he held it in his hand. He sat down on the stool, thinking about all that had been said, and closed his eyes. *Lord, please heal Richard's physical and spiritual wounds and help him find his way back to you.* Several minutes had passed when the tent flap was pulled back, and Rodrigo looked up as Geoffrey walked into the tent.

"He will not listen to me either," Geoffrey said as he let out a sigh of frustration and sat down. "You are right. It is going to take some time, and we will have to wait. Jean is still angry, but he agreed to leave Richard alone as well."

Rodrigo nodded as he closed his hand around Richard's cross. "We can try talking to him again in time, but only Richard can decide if he will turn from this path and find his way back to God."

17

THE HOLY LAND

The shouting of men could scarcely be heard above the howling winds as they struggled to save one of their own who had lost his footing on the treacherous path that snaked its way through the mountainous terrain. The man desperately clung to the rocks at the end of a slippery slope, with the lower half of his body dangling over the edge of the cliff. Far below him, his horse and two other pack animals tethered together lay broken on the rocks, their bodies twisted and mangled from the fall. The precarious trail had become deadly in the higher altitudes, with the freezing cold and ice on the ground causing men and beasts to lose their footing, and had claimed the lives of several men over the last few days. The bitterly cold wind lashed the men during the rescue attempt that evening, stinging their eyes and hindering their efforts.

"Take my hand!" Rodrigo yelled as he stretched out his arm. The Crusaders had formed a human chain, and Rodrigo was at the very end, clinging to a lance. Straining with all his might, with one hand outstretched and the other grasping the end of the lance, Rodrigo desperately tried to reach the man whose life depended on him. Rodrigo had moved his grip to the very end of the lance, but he knew it might give out at any moment, sending both himself and the other man over the side of the cliff. Gritting his teeth, he closed his eyes and said a silent prayer to God for help. Then at last, he felt the man's hand upon his own. "Hold on!" he yelled. With renewed hope, he felt the man's grip tighten, and turning his head toward the others, he shouted, "Pull!"

Slowly, Rodrigo felt himself moving upward, away from the edge of the cliff. His grip on the end of the lance held as he dragged the man along with him. Finally, he felt other hands upon him, pulling him up, and a flood of relief came over him as he realized both he and the other man were safe.

Breathing heavily and exhausted from the ordeal, Rodrigo sat down upon the rocky path, pulling his cloak about him to shield himself from the freezing wind and cold. Several Crusaders around him patted him on the back in gratitude. The man whom Rodrigo had helped rescue approached him. "Thank you," the soldier said, placing his hand on Rodrigo's shoulder. "I thought I was going to die. Thank you for risking your life to save me. Might I know your name?"

"I am Sir Rodrigo . . . of Castile," Rodrigo managed to say between breaths.

"Rodrigo!" a familiar voice called out to him. Rodrigo stood up to see Geoffrey walking toward him.

"Thanks be to God, brother! I saw what happened. I wanted to help, but I could not come to your aid lest I lose my own footing and send all of us to our deaths." Geoffrey grimaced and shook his head. "By the blood of Christ, our shite-for-brains leaders must have been piss-drunk when they made the decision to cross these cursed mountains!" he swore angrily.

"What's done is done," Rodrigo said, struggling to his feet. "All we can do is try to see that as many of us as possible safely make it through these mountains into the Holy Land."

The bellowing voice of one of the commanders cut through the howling wind as he shouted his commands. "Men! We will stop here for the night! We will move again at dawn!" The command was echoed by the various commanders as it moved down the column of men and animals that wound for miles up and down the mountain pass. Too narrow for a wide column, the pass had restricted their movement to a single-file line that stretched far into the distance until it faded from sight. Wrapping his cloak about him tightly, Rodrigo and the others sought out what little shelter they could find from the freezing wind and bitter cold, nestling down between outcroppings of rocks along the rugged path and waiting for the dawn to break.

✠

Rodrigo tried to open his eyes but found he could not. He opened his hand, which was still gripping his cloak, and pain began to flood into his numb fingers as he moved them. His cloak was stiff and crackled like brittle paper as he opened it, still lying on his side. Slowly, he brought his hands up to his face, and touching his eyelids, he felt a thin crust of ice covering his eyes, which he wiped away with his hands. Opening his eyes fully, he could see the sun beginning to rise above the mountains to the east.

Slowly, he rose from the ground as pain shot through his limbs and joints, which were still stiff from the cold. He stretched his arms above his head and looked out into the valley. The sky was clear, and from the path, he beheld a magnificent view. Far off in the distance, beyond the mountain range, he could see a wide open plain, and he realized it was his first glimpse of the Holy Land. It was a sign of hope, and silently he gave thanks to God as he felt his spirit renewed. Turning around, he looked ahead and behind him on the path. Men were beginning to stir and rise from their icy slumber. The first rays of dawn began to crest the mountains and cast their warm glow upon the cold and weary Crusaders.

Rodrigo began to walk around, treading carefully upon the melting ice on the path, to find Geoffrey. At last he found him, nestled tightly between two large boulders just above the path. "Wake up," he said, kneeling and shaking Geoffrey's arm. For a moment, Geoffrey did not stir, but then he slowly lifted his hands to wipe his face and blinked his eyes to clear his vision.

"It was so cold I did not think I would be able sleep," Geoffrey said. He began to move his limbs and struggled to sit up as Rodrigo helped him. He grimaced. "It feels like my whole body is being pierced with needles."

"I felt the same," Rodrigo said with a laugh. "It will soon pass." As he helped Geoffrey to stand, he pointed out into the distance. "Look."

Squinting to see past the light of the dawn, Geoffrey peered into the distance beyond the mountains. "I see a wide plain. These cursed mountains are coming to an end."

"It is the Holy Land," said Rodrigo.

Geoffrey thought for a moment. "You are right! Just beyond these mountains lies the Holy Land and the holy city of Antioch!" His face lit up with a smile. "Praise be to God! We are nearly there."

With renewed energy and spirit, Rodrigo and Geoffrey joined the others as the signal came for the columns to form and begin the day's march. For many, however, the light of the new day did not bring a renewed spirit and energy. Several men lay still and silent upon the ground, frozen where they lay, never to rise from their eternal slumber. There was no time for burials, so the bodies were hastily covered with rocks, and the priests gave a few quick words over the rocky mounds as they passed by. A trumpet blast at the head of the column echoed through the valley, and the long column began to slowly move down the mountain pass.

✠

The Crusaders' march through the unforgiving Taurus Mountains was entering its third week. The highest peaks of the range were at last behind them, and now they were moving into the valleys below. Men and beasts had been lost all along the way; some had lost their footing on the treacherous mountain passes, others had succumbed to the freezing temperatures of the night, and still others had been swept away attempting to ford the raging rivers that ran through the valleys. Food for both men and beasts had nearly run out, and many of the animals had been slain to provide food over the past few days.

"This is embarrassing," Jean declared as he sat behind Geoffrey, riding double on Geoffrey's mount. "What is a knight without a horse?"

"A foot soldier!" Rodrigo answered with a grin as he trotted up beside them on his mount.

Jean muttered under his breath.

"Perhaps you could purchase an ox or a mule if you wish to ride on your own," Rodrigo suggested. "I do not think there are too many horses left in the cavalry."

"Can you imagine riding an ox or a mule into battle?" Geoffrey asked.

"You would have one advantage at least," Rodrigo said with a broad grin. "The Turks would be laughing too hard to mount a serious charge."

"Thank you, Rodrigo, for creating humor out of my misfortune," Jean said with disgust. "When I began this journey, I knew of the possibility of losing my mount, but I thought it would be in battle, not from a broken leg on a mountain pass. And never did I imagine I would have to eat it for food!" he said, his voice rising. Geoffrey covered his mouth to try to contain his laughter, but both he and Rodrigo began laughing out loud.

Jean continued to frown. "Laugh all you want, but I will be the one laughing when your mounts are roasting on the spit!" he yelled as Rodrigo and Geoffrey struggled to compose themselves.

"You may be right, brother. The way the supplies are going, you may be right," Rodrigo said with a smile as the three continued down the path at the base of the mountains.

✠

A few more days had passed, and the mountainous valleys had finally given way to a broad plain flanked by coastal mountains to the west and rolling hills to the east. The Crusaders had set up a full camp at the base of the mountains to recover from their ordeal as they formulated plans for moving forward. The leaders decided that their first goal upon entering the Holy Land would be to retake the city of Antioch from the Turks. They also awaited a small force of Crusaders led by Tancred and Count Baldwin that had split off from the main group when they entered the Taurus Mountains. The small force had traveled down the coast and were to later rendezvous with the main Crusader army.

Rodrigo, Geoffrey, and Jean had been summoned to Adhemar's tent. As they walked, they discussed the rumors being spread about the group led by Tancred and Baldwin.

"I heard that they were going to scout an alternate route in case the mountains were impassable and we had to turn back," said Geoffrey.

"Scout an alternate route? More likely they were out to grab land for themselves," Jean said with a smirk.

"Do you really think that was their intent?" asked Rodrigo.

"Did you not hear? Count Baldwin's wife died on our march through the desert after the battle at Dorylaeum," Jean said. "It is well known that she and her family were the main source of his wealth in Boulogne. Without her, his fortunes have dried up and he has nothing to go home to. Why would he not use this opportunity to grab land and wealth while in a foreign land?"

Rodrigo remained silent as he thought about what Jean had said. *If this is true, what does it say about the intentions of our leaders? How many of them have embarked upon this journey to answer the Pope's call to liberate Jerusalem, and how many have come to grab land and wealth? What will happen to the army if we begin to lose our leaders along the way as they seek to establish their own kingdoms?*

"Knights of the Crucem Auream!" a servant of Adhemar bellowed as they approached Adhemar's tent. "You may enter. He is expecting you."

Rodrigo, Jean, and Geoffrey entered the tent and stood silently as Adhemar greeted them and began to speak. "God has seen our army safely through the mountains and into the Holy Land, ever closer to our destination. We must focus our efforts now upon our goals and never lose sight of our mission. Tancred and his men have arrived this morning, and we will break camp in two days. Until then, we will gather as many supplies as we can before we move toward the city of Antioch. Your camp duties will continue, as well as your daily reports. Are there any questions?"

"About our mission, Bishop Adhemar . . . we are now only three. Richard . . ." Geoffrey began.

Adhemar cut him off. "Yes, I am aware of Sir Richard," he said with a frown. "I have been keeping a close eye on him after what happened at Dorylaeum. I have spoken to him about his decision, but he will not turn from this path. You must all pray for him, and if your faith and prayers are strong enough, he may yet return to God's flock. If not, he will die forever lost."

Rodrigo lowered his head and bit his lip as he listened to Adhemar's words. *Again, we are to blame if Richard does not return to our group? Is he not responsible for his own decisions?*

Adhemar turned to Rodrigo. "Richard said he left his golden cross with you. Is that correct?"

"Yes, I have it," Rodrigo answered.

"Keep it for now. If he returns, you may give it back to him. Now, were there any questions before you are dismissed?" Adhemar asked.

Jean turned to look at Rodrigo and Geoffrey before speaking. "Bishop Adhemar, what of Count Baldwin? Did he not return with Tancred?"

"He and his men have traveled farther east, to the city of Edessa," Adhemar said. The three glanced at one another. "If there is nothing else, you are dismissed."

The three knights exited Adhemar's tent, and as soon as they were outside, Jean spoke. "See, I told you. Count Baldwin is out to grab new land and establish a kingdom for himself."

"Unfortunately, I think you may be right," Rodrigo said with a frustrated sigh. "And with him go all of his men, further weakening our army. If this becomes the pattern of our leaders, then our numbers will be greatly depleted by the time we get to Jerusalem."

"Then let us pray that it does not," Geoffrey said as the three walked through the camp back to their tent. The noonday sun was high in the sky as the Crusaders began preparations to move farther into the Holy Land toward an uncertain future.

✠

"Bishop Adhemar," said the servant, entering the tent after the three knights had left. "Count Raymond arrives."

"See him in," Adhemar replied, retiring to a couch nearby. "And bring some wine."

Count Raymond entered the tent and approached Adhemar. "I see your men have just left. I trust that all is still going well?" he asked.

"Yes. However, they remain only three. I have recovered the knight who was captured by the Turks through a prisoner exchange, but he has lost heart and refuses to return to the mission," Adhemar said as the servant filled his wine goblet. "He may yet return, but it will likely take some time."

"I am glad to hear that your knight was among those recovered in the exchange," Raymond said. "It must have been quite a difficult ordeal for those men, to have remained prisoners of the Saracens for so long. With time, rest, and proper care, however, I trust that he and the others will recover their strength and their spirit." He pulled up a chair and sat down next to Adhemar.

"Indeed, my lord," Adhemar said. *A difficult ordeal, yes, but perhaps it was necessary. It should serve as a deterrent for him and the others should they ever again consider disobeying my orders.* "Have you received a report from Tancred and Baldwin's expedition?" he asked.

"I have. Apparently, they were at each other's throats most of the time during their absence, squabbling over cities and territory that they captured." Raymond's brow creased with concern. "Now, Count Baldwin travels farther east to the city of Edessa, and it is likely that he will not return. I understand his desire to capitalize on this newfound opportunity, but our oaths to the Pope to recapture Jerusalem should remain our foremost priority. I knew it was a mistake to allow the younger leaders to go off on their own."

Adhemar pondered Raymond's words as he sipped wine from his goblet. *Troubling news, yet not entirely unexpected. I assumed Count Baldwin would do something like this, but not so soon. Perhaps Count Raymond still favors Antioch for himself?* "What of Antioch, my lord?

Do you still believe that the emperor would consider making you the city's governor were we to take it for him?"

Count Raymond thought for a moment before replying. "I think the chances are still good, but it will be no easy feat to take the city. Scout reports indicate that it is exceptionally large, much larger than Nicaea, and heavily fortified. Should we succeed, however, the emperor would be exceedingly *grateful*, and it would all but secure direct passage to Jerusalem."

A smile crept across Adhemar's face. *If Count Raymond were appointed governor of Antioch, then it would vastly increase our power and influence.* "Well then, may God grant us a swift victory, my lord," Adhemar said, raising his wine goblet.

18

AN INTIMIDATING PROSPECT

I t was October of 1097 when the Crusader army reached the massive walled city of Antioch. Word of the approaching Crusaders had reached the city well in advance of their arrival. Scouting parties reported that hoards of supplies were being brought into the city, and riders were seen heading south, which meant that the inhabitants were settling in for a long siege, or at least until a relief force could be gathered and come to their aid.

As the Crusaders approached the city from the north, they looked up in awe at the formidable defenses and the sheer size of the walls and the city itself. More than twice as large as Nicaea, Antioch stood like a stone sentinel, towering above the plain, dwarfing the Crusader army in its shadow. In addition to its intimidating size, natural defenses also aided the city; the rapidly flowing Orontes River lay on its western flank, and the walls of the eastern half of the city stood atop the rocky cliffs of Mount Silpius, rising over a thousand feet into the sky. Overlooking the city, occupying the highest part of the mountains on its eastern side, was a citadel where a Turkish lord named Yaghi Siyan presided over all.

"God help us," said Jean, staring up at the citadel as he sat behind Geoffrey on his mount. "We must look like ants to them down here. Even if we do somehow manage to breach the city walls, how can we ever hope to take such a fortress, unless we grow wings and fly?"

Rodrigo glanced at the citadel high on the cliffs as he rode beside them. "I agree, it is quite intimidating. It would seem impossible to take such a well-fortified position. But do not lose heart, Jean, for no fortress is completely unassailable if you use the correct strategy," he said with a grin.

"The correct strategy?" Jean asked as he narrowed his gaze at Rodrigo. "If you are going to remind us again about your strategy in Count Raymond's tournament, you can save your breath. It would be useless here," he said with anger in his voice.

Rodrigo's grin quickly faded. *Why such an angry response? I only spoke in jest.* "If you had studied your history, Jean, you would know that many seemingly impenetrable fortresses have fallen when the opposing army's will was coupled with ingenuity and courage," he snapped back.

"What are you going to do, Rodrigo? Scale the walls of Antioch and open the gates for us?" Jean asked sarcastically.

"If I have to, I will," Rodrigo said, his voice rising.

"Here is another idea, Rodrigo. You speak the language of the Saracens, do you not?" Jean asked. "Perhaps you can knock on the gate and negotiate a truce for us," he said with a laugh.

Trumpets sounded in the distance, signaling for the Crusaders to halt and set up camp as nearby troop commanders began barking orders. "Enough, you two," Geoffrey said as he dismounted. "It is time to set up camp."

✠

The Crusaders set up their camp around the northern part of the city, but Antioch was far too large for them to completely surround without spreading themselves too thin. The eastern half of the city was naturally protected by Mount Silpius, and around the other half, there were a total of five city gates: two on the northern side, two on the western side, and a lone gate to the south. With the setup of their camp, the Crusaders were only able to block three of the five gates—the two northern ones and one on the western side—leaving the other western gate and the southern gate wide open. To make things even more difficult, they had to cross the Orontes River to reach the two unblocked gates.

The ladders and siege equipment from Nicaea had been lost in the mountains or burned for firewood. With no siege equipment, the Crusaders would have to starve out the inhabitants by denying them food and water. However, with the city full of supplies and the Crusaders unable to completely cut off entry and exit, it seemed as though a lengthy siege attempt would be unlikely to succeed. What was likely at some point, however, was the arrival of a Turkish relief force to break the siege.

✠

Three days had passed, and many of the Crusader knights and warriors were becoming restless as their leaders debated a plan of action. The Turks inside the city remained on high alert, guarding the walls and towers for the assault that had yet to come. Some of the Crusader soldiers began foraging the land surrounding the city for food and supplies. Rodrigo, Geoffrey, and Jean decided to join a group of Crusaders heading to the Orontes River on the afternoon of the fourth day to gather water for the camp and look for potential ways to cross.

"What kind of siege only blocks *some* of the city gates?" asked Geoffrey as he and the others walked from the camp toward the river.

"I agree, it is a useless strategy," Rodrigo said. "As long as two of the city gates remain open, this siege will never end. In time, perhaps, we can build a bridge across the river, allowing greater access to the other gates. That would allow a smaller group to block those gates without being cut off from the main camp."

"You two are aware that Adhemar has forbidden us to go on scouting missions, are you not?" Jean asked.

"That is true, but he did not forbid us to go foraging or gather supplies. So that is what we are doing," Rodrigo said as he glanced back at the city walls. "I don't know about you two, but I am growing weary of staring up at the Turks who are staring down at us, wondering what kind of army lays siege to only part of a city," he said with a laugh as the three neared the banks of the river. Some of the soldiers had already gone down to the river's edge and were filling buckets they had brought with them.

"Riders! Riders are approaching the river!" a voice from the riverbank cried out. Rodrigo and the others immediately stopped to look beyond the foliage at the riverbank to the other side of the river. A large group of horsemen was galloping toward them in the distance.

Rodrigo dropped his bucket and quickly began to unsling his shield from across his back as his mind raced. *If the Turks are able to cross the river, they will cut us down one by one as we try to flee back to camp.* His heart began to pound as he drew his sword, raised his shield, and called out to the others at the riverbank. "Leave the water buckets! Form a shield wall! Hurry!" he yelled.

The men at the riverbank dropped whatever they had in their hands and began scrambling to grab their shields and weapons as the horsemen swiftly approached. Many of the Crusaders heeded his call and joined Rodrigo, Jean, and Geoffrey as they interlocked their shields to form a defensive wall with spears and swords at the ready. Some of the men behind them had already begun fleeing back to the camp.

Peeking above his shield, Rodrigo could see that a group of Turkish warriors, perhaps twenty, had reached the opposite side of the river and were notching and firing arrows at them from their horses. Rodrigo quickly ducked behind his shield as the air around them filled with the whistling sounds of arrows. He could hear the thud of the iron-tipped arrows as they bit into their wooden shields and felt the shock of their impact. Then a cry rang out just in front of them.

One of the last Crusaders to come up from the river was running toward them when he went down, struck in the back of the leg with an arrow. Rodrigo knew that the Turks had them in their range, and the subsequent volleys would become increasingly deadly. He turned to Geoffrey and Jean beside him. "We need to get him! He will die if we don't!"

Jean and Geoffrey nodded, and the three broke off from the wall, crouching behind their shields as they quickly moved toward the fallen Crusader. In moments, they reached him, and they set their shields down around him just as another volley of arrows hit, this time with deadly accuracy. Several arrows struck their shields, some of them punching through the leather and wood with the force of their impact. Rodrigo heard Jean gasp with pain, but knew they had no time to waste before the next volley. "Grab his arms and pull!" he yelled.

Still holding their shields up for protection, they began to move back toward the others, dragging the wounded Crusader along with them and trying to protect both themselves and the fallen Crusader from the deadly rain of arrows. The thud of the arrows hitting their shields continued as the defensive wall opened to let them in and then closed around them. "Back to camp!" Rodrigo shouted. The men forming the shield wall maintained their defensive stance as they began to move back, away from the river.

Rodrigo and the others continued to drag the injured man, who writhed in pain, leaving a red trail across the grassy plain behind them. At last, the rain of arrows ceased as they moved out of range. Lowering their shields, they could see the Turkish horsemen leaving the riverbank and riding back toward the southern gate of the city. They finally released their grip on the wounded man as several other Crusaders came to their aid.

Slinging their shields across their backs, some of the Crusaders picked up the wounded soldier and began to carry him back to camp. Rodrigo, Jean, and Geoffrey stood on the plain outside of camp for a moment, but then Geoffrey noticed that Jean was clenching his teeth in pain. "What happened? Were you hit?" Geoffrey asked.

Jean extended his arm downward while holding his shield and turned it to expose his arm underneath. An arrow had penetrated a weak spot in the shield and had gone completely through his forearm. The bloody tip was protruding from the wound, and steady stream of red droplets showered the ground. "One of the arrows went through," he said, wincing in pain. "My shield is pinned to my arm. I cannot put it down."

Rodrigo grimaced as he studied Jean's wound. *It does not look good, and it is bleeding heavily. We must get him back to camp to see a surgeon.* "Your coat of mail might have stopped the arrow," he said to Jean.

"I did not think I would need it," Jean muttered, shaking his head.

"Come, let's return to camp. We will see you to the surgeon's tent," said Geoffrey, slinging his shield across his back. The heat of the afternoon sun beat down as the three made their way back to camp.

Rodrigo frowned as they walked in silence. *We were able to save a man's life this afternoon, but at a high cost. Jean was already disheartened by the loss of his mount, and now with the loss of his arm, at least for a while, his struggle may worsen.* Rodrigo glanced again at the walls of the city. *Not only will this siege never end, but now the Turks will start harassing and attacking us whenever we search for food. Our situation is beginning to look bleak. I think we will need to place all our faith in God, as placing faith in our leaders is proving to be folly.*

19

THE SEEDS OF HATE

By mid-November, the Crusaders were finally able to experience some success by capturing the lightly defended port town of St. Symeon, which lay on the coast a half day's march from Antioch. Rodrigo and the others had to bide their time with camp duties, as they were expressly forbidden to take part in the attack and had been ordered to stay put after Adhemar had been informed of Jean's injury. Rodrigo's frustration continued to grow as they spent their days attending to the mundane duties of camp life while their food and supplies slowly dwindled and their leaders sat idle.

Ships were dispatched to Europe and the Byzantine Empire with urgent messages that the Crusader army was in dire need of supplies. Foraging parties, under heavy guard after what had happened at the river, continued to scour the countryside outside the city for food, but each party returned with fewer and fewer supplies. The Crusaders and the animals that were left were forced to survive on less as the weeks went on. Around mid-December, some much-needed supplies finally arrived by sea on Byzantine ships from the nearby island of Cyprus. However, the Crusaders knew the supplies would not last long, and by late December, they were almost completely out of food.

ⴕ

The full moon shone down from above, guiding their way, as Rodrigo, Jean, and Geoffrey walked through the camp. The mist from their breath was visible in the cold night air. It was Christmas Eve, and they were returning to their tent from Mass that evening. Jean and Geoffrey were discussing the priest's message while Rodrigo walked in quiet contemplation. *I never would have thought that Christmas here in the Holy Land would feel so depressing.* He closed his eyes for a moment and thought of the last Christmas he had spent in Castile with his family. He could smell the roasting meats in the feasting hall, taste the wine in his goblet, and hear the laughter of the joyous occasion. A cold gust of wind upon his face brought him back to the present and their conversation as they walked.

". . . I was also hoping for a more inspiring message. The priest seemed to be as disheartened as all of us and just going through the motions," Jean said with a sigh. He walked with his arm in a sling, his wound not yet fully healed.

"Adhemar was supposed to give the message for Christmas Mass this evening, was he not?" asked Rodrigo. "I wonder what happened?"

"The priest said something about Adhemar having taken ill," Geoffrey said. "I suppose that would explain why he has not requested any reports or summoned us these last few weeks."

"Perhaps we should visit him, and bring him some Christmas cheer?" Jean suggested with a grin.

"Ha! Have you ever seen Adhemar cheerful?" Rodrigo asked with a smirk. "He is none too pleased with us at the moment. I think we should let him rest and fully recover before showing our faces again."

"Which way now?" asked Geoffrey as the three stopped and looked around, having become momentarily disoriented during their conversation. Surveying their immediate surroundings, they realized they were on the border of the Crusader army's camp, next to the tents of the camp followers. Not far away from where they stood, they could hear many voices cheering and chanting in unison from a large tent on the camp followers' side.

"What is that?" asked Geoffrey. They paused for moment in silence as they listened.

"I don't know, but it sounds like they are having a good time," Jean answered. "Those are the tents of the camp followers, so perhaps they are having a Christmas celebration. I cannot speak for you two, but I could definitely use some cheer and celebration after the depressing Mass we just came from. Perhaps we could see what all the commotion is about?" The others agreed.

As the three approached the large tent, loud voices could be heard from within, and the shadows of many people inside could be seen on the ground from the light that escaped the entrance. Moving the tent flaps aside, the three entered and had to squeeze in among the soldiers in the back of the crowded tent, which was alive with energy and excitement. Rodrigo looked around at all the Crusaders, who seemed transfixed by something toward the center of the tent. From there, he heard a familiar, unmistakable voice.

". . . and so I ask all of you, ye faithful children of the most-high God: will you bow to the filthy Saracen cowards who reside within the city walls?" It was Peter the Hermit, standing on a table in the center of the tent with his hands in the air, preaching his message to all those inside. "No!" the crowd within the tent shouted in unison. The smile on Rodrigo's face immediately fell, turning to a frown of disgust as he watched. *It is despicable that Peter the Hermit is preaching his foul message of hate on one of the holiest days of the year.*

"The Saracen vermin who sit atop these city walls, polluting the holy city with their presence, mock you with their every breath. Do not lose hope! Do not let your faith in God be shaken by our difficult situation. God will test us! Indeed, he will. But in the end, he will deliver unto us the accursed Saracen horde that cowers behind these city walls, so that they may be crushed beneath our heels like the vermin they are!" Peter yelled, stomping and grinding his foot on the table.

A great cheer of approval went up from the crowd within the tent as Rodrigo and the others stood and looked on in stone silence. The memories of the crowds in Toulouse who were mesmerized by Peter the Hermit's words flashed back in Rodrigo's mind. *Peter the Hermit's influence has only led to death and destruction in the past. Will the consequences be the same if it is allowed to happen again?*

Peter paused for a moment and moved to one side of the table before speaking again. "With me this holy night is a man whose testimony will stir your very souls. I found him not long ago, broken, tormented, and without hope for the future. Under my guidance and direction, this man has once again found God and renewed his faith to fight for our cause!" Some of the Crusaders began to part, and a man stepped out of the crowd and approached the table. It was Richard. Rodrigo and the others were stunned at what they saw. Staring with wide eyes, Rodrigo felt his heart sink into his stomach. *Richard, do not be a fool! Do not allow yourself fall under the spell of this evil man!* he wanted to cry out.

Climbing onto the table and standing alongside Peter the Hermit, Richard began to speak to the crowd. "I am Sir Richard of Hastings, a knight from Normandy. I began this journey like so many of you, a warrior longing for a chance for adventure, to earn honor in combat, and above all, to answer the Pope's call and fight to reclaim the Holy Land and Jerusalem for all of Christendom."

A murmur of agreement went up from the crowd in the tent. Rodrigo stared at Richard, whom he had not seen in several months. He appeared very different than the last time they had spoken. The physical strength and vitality of the old Richard had returned, yet the anger and pain in his eyes and face remained as he continued to speak to the crowd. "Those hopes and dreams and my very faith in Christ and the holy Church began to crumble when I was captured and held prisoner by the Turks at Dorylaeum. I was beaten, tortured, and humiliated by my Saracen captors. For weeks, I endured and prayed to God fervently every day for a release from the relentless pain and suffering, which never came. In the end, my faith was shattered and broken."

Rodrigo looked around the tent, which had fallen into utter silence. On the faces of those around him, an initial sense of pity began to transform into anger and hatred as Richard continued.

"The Saracens spat upon the cross and demanded that I renounce my faith in God and Christianity and accept their faith as my own," Richard said, looking down. "I am ashamed to admit before all of you . . . that I did."

Gasps went up from the crowd at Richard's confession, and whispers of disapproval could be heard as Peter the Hermit placed his hand upon Richard's shoulder.

Richard raised his eyes and gazed into the crowd as he continued. "It was not long after that Bishop Adhemar secured my release along with my fellow prisoners, and I was returned to all of you. God had finally shown me mercy, but I was a broken man, my faith was gone, and I did not know what to believe. I did not care at that time whether I lived or died. It was in this dark place that God led me to Little Peter," Richard said, glancing down at Peter, who was staring back at him.

Rodrigo's frown deepened, and he clenched his fists as he watched. *Can you not see that he is just using you?*

"It was through Little Peter and his teachings that I was able to find God again," Richard said as another murmur went through the crowd, this time showing approval. "Having come back into the light, I know now the depth of the evil that had befallen me and kept me trapped in the darkness." Richard's face and tone began to change as he spoke. "I know now the depth of the evil that has crept into the Holy Land and polluted its cities with its foul presence!" Richard's voice began to rise, and the voices in the crowd began to build along with his. "Little Peter has shown me that God wants us to rid the Holy Land of this evil and cleanse its cities with Saracen blood!" he yelled as the voices in the tent reached a fever pitch.

"Who among you still has faith?" Peter shouted as a roar went up from the crowd in the tent. "Who among you still believes that God will deliver the Holy Land unto his faithful?" Raising Richard's hand along with his in triumph, Peter shouted, "Together, we shall cleanse the Holy Land with the blood of the Saracens and any non-believers! *Deus vult!* God wills it!" The crowded tent erupted in cheers as the Crusaders began chanting, *"Deus vult! Deus vult!"* Rodrigo turned and pushed his way through the cheering crowd and exited the tent, tossing the flaps aside. *I will not listen to any more of this!*

Jean and Geoffrey caught up to him as he walked away. "Rodrigo, wait!" Geoffrey called out. Rodrigo stopped and turned around.

"I am sorry, but I have heard enough. I cannot stand to listen anymore," Rodrigo said, looking down in frustration.

"I know your disdain for Peter the Hermit, but what about Richard?" asked Jean. "It seems he has overcome his injuries and his health has returned. Perhaps now we should try to talk to him?"

Rodrigo looked up with an exasperated sigh. "I don't know, brothers. I think Peter the Hermit took advantage of Richard while he was weak and vulnerable, and now his seeds of hate have found a fertile ground. It is obvious he is just using Richard for his own ends, but it seems that Richard does not care. It also pains me to see how many others are falling under Peter the Hermit's influence."

The three stood in silence for a moment.

"Let's find our way back to our tent," Geoffrey said at last. "Perhaps in the morning, we will have a better idea what we can do." The others agreed, and they slowly made their way to their tent, the cold light of the full moon guiding their way.

Rodrigo lay in his cot with his hands behind his head, replaying the events of the evening. Richard's words continued to echo in his mind as he thought. Whether or not the Pope's words were true, Richard's original intentions for journeying to the Holy Land had been honorable. Now, what had become of those honorable intentions? Peter the Hermit's words had twisted and perverted them into hate and anger for all Saracens, along with any non-believers, just as he had against the Jews—all to spread his deplorable influence over the masses, thereby gaining power and control over them.

He turned on his side and tried to push the thoughts from his head, but he could not. He lay awake on his cot until the early hours of the dawn, when at last he fell into an uneasy slumber.

20

ALEA IACTA EST

I t was the end of January in the year 1098 when the Crusader army ran out of food and began to starve. Weeks earlier, Prince Bohemond and Count Robert had left camp with their men on a long-range foraging mission, and had unexpectedly encountered and defeated a Turkish relief force led by Duqaq of Damascus in a valley east of the city. Although the foraging mission had been successful, all the food and supplies they had brought back were now completely exhausted. The mood in the camp was bleak, and the hungry Crusaders did not wish to risk another long-range foraging mission, as rumors were spreading about another imminent attack. A sultan named Ridwan was allegedly amassing forces in the Turkish city of Aleppo, some ten days' march from Antioch.

Orders came down that all nonessential pack animals were to be slaughtered and the meat distributed among the troops. The only animals that were to be spared were the warhorses of the cavalry units, only some seven hundred of which were left, as many had either died in battle or succumbed to starvation. To make matters worse, several tents around camp were discovered to be emptied of their inhabitants and their belongings. Many of the Crusaders were deserting, taking all their belongings and leaving camp in the dark of night. Some had decided to take their chances by heading north, back through Anatolia, rather than starve and wait to be attacked while continuing the siege.

To counter this problem, the leaders ordered extra guards outside of camp, not only for protection, but to keep any more Crusaders from leaving. Anyone caught leaving would be severely punished, as such actions were considered the highest form of cowardice and meant they were abandoning their oaths to the Pope. Corporal punishments such as whipping and flogging were meted out, and some were publicly humiliated, forced to wear signs denoting their cowardly actions. Despite all of this, the number of desertions grew, and the commanders were forced to begin taking daily accountability of their troops.

Although it was shocking to some, it came as no surprise to Rodrigo when Peter the Hermit and one of his trusted deacons were caught by Tancred trying to desert the Crusader camp. While Peter the Hermit largely escaped punishment due to his widespread influence and status as a holy man of God, his deacon did not. Peter had to publicly beg God's forgiveness for his weakness of faith, while his deacon was forced to endure humiliation and corporal punishment.

By the first week of February, the Crusaders were being rationed to one meal per day, which consisted of scant bits of heavily salted meat. At last, some good news arrived by sea. Several Byzantine ships from the nearby island of Cyprus had arrived in St. Symeon loaded with food and supplies. The news of the coming supplies was a huge boost for camp morale after the weeks of near starvation and desertions.

Just one day later, however, it was overshadowed by dire news from long-range scouting parties that had returned to camp. They reported that Ridwan and his army from Aleppo were approaching the city from the west and were only one day's march from Antioch. The estimated strength of his forces numbered around twelve thousand infantry and cavalry. The Crusader leaders quickly assembled to discuss plans of action, and finally agreed to a plan put forth by Prince Bohemond. His plan was bold and extremely risky, but the reward was high if they succeeded.

✠

Rodrigo had returned to their tent from a cavalry muster and had begun preparing his armor and weapons as he talked with Geoffrey. Jean had left that morning with a group of Crusaders traveling to St. Symeon to collect the food and supplies that had arrived. Rodrigo's warhorse was the only one that still remained of the three knights, as Geoffrey's had not survived the lean winter months.

"This is not a plan, it is suicide!" Geoffrey declared. "You are always speaking of strategy, Rodrigo. How could you expect such a plan to work?" he asked, raising his arms in the air.

"We do not have much of a choice at this point," Rodrigo said as he continued to prepare his belongings. "The only other option is to wait for them here at Antioch. That would mean that we would have to lift the siege, which would likely embolden Yaghi Siyan to attack us as we prepare to defend against Ridwan. Then we would be forced to fight two enemies at once, which would be a huge disadvantage."

"So how is Prince Bohemond's plan any better?" Geoffrey asked. "A heavy cavalry charge of seven hundred knights against an army of twelve thousand? You will be outnumbered more than twelve to one, with no infantry support. How is this plan not suicidal?"

Rodrigo stopped for a moment and looked up at Geoffrey. "Do you remember the lake to the north of the city that we passed when we first arrived?" he asked.

Geoffrey nodded.

"If you recall, the position is perfectly suited for a heavy cavalry charge," Rodrigo said. "It is protected on both flanks, one by the lake and the other by the river, and we will be charging downhill at the enemy. If we catch them by surprise before they have time to form a defensive line, the charge will be devastating. But we can only get to that position in time if we leave immediately. Bringing infantry with us would only slow us down." He finished strapping his sword and scabbard about his waist. "You have seen the damage a heavy cavalry charge can do and its effect on the morale of the Turkish troops. If we hit them hard and fast enough, perhaps we can break their spirit before they are even in the fight."

"And if you do not?" Geoffrey asked with raised eyebrows.

"Then at least we will have dealt enough damage that they will be easier to defeat once they reach Antioch," Rodrigo answered, slinging his shield across his back.

"As I said, it is a suicide mission," Geoffrey asserted solemnly. "It seems as though Prince Bohemond is taking an unnecessary gamble."

"We are in a difficult situation, brother. This is a gamble we must take," Rodrigo said with a sigh of frustration. "*Alea iacta est,*" he stated as he finished his preparations and stood in the middle of the tent.

"What does that mean?" asked Geoffrey.

"It means 'the die has been cast.' There is no going back now. Julius Caesar said it before crossing the Rubicon into Rome."

"So history teaches us to gamble with our lives?" Geoffrey asked skeptically.

"History teaches us that at times, great risk is required for great reward. Besides, if victory is God's will, as the men always say, then what do the odds matter?" asked Rodrigo. "I must go. We ride out this evening if we are to reach the bridge before dawn." He lifted his saddlebags over his shoulder.

"I still do not agree with this plan, but I admire your courage and conviction, Rodrigo. I only wish I could go with you," said Geoffrey as he moved forward and gave Rodrigo a quick farewell embrace. "God be with you, brother. You and all the others will be in our prayers."

"Thank you, brother. I hope to see you and Jean again. If not, then may God be with both of you as you continue our mission," said Rodrigo as he exited the tent. Outside, he had left his horse hitched to the tent post. He breathed in the cool evening air as he secured his saddlebags, lance, and shield and then mounted his horse. *Caesar knew he was taking a gamble when he crossed the Rubicon. Just as it was for him, so it is for us.* Rodrigo looked up at the evening sky and then bowed his head in prayer. *Lord God, I know not what the outcome of this battle will be. I do not want to die, but if our victory is your will, then I know that nothing can stand against us.* Rodrigo opened his eyes, then rode to the outskirts of camp to join the other cavalry.

Bohemond waited until cover of darkness before giving the orders to move out as he led the seven-hundred-strong cavalry detachment out of the camp toward Lake Antioch. He needed to be sure that the Turks in the city were not aware of the plan, lest they were somehow able to get word to Ridwan and warn him of the attack. A major part of his strategic gamble would be catching the Turks off guard with a surprise attack. The Crusader cavalry rode most of the night, finally crossing the bridge and reaching the high ground near the lake just before dawn. Below them lay the open plain upon which Ridwan and his twelve thousand Turkish soldiers would soon be approaching.

Bohemond arranged the cavalry into six squadrons. Each squadron held around 120 heavy cavalrymen, and they would attack in two waves, three squadrons in each. The first wave would charge the enemy center and both flanks. After the shock of the first charge wore off, Bohemond would lead the second wave of cavalry into battle before the Turks could regroup. Like successive waves crashing into the open surf, Bohemond hoped to tear the Turkish lines apart, sending them fleeing in panic back through their own ranks, creating disorder and confusion. If the Turkish lines held, their far superior numerical advantage would quickly overwhelm the Crusaders, and all would be lost.

The squadrons were formed, and Rodrigo was in the very center of the first wave to charge at the enemy. Rodrigo recalled that the coldest and darkest part of the night is just before the dawn as he turned to look down the long rows of Crusader cavalry that sat in stoic silence against the dusky night sky. The sound of the rushing river, the squawk of birds taking flight from the lake, and the mist from the horses' breath and their riders' in the chilly night air painted a surreal picture in his mind. He did not feel tired from the long night's ride, nor did he feel the cold. Only the anticipation of what was to come filled his body and his senses. Rodrigo realized that never in his life had he felt more alive than at this moment, against nearly insurmountable odds, facing almost certain annihilation.

Time seemed to stand still in that moment and yet moved quickly as the first rays of dawn crept over the eastern mountains and began to brighten the night sky. Rodrigo felt his heartbeat quickening and the blood pulsing in his temples as the footfalls of thousands of Turkish warriors marching in cadence to the war drums became louder in the distance.

The light of dawn slowly began to transform the darkened sky into a beautiful iridescent red, with streams of sunlight peeking through the clouds like a crimson cloak imbued with magnificent strands of gold. Bohemond had ordered that each cavalryman attach a banner to the back of his saddle that would fly the Crusader cross above him as he rode. Riding out in front of the first wave of cavalry, Prince Bohemond looked like a giant atop his warhorse. He studied each soldier with a fearsome gaze as he rode to the center of the group and stopped.

His booming voice cut the silence like a knife. "Men! Listen to me and hear my words! Below us on the plains are thousands of Saracens who put their trust in a false god, hoping in vain that he will hear them and answer their prayers. How sad it is for them, but how fortunate it is for us! We are the warriors who fight for all of Christendom and the one true God!" he shouted, as a raucous cheer arose from the cavalry.

Rodrigo cheered loudly along with the others, feeling all the anticipation and excitement begin to pour out like water bursting from a dam as Bohemond continued. "God will hear us and be with us as we ride into battle! This day, there will be no retreat, and there will be no surrender. I will not promise you victory. But I will promise you this: if we die this day, we die with the knowledge that an eternity in heaven awaits us! If they die today, they will rot in the ground and return to dust along with their false god! Look at them! They are like thousands of strands of wheat waiting to be cut down by our swords and lances. Show them the fierceness of your heart and the strength of your faith! Show them that we are not afraid to die for our faith in God!" With that, he drew his sword and galloped down the rows of the first wave of cavalry as a trumpet blared behind them, and a thunderous roar went up from the cavalrymen waiting upon the hill. The sudden clamor and the sight of the Crusader cavalry on the hill above them sent chills down the front lines of the Turks as their march came to an abrupt halt.

Rodrigo's heart was racing as the Crusader cavalry began their charge down the sloping hill toward the front ranks of the Turkish warriors, who were scrambling to form a defensive line. Caught completely by surprise, the Turkish lines were still moving to follow the frantic orders of their commanders while the first wave of Crusader cavalry came barreling toward them.

The clatter of the horse's hooves was deafening, and a terrifying shout went up from the Crusaders as they charged toward the Turks at full speed, lowering their lances in unison, their banners emblazoned with the cross fluttering behind them. Panicked and unprepared for such a violent onslaught, the frontal Turkish units crumbled instantly as the Crusader cavalry crashed through them like a rotted doorway and burst through the other side of their lines with most of their lances still intact. Rodrigo heard the cries of men being trampled and crushed beneath the hooves of his galloping warhorse, but his lance had not yet found a home as he continued his charge through to the second line of Turkish warriors.

The second line was no better prepared than the first to defend against the Crusader charge. Inexperienced and unprepared soldiers in the front lines had begun to fall back upon seeing the enemy cavalry and had disrupted the second lines while trying to flee. Charging into the second line of Turks, Rodrigo's lance impaled a Turk who had just reached the line. The force of the blow lifted the Turk off the ground and carried him face-first into the shields and spears of the Turkish warriors ahead of him.

The charge carried them deep into the secondary lines, but like a giant boulder rolling downhill into a field of wheat, the devastating charge finally lost its momentum and ground to a complete halt. There was now little room to move as Rodrigo and most of the Crusader cavalry found themselves packed tightly in the middle of the Turkish ranks and had to begin fighting from horseback with their swords and axes. Rodrigo drew his sword and began hacking and slashing at the limbs, heads, and torsos of the Turkish warriors around him. Rodrigo could tell that the Turks were still in disarray, as they were all facing different directions around him and could not mount a coordinated defense against the Crusaders on horseback.

Limbs went flying as they were hacked off, the screams of the dying filled the air, and horses and men were spattered red with blood from the carnage. The muscles in Rodrigo's sword arm were burning with exhaustion when the second line of Turks finally broke and began fleeing back toward the third and fourth lines of the Turkish army. Knowing that this panic would cause disruption among those lines, Rodrigo was determined to use that window of opportunity to penetrate the existing defenses. Failing to do so would give the Turks the opportunity to coordinate an effective defense and then overwhelm the Crusaders with their sheer numbers.

Breathing heavily, his voice dry and hoarse from exhaustion, Rodrigo raised his sword and yelled at the cavalrymen around him to charge into the Turkish third ranks while those from the second rank were fleeing in panic. A handful of Crusader cavalry close enough to hear him listened and spurred their horses as they followed him toward the next line of defenses. Their actions served as a catalyst, prompted others to do the same. Just as the fleeing Turks reached the ranks of the third line, causing them to lower their spears and weapons lest they kill their own troops, Rodrigo and the other cavalrymen were upon them, smashing into their ranks, trampling soldiers beneath their hooves.

This time, however, their penetration was not as deep, and they were quickly being surrounded. Rodrigo hacked with his sword at the Turks around him and ducked to one side as a spear thrust narrowly missed his head. Nearing total exhaustion, his sword felt as though it were made of lead as he struggled to wield it. He and the other Crusaders were now surrounded.

Suddenly, a thunderous clamor of hooves and yelling warriors filled the air behind him. Arriving just in time, the second wave of Crusader cavalry led by Prince Bohemond smashed into the third ranks of Turkish warriors, splintering their lances upon the Turkish infantry just as they had begun to regroup and overtake the first wave.

The violent impact from Bohemond's charge tore apart the third rank of the Turkish warriors, and those still standing were being hacked apart and trampled beneath the hooves of the warhorses. Shattered by the second wave of charging Crusaders, the remnants of the third line of Turkish forces crumbled into disarray and began to retreat. The fourth line of Turks, having witnessed everything that had happened, turned and began to flee, ignoring the voices of their commanders ordering them to stop and face the Crusaders. Had there been more discipline among their ranks, the Turks might still have been able to turn the tide of battle in their favor, but it was too late.

The second wave of Crusaders, still fresh and unfatigued from battle, gave chase to the fleeing Turks and cut them down in droves as they fled. The Turkish sultan Ridwan, seeing that his army had been routed, sounded the retreat before the quickly advancing Crusaders were upon him.

The Crusader cavalry gave chase to the Turkish army during their retreat, cutting them down in their wake. Like dried wheat before a scythe, the Turkish warriors fell, littering the ground nearly as far as the eye could see. Rodrigo declined to join the chase and lowered his sword as he watched the other Crusaders pursue the fleeing Turks in the distance. He was elated, but his body was reeling from exhaustion. Looking behind him, he saw thousands of Turkish dead lying upon the ground. In the wake of their fleeing army, the Turks had also abandoned wagonloads of food, supplies, and weapons, which were now spoils of war. The battle was over. Against overwhelming odds, it was a total victory.

THE HIGH AND THE LOW

The Crusader cavalry returned to camp a few days later following their victory over the Turks at Lake Antioch. Along with their victory, they had brought with them wagons full of food, supplies, and weapons. Honor was heaped upon Prince Bohemond for flawlessly executing his daring plan and pulling off a heroic victory. The Crusaders had sustained few losses, while the entire Turkish army was completely routed. More food and supplies had arrived in the camp one day earlier from Byzantine ships at St. Symeon. The mood and morale of the Crusader camp had changed dramatically, and it seemed as though their fortunes had finally begun to change.

"We did it! We defeated Ridwan's army! Prince Bohemond's plan was a success!" Rodrigo announced, beaming with pride as he entered the tent. Met with only silence, he paused and looked around for a moment, and he noticed that Geoffrey was seated, looking down and holding something in his hand. Geoffrey looked up from where he was sitting and seemed to force a smile. "You were right, brother. With great risk comes great reward," he said with a somber tone.

Rodrigo's smile quickly faded. *Something must have happened.* "What is wrong? What are you looking at, and where is Jean?"

Geoffrey did not reply, and his gaze returned to the items he held. In one hand, he had a piece of parchment with writing. In his other, he held a small leather pouch. He upended the pouch, and a necklace with a golden cross fell out into his other hand. "It belongs to Jean," Geoffrey said at last. "The pouch and the letter were given to me by a soldier who said he had received payment to deliver it. It came just before you arrived, and I have just now finished reading the letter. Here," he said, holding the up parchment.

Rodrigo took the parchment from Geoffrey and read the letter:

To my brothers in arms,

With a heavy heart, I am writing to inform you that my journey to the Holy Land and my mission as a Knight of the Crucem Auream are now over. Though it fills my heart with sadness, I have prayed many nights about what I should do, and I finally feel I have the answer.

I know that my time as a knight in the service of this great Christian army has come to an end. My wound has failed to heal properly, and I can no longer hold a shield or wield a weapon with that arm. What good is a one-armed soldier? None, I am afraid, and that is why I have been searching and praying to God for an answer.

Word has come from the Byzantine sailors here at St. Symeon that ships from Europe will soon arrive, loaded with food, supplies, and timber for siege equipment. I know that this long siege will soon be over, and that God will grant us victory over the Turks. I feel comfort knowing that I am not leaving you in a desperate situation, and that victory will soon be ours.

I have decided to stay here in St. Symeon until the European ships arrive. Because of my injury and inability to fight, I have been granted permission by the naval commander to embark back to Europe along with other Crusader wounded who can no longer fight and have become a burden to the camp and our cause.

I will return to my home kingdom in Saint-Léger, Aquitaine. Perhaps I will someday chronicle our adventure as Crusaders in the Holy Land. I wish that I could be with you as you continue your journey, but know that you will be in my prayers daily, and I will never forget the time we spent together.

Good luck and farewell. God be with you always.

Sir Jean of Saint-Léger

Rodrigo lowered the parchment, and his gaze fell to the ground. The joy and elation he had felt moments ago were gone, replaced by a somber mood. *It is difficult to see Jean go, but I think he is making the right decision.*

"Do you think we should go to St. Symeon and speak to him about this decision?" asked Geoffrey, the chain of the cross still dangling from his fingers.

"No," Rodrigo said. "He prayed about it and made up his mind. I agree with his decision. With only one good arm, he is not much use in battle, and being relegated to performing camp duties is not good for a knight whose honor and pride are rooted in battle. It would eventually wear him down. I think we should let him go, but he will be missed."

"I suppose you are right," Geoffrey said with a sigh.

"I will keep his cross with the others," said Rodrigo, taking it from Geoffrey and placing it in a pouch on his belt containing William and Richard's crosses. "No doubt Adhemar will tell us to keep it as a reminder that we are somehow responsible once we give him the news," he said sarcastically. "Speaking of Adhemar, has there been any word from him since I was gone?"

"None," Geoffrey said.

"I hope he is well. Were we to lose Adhemar also, I do not know what would become of our mission," said Rodrigo. "We are the last, brother. I just pray that we are able to see this through to the end."

DIMINISHING CONTROL

Weeks passed, and by mid-March, just as Jean's letter had foretold, a fleet of ships from Europe had arrived, loaded with food, supplies, and building materials. Rather than using the building materials for siege equipment, however, the leaders decided to use them to construct small fortifications around the city near each gate and build a bridge that would allow troops to cross the Orontes River. Instead of trying to storm the city and take it by force, they would elect to apply a choke hold on the city and cut off any possible means of gathering supplies from the outside. Although blocking two more gates meant spreading their forces somewhat thin, the fortifications now gave the Crusaders considerable protection from any sorties or attacks launched from the city. The bridge across the Orontes also allowed for reinforcements to quickly come to their aid from the main camp if necessary.

The plan was working, and by April, the supplies inside the city were running low and the inhabitants were beginning to feel the strain of the Crusaders' hold on the city. The siege was finally beginning to turn in favor of the Crusaders. The weather was also beginning to warm with the arrival of spring, and at last Rodrigo and Geoffrey were summoned by Adhemar after months of silence. It was late in the morning when the two stood outside his large tent, waiting to enter. Rodrigo stood in silence, staring at the ground in thought as they waited. *I wonder if he is aware of Jean's departure. And if he is, will he place the blame on us?*

One of Adhemar's attendants moved back the tent flap, and a voice came from within: "You may enter." The voice was Adhemar's, but it was weak and hoarse, scarcely recognizable from their previous meetings. Rodrigo's brow furrowed as he entered. *He does not sound well.*

Rodrigo and Geoffrey walked into the luxurious tent, noting the furnishings, the Roman Catholic décor, and the ornate rugs that covered the ground. Rodrigo had nearly forgotten how grandiose Adhemar's living quarters were compared to their own—though in the past, even that grandiosity had been overshadowed by Adhemar's powerful and sometimes intimidating presence. Now, however, that presence was strangely missing. It was like walking into a lavish feasting hall absent any guests.

In the middle of the tent, in a large bed, Adhemar was resting with his back against some pillows and his attendants by his side. "Come forth," he commanded in a hoarse, shaky voice. Rodrigo and Geoffrey silently walked to his bedside.

"Bishop Adhemar," Rodrigo said as he approached, "it is good to see you, Your Excellency, after so many months. We were beginning to worry." *He looks very weak. It is obvious he is struggling to retain an air of authority.*

"Silence," Adhemar replied with disgust. "Leave us," he commanded to his bedside attendants. Quietly, the attendants withdrew and exited the tent. Once they were gone, Adhemar began to speak. "My health has not fared well during the many months of hardships during this long siege. In the last few weeks, however, I feel my health and strength beginning to return, just as our army grows stronger and our enemies grow weaker. Fervent prayers and faith in God and the holy Catholic Church have reversed the fortunes of our army and will continue to do so!" he said with a raised voice, coughing hoarsely afterward. Reaching over to grasp a

149

goblet beside his bed with a shaky hand, he slowly took a drink before continuing.

"I am aware that Sir Jean has departed back to Europe and that you two are the last of the Knights of the Crucem Auream. However, I still have faith that Sir Richard will return to the mission for which he was chosen. It has come to my awareness that Little Peter has brought him back to the flock of the Church, and he continues to grow under his tutelage."

Rodrigo glanced at Geoffrey but said nothing. *Growing under his tutelage? His mind and spirit are being warped and twisted by Peter the Hermit's influence, as are all who adhere to his teachings.*

"I hope that the high cost of your rebellious and insubordinate behavior is becoming clear to both of you," Adhemar continued. "A death of one knight, the desertion of another, and one who nearly lost his faith in God." He momentarily lost his voice as he coughed heavily. Rodrigo frowned. *I weary of this constant guilt being laid upon us. I will not accept responsibility for the actions of our brothers!*

When his coughing subsided, Adhemar took a moment to compose himself before continuing. "We may yet reach the holy city of Jerusalem, and there you will have the opportunity to fulfill your vows and complete your mission, but only if you submit yourselves to my authority and that of the holy Catholic Church. Is that understood?"

"Yes, Bishop Adhemar," Rodrigo and Geoffrey answered.

"You will be assigned as guards to the outpost by the gate near Count Raymond's camp. I shall be in contact with you weekly. Pray for the souls of your lost and departed brothers. Pray for forgiveness for your rebellion against the Church. Pray, and never lose sight of the mission for which you were chosen. You may go," he said with a wave of dismissal.

As Rodrigo and Geoffrey walked back to their tent, Geoffrey began to speak. "It is strange to see how weak Adhemar has become. He is quite unlike the Adhemar we have grown accustomed to. His message is still the same, however," he said with a smirk.

Rodrigo nodded. "I agree. He now appears weak and frail, but also desperate to cling to authority and control with his usual methods. I do not care about the duties to which we are assigned, nor humbling ourselves to his authority, but I refuse to accept any of the guilt and responsibility that he continues to lay upon us for the loss of our brothers."

"Nor do I," said Geoffrey.

"My only fear is that if Adhemar's health declines again and we were to lose him, what would become of our mission? How would we carry on without his backing and support?" Rodrigo asked.

"Perhaps Count Raymond would take Adhemar's place and assume control of his men and our mission," Geoffrey said.

Both men noticed a large tent near the edge of camp where many Crusaders were gathering. The sight and sounds of the tent reminded Rodrigo of the place where they had last seen Richard and Peter the Hermit, and a feeling of unease came over him. *Worse yet, our mission could fall into the hands of someone who would use it for their own personal greed and lust for power.* "I sincerely hope, then, should Adhemar pass away, that our mission will be passed to someone worthy like Count Raymond," Rodrigo said as they reached their tent. "We should probably get some rest. We have a long night of guard duty ahead of us."

THE MESSENGER

Oone month had passed since their meeting with Adhemar, and Rodrigo and Geoffrey had been spending their nights in a guard tower of the outpost at the southwestern gate, keeping watch until the early morning hours and then sleeping the better part of the day.

"At least we don't have to spend our days doing camp duties," said Geoffrey as he gazed out into the darkened plain between the tower and the city gate.

"I don't mind camp duties," Rodrigo said, leaning back against the walls of the tower. "It gives us something to do, rather than just sitting here staring into the dark."

"Some of the camp duties I don't mind. As for some of the others, I think I would prefer to sit here and stare into the dark," Geoffrey said with a laugh as the torchlight flickered in the light breeze, causing shadows to dance upon the tower floor. Just beyond the outpost was the Orontes River, which flowed past the southwestern gate of the city. On bright, moonlit nights, the walls of the city shone like a stone beacon, but now the crescent moon was waning, and the darkened walls were scarcely visible, save for the light coming from the watchtowers far above.

The silence was suddenly broken as the ladder to the guard tower creaked with the weight of someone ascending it. Rodrigo and Geoffrey both turned to see a man enter the tower dressed in full armor and wearing a blue tunic with a red cross. The man was tall and bore a striking resemblance to Prince Bohemond, but with a more youthful appearance and slender build. His bearded face had a noble look, yet was strong and hardened by years of battle.

Following him, two more men entered the tower. One was also dressed in full armor with a white tunic, and the other man was Turk, though his colorful silken garb denoted wealth and status. While it was not unusual to have officers and other soldiers visit the tower during the night, none had ever brought a Turk with them, especially one so finely dressed. Turkish merchants were sometimes allowed in camp, but normally the only other Turks in the company of Crusaders were translators. Rodrigo and Geoffrey stared at the men in silence, unsure what to make of the strange and unexpected visitors. *One appears to be an officer or minor nobility, the other a knight, and the other a Turkish emissary or merchant. What could possibly be the purpose of this strange visit?*

The tall man spoke, breaking the awkward silence. "I can see by your faces that you are wondering who we are, and what reason we have for visiting this tower in the middle of the night," he announced to Rodrigo and Geoffrey. "Forgive this unexpected intrusion, and allow me to introduce myself and my men. I am Tancred of Hauteville, and this is Sir Roger, one of my knights, and Ahmed, a Turkish translator."

Tancred was a minor Norman lord from southern Italy, along with his uncle, Prince Bohemond. He was a brilliant tactician and a brave warrior, often leading long-range scouting parties deep into enemy territory and being the first to charge into battle. He was man of strength and courage, and well respected among the other Crusader leaders. It was rumored, however, that he sought to establish his own kingdom and longed to break free of his uncle's shadow, which eclipsed his own accomplishments and heroics.

Rodrigo's eyes widened at Tancred's introduction. *He is a noble and one of the Crusader leaders, no less!* "It is an honor to meet you, Lord Tancred," he said as he and Geoffrey introduced themselves.

"We have heard of you. Your reputation as a brave warrior and leader are known throughout this army," said Geoffrey.

"Sir Geoffrey and Sir Rodrigo?" Tancred said, looking at both men with a furrowed brow. "You are knights? Why does Count Raymond have men of such status guarding his tower in the middle of the night?"

Geoffrey glanced at Rodrigo as he quickly considered his explanation. "We are part of Count Raymond's army, but we are under the personal command of Bishop Adhemar as members of his cavalry unit. As knights, we are highly motivated to seek honor through combat and bravery on the battlefield. Bishop Adhemar, however, prefers to . . . keep our personal motivation and ambitions in check by assigning us such humbling duties."

"Ah, now I understand," Tancred replied. "I am familiar with Bishop Adhemar and his strict demeanor. I too am often called upon by the other Crusader leaders to humble myself for the good of our army and to set aside my personal motivation and . . . *ambitions*," he said with a laugh.

"Indeed, my lord. For what reason do you honor us with your visit this night?" Rodrigo asked.

Tancred did not immediately reply, but walked to the edge of the tower and leaned out, looking over the edge toward the city. The light of the waning moon was faint, and the walls of the city were scarcely visible. He stood for a moment in silence, listening to the sound of the river in the distance, and then turned back toward the others in the tower. "My uncle, Prince Bohemond, has established a contact within the city. So far, their communication has only been through written messages exchanged at a secret location outside the city walls. Tonight, his contact agreed to send his personal messenger to meet with us to give us information and as a show of good faith."

Both Rodrigo's and Geoffrey's eyes widened as they stood in momentary silence. *This is incredible news!* Rodrigo thought. "Why meet here, at Count Raymond's outpost, my lord? Why not meet closer to your own fortifications outside the southern gate?" he asked.

"It was the desire of the contact to meet at this location," Tancred replied. "Now that I am here, I can see why. The proximity of this outpost to the river conceals any noise that may come from our meeting, and it is far enough away from the walls to make it difficult for anyone on top to see, especially on a night like tonight." Tancred then drew a white cloth emblazoned with a red Crusader cross from a pouch on his tunic and hung it outside the wall of the tower toward the city. "This is so the messenger can correctly identify which tower to contact."

Rodrigo walked to the edge of the tower beside Tancred and peered out into the darkness. "Yes, I can see why they wanted to meet here. Is there anything Geoffrey or I can do to do to assist you?"

"No," Tancred said, shaking his head. "It was agreed that we would only bring three people to the meeting. My uncle is being deliberately secretive about his contact, so only those who need to know are aware of it. That is why I am here, as he knows he can trust me. I brought Sir Roger to act as my bodyguard, and of course I need Ahmed, as neither of us speak or understand the Turkish language."

"The Turkish language is quite similar to Arabic, which I can speak and understand," Rodrigo replied. "Although the dialect I am most familiar with is a bit different than that of the Turks, it is close enough that I am able to understand when I listen to them."

Tancred stared at him with raised eyebrows. He then turned to the translator. "Ahmed, speak to him in Arabic," he commanded, pointing to Rodrigo. Tancred, Geoffrey, and Roger all watched in silence as Rodrigo and Ahmed engaged in a brief conversation.

"He said he is surprised that I can speak and understand their language," Rodrigo announced after their conversation ended. "He said that he was formerly a merchant and has done a lot of business with the Franks and learned to speak Frankish because of it. He also said that you pay him very well for his services."

"That is all very true!" Tancred said with a laugh. "So tell me, Rodrigo, how did you learn to speak Arabic?" He listened as Rodrigo told them of the time he had spent in the Moorish kingdom of Zaragoza during his youth, and his exposure to the Arabic language and Saracen culture. "A knight from Castile who speaks the language of the Saracens," Tancred said with a smile of approval. "You are quite unique to this Crusader army. I know of no others from your region, and the only Crusader I know who can speak Arabic, besides yourself, is my uncle." The torchlight flickered in the guard tower as he paused for a moment. "Perhaps you can be of assistance to me after all," he said with a smile.

✠

The night passed quietly as the five men sat in the tower, engaged in conversation while waiting for the signal from the messenger. Rodrigo and Geoffrey shared their stories of how they had come to be part of Count Raymond's army and listened with great interest to Tancred's story of his expedition with Count Baldwin when they had split from the main Crusader army. Impressed by what he had heard and seen that evening, Tancred decided to replace Ahmed with Rodrigo, who would serve as an extra bodyguard as well as a translator. *Truly, it is a great honor to assist in what may be our chance to finally take the city and end this siege,* Rodrigo thought, excited for the chance to be part of the meeting.

The conversation continued into the night until the dull thud of a rock hitting the dirt in front of the tower caught their attention. Ceasing their conversations, they peered out along the edge of the tower, searching the darkness for another sign from the messenger.

Looking out toward the city, Rodrigo saw a tiny flash of light about halfway between the tower and the city walls. "Look there. Did you see that?" he asked, pointing in the direction where he had seen the flash.

"I saw it," Tancred said as he turned from the edge of the tower and walked to the ladder. "That is his signal. Let us depart and meet with him," he said to Rodrigo and Roger.

The three quickly descended the ladder and exited the protection of the outpost, disappearing into the night. They walked slowly, as the absence of moonlight made it nearly impossible to see more than a few feet in front of them. When they reached the area where the flash of light had come from, Tancred gave the order to stop and wait.

Rodrigo felt his heart beating faster, and he placed his hand on the hilt of his sword. He turned to look around, straining to see anything in the darkness or hear anything above the rush of the river nearby. *We are very exposed out here in the open, far from the safety of the outpost. Any cries for help will be drowned out by the sound of the river. Prince Bohemond must have reason to trust this contact. Otherwise, we are placing ourselves at great risk of being killed or captured.* Behind them, far off in the distance, Rodrigo could see the torchlight in the watchtowers framing the silhouettes of the men as they stood guard.

A voice suddenly hissed at them from behind, causing the men to turn, and then, like an apparition in the night, a man appeared out of the darkness. He wore black garments from head to foot, and a black cloth was wrapped about his head and face so that only the whites of his eyes were visible. The man stood silently in front of the group and then began to speak in a hushed tone in Turkish. "I bring a message from Captain Firouz to Prince Bohemond."

"This is Lord Tancred, who is here on behalf of Prince Bohemond," Rodrigo replied in Arabic.

The man studied Rodrigo for a moment and then replied in Arabic. "Firouz accepts the deal offered by Prince Bohemond. He will allow access to the city gates, but he wants more. One hundred pieces of silver and safe passage out of the city for not only him and his family, but ten additional people, his servants and personal guard."

Rodrigo turned to Tancred, who listened while Rodrigo translated the message. "If we accept, then what?" Tancred asked.

Rodrigo asked the messenger, who then continued. "If these terms are agreed upon, then on the night of Bohemond's choosing, Captain Firouz will have five ropes lowered from the southernmost city walls. Bohemond's men must climb the walls, make their way down to the city gates, dispatch the guard, and then open them for your armies to enter."

"Why must we climb the walls? Why does Firouz not just open

the gates himself?" Tancred asked after hearing Rodrigo's translation.

The man's eyes narrowed when Rodrigo asked him Tancred's question, and he growled his response in a hushed, angry tone. "Yaghi Siyan does not trust Firouz or any of his captains. There are rumors of treachery among the city guard. All the gates are now manned by Yaghi Siyan's personal soldiers. Only the towers are allowed to be controlled by the city guard, and only Captain Firouz knows about this plan. Because of the great risk he is taking, Firouz wishes to receive the hundred pieces of silver in advance."

Rodrigo translated the message, and after listening, Tancred loosened a pouch tied to his belt. Handing the sack to the messenger, Tancred said, "Firouz will receive fifty pieces of silver now and fifty more pieces after it is finished. Prince Bohemond will need to decide if he agrees to the plan to scale the city walls."

Rodrigo translated Tancred's words, and the messenger began to walk about the group like a stalking animal. Rodrigo followed him with his eyes, keeping his hand upon the hilt of his sword as the messenger spoke. "Prince Bohemond must decide quickly! Yaghi Siyan has already executed two captains for plotting against him. Captain Firouz may not have much time before he is next!" As soon as he had finished speaking, he abruptly turned and vanished into the darkness.

Rodrigo translated the final message, and the sound of the rushing river dominated the silence as the three stood in the dark for a moment. Then Tancred spoke. "Sir Roger and I will go now to the main camp to discuss this information with my uncle. You may return to your guard tower and instruct Ahmed to go to my outpost and wait for me there."

"Yes, my lord," Rodrigo answered calmly. Inwardly, however, he could scarcely contain his excitement about what he had heard from the messenger. *A plan to scale the walls of Antioch and open the city gates? This is extraordinary!*

"Thank you for your assistance tonight," Tancred said, moving closer and looking Rodrigo in the eye. "But there is one more thing I require. I need you to swear to keep all of this information a secret and tell no one. Doing so could jeopardize my uncle's weeks of planning and forfeit our opportunity to take the city."

"Yes, my lord. I swear I will tell no one," Rodrigo answered. "However, I would ask one small favor in return. If this plan comes to fruition, and the selection begins for the men to climb the walls and open the gate, I would like to be considered from among them."

A faint smile came across Tancred's face. "It is an honorable request. However, that will be up to my uncle. I will inform him of your services this night *and* your request. We must go now." He and Roger turned and began walking north toward the main Crusader camp while Rodrigo made his way back to the outpost.

The first rays of dawn had begun to brighten the sky when Rodrigo and Geoffrey returned to their tent after being relieved from their long night of guard duty in the tower. Geoffrey lay in his cot with his arms folded behind his head. "Have you thought about what might happen if this turns out to be a trap or does not go as planned? You may be captured and executed or held for ransom. Or they may simply cut the ropes before you reach the top of the wall and laugh as you fall to your death."

"True, those are all possibilities, but I think the chances of this being a trap are low," Rodrigo answered as he lay down on his cot. "I do not think the Turks would create such an elaborate plan to kill a handful of soldiers. From what the messenger said, it sounds like some of the officials within the city are growing desperate and are looking for a way out."

"It is still a risky plan. Why not let Prince Bohemond's men scale the walls and open the gates? Why did you volunteer to go?" asked Geoffrey.

Rodrigo paused for a moment. "I believe that this plan is the best chance we have of taking the city and ending the siege. If I can do something to help that plan be successful, then I am willing to do whatever it takes."

"Well, if you are chosen to go on that mission, then for your sake, I hope that it works," said Geoffrey as he turned on his side to sleep.

Rodrigo lay staring at the ceiling of the tent for a while, then closed his eyes. *Lord God, I pray that this long siege will soon come to an end. If this plan does come to pass, whatever the outcome may be, I pray that your will be done.*

2 4

VYING FOR POWER

One week had passed since Rodrigo and Geoffrey had spoken to Tancred, but no word had come regarding the mission. It was now the end of May, and news arrived in camp that sank the Crusaders' morale just as it was starting to rise. Word had come from the city of Edessa to the east, now being governed by Count Baldwin, that they had been besieged by a massive Turkish army under the command of Kerbogah of Mosul.

Kerbogah had joined forces with Ridwan of Aleppo and Duqaq of Damascus, both of whom had suffered recent defeats by the Crusaders and were hungry for revenge. Their combined army numbered around thirty-eight thousand men. Growing frustrated with the stubborn defense of Edessa by Count Baldwin, Kerbogah decided not to waste any more time and lifted the siege after just three weeks and headed straight for Antioch.

Long-range scouts reported that the Turkish army would arrive in four days, prompting the Crusader leaders to hold an emergency meeting in the camp of Count Raymond. All the leaders were present to discuss a plan of action around a large table in the middle of the tent. At the head of the table sat Count Raymond, and next to him, Bishop Adhemar. Adhemar, who normally was a commanding presence and an outspoken voice in the leaders' meetings, now sat quietly subdued with attendants by his side. He was only able to voice his opinion through Count Raymond, whom he had to lean over to speak with in a hoarse whisper.

Adhemar scowled as sat quietly, frustrated by his diminished sense of power and the position he had been relegated to due to his failing health. *I trust that Count Raymond can hold his own in this meeting, but some of the other leaders may seek to take advantage of our weakened position and impose their will.*

It had been rumored that the wealthy Count Stephen of Blois was growing weary of the long siege, and he was the first in the group to stand and propose a plan of action. "My fellow leaders, it is clear that we must lift the siege immediately and arrange a defensive position near the lake where Prince Bohemond defeated Ridwan. This must be a completely unified effort, as we cannot divide our forces and hope to defeat Kerbogah's army." Many leaders in the group nodded and muttered their approval.

Adhemar leaned in close to speak with Raymond. "This is a sound plan, my lord, and similar to our own. Once we have eliminated this threat, then nothing will stand in our way of taking the city," he whispered. *Then we will be able to offer the city back to the emperor, and Count Raymond may appeal for governorship of Antioch.*

No sooner had Stephen sat down than Bohemond rose from the table to offer his own opinion. "I disagree with this plan. Lifting the siege will wipe out many months of effort that we have already put into it. The Turks will destroy our fortifications and resupply the city while we are away. Even if we defeat Kerbogah's army, we will have to start the siege all over again. It will take many more months before their supplies are again exhausted, and that is only if our own supplies hold out. It is likely they will not."

"This may be true, my lord," Adhemar whispered to Raymond, "but once the threat is removed, we will be able to expand our search for food and supplies as we wait for more to arrive by sea." He stared at Bohemond. *Prince Bohemond must be planning something to dissent to such an obvious choice for a plan of action.*

Stephen rose again in response to Bohemond's statement, and

both now stood at the table across from each other. "What choice do we have, then? You were only able to defeat Ridwan with a much smaller force because you were able to catch him by surprise. Do not be so foolish as to think that they will make the same mistake twice. They will be better prepared, and in order to defeat such a large army, all of us will need to combine our forces and face them in open battle. This plan is the only option!" he said, raising his voice in opposition as he looked to the other leaders for approval.

"It is *not* the only option!" Bohemond loudly asserted as he stared at Stephen in defiance.

Adhemar's scowl deepened. *What is he hiding from us?*

"It is not the only option?" Stephen asked with raised eyebrows as he turned to look around at the other leaders in the tent. "Come then, Prince Bohemond, why don't you entertain us with another one of your grand strategies." He raised his arms in mock praise, to the amusement and laughter of some of the other leaders.

A loud bang shook the large table, and the laughter ceased immediately as Bohemond withdrew his massive fist, looking at the other leaders with an intense scowl. "I know a way we can take the city in two days," he said in a loud, commanding voice. "I have established a contact inside the city, with whom I have been able to negotiate a deal. In two days, the gates will be opened, and we will be able to storm inside and take the city by force." Bohemond's bold claim was met with much surprise and skepticism from the other leaders and triggered a flurry of conversation around the table.

At last, Prince Bohemond's bid for power is revealed, Adhemar thought as he leaned in close to Raymond. "My lord, do not agree to this plan. He seeks the city for himself." His words came as a hoarse whisper, and he began coughing heavily afterward. His servants quickly brought water for him to drink.

When the conversations around the table began to subside, Stephen challenged the bold claim. "If this is true, Prince Bohemond, why were we not informed of this plan earlier? Why should we believe you now?" he demanded. All conversations had ceased as the group waited for Bohemond's response.

"It took time to establish this contact and to complete our

negotiations," Bohemond answered. "I did not want to inform the rest of you until the preparations were complete and the plan was ready to be executed."

After Bohemond had finished, Count Raymond rose from his seat to speak, having conferred with Adhemar. "If it is true what you say, Prince Bohemond, that you have established a contact inside the city and have an agreement with him, what assurances do you have that your plan will work?" he asked.

"I have no assurances," Bohemond calmly admitted to all the leaders. "Should my plan fail, then I will agree to lift the siege and march out to face Kerbogah's army. However, should the plan succeed, because it is mine alone, I will ask all of you to agree that Antioch should be mine to rule once it falls into our hands."

Immediately following Bohemond's statement, cries of outrage erupted from the other leaders in the tent. Adhemar stared in contempt at Bohemond as he gripped the arms of the chair tightly in anger and frustration, but he remained silent. In the past, he would have unleashed a fiery rebuke to such a brash statement and called upon the wrath of the Pope and the holy Catholic Church, but in his weakened state, there was nothing he could do but quietly voice his opinions and offer counsel to Count Raymond.

Count Raymond again spoke up after consulting with Adhemar. "Prince Bohemond, what about your vows to return all reclaimed lands and cities to Emperor Alexios? What you are asking us to do defies the vows that all of us took before embarking upon our journey to the Holy Land." Many in the group voiced their agreement.

"We gave Nicaea back to the emperor, and all the land we have crossed until now," Bohemond said. "We have fought many battles, lost many men, and suffered a long and difficult siege, all without his help. I say that we have fulfilled our vows to the emperor and owe him nothing more."

Again, the table erupted into arguments and debate. Some of the leaders agreed with Bohemond, while others did not. One of the leaders at the table, General Tatakios, the Byzantine general who had been with the Crusaders since they left Constantinople, got up and walked out of the tent.

Stephen stood and glowered with indignation at Bohemond. "Not only do you ask us to break our vows to the emperor with this disgraceful act of selfishness, but you want us to waste days of valuable preparation while you attempt some ridiculous scheme with no assurances that it will even work? I will not stand to listen to any more of this arrogance and foolishness!" he shouted, storming out of the tent. Another leader, Count Hugh of Vermandois, the wealthy son of the French king, also got up and left.

The rest of the leaders remained for a time, engaged in heated discussion, as they considered Bohemond's proposal. "My lord, we cannot agree to this plan," Adhemar whispered to Raymond. "It would be better to leave and join Count Hugh and Count Stephen in their dissent. It would place an immense amount of pressure on Bohemond to abandon his scheme." *He cannot possibly move forward with this outrageous plan without Count Raymond's support!*

Raymond remained silent as he thought for few moments. At last, he leaned over to Adhemar to speak. "I cannot join with those who choose to divide our army and thus weaken our forces. If I walk out now and the rest agree to his plan, then I may be forced to capitulate, and will then appear weak to the other leaders. We must wait and see what the others think. I will continue to place pressure on him to relinquish his demands by reminding him and the others of our oaths to the emperor."

Adhemar said nothing, but sat back in his chair, disgusted by Raymond's response. *Prince Bohemond does not care about his oaths to the emperor! Reminding him and the others will do nothing to change his mind!*

When the discussions had concluded, Bohemond spoke again. "I would not ask the rest of you to put your trust in me if I were not confident that my plan will succeed. With any plan, however, there is always the risk of failure. Should it not succeed, we will still have two days to break camp and assemble our forces near the lake. If we are successful, then this long and difficult siege will be over, and the city will be ours because of my plan. If this happens, I do not think it is too much for me to ask that Antioch be placed under my rule."

The leaders took a vote, and all who were present agreed that they would follow Bohemond's plan and honor his request, save for Count Raymond, who continued to insist that the city be turned over to the emperor. Count Stephen, General Tatakios, and Count Hugh, however, broke camp the following day and, taking thousands of soldiers with them, began heading north to Constantinople.

25

THIEVES IN THE NIGHT

The next evening on June 2, much to Rodrigo's surprise and excitement, his request was granted, and he was summoned to Tancred's outpost while the rest of the Crusaders were ordered to prepare their armor and weapons and stand at the ready inside the camp and outposts. Inside the fortifications at Tancred's outpost, Rodrigo joined Bohemond and fifty of his soldiers that had he handpicked for the mission.

They were only allowed a thin coat of mail for protection and given dark tunics that would not reflect any light. They wore no helmets, their swords were strapped to their backs, and each carried a dagger in his belt. Bohemond had given them their instructions. They were to climb the walls when the ropes were lowered and wait until all fifty were atop the battlements. Bohemond himself would be leading the group, and from there they would make their way down to the ground level of the southern gate, kill the guards, and open the gate for the Crusaders waiting outside.

Around midnight, the lamps in the southern tower went dark; it was their signal to begin. Like thieves in the night, they stole across the open plain in the darkness to an area below the southern tower. At the base of the wall near the tower, five ropes were waiting to meet them. One by one they ascended the ropes, pulling themselves up, arm over arm, struggling to make as little noise as possible. If anyone slipped or lost their grip and fell, the noise and clamor could jeopardize the entire mission.

Rodrigo now knew why they were only allowed the barest essentials of armor and equipment. The muscles in his arms, shoulders, and back were burning and he was breathing heavily by the time he reached the top of the thirty-foot wall. Helped by those on top, he climbed over the top of the battlements onto the walkway and looked down into the city below as he waited for the others. The many houses, buildings, and market squares seemed calm and quiet, completely unaware that the entire Crusader army lay in wait just outside the gates. Like a flock of sheep, the inhabitants slumbered peacefully inside the city that evening while a hungry predator waited outside in silence for the kill.

At last, all fifty had made it onto the walkway without making a sound. Drawing his sword as the others did the same, Bohemond led the group to the door of the southern tower. He pulled slowly on its handle, and it opened silently to reveal a dark chamber. Motioning the soldiers behind him to follow, he entered the pitch-black room and drew an unlit torch from a sack. Once inside, the men huddled around the torch in silence while Bohemond lit it by striking a piece of flint and steel. The intermittent flashes in the darkness illuminated the deadly serious countenances on all the men in the circle. The torch sputtered to life on the third strike, brightening the interior of the stone chamber.

On the opposite side of the chamber, a stone staircase descended downward. Holding the torch in one hand and his sword in the other, Bohemond warily led the men down the staircase in single file. Two more torches were lit, one in the middle of the line and one in the back. The stairs led down to another chamber, which held another staircase leading downward. Rodrigo felt his heart pounding, as he expected to encounter the enemy at any moment, but each successive chamber that they passed through was empty.

Finally, they reached the chamber on the bottom floor. There were no more staircases, only a door leading out into the city. Bohemond waited until all the men had reached the bottom floor. They could hear noise from men speaking in Turkish outside the door. Speaking as softly as he could, but loud enough for everyone to hear, Bohemond gave the orders. "This is it, men. If we open the city gates, victory is ours. If we fail, we die. Fight with everything you have, for everything you have is at stake." Bohemond kicked the door with his boot, flinging it open, and sprang upon two unwitting Turkish guards like a lion ambushing its prey.

Both guards fell to Bohemond's sword, and before the others knew what happened, the rest of the Crusaders had burst out of the doorway, yelling their battle cries as they attacked the startled guards. Rodrigo rushed at a guard near the gate, who lowered his spear in defense. Gripping his sword with both hands, Rodrigo quickly knocked the spear aside and then swung with all his might on his recovery, slicing open wounds across the arms and chest of the Turkish warrior. The guard dropped his spear and fell to the ground as Rodrigo came to a stop. Standing over the downed guard, Rodrigo swiftly planted his sword in the guard's chest.

The Turkish guards at the gate were caught by surprise and were quickly overwhelmed by Bohemond and his men. The element of surprise was now gone, however, and cries of alarm could be heard from atop the walls and all around them. Rodrigo knew they had little time to get the gates open before thousands of Turkish warriors would descend upon the mere fifty Crusaders inside the city. Sheathing his sword, he began working with others to remove the heavy timbers that reinforced the gates as Bohemond ordered the rest to form a perimeter around the gate.

Almost as soon as the perimeter was formed, Rodrigo could hear the clash of swords and the sounds of battle behind him as the first wave of Turkish warriors arrived at the gate. Time was becoming critical, and the gates proved to be well fortified. Rodrigo grunted with effort as he and the others worked desperately to open the gate. Out of the corner of his eye, he could see the giant form of Prince Bohemond coming to aid their efforts, and the sounds of fighting around them intensified as more and more Turks arrived to defend the gate.

Putting his shoulder into the last of the massive timbers barring the gate, Rodrigo strained with all his might and felt it starting to move. "It's moving!" he yelled. Others nearby grabbed the timber as he strained again and felt it move away from the gate and fall on the ground. Like a dam starting to burst, the huge city gates slowly creaked open by the force of the Crusaders pushing from the outside. Rodrigo moved out of the way as the gates opened wide and the Crusaders began flooding into the city.

The Crusader army had massed outside the city walls and was now streaming into the wide-open southern gate. Rodrigo and the others had been moments away from being overtaken when the gates opened and the incoming Crusaders engaged the Turkish soldiers within. More Turkish soldiers had arrived at the gate, but it was too late. The Crusaders were now in the city, and the bloody chaos was about to begin.

26

THE MASSACRE

R odrigo ran down the city streets with a small group of soldiers with the goal of finding and opening another one of the city gates. A steady flow of Crusaders was now pouring into the city from the south, and groups of marauding soldiers began stalking the city streets, causing fear and panic among the residents, who were awakening from their slumber into a living nightmare.

A woman's scream of terror behind him brought Rodrigo to a sudden halt as the rest of the group continued without him. The scream sent a chill down Rodrigo's back as he spun around to see where it had come from. Behind him, he could see some of the city's inhabitants—a man, a woman, and a young boy—being dragged into the street by some Crusaders who had entered a building. The young woman was screaming and kicking as she was dragged by her hair, and the man and boy were thrown to the ground.

Rodrigo grimaced, and his grip on his sword tightened as anger and revulsion gripped him at the heartlessness of their actions. "What are you doing? These people are civilians!" he yelled as he began to move toward the men. Suddenly, his eyes went wide as he froze in his tracks. "No!" he cried out in horror as the Crusaders raised their swords and axes. The screams and cries abruptly ceased, replaced by the dull thud of metal cleaving flesh as the Crusaders ruthlessly butchered the helpless victims in front of him.

Several more Crusaders were coming down the street and stopped by the men where they stood, the blood still dripping from their weapons. Leaving the bodies behind, all the men began running toward Rodrigo, who stood motionless, stunned by the savage brutality he had just witnessed. More cries and screams of the city's helpless inhabitants began to ring out from all directions. "What are you waiting for? The city is ours!" one of the Crusaders yelled at Rodrigo as the group ran by him down the street. Rodrigo said nothing, but stared at the faces of the Crusaders as they ran by. Their wild eyes and elated expressions revealed a perverse sense of satisfaction with what they had done. It was obvious that they were hungry for more.

Rodrigo looked at the lifeless bodies behind him for a moment, then turned to follow the group down the street toward the next gate. He began to feel sick to his stomach as he ran, and the revelation of what was occurring all around him began to sink in. *The entire population of this city is going to be massacred!* Outrage and a sense of helplessness began to well up inside him as he continued to move down the street. He knew there was nothing he could do to stop the slaughter that was now taking place within the city.

Screams of terror and the cries of the dying began to fill the city as the night went on. Doors were kicked in, and soldiers rushed inside the houses and other buildings, searching for loot and killing whomever they found. The Crusaders were met with armed pockets of resistance from the Turkish troops in various sections of the city, but with no way to mount a coordinated defense, all were quickly overrun and fell to the Crusader onslaught. Following the street close to the city wall, Rodrigo soon reached the southwestern gate. The Turkish soldiers guarding it had been overrun just as he arrived, and the Crusaders were now working to open the gates for the yelling, frenzied mob that waited outside.

A building close to the gate caught Rodrigo's eye as several Crusaders ran past him, their passions ignited with the prospect of loot and a lust for blood. Rodrigo stood still for a moment as he stared, and his brow began to furrow. The building was clearly marked with a Christian cross that stood above the doorway. A group of Crusaders had already begun hacking away at the locked doors with their axes, attempting to gain access. *Do they not realize this is a Christian church? I will not allow this to happen!*

"What are you doing? This is a church!" Rodrigo yelled out to the men, pointing to the cross above the doorway as he approached. Paying him no heed, they continued their efforts, and the door began to break apart under the weight of the heavy axe blows. A woman's scream could be heard as the first of the men entered through the shattered doorway. Rodrigo ran to the building's entrance and followed the rest of the Crusaders, who had gone inside.

Upon entering, Rodrigo saw a group of people huddled in the corner of the sanctuary, surrounded by four Crusaders who had their weapons drawn. Sheer terror filled the faces of the men who stood in front of the group and the women behind them. Some of the men were on their knees, pleading and holding up wooden crosses for the Crusaders to see. They were speaking frantically in a foreign tongue and seemed to be professing to be Christian while the men with crosses emblazoned upon their bloodstained tunics began to close in. The horror that Rodrigo had felt earlier that night transformed into rage at the sight of sacrilege that was about to occur.

"Stop!" Rodrigo yelled, as the four turned to face him. "This is a church! These people are Christians!" Rodrigo felt his heart about to beat out of his chest as he gripped his sword so tightly he nearly shook.

Rodrigo could see the same wild look in the eyes and the faces of the men. They were out for loot and plunder and did not care where they found it or how they obtained it. "The city is ours! We will take what we want and kill anyone that stands in our way!" said one of the Crusaders as he approached Rodrigo with an axe.

"Then you will have to kill me!" Rodrigo angrily asserted, raising his sword. The Crusader lunged forward and took a wild swing at Rodrigo with his axe. Rodrigo easily avoided the swing and struck back with a cracking blow to the side of the man's head with the flat of his sword. Immediately knocked unconscious by the blow, the man, carried forward by the momentum of his swing, crashed into the wooden pews as Rodrigo stepped out the way.

Turning quickly to the others and pointing his sword at them with a menacing glare, Rodrigo angrily rebuked them. "You wear the cross and call yourself Christians, yet you would loot and kill innocent civilians inside a church?" he yelled. "I swear that any of you who lay one hand on these people or take one item from this church will stand in judgment this day before God!"

The men looked at Rodrigo and then over to their fallen comrade, who lay on the floor. The wildness had fled from their faces as they lowered their eyes and their weapons. "We did not realize this was a church. We were only following the orders of our captain," said one of the soldiers, motioning to the man whom Rodrigo had knocked unconscious.

"All of you, listen to me well," Rodrigo said through clenched teeth. "Enter buildings in the city as you wish, but leave the churches alone! Kill or capture any Turkish warriors you find, but spare the city's inhabitants! Do you understand?" Rodrigo growled, glaring at the men. The soldiers stood still for a moment and then nodded in agreement.

"Now leave! And take your captain with you," Rodrigo ordered, stepping away from the unconscious man who lay between the fallen benches. The Crusaders picked up their captain and exited the church without a word. Some of the men and women in the church immediately fell to their knees and wept with joy and relief, praising and thanking God for their salvation. Others walked over to Rodrigo and began to speak to him in a language he did not understand. Rodrigo spoke Arabic to the group, asking if anyone understood.

"I understand," said a young woman as she approached him.

"Who are all of you?" Rodrigo asked.

"My name is Milena. We are Armenian Christians, and this is our church," said the woman. "Thank you for saving our lives. The soldiers would surely have killed us."

Rodrigo silently nodded in acknowledgement as he looked at the people in the church. *Had I not arrived when I did, no doubt they would have. God must truly be watching over these people.* "Are there many other Armenian Christians and churches within the city?" he asked.

"There are some," Milena replied. "Although many of our community left the city over the last several months. The Turks became less and less tolerant of us as the siege wore on because we share the same faith as you."

"Where in the city are they located?" Rodrigo asked. He turned and began walking toward the entrance of the church. "Perhaps I can try to reach them before they are looted."

"Wait, where are you going?" Milena asked aloud, running up to Rodrigo and catching his arm. "If you leave, more soldiers will come. We will not be safe here alone!" she said, suddenly shrinking back as more Crusaders arrived at the doorway and peered inside.

"This is a Christian church! There is nothing here for you!" Rodrigo yelled angrily, walking toward them with a menacing look in his eyes. The men lingered momentarily at the doorway and then left. Rodrigo walked through the ruined doorway and frowned as he peered out at the city, which had fallen into a state of chaos and anarchy. *We risked our lives to open the city gates, for what? So that our army could butcher the innocent civilians within? We bring shame and dishonor upon ourselves by these deplorable actions.*

"Please, sir," Milena said as she stepped outside the church and stood by his side. "Please do not leave us." She put her hand on his arm and looked up into his eyes.

Rodrigo felt torn as he looked down at Milena and then back out at the city. *How many more churches are being looted in the city and innocent civilians being slaughtered? But if I leave, something may happen to these people. I cannot abandon them to their fate.*

"I will stay until the city is secured. You will be safe then," Rodrigo said, looking back down at Milena.

"Thank you, thank you," Milena said as she breathed a sigh of relief and walked back inside to tell the others.

The looting in the city and the massacre of its population continued throughout the night. Rodrigo stood guard outside the church, turning away several more groups of Crusaders who sought entrance during his watch. Dawn broke at last, casting the cloak of night aside, revealing the slaughter and devastation that had taken place inside the city. Corpses littered the streets, entrances to buildings and houses were broken in, and their interiors ransacked. Groups of prisoners, both Turkish soldiers and civilians, were being marched out of the city in the early morning hours.

Rodrigo entered the church to find many of the group sleeping on the floor. Only Milena and a few others were still awake, sitting on a bench. Rodrigo approached Milena. "Wake the others and tell them to gather any belongings they have."

"Why? What will happen to us?" Milena asked.

"All captured Turkish warriors and civilians are being moved outside the city at this time," said Rodrigo. "The Turkish soldiers will become prisoners of war, but the civilians will most likely be set free. However, you must take everything you can carry with you, for you may not be allowed back in."

"I understand. Thank you for what you did last night and for staying and protecting us. What is your name, sir?" Milena asked. "You never told me."

"I am Sir Rodrigo of Castile."

"Thank you, Sir Rodrigo. You will not be forgotten. God be with you," Milena said with a smile of gratitude as she turned and began to wake the others.

"God be with you as well," said Rodrigo as he exited the church and headed toward the city gates.

✠

The Crusaders' victory celebration was short-lived, as Rodrigo and the other Crusaders were immediately ordered back to camp with instructions to break it down as quickly as possible and move everything inside city. Kerbogah and his massive army were only two days away, and the Crusaders had to work quickly to refortify the gates and set up the city defenses. When he arrived back at camp, Rodrigo walked into his tent and met Geoffrey, who was already packing his belongings.

"Rodrigo!" Geoffrey said, smiling as he stood to greet him. "So returns the liberator of the great city of Antioch from the hands of the Saracens! I am glad to see you safe and well!"

Rodrigo glanced at Geoffrey but said nothing. He sullenly walked across the floor and sat down on his cot, hunched over with his head down and his forearms on his knees. He was exhausted from the long night, and the horrors he had witnessed continued to haunt him as they replayed in his mind. "Safe and well," he said at last, after musing over Geoffrey's words. "If only the same could be said of the innocent inhabitants of the city. Had I known the cost of victory, brother, I would have gladly let them keep it."

Geoffrey's smile faded as he moved his belongings aside and sat down on his cot facing Rodrigo. "I understand what you are feeling. I, too, witnessed many terrible acts of savagery inside the city last night after we entered and the looting began. Count Raymond had given the order that all civilians were to be spared and detained, but those orders went unheeded once we were inside the city and the soldiers began to run amok," Geoffrey admitted, looking down. "I do not believe there is anything we could have done to stop it."

"I tried," Rodrigo said, looking up. Geoffrey listened as Rodrigo told him what had occurred at the church of the Armenians that night. ". . . had I left them, it is doubtful they would have made it through the night."

"I believe you made the right decision, then," said Geoffrey as he contemplated Rodrigo's words. "Even if you were able to save a few, then your actions were not in vain."

Rodrigo stood up from the cot, frowning, as he hastily unstrapped his sword from his back and his dagger from his belt. "Is this why we came to the Holy Land?" he yelled in frustration, throwing his weapons down onto his cot. "To loot and to kill innocent civilians, even our fellow Christians?"

Geoffrey continued to sit and think for a moment. "You had mentioned once, in a conversation with Richard, about the reality of war. Is it not true that the loss of innocent life is simply a part of this war?" Geoffrey asked.

Rodrigo's frown deepened as he slowly shook his head. He paced the length of the tent as he pondered Geoffrey's question in silence for a time before answering. "I believe that sometimes it is inevitable that innocent lives are lost when caught in the violence of war. However, I *do not* believe that massacring an entire city's population is part of that inevitable reality. With strict orders from our leaders and more discipline among our soldiers, most of the bloodshed could have been avoided. We are supposed to be a *Christian* army!" Rodrigo yelled, clenching his fist. "Last night many of our soldiers committed unspeakable acts of violence on innocent civilians, something no *true* Christian would ever do!"

Geoffrey looked down and nodded. "With spiritual leaders in the Church like Peter the Hermit, is it any wonder?" he asked, looking back up.

"Very true, brother," Rodrigo replied. "The poisonous fruit from Peter the Hermit's seeds of hate is beginning to ripen, and the wanton slaughter of innocent people is the result." He sat back down on his cot and stared at the ground. "Unfortunately, I fear that as long as he is allowed to preach his vile message, it will continue."

"I completely agree," said Geoffrey. "In fact, I saw clear evidence of that last night. I witnessed an atrocity that was far greater than anything else I had seen. It took place at a large mosque in the interior of the city."

"What happened there?" Rodrigo asked.

"After we entered and fought our way to the city interior, many of the Turkish soldiers began to flee toward the citadel, while some sought refuge in a large mosque. I was there when several groups of Crusaders surrounded the mosque. It was already full of Saracen civilians, and the Turkish soldiers who fled there threw down their weapons before they entered. Apparently they thought, as did I, that such places of worship were deemed sanctuary and they would not be harmed."

Rodrigo said nothing but listened intently.

"They were wrong," said Geoffrey. "A large group of Crusaders entered the mosque, weapons drawn, and the savagery of what occurred was unlike anything I have ever witnessed as I listened to the screams of those being butchered inside. I, along with some others, attempted to enter the mosque, but the doors had been barred from the inside. Whether it was to keep us out or prevent anyone from escaping, I do not know. When they finally exited the mosque, most were carrying loot and covered in blood. One of those Crusaders I saw coming out of the mosque was Richard."

"You saw Richard? Did he recognize you?" asked Rodrigo, his eyes widening.

"If he did, he said nothing. He walked right past me, covered in gore from head to foot, and his entire tunic was stained red. It was the look on his face that I cannot forget. He seemed to have taken great pleasure in what they did, and his eyes were hollow and soulless. I believe the Richard we once knew is gone. He has become something else," said Geoffrey, shaking his head.

"No doubt the *close personal tutelage* of Peter the Hermit has helped to facilitate Richard's transformation," Rodrigo said with disgust. "He has now become an instrument Peter uses to commit acts of hate and violence, all with impunity and the blessing of a so-called leader in the Catholic Church. It turns my stomach to think about it."

"Mine as well," said Geoffrey as he stood up from his cot and looked around the tent. "We need to finish packing and break down the tent. It has been a long night for both of us, and we have much work to do before the day is over."

27

A TWIST OF FATE

Two days had passed, and the besiegers had now become the besieged. Kerbogah's army had arrived and conveniently occupied the fortifications around the city that had been abandoned. The defense of the Turkish-held citadel within the city was strong and had prevented the Crusaders from taking it. The citadel was cut off and isolated, but knowing that a massive relief force lay just outside the walls of the city, the Turkish warriors who took refuge there refused to surrender. The irony of their current situation was not lost on Geoffrey and Rodrigo, who were tasked with defending the western walls. Though the horrors of the massacre that had taken place just days ago were still fresh in Rodrigo's memory, the gravity of what they now faced forced him to push such thoughts aside and focus on the task at hand.

"So, now we are laying siege to a citadel defended by the Turks . . . inside a city that is besieged by the Turks . . . which we laid siege to just two days ago, but we are now defending," said Geoffrey as he leaned against the battlements on the city walls and looked down at the Turkish camp below.

"That is correct. A bit confusing, but correct," Rodrigo replied with a slight grin as he sat on the walkway with his back against the battlements. Next to him, leaning against the battlements, was a large two-handed mace.

"A strange twist of fate, is it not?" asked Geoffrey.

"It is," said Rodrigo, standing up. "In truth, I did not expect to be on this side of a siege this entire campaign. It is a welcome change, at least for now," he said as he grabbed and hefted the heavy mace, feeling its weight in his hands.

"Where did you get that?" asked Geoffrey, staring at the intimidating weapon.

"From the city armory," Rodrigo answered. "Weapons were being taken from there yesterday and distributed among the soldiers. This immediately caught my attention when I saw it, so I decided to try it out. It is quite heavy."

"I can see that. I would hate to be on the receiving end, especially after climbing to the top of a ladder with the ground thirty feet below," Geoffrey said with a smile.

"I was thinking the same thing," said Rodrigo. He gripped the mace firmly and grunted with effort while giving it a practice swing. "I believe it will be more effective for defending the walls than a sword. We will see what kind of damage it can do."

"I do not think you will have to wait long to find out," said Geoffrey, looking over the battlements. "They seem to be preparing to assault the city as we speak."

"I guess Kerbogah is not one for wasting any time," said Rodrigo, peering down at the Turkish camp, which was alive with movement and activity.

✠

Late that morning, horns began blaring in the camp below as the Turkish soldiers started to mass in various areas around the city. There were no siege towers, but battering rams could be seen moving into place near the gates, and many ladders were being distributed among the groups of Turkish warriors as they prepared to assault the city.

"Get ready, men!" barked a commander from a nearby guard tower.

The battle horns sounded the beginning of the assault as the Turkish troops rushed toward the city with a roar. The Crusaders pelted the Turkish troops below with arrows, rocks, and anything heavy and expendable that they could find. Ladders went up from the ground but were being pushed off the walls with poleaxes and spears with hooks. For every ladder that was pushed off, however, two more would go up in its place.

Some of the Turks managed to make it over the walls but were quickly killed and thrown back over the wall. Rodrigo did not even bother to push away the ladders, preferring instead to swing the heavy mace at the easy targets reaching the top of the ladder or hammering those who managed to make it onto the battlements. The weapon proved brutally effective as he sent man after man crashing down to the ground with shattered skulls and broken limbs.

The tactics seemed to have a demoralizing effect on the troops below, and after they had assaulted the city walls without success for the entire morning, the horns sounded again, withdrawing the troops back to camp. The efforts with the battering rams continued, and the booming from the heavy blows resounded on the gates as the Crusaders rained down rocks and arrows from above. The gates held strong, however, and with neither tactic finding success, the battering rams were also withdrawn in the early afternoon.

Rodrigo was breathing heavily, dripping with sweat, and took a long drink from the water skin that was being passed around. "This weapon is extremely effective, but it takes a tremendous amount of energy to wield and control it," he said while sitting and resting with his back against the battlement.

"That is true, but whenever one of your swings connects, the damage is devastating." Geoffrey laughed. "If I were a Turk going up the ladder and saw what was happening to those at the top, I might hesitate before going any farther."

"I had noticed that they stopped coming up as fast after a while," Rodrigo replied with a grin.

"Do you think they will continue to assault the walls?" Geoffrey asked, taking the water skin from Rodrigo.

"I think they will," Rodrigo said. "Even if the assaults have not been successful thus far, I think they will continue until they have lost enough men. Commanders are always stubborn, because they are not the ones climbing the ladders. They only care about the troop numbers, and once they have lost enough, most likely they will resort to starving us out like we did to them."

"So you do not believe their assaults have any chance of succeeding?" asked Geoffrey.

"They have many warriors, but these walls are high and easy enough to defend," Rodrigo said. "If they had siege towers, they might have a chance, but not with ladders. So long as the gates hold, which I think they will, then I believe their attempts to assault the city will fail. Starving us out, however, may not prove to be too difficult for them. The supply stores within the city, from what I have seen, have mostly been depleted, and we only had a couple days to bring in supplies from the outside. If this siege lasts long, it will not go well for us."

"Let us pray for some divine intervention then, and that the siege does not last long," said Geoffrey as the battle horns sounded from below, signaling the next assault to begin.

28

THE HOLY LANCE

The Turkish assault on the city lasted for two more days, but the Crusader defenses held strong, and with mounting losses, Kerbogah called off the assault and settled in for a long siege. In just three weeks, however, the Crusader army had completely exhausted the supplies within the city and had resorted to slaughtering the last of the cavalry's warhorses to fend off starvation.

Rodrigo and Geoffrey were standing in line near the city barracks where they now resided, waiting for their ration of horsemeat, which was roasting on a large spit. "Jean would be laughing if he could see us right now," Rodrigo said with a smirk. "His prediction has come true. Here we are, waiting to eat our mounts. I wonder if that one is mine?"

"Well, I am glad you can find humor in all of this," Geoffrey replied as he waited behind Rodrigo with folded arms. "I wonder where Jean is right now?"

"No doubt relaxing in the comfort of his family's castle in Saint-Léger, feasting on duck, pheasant, and roasted boar with apple," Rodrigo said as he held out his wooden plate for piece of roasted horseflesh.

"Perhaps his injury turned out to be a blessing after all," Geoffrey mused as they began walking back to the barracks holding their plates of food. "It is not the taste of horseflesh that I can't get used to, it's the toughness." He pulled on a piece of meat, trying to tear it with his teeth.

"Meat is meat, brother. We should enjoy it while we still can. After it runs out, then what? Will we be forced to eat the leather of our shoes?" Rodrigo asked with a grin.

"It may be less difficult to chew," Geoffrey said, releasing his bite on the piece of horsemeat and putting it back on his plate. "Well, there may yet be hope. Before we took the city, I heard rumors in camp that Emperor Alexios was preparing to march his army to Antioch to relieve us." They reached the barracks and sat down outside among other Crusaders to eat their meal.

"I heard those rumors too," said Rodrigo, chewing his food with effort. "Even if it is true, what do you think will happen when the emperor encounters General Tatakios and the other Crusader lords on their way back to Constantinople with the news that Prince Bohemond has claimed Antioch for himself? I doubt that the emperor will take that news favorably, especially after hearing it from his own general."

"Yes, I suppose that is probably true," Geoffrey admitted with a sigh while rolling his eyes. "Thank you for dashing my hopes upon the ground." He set his plate aside.

"Better to hear the truth than rely on false hope, brother," Rodrigo replied as he continued to gnaw on a piece of meat.

✠

Another week had passed, and it was nearing the end of June. The last rations of horsemeat had been given out, and the Crusaders' situation had grown desperate. Their leaders had begun negotiations with Kerbogah as a last resort, but with little to bargain with, the negotiations had stalled. The Crusaders' morale was low, and it truly began to seem as though their only hope for salvation would be through divine intervention.

Rodrigo was awakened early that morning to the sounds of many voices and movement within the barracks. He rose from his cot and sat up as he rubbed his eyes and began to listen to the excited voices of many soldiers who were talking in small groups. He looked over at Geoffrey, who was still asleep in his cot.

"You there," Rodrigo called out to a soldier walking nearby, "what is all the commotion about?"

"A holy relic has been discovered in the city!" the man said enthusiastically. "Come and see for yourself!" Rodrigo could see that many men were beginning to exit the barracks. He immediately got out of his cot and walked over to Geoffrey.

"Wake up!" Rodrigo said loudly, shaking Geoffrey's shoulder.

"What is it?" asked Geoffrey as he startled awake. "Are we being attacked?"

"No. I just heard that a holy relic has been discovered inside the city!" Rodrigo answered excitedly. "Perhaps it is a sign from God. I think we should go investigate."

Geoffrey paused for a moment while the news sunk in, then threw off his blanket and grabbed his clothes and boots from under his cot. "What are we waiting for, then? Let's go and see for ourselves!"

Rodrigo went back to his cot and sat down to put on his clothes and boots when he noticed a priest inside the barracks, talking to some of the men. The priest turned, and when he saw Rodrigo and Geoffrey, he began walking toward them. "Are you Sir Rodrigo and Sir Geoffrey?" he asked.

"Yes, Father," Rodrigo answered as he finished dressing and stood up.

"I bring word from Bishop Adhemar," the priest announced.

The priest told them the news that was spreading rapidly around the city and causing an instant fervor among the Crusaders. Peter Bartholomew, one of Count Raymond's priests, had purportedly received a vision in the night from Saint Andrew. In the vision, Saint Andrew had revealed that the Holy Lance, the spear that pierced Christ's side during the crucifixion, was buried beneath the Church of Saint Peter in Antioch. Immediately after receiving the vision,

Peter Bartholomew had sought audience with Bishop Adhemar and Count Raymond, who ordered an excavation at the church at once to locate the relic.

The priest told Rodrigo and Geoffrey that Adhemar had ordered them to be at the church during the excavation as part of their mission to secure any holy relics that might be discovered. They were to report to Count Raymond once there, and he would be expecting their arrival. As soon as the priest finished his message, the two left the barracks and eagerly began walking down the city streets toward the Church of Saint Peter.

"The news is extraordinary, but I cannot seem to make sense of it," Geoffrey said as they walked. "Why would the Holy Lance be buried under a church in Antioch?" he asked skeptically.

"I don't know, brother," Rodrigo answered. "It does seem rather strange. I suppose we will soon find out." Rodrigo thought about Geoffrey's question as they walked, and his brow began to furrow. *Geoffrey is correct. Why would such a relic be buried under a church here in the city? The fortuitous nature of Peter Bartholomew's vision seems a bit suspicious, given our current situation.*

The sun had scarcely risen that morning when they arrived at the church, but a great number of people were already outside, excitedly discussing the news of Peter Bartholomew's vision and the excavation. Many soldiers, clergy members, and camp followers were crowded around the church, blocking the entrance. Some were praising God out loud, with their eyes fixed toward the heavens, but some stood with folded arms, frowning in their conversations with others. Rodrigo noted a mixture of excitement and skepticism within the crowd as he looked around. *Apparently, not everyone believes in Peter Bartholomew's vision of this holy relic.*

"We need to get inside," Rodrigo said to Geoffrey as the two began weaving their way through the crowd toward the church entrance.

"Halt! No one else is allowed inside save for priests and nobility," said a soldier who was standing guard outside the doors when they finally made it through to the entrance.

Geoffrey reached inside a pouch on his belt and handed the

guard a piece of parchment as he spoke. "We are here on orders from Bishop Adhemar. We need to go inside."

After examining the parchment stamped with Adhemar's seal, the guard stepped aside, allowing them entrance. Rodrigo and Geoffrey walked through the double doors into the large church, which was completely made of stone, unlike the small wooden church Rodrigo had encountered at the city entrance. As they walked into the wide-open sanctuary, they noted the beautiful frescos painted on the domed ceilings of the archways between the pillars and the tall stained-glass windows that illuminated the inner sanctuary. *It certainly seems old enough to harbor an ancient relic,* Rodrigo thought as he studied the interior.

All of the wooden pews in the middle of the sanctuary had been pushed aside, and there in the middle of the floor, a giant pit was being excavated by men using spades and shovels. The heavy stones that had covered that section of the floor had been removed and, nearly ten feet down inside the pit, a dozen workers were busy filling buckets of dirt that were handed up and sifted through.

"They must have started the excavation last night, right after the vision was revealed," Rodrigo remarked, looking down into the pit. Standing around the pit, watching and supervising the labor, were several of Raymond's priests. Rodrigo sneered with disgust when he noticed that one of the priests looking down at the edge of the pit was Peter the Hermit, who was standing next to a man whose only garment was a long white bed shirt. *Of course Peter the Hermit is here. He is probably scheming at this very moment about how best to use this situation to his advantage. I wonder if he has anything to do with this?*

Rodrigo leaned over to Geoffrey and whispered. "I see that Peter the Hermit is here, but who is the man wearing only the white bed shirt standing next to him?"

"That is Peter Bartholomew," Geoffrey said. "I recognize him from a Mass that I attended recently."

"It appears that Peter Bartholomew was so excited to share his vision of Saint Andrew with others that he forgot to put on his pants," Rodrigo whispered as Geoffrey laughed.

"Sir Rodrigo and Sir Geoffrey?" asked a soldier who approached them from behind.

"Yes?" Rodrigo answered.

"Count Raymond requests your presence. Follow me," said the soldier as he turned and walked away.

Rodrigo and Geoffrey followed the soldier to the back of the sanctuary, where they encountered Count Raymond sitting at a table. Around him were some servants and other soldiers acting as guards. There was a plate of bread and some fruit on the table next to a goblet of wine. Rodrigo's stomach began to growl as he looked at the food. It had been a nearly a full day since his last meal. Though most of the soldiers had to make do with scant rations only once per day, it was not so for the upper nobility.

"Your Excellency, this is Sir Rodrigo and Sir Geoffrey," said the soldier as they approached the table.

"Thank you. You may leave," Raymond said, waving the soldier and the other servants away. He turned back to Rodrigo and Geoffrey. "Are you hungry? There is food and wine. Please, help yourself."

"Yes, thank you, my lord," said Geoffrey as they sat down and took some of the bread and fruit from the plates.

Though extremely hungry, Rodrigo took only a bit of fruit and a small piece of bread, as he was keenly aware of the hungry eyes of the soldiers and servants around them who were watching. He bowed his head and prayed silently for a moment before he began eating. "Thank you, my lord. It has been almost a full day since we have eaten anything," he said between bites. "You requested to see us?"

"Yes," Raymond said, studying them for a moment. "You are members of Bishop Adhemar's Knights of the Crucem Auream, but originally there were five of you, correct?"

"Yes, my lord, that is correct," Rodrigo said. "Now there are only two of us. The others have become casualties of this difficult campaign, I'm afraid."

"Yes, I understand." Raymond nodded and paused for a moment in thought. "It has been a difficult journey thus far, and we have all suffered losses along the way," he said as he took a flask and poured some wine into his goblet. "Speaking of difficulties, Bishop Adhemar had dearly wanted to be here after hearing about Peter Bartholomew's vision, but he is still quite weak and asked me to meet with you in his place. He and I have become quite close, and I am fully aware of the mission for which you have been chosen. Any holy relics that are acquired will be kept by Bishop Adhemar and myself until we can safely deliver them to the Pope." Raymond took a drink of wine and set his goblet down. His eyes were heavy and tired, and his countenance lacked any of the excitement and enthusiasm of those around him. "We shall see if anything becomes of Father Bartholomew's . . . *vision*," he said as a sigh escaped from his lips.

Rodrigo and Geoffrey stopped eating for a moment and glanced at each other. "You have doubts about the vision, my lord?" asked Geoffrey.

Raymond sat up, leaned in bit closer to Rodrigo and Geoffrey, and spoke in a lowered voice. "Father Bartholomew is a mystic as well as a priest. He has had visions and premonitions in the past. Although, shall we say, they are not always entirely accurate. We shall see if this one has any merit. He certainly believes in it, however," Raymond said as he leaned back in his chair.

Rodrigo said nothing but continued to eat his meal. *This is interesting. It seems as though even Count Raymond is skeptical about Father Bartholomew's vision. If he truly did not believe it, however, would he have gone through all of this effort to find it? Perhaps there is chance that it may be found then, and if so, it will undoubtedly have a huge effect on the morale of the men.*

One of the workers approached the table, escorted by Raymond's guard. His clothes were covered in dirt from head to foot and stained with sweat. He had dark circles under his eyes and a look of exhaustion on his face. "Forgive my intrusion, my lord," he said meekly.

Raymond put his goblet down. "It is fine, you may speak. Have you found anything yet?"

"No, my lord. We have already dug nearly twelve feet down and twenty feet across, right where Father Bartholomew instructed us to dig," the worker answered. "We have sifted through every inch of dirt that we have dug up, and still nothing. The men are exhausted, my lord. We have been working nonstop throughout the night and into the morning."

"Very well," Raymond replied. "We have done as much as we can. Call off the search, and I will make the announcement. The Holy Lance has not been found."

"Yes, my lord," said the worker as he turned to leave.

"I will inform Bishop Adhemar of your presence here and give him the news," Raymond said to Rodrigo and Geoffrey as he sat back in his chair. "You may leave."

"Yes, my lord. Thank you for the meal," said Rodrigo as he and Geoffrey got up from the table.

In the sanctuary behind them, the man who had come to the table could be heard making the announcement to the other workers and those around the pit who were watching. "By order of Count Raymond, the excavation is over. All sappers and miners here today shall be compensated for their work."

Those around the pit turned to each other to discuss the announcement as those inside began handing up their spades and shovels and climbing out. As Rodrigo and Geoffrey walked by the pit toward the doors at the end of the sanctuary, they heard a single voice of protest call out above the rest. "Not yet! Not yet! Keep digging! We are too close! It is here, I swear it!"

The voice came from Peter Bartholomew who, without warning, jumped into the pit from the side. Seeing the white robe suddenly disappear into the giant pit, Rodrigo and Geoffrey hurried back to see what had happened. Standing at the edge of the pit and looking down, they saw Peter Bartholomew below them on his hands and knees, digging into the dirt with his bare hands. The onlookers stood in stunned silence, watching the bizarre scene unfolding before them. At the top of the pit, the line of onlookers parted as Count Raymond approached the edge, frowning as he looked down into the pit. "Father Bartholomew!" he called out with an angry voice. "Come out of there at once!"

The command went unheeded, and Peter Bartholomew continued to frantically scoop out dirt with both hands, staining his white shirt brown as he clawed into the dirt and flung it behind him. Raymond looked at his guards and gave them a silent nod, and two soldiers beside him climbed down into the pit. Once at the bottom, they walked over to Peter Bartholomew, and just as they were about to place their hands on him, he stopped digging and called out, "I found it! I found it! The Holy Lance! It is here!"

His eyes were wide, and his face was beaming as he stood and held up what appeared to be a rusted piece of metal to the surprise and gasps of those above. Count Raymond continued to frown as he looked down at the scene and called to his guards in the pit. "Bring him up!" he ordered. The guards escorted Peter Bartholomew to the edge and helped him up as those near the pit crowded around them to catch a glimpse of what he had found.

"Let's take a look," Rodrigo suggested to Geoffrey, and they walked over to the crowd around Peter Bartholomew. Raymond had walked back to the table and seated himself, and once Peter was out of the pit, the guards escorted him to Raymond with the crowd following closely behind.

Standing in front of Raymond and flanked by guards, Peter Bartholomew held out his trembling hand to reveal a rusted spike a few inches in length. Raymond took the spike and examined it. Looking back up at the crowd around him, he spoke. "Give us a moment." Hearing his request, the guards began to push the crowd back several feet, leaving Raymond and Peter alone. Scanning the onlookers, Raymond spotted Rodrigo and Geoffrey in the crowd and waved them forward to come and look at the object. "Let them through," he told his guards.

Rodrigo and Geoffrey came forward and stood beside Peter in his soiled nightshirt. Peter's wrinkled forehead and nervous face were accentuated by his disheveled gray hair and beard and the dark circles under his eyes.

Raymond handed the rusty spike to Rodrigo, who turned it over as he looked at it. "The Holy Lance?" Raymond asked with raised eyebrows and a note of skepticism in his voice.

Rodrigo looked at the rusty metal spike in his hand as he spoke. "It is difficult to tell exactly what it is, my lord, as it is so small. From its shape, I suppose it could be the tip of a Roman pilum," he said, handing the spike to Geoffrey. *Or it could simply be a rusty nail used in construction. It is impossible to tell what it really is.*

"What is a pilum?" Geoffrey asked, examining the object.

"A Roman spear with a long, thin point," Rodrigo explained as Geoffrey handed the spike back to Raymond. The look on Raymond's face remained unchanged, but he managed a sympathetic smile as he turned to Peter standing next to him. "You knew right where to dig, didn't you, Father Bartholomew?" he asked as a father to a child.

"I did, my lord," Peter Bartholomew answered timidly. "It was exactly where Saint Andrew showed it to me in my vision." For a moment, the three stood in silence, staring at the rusty spike, which Raymond held in his hand while seemingly deep in thought.

"Indeed, it was located exactly where you described in your vision," Raymond said at last. Turning to the crowd once again and raising his voice, he loudly proclaimed, "Spread the news! The Holy Lance has been found!" The announcement drew gasps of awe from the crowd. Many looked to the heavens and began praising God aloud, while the priests made the sign of the cross. Rodrigo looked at Raymond with raised eyebrows and then back over at the excitement and enthusiasm of the crowd. *Does Count Raymond really believe this is the Holy Lance? Or is he just using this situation to his advantage? I suppose I cannot really blame him, given the low morale of the men and our current situation. But what does that say about the integrity of our mission? Is anything we have been led to believe truly as it seems?*

"Thank you, Father Bartholomew," Raymond said with a smile. "I shall deliver the holy relic to Bishop Adhemar. Why don't you go and get some rest? You look extremely tired." He put his hand on Peter's shoulder. "I shall summon you later this evening."

"Yes, my lord. Thank you, my lord," said Peter Bartholomew meekly as he bowed and turned to leave.

"Thank you for sharing your thoughts on this matter," Raymond said to Rodrigo and Geoffrey. "Your presence here has been helpful.

Now you can help me further by going and spreading the news that the Holy Lance has been found and that it shall stay in my safekeeping."

"Yes, lord," Rodrigo and Geoffrey replied. As they began walking away, the guards released the crowd, which quickly moved forward, eager to catch a glimpse the holy relic that had been discovered. Rodrigo was looking at the excitement in their eyes as they walked by when his gaze unexpectedly met Peter the Hermit's. His eyes unconsciously narrowed, as his memory flashed back to when he had held the cowering Peter the Hermit in his grasp when he confronted him in Constantinople.

Their eyes locked on each other for a moment as they passed, and a flood of recognition seemed to wash over Peter the Hermit as he stopped in his tracks. Rodrigo broke their gaze and looked straight ahead as he and Geoffrey continued to walk toward the church exit. *Did he recognize me? If so, perhaps he will seek retribution for what occurred between us in Constantinople.* Rodrigo stole a glance backward and could see Peter the Hermit still staring at him as he and Geoffrey walked through the doors.

"I think Peter the Hermit recognized me," said Rodrigo as they walked out of the church.

"Well, if he did, I am sure he was surprised to see you again, and certainly not expecting you to be offering counsel to Count Raymond," Geoffrey said with a grin. "No matter. What occurred between you two happened a long time ago."

"I agree," said Rodrigo. "I think we have much greater concerns right now anyway."

"Do you think Count Raymond really believed that rusty spike was the Holy Lance?" asked Geoffrey as they began to make their way back to the barracks.

"It did not seem so," Rodrigo answered, shaking his head. "I think he may just be taking advantage of the situation to boost the morale of the men."

"Yes, that is probably true," Geoffrey said with a sigh. "I was truly hoping for a miracle."

"As was I," Rodrigo said.

"So, Count Raymond has found the Holy Lance. What happens now, I wonder?" asked Geoffrey.

"I don't know. I suppose we will have to wait and see what our leaders decide to do next," Rodrigo said as they reached the barracks. "We are here. Come, let's spread the news as Count Raymond asked us to."

29

THE HOUR OF RECKONING

The news of the vision and discovery of the Holy Lance spread quickly through the city and was a huge boost to the morale of the Crusaders. Their leaders held a meeting that evening to discuss their situation in the city palace. They had gathered in a large chamber and sat around a long table, in the middle of which was a white cloth displaying the holy relic found by Peter Bartholomew. Sitting in front of the holy relic was Count Raymond. He was alone for the first time in the leaders' meeting without Bishop Adhemar, who was too weak to leave his living quarters. Raymond looked around at the faces of the other leaders, many of whom wore frowns of skepticism and were whispering to one another in suspicion. He sat calmly, and his eyes moved back to the object that lay before him. *I care not for their opinions. This object has given the men hope, and that is all that matters.*

Sitting across from Raymond was Prince Bohemond, who was the first to offer comment among the leaders. "This is the Holy Lance that was found by your priest?" he asked with an intimidating stare as he stood up and reached across the table, picking up the rusty spike from the cloth. The lamps that illuminated the chamber behind

Bohemond cast a giant shadow over Raymond as Bohemond examined the spike with a frown.

"It is," Raymond confidently answered. *Prince Bohemond cannot intimidate me. I know my decision to declare the discovery of the Holy Lance was the right thing to do.* Murmurs and whispers could be heard among the other leaders in the room.

"Did your priest offer explanation as to why the holy relic was buried so far underground beneath a church in Antioch?" Bohemond asked with a raised eyebrow as he passed the relic on to be examined by the other leaders.

"He did not," Raymond answered flatly.

"Do you truly believe this rusty nail is the Holy Lance that pierced Christ's side?" Bohemond growled while leaning forward and looking at Raymond with both hands on the table. Raymond did not immediately answer but retained his air of confidence as the other leaders waited in silence for a response.

"I believe that its discovery has been auspicious, and that God comes to the aid of his faithful in their time of need," Raymond replied, raising his voice as he returned Bohemond's stare. "We are in need right now, Prince Bohemond, are we not?"

Bohemond took his hands off of the table and stood up straight. The faintest of smiles could be detected under his bushy beard and furrowed brow, a rare hint of approval distinct from his normally scowling countenance. "On that, Count Raymond, we can agree!" he said loudly, turning to the other leaders around the table. "Whether this object is truly the Holy Lance or something that was discarded during the construction of the church, it matters not! The men need something to believe in right now, and you, Count Raymond, have done well to give it to them." Bohemond then turned to Count Robert. "How are the negotiations going with the Turks?"

"All of our negotiations have failed. They will not accept our terms, and Kerbogah continues to demand our complete surrender," Robert answered. "We have also not made any progress toward capturing the citadel."

"What about our food and supplies?" Bohemond asked, turning next to Duke Godfrey.

"At the current rate that we have been rationing them, we have only a few days before there is nothing left," Godfrey said.

Bohemond pondered the grim reports for a moment and then spoke. "This is what I will propose. The men's morale has been lifted by Count Raymond's discovery of this . . . relic. We will give out the rest of the food and supplies tonight and not hold anything in reserve. A good meal and a full stomach will boost the men's morale even further. Also, we will tell them that tomorrow we will begin a three-day fast for a *spiritual cleansing* to honor the discovery of the Holy Lance. This will give us time for a final attempt to negotiate with the Turks, and if it fails, which is likely, we will draw up plans to sally forth from the city and face the Turks in open battle."

There was silence in the chamber while Bohemond looked around at the other leaders at the table, studying their faces. "I cannot speak for all of you, but this I will say for myself. I will not lay down my sword and surrender to the Turks, nor will I cower behind these city walls and slowly starve to death. If I must die, then I will die in battle. What say the rest of you?"

Raymond sat back in his chair as the relic was returned to him and placed back on the cloth. *For once, Prince Bohemond and I agree. There is nothing more we can do, and we should take advantage while the men's morale is still high.* "I agree with Prince Bohemond's proposal," he announced to the others.

The rest of the Crusader leaders looked at each other, and one by one they unanimously agreed to Bohemond's plan. That evening, the last of the food and supplies were dispersed among the Crusaders. An announcement was made that the following day, they would begin a three-day fast. Over the next two days, the final negotiations with the Turks failed, as expected, and the leaders convened again to draw up battle plans. On the evening of the third day, the Crusaders were ordered to prepare their armor and weapons. Though they had not eaten for three days, their hunger had not gone without purpose, and the morale of the Crusaders was still high, knowing that the hour of reckoning with the Turks was upon them.

✠

On June 28, 1098, the entire twenty-thousand-strong Crusader army marched out of Antioch on foot, as not a single horse remained. Only one-third of their original number since beginning their journey, they now faced a Turkish army nearly twice as large with infantry, cavalry, and horse archers.

The Crusaders were led out of Antioch by Count Raymond, and with him he carried the Holy Lance. Prince Bohemond followed in the middle and would lead the army forward once they were positioned on the field. Count Robert and Duke Godfrey brought up the rear and would form the right flank. Rodrigo and Geoffrey were in the front with Count Raymond. Though Bishop Adhemar would not be joining them, they were ordered to protect Count Raymond and the Holy Lance at all cost.

The Crusader army marched out over the bridge of the southwestern gate and onto the fields outside the city. The main body of the Turkish army, some thirty-eight thousand men, were in camp north of the fields. The move to sally forth came as a surprise to the Turks, but with an army nearly twice as large as the Crusaders', Kerbogah and his commanders welcomed the opportunity to face them in open battle. The Turks quickly began forming their battle lines north of the fields. The order was given to the commanders to allow the Crusaders to completely exit the city before attacking, thus ensuring their complete destruction by not allowing any to escape back inside.

By midmorning, the Crusader army completed their battle formations on the field and were ready for what lay ahead. The massive Turkish army was waiting for them to the north, and behind them, the smaller Turkish units that had occupied the fortifications on the southern end of the city had a combined force of two thousand men. The sun shone brightly in the sky, and the sunlight gleamed and sparkled on the polished steel of the spears, swords, and helmets of the Crusaders.

Rodrigo and Geoffrey listened as Count Raymond began to speak to the troops around him. "My faithful warriors and servants of the most-high God! This is our moment of truth! God has granted us possession of the Holy Lance, the spear that was thrust into his son's side as he hung from the cross. His son's death has cleansed us of our earthly sins, assuring us an eternity with him in heaven! It is a sign from God that he is with us and will be watching over us this day!" Looking up to the heavens, Raymond raised his sword in one hand and the Holy Lance in the other. "The angels and saints in heaven are all around us, protecting us, and will guide us to victory!" he shouted to the cheering of his men. The Crusaders raised their spears and swords with their eyes fixed firmly forward on what lay before them, signaling to their enemy that they were ready and willing to die for their belief in Christ and God above.

Rodrigo and all those around Count Raymond let loose a fearsome battle cry that echoed down the long lines of the Crusader army as all the leaders finished their pre-battle speeches and whipped the hungry and half-starved soldiers into a religious frenzy. Rodrigo felt the familiar pounding in his chest as the adrenaline began to flow. The trumpets blared, and the long battle lines eagerly began marching forward into the jaws of the enemy that lay in wait before them.

Then something strange began to happen, something that no one had ever witnessed or heard of before. It began with some of Count Raymond's men closest to him. They began singing hymns and praising God aloud as they marched. Those in the ranks next to them joined in and started singing and shouting praises to God, which gradually continued down the lines and throughout all the ranks of the soldiers. The more that joined in, the louder the praises and singing became, until the entire twenty-thousand-strong Crusader army was singing hymns and shouting praises to God at the top of their lungs in a religious exultation as they marched toward the Turks.

The Turkish troops who were witnessing the bizarre behavior of the Crusaders looked at one another in confusion and then turned to their commanders, who had no answers for them. Determined not to let the strange behavior of the Crusader army rattle him or alter their battle plans, Kerbogah gave the order for the Turkish army to stand their ground and wait for the command to engage the Crusaders. However, the other leaders of the Turkish army did not feel the same way. Duqaq and Ridwan, incensed by the actions of the Crusaders and hungry for revenge and personal victory, ordered their troops on the front lines forward to meet the Crusaders head on. At their commands, the front lines of the Turkish army began to peel off from the main body and move forward.

Seeing what was happening, Kerbogah immediately sounded the battle horns, ordering the units to return. The orders fell on deaf ears, however, as the other Turkish leaders ordered their troops to ignore Kerbogah's commands and continue their march. The Turkish troops behind the Crusaders, seeing the frontal units advancing, rushed to engage the Crusader army, deciding to attack them on the flanks.

Pausing their march momentarily to defend against the attack, Rodrigo, Geoffrey, and the others turned to face the Turks who attacked them from behind. The heavily armored Crusaders quickly overwhelmed the Turkish light infantry units and hacked them to pieces with a religious zeal. The bloody skirmish lasted only minutes and ended with the Turks fleeing back to the south, broken and battered. The emboldened Crusaders regrouped and began their march again, singing their hymns and praises to God even louder than before.

Moments later, several of the main Turkish infantry lines had reached and began to clash with the advancing Crusaders. However, it was as if they had hit a solid wall, and the flashing blades and spears of the Crusaders cut down the Turkish troops like blades of grass in their path. Those that fell were crushed and trampled upon by the seemingly unstoppable force. To the Crusaders, the angels and saints in heaven were all around them as Count Raymond had said, protecting them and urging them ever onward. Line after line of Turkish infantry broke against the impenetrable wall of advancing Crusaders, whose singing and praises to God in the midst of the battle began to unnerve many in the Turkish ranks.

Kerbogah, angered and frustrated by the insubordination of the other leaders, again reissued the command for the Turkish forces to remain in their positions and await orders to engage. The Crusaders were well within range of the Turkish archers, who were waiting to unleash their deadly volleys at the massive wall of soldiers moving toward them as the sounds of singing and praises became louder and louder. So long as Turkish infantry units kept moving forward to engage the Crusaders, however, Kerbogah could not begin the lethal rain of arrows lest he cut down his own men.

Duqaq and Ridwan, now realizing their mistake in not sending enough troops forward, ignored Kerbogah again and gave the orders for more troops to advance as the Crusader army marched ever closer. As the additional troops moved forward, they were met with Turks fleeing from the units that had been routed, which had a demoralizing effect on them. The wall of Crusaders was closing in, and the sounds of the singing and cries of praise had grown to a fever pitch, terrifying the Turkish army. Willing to sacrifice his own men, Kerbogah readied his archers to unleash their arrows upon the Crusaders, but it was too late—their enemy was upon them.

The trumpets blared behind the Crusaders, signaling a charge on foot. The singing abruptly ceased as the Crusaders let out a furious battle cry and rushed at the enemy. The Turkish units sent to reinforce the others barely put up a fight before turning and fleeing in panic. The massive wall of Crusaders, now in a battle frenzy, crashed into the main body of the Turkish army, who were already demoralized and confused by the many contradictory commands of their leaders. The battle was over almost as soon as it had begun. The whole of the Turkish army began to rout and flee back toward its camp. Kerbogah, stunned by the sudden defeat, gave the order to retreat as he turned and rode back toward camp. Having no time to gather any valuables or supplies, he ordered the cavalry to set the camp ablaze as they turned and fled to the north.

The Crusaders pursued the fleeing Turks and hacked them down, killing thousands, leaving a trail of human destruction all the way to their camp, which was already in flames. The move to fire the camp only served to doom many of the retreating forces, who were now faced with the prospect of certain death at the hands of the Crusaders or taking their chances in a blazing inferno. Many chose the latter, and few made it out alive.

Yaghi Siyan's son and his Turkish warriors watched the battle from above in the citadel and stared in utter disbelief while witnessing the crushing defeat of the Turkish army. The only explanation, they concluded, was that God must truly be on the side of the Crusaders, and with no relief coming, they surrendered the citadel immediately. It was yet another miraculous victory for the Crusaders against overwhelming odds. They had only suffered minor losses, while the Turkish dead were in the tens of thousands.

30

THE BLACK DEATH

Three months had passed since the great Crusader victory over Kerbogah and his Turkish army. The city of Antioch had been secured, and the road to Jerusalem now lay open, but a rift had grown between Bohemond and some of the other leaders, and it had come to an impasse. They could not agree on a way forward to Jerusalem, and Bohemond, now the self-proclaimed prince of Antioch, had cut off communication with the other leaders and was content to reside in the citadel high above the city, away from everyone else.

The momentum gained by their triumphant victory had been lost, and a feeling of stagnation and restlessness had crept into the Crusader army as they awaited the decision of their leaders to move forward to Jerusalem. Food and supplies were no longer issues, but the stagnant environment within the city gave birth to other problems, and soon there were reports of plague in some areas, which, if not contained, could quickly spread to others.

To combat the issue, the leaders issued strict orders on movement within the city. Areas that were affected by the plague were sealed off from the rest. Food and supplies were brought to the inhabitants of these areas, but no one was allowed to enter or leave for weeks until no new cases of the plague had been found. A black cross was marked on the doors of houses and buildings with infected inhabitants, and those who died of plague were quickly taken outside the city and burned, along with all their clothes and belongings.

The soldiers were mostly confined to the barracks. They were constantly tasked with cleaning the buildings and ordered to maintain strict rules of personal hygiene and cleanliness. Twice per day, priests would enter the barracks and burn incense to purify any infected air, and the church bells rang day and night to ward off the plague. The morale of the Crusaders was beginning to plummet, as many saw the plague as a sign of displeasure from God at the inability of their leaders to get along and their refusal to move forward toward Jerusalem.

Rodrigo lay on his cot with his arms folded behind his head, staring at the ceiling of the barracks. His mood began to foul, and he squeezed his eyes shut as he contemplated all of the events since beginning his journey that had led him to this point. *Our leaders have proved time and time again that they cannot be trusted. It is obvious that most, if not all, have journeyed to the Holy Land to find new kingdoms and wealth and nothing more. And now I know that Marcellinus was telling the truth. The Pope's words have proved false, as Christians and Saracens were coexisting peacefully together in the city before we arrived, and the only atrocities have been committed by us!*

He placed his hand on his face and slowly dragged it across in frustration. *Adhemar's only concern is finding holy relics, and the only relic that has been found is likely nothing more than a rusty nail! Evil men like Peter the Hermit are allowed to spread their influence and corrupt the masses, and the Church will do nothing to stop it.*

He opened his eyes, lifted the golden cross from the chain around his neck, and held it in his hand, staring at it for a moment before clenching his fist around it so tightly that the ends of the cross dug into his flesh. He felt a growing urge to rip it from his neck and throw it across the room, but then the thought of Richard doing the same flashed back in his memory. The thought gave him pause, and he began to reflect on what had become of Richard since that time.

He slowly released his grip on the cross as a long sigh escaped from his lips and his frown began to melt away. He let the cross fall out of his hand and back onto his chest as he closed his eyes. *Forgive me, Lord, for these troubling thoughts that fill my mind. But I am feeling lost, Lord, and I ask that you please help me to find my way.*

The sound of someone beside his bunk caused him to open his eyes. He looked up to see a priest in brown robes staring down at him. "Are you Sir Rodrigo?"

"I am, Father. What is it?" Rodrigo asked.

"Please come with me. It is a matter of some urgency," the priest said with a grim expression.

"Why? What is wrong?" asked Rodrigo, sitting up with his eyes wide open.

"It is Bishop Adhemar. He is . . . dying," the priest replied in a somber tone. "He has requested to speak with you and Sir Geoffrey."

Stunned by the news, Rodrigo quickly rose from his cot. "Geoffrey is helping to clean the barracks. If you will wait for me here, Father, I will go find him and return." As he walked away to search for Geoffrey, his brow creased with concern. *Bishop Adhemar is dying? What will we do without him? Could this be a sign from God that he wants us to abandon our mission?*

It was not long before he found Geoffrey and told him the news as they walked back to the priest. Together, they left the barracks and walked through the city to where Adhemar had been residing, close to the palace. As they walked through the streets, obvious signs of the plague could be seen around them. Streets leading to some areas of the city were barricaded, and armed guards were posted to make sure no one went in or out. A wooden cart being pulled by a mule passed them, heading toward the city gates. Glancing at the contents of the cart as it passed, Rodrigo could see a hand protruding from under the sackcloth that was thrown over the bodies stacked inside. The streets themselves were generally empty and barren of activity, and those that passed them kept cloth coverings over their mouths and hoods over their heads.

At last, they came to the street where Adhemar resided and passed through a barricade after the priest spoke to the guard. When they came to a building marked with a black cross, the priest stopped. "Adhemar is inside and wishes to speak to you. However, he is extremely weak, and you are advised to cover your mouths and not to touch him or get too close, for your own safety," he warned.

Rodrigo and Geoffrey nodded as they accepted cloths from the priest, which they used to cover their mouths as they entered. The cloth had been dipped in an aromatic oil, and as Rodrigo brought it to his face, his sense of smell was quickly overpowered by the scent. Once inside the residence, they walked straight through to the bed chamber. Incense was being used to purify the air, and the smoke drifted around the room, creating a hazy, dreamlike atmosphere. The large room was richly decorated with Adhemar's usual furnishings, and in the middle of the room was a bed.

Several feet away from the bed, a number of priests had gathered. Although the men stood silently with their mouths covered, Rodrigo easily recognized two of the priests, Peter the Hermit and Peter Bartholomew. Rodrigo stared at Peter the Hermit with contempt, but only for a moment, and avoided making eye contact. *There he is, perched beside Adhemar's bed like a hungry vulture, waiting to devour the carcass the instant life has flown from his body. Peter the Hermit does not weep for Adhemar. His only desire is to feed off of others to bring strength and life to himself.*

Rodrigo and Geoffrey approached the side of Adhemar's bed. He looked pale and gray, and black boils covered his face and his hands. He slowly turned to look at them and offered a faint smile of recognition between labored breaths. As they stood at his bedside, Adhemar began to speak in a near whisper. "Just as Moses led his people to the promised land but was not allowed to enter . . . so too has God called me to his kingdom before reaching . . . Jerusalem. I will no longer be able to guide you . . . but do not lose sight of your . . . mission. Continue the mission for which . . . you have been chosen. Count Raymond and . . . my successor will continue . . . to guide you on your way. God be with you . . . my sons."

The once powerful and intimidating presence was gone, and in its place was a weak and feeble man on his deathbed uttering his last request. Rodrigo felt overcome with pity in that moment, and his eyes became watery as he stared at Adhemar. Distant memories came bubbling up from the past, and he saw himself as a young boy at his father's funeral, staring at the lifeless body, feeling helpless and alone. He had never gotten the chance to say goodbye to his father, and he would not lose that chance again.

Rodrigo lowered his cloth as he spoke, ignoring the priest's warning. "God be with you as well, Bishop Adhemar, as you journey to the next life. Know that we will be faithful to our mission." Adhemar looked up at Rodrigo with another faint smile of approval and nodded as Rodrigo returned his smile. *Adhemar has been a difficult man to serve, but I believe we must honor his last request to keep our vows and follow through with our mission.*

Following Rodrigo's lead, Geoffrey also lowered the cloth covering his mouth and said his final farewell to Adhemar and renewed his vow to fulfill their mission. When he finished, they stepped back from the bedside and were escorted by the priest back outside the building. "Thank you for coming," the priest said. "Bishop Adhemar's successor as spiritual advisor to Count Raymond has yet to be chosen. You will be notified when that occurs. For now, you may return to your quarters at the city barracks. Be sure to wash thoroughly upon arriving there, as a general order given by Count Raymond to avoid any contamination of your living quarters."

"We will. Thank you, Father," said Geoffrey as he and Rodrigo turned to leave. For a time, Rodrigo and Geoffrey walked in silence, until at last Geoffrey spoke. "So, who do you think will succeed Adhemar as Count Raymond's new spiritual advisor?"

"Who that will be, I do not know. All I know is who it *should not* be," said Rodrigo.

"Rodrigo! Geoffrey!" a gruff, angry voice called out to them from behind, and they stopped in their tracks and turned.

A tall soldier was walking quickly toward them down the street, and as he drew closer, they suddenly realized it was Richard. Rodrigo and Geoffrey glanced at each other as he approached, unsure of what to do or say. Richard seemed even taller than Rodrigo's last memory of him, and he was carrying a sword and dagger in his belt. He approached them with a menacing glare. *What does Richard want with us? He is obviously not here to exchange pleasantries.* Richard stopped in front of them, and all three stared at each other for a moment in tense, awkward silence.

"It has been quite some time, Richard," said Rodrigo, breaking the silence. "When last we spoke, you made it quite clear you wanted nothing more to do with us. So what do you want?"

Richard scowled. "If given the choice, I would prefer that we never crossed paths again," Richard replied harshly. "However, it is necessary that I speak to you about the mission given to you by Bishop Adhemar."

"Our mission?" Geoffrey asked, stepping into the conversation. "What of it, and why would it matter to you? You are no longer part of our mission."

"On the contrary," Richard replied, turning his menacing gaze toward Geoffrey, "It is *you* who are no longer needed for the Pope's mission."

Rodrigo's eyes narrowed, and he felt his pulse quicken. *What is this all about, and why is he behaving like this? I will not be bullied or intimidated by Richard.* "I do not care for your words, Richard, nor the manner in which they are delivered," Rodrigo said. "You had better explain yourself."

Richard rested his hand on the hilt of his sword, emphasizing the fact that Rodrigo and Geoffrey were unarmed. "Your mission will end with the death of Bishop Adhemar," he said as his scowl transformed into a mocking grin. "Little Peter of Amiens is in line to become Count Raymond's spiritual advisor, and when he does, your services will no longer be needed."

Rodrigo stared at Richard for a moment. *I see that Peter the Hermit is making his move even before Adhemar's blood is cold and is using Richard as his personal messenger.* "I am disappointed, Richard, to see how you have become a *lackey* for that snake," Rodrigo said with a smirk as he taunted Richard. "I am assuming that you have broken your vow of secrecy and divulged the Pope's mission to that coward and liar."

Richard's mocking grin disappeared, and his intense scowl

returned. "I am no longer bound by such vows, Rodrigo, and it is you who are the coward and the liar!" he yelled, pointing his finger at Rodrigo.

Sensing that Richard was growing frustrated at his inability to intimidate them, Rodrigo said nothing, but continued to stare at him. Geoffrey folded his arms as he spoke. "Richard, we have just come from visiting Adhemar on his deathbed. I believe we can discuss these matters later. This is not an appropriate time for a confrontation," he suggested, attempting to cool the situation.

"Ha! You seek to lecture me on confrontations? Perhaps this is something you should discuss with Rodrigo!" Richard said loudly, looking Rodrigo up and down. "Little Peter recognized you when the Holy Lance was discovered and told me what occurred between you two in Constantinople. He said you attacked him in his own church, threatened his life, and then threw him upon the ground. At first, it was difficult to believe such an act of cowardice, but it was confirmed by his deacon, who bore witness to the whole ordeal," he said with disdain.

Rodrigo remained silent for a moment, and he felt his anger rising at the accusation. He tightened his fist and pointed a finger back at Richard as he growled his response. "You would accuse *me* of cowardice? *You*, a murderer of innocent men, women, and children in their place of worship and refuge?"

"A murderer of innocent men, women, and children? I have done no such thing. You are a liar as well as a coward, Rodrigo," Richard scoffed.

"I was there, Richard," Geoffrey said, "when you came out of a mosque after butchering innocent civilians and unarmed soldiers when the city fell. Did you not see me? You walked right past me, covered in blood from head to foot, and I will never forget that horrible look of satisfaction upon your face," he said with disgust.

Richard glared at Geoffrey for a moment before speaking. "Killing the Saracens and ridding the Holy Land of their presence is part of the mission called upon by the Pope," he replied flatly.

"I have told you before, Richard—the Turkish warriors are our enemy, not the innocent civilians. You know this to be the truth," Rodrigo said.

"They are one and the same, and anyone who does not understand that is a fool!" Richard yelled. He waved his hand dismissively. "I care not for your weak-minded opinions. All you need to understand is this: the mission to recover the holy relics is no longer your concern. The mission will be carried out by Little Peter and his men for the Pope and the holy Catholic Church."

Rodrigo folded his arms and glanced at Geoffrey as he spoke. "It is now clear what this is all about. I am not surprised that snake would try to use our mission to further his own ambitions," he said as he stared defiantly at Richard. "Peter the Hermit is free to pursue the holy relics if he likes, but we will *not* abandon our mission."

"Ha! What can you do?" Richard replied in a mocking tone. "Without Adhemar, you are only two, while Little Peter's influence is growing by the day, and soon he will be the spiritual advisor to Count Raymond. You had best take my advice and forget about the mission. If you choose to persist and interfere, things will go very badly for you." He again placed his hand on the hilt of his sword.

"Is it not clear by now, Richard, that we are not intimidated by your threats?" Rodrigo asked.

"You are a very stubborn man, Rodrigo," Richard said as he and Rodrigo stared at each other. "The Bible says, 'A man who persists in his stubbornness will someday be *crushed* and never recover.' You would do well to take heed of that proverb." When he finished speaking, he turned and walked back toward Adhemar's residence. Rodrigo and Geoffrey watched him leave in silence, pondering Richard's threatening words and their mission, which now lay in jeopardy.

☩

Later that afternoon, Rodrigo and Geoffrey sat on their cots in the barracks discussing the difficult situation they now found themselves in. "So, assuming that Peter the Hermit becomes spiritual advisor to Count Raymond and takes over the mission to find and secure the holy relics, what are we to do?" Geoffrey asked.

"I do not know, brother," Rodrigo said as he leaned back in his cot. "All I know is that we cannot allow it to happen. We cannot allow an evil man who masquerades in the robes of a priest to acquire such sacred and powerful holy relics."

"How do we know they even exist? And even if they do exist and are recovered, will they not be turned over to the Pope anyway?" Geoffrey asked with frustration.

Rodrigo sat up as he pondered Geoffrey's question. "It is possible that they may not exist, or may not be found, but what would happen if they *do* exist and are recovered?" he asked. "An evil man like Peter the Hermit will only use them to further his own ambitions for power and status within the Church. Look how he used the Pope's proclamation to create his own 'People's Army' and the destruction and damage it caused before ultimately being destroyed. If only he had perished along with it." He shook his head.

"I suppose that is true," Geoffrey admitted. "But it is also true what Richard said, that we are only two. If Peter the Hermit becomes Count Raymond's spiritual advisor, he will gain a tremendous amount of power."

Rodrigo nodded as he stood up. "It is times like these when we must rely on faith, brother, and believe that God is on our side and will help us. Come, let's find something to eat," he suggested. "It is afternoon already."

"On that, at least, I can agree," said Geoffrey as he stood up to follow Rodrigo.

THE SIEGE OF MA'ARRA

Two months had passed since the death of Adhemar as the Crusader army continued to languish inside the city. The communication between the leaders had come to a complete standstill as the various groups became more and more isolated for fear of being exposed to the plague. To make matters even worse, winter was coming, and supplies in the city were now running low. The port of St. Symeon had not been spared from the plague and was being avoided by all passing ships for fear of contamination. No ships came in and no ships were allowed to depart in order to stop the spread of the disease.

With nowhere else to turn, Count Raymond appealed to Emperor Alexios for supplies and troops to continue their quest to take Jerusalem. Months later, he finally received a reply from the emperor: a formal refusal along with a rebuke for not having honored their vows to relinquish Antioch to the Byzantines. Their situation began to seem hopeless.

At the end of November, a three-thousand-strong Crusader detachment began an expedition south to the city of Ma'arra on the road to Damascus. There was little food or supplies to be found in the villages and fields around Antioch. Ma'arra was a large, walled city with a population nearing ten thousand civilians. It was said to be lightly defended by a small Turkish garrison. Untouched by any recent sieges or battles, the city was likely to be full of food and supplies. Rodrigo and Geoffrey volunteered to join the detachment, grateful for the chance to get out of the city and to do something with their time other than cleaning the barracks and trying to avoid the plague.

"Even if we are not going all the way to Jerusalem, at least we are going in the right direction," Geoffrey joked as he and Rodrigo marched in the long columns down the road that afternoon.

"Yes, I agree. If we had been ordered to clean the barracks one more time, I believe I might have gone mad and burned the whole building down," Rodrigo said.

Geoffrey laughed. "At least that is one way to be sure the plague does not contaminate the building," he said with a grin as they continued to march. "I was just thinking—it seems strange that this expedition is being led by ordinary troop commanders, and not one of the Crusader leaders has joined us."

"I think our leaders are too busy sulking and complaining about each other to take any kind of meaningful action," Rodrigo said, looking down the road ahead of them. "This city, Ma'arra, what have you heard about it?"

"I heard that it is large, with a population of several thousand. I also heard that its walls are strong, but not too high and lightly defended. With three thousand soldiers, we should be able to take the city without too much difficulty," Geoffrey said.

"I hope so, for if we are to take Jerusalem in the future, then we cannot afford to lose too many men," Rodrigo said as they marched down the long, winding road.

Earlier that year, in July, a smaller expeditionary force had tried to take the city with several hundred men. The city defenders had been able to repel the assault, which was severely hindered by the lack of siege equipment, and soon after, the Crusaders had abandoned their efforts due to a lack of supplies. The current detachment only had enough food and supplies to last two weeks and were also without siege equipment, although the surrounding forests and hills provided plenty of raw materials for their construction.

On the third day of the expedition, the Crusader detachment reached the city of Ma'arra and set up camp outside the city gates. The walls were broad and strong, nearing fifteen feet from the ground, and much to the Crusaders' surprise, additional fortifications had been created around the city. Large mounds had been constructed with ditches behind them, preventing the deployment of siege towers, and sharpened stakes were positioned between the mounds.

The unexpected improvements to the city defenses seemed to frustrate the commanders of the Crusader detachment, and as the days went by, no plan of attack was announced. The obvious hesitation to attack emboldened the city defenders, who began to hurl insults and taunt the Crusaders from atop the walls. On the morning of the seventh day of the expedition, Rodrigo and Geoffrey stood at the edge of camp, staring at the men on top of the city walls, who had launched a withering barrage of insults and disparaging remarks against the Crusaders all morning. Several of the men on the walls had dropped their britches and exposed their backsides, confident enough to add visual as well as verbal mockery to their arsenal.

Geoffrey was laughing as he turned to Rodrigo and pointed to the men on the walls. "My God, look at them. Have you ever seen such a thing?" He grinned and shook his head. "They truly have no fear of us."

"Not exactly professional soldiers, are they?" Rodrigo said with a smirk as he scanned the men above. "I do not see any real Turkish warriors among them. I think we are being humiliated by simple townsfolk as we camp outside their walls and idly stand by like imbeciles." He breathed a sigh of frustration.

"What do you think the commanders are doing in their tents all day? Why haven't they proposed a plan of action?" asked Geoffrey, raising his arms.

Rodrigo glanced at the tents of the commanders at the far end of the camp. "I would guess that this what happens when you have inexperienced commanders in charge of an army. They are used to taking orders from our leaders and simply echoing their commands, with no real thought or input of their own."

Geoffrey nodded in agreement as he thought about their situation. "That is true, but it has been four days already since we arrived. Surely they have come up with some sort of a plan by now."

"Perhaps they have, but cannot agree and are too afraid to settle on one. If they all agree to one plan and we are defeated, then we will be forced to return to Antioch, and the commanders will be humiliated and dishonored," said Rodrigo, looking back out at the mounds and pits of the city defenses. "In any case, we only have enough supplies to last one more week, so they will probably settle on a direct assault of the walls out of desperation. That is unlikely to succeed, I think, given the strong defenses, and even if it does, we would probably lose many men in the process." He frowned. *If that happens, then it will hinder our path forward to Jerusalem.*

"Unfortunately, I think you are correct," Geoffrey replied.

Rodrigo stared intently at the city defenses for a moment, deep in thought. *Trusting our leaders to make the right decision has proven folly too many times. It is time to start trusting our own instincts and relying upon ourselves.* "I think we should take matters into our own hands and try to come up with something on our own. The outcome of this siege is too important to leave in the hands of our commanders. I have an idea." He pointed to the city. "Let's go on a scouting mission and have a look at other areas around the city. I want to see for myself if our commanders have overlooked any areas of weakness in the defenses. I highly doubt the thoroughness of their initial inspection and assessment."

"Do you think the guards will allow us to leave camp on an unauthorized scouting mission?" Geoffrey asked with raised eyebrows.

"Camp security has been fairly light from what I have seen. I doubt anyone will even notice if we leave," Rodrigo said. "If we are questioned, however, we can tell them that we are going to forage for food and firewood. I doubt anyone will object to that."

✠

The mood inside the camp that afternoon was one of restlessness due to inactivity, and many of the Crusaders were engaged in various diversions as an outlet for their energy. Rodrigo and Geoffrey were able to easily slip out of camp without anyone noticing. Rodrigo glanced back as they walked away from the camp. *The lack of security in this camp is yet another sign of the incompetence of the commanders. It is fortunate that we are not facing a cunning and dangerous enemy.* The walk around the entire city took most of the afternoon, and they stopped at various points to take visual notes and discuss ideas. The sun was beginning to dip down in the sky when they returned to camp, unchallenged and unquestioned as to their whereabouts.

When they had finished their evening meal, Rodrigo and Geoffrey decided to appeal for an audience with the commanders of the detachment to discuss what they had found on their scouting mission and share their ideas for a strategy to take the city. They approached a soldier who stood guard outside the commanders' quarters. The guard was initially hesitant to disturb the commanders during their evening meeting but soon relented after Rodrigo explained the purpose of their request. *I think everyone in camp has grown frustrated and lost faith in our commanders at this point,* Rodrigo thought as the guard led them to one of the tents.

As they approached a large tent, heated arguments and shouting could be heard emanating from within. "Wait here," the guard instructed Rodrigo and Geoffrey before turning to enter. The yelling and shouting inside ceased for a moment. Although they were waiting outside, the voices inside the tent were loud enough for Rodrigo and Geoffrey to hear every word. "My lords, forgive the interruption," said the guard.

"What is it?" said an angry voice from within.

"Two knights from Count Raymond's army beg an audience with you, my lords," the guard said. "They claim to have information from a scouting mission that may aid us in taking the city."

"A scouting mission? Who allowed these knights to go on a scouting mission?" the angry voiced demanded and was met with silence. "Bring them in!" the voice commanded. "If they went on a scouting mission without the authority to do so, they will be severely punished!"

The tent flap opened, and the guard came out with a frown. "I would tread lightly with your words, if I were you," he muttered as he walked them to the entrance and held back the tent flap. "They will see you now."

Rodrigo and Geoffrey entered the tent, and Rodrigo looked around, noting his surroundings and the men within. The tent was lavishly furnished as was typical of the Crusader leaders and nobility, but the interior was in complete disarray. Wine bottles, utensils, goblets, and bits of trash littered the furniture and the floor. Plates of half-eaten food were left on one of the tables, covering a map of the city. The interior of the tent reeked of wine and rotting food. *It is no wonder these commanders have not been able to devise a battle plan. They cannot even organize their own living quarters.*

A younger man of medium stature and a slight build stood near the table in the middle of the tent. A thin beard and blonde hair framed his scowling face. He came around the table toward Rodrigo and Geoffrey as two other men who were seated at the table put down their goblets and stood up.

The scowling man came to stand directly in front of them, leaning forward as he spoke. "Who gave you the authority to go on a scouting mission?" he demanded in a loud voice.

"No one gave us permission," Rodrigo answered calmly, unimpressed at the man's attempts at intimidation. "We grew weary of listening to the taunts by the men on the walls, so we decided to have a look around at the city's defenses to see if there were any weaknesses."

"So you decided to ignore the general orders of your commanding officers and leave camp on your own?" the man asked as he walked around Rodrigo and Geoffrey. "Tell me, why should I not have you severely punished for this act of insubordination?" Fighting the urge to make a sarcastic remark, Rodrigo remained silent. *It is obvious this man is acting this way to make up for his lack of control of the situation.*

"Enough, Girard," said one of the other men. Rodrigo noted that all three commanders were young, and judging from their fine clothes and superior demeanor, they appeared to be nobility. "You are just angry because we have been here a week, we are running low on supplies, and we still have no plan. I would like to hear what they have to say," he said, turning to Rodrigo and Geoffrey.

"As would I," said the third man.

Girard glared at the others and then backed away from Rodrigo and walked to one of the tables. Muttering to himself, he grabbed a bottle of wine and began filling a goblet.

Rodrigo and Geoffrey looked at each other for a moment before Geoffrey began to speak. "My lords, before we begin, if the information we present is useful and leads to the fall of the city, then we have but one request."

"Ha! I knew it! This is simply a scheme to fatten their own pockets," Girard said loudly as he leaned on the table and sipped his wine.

"We seek no compensation nor monetary reward for this information," Rodrigo assured the men. "We only ask that if you are able to use it to take the city, we spare its inhabitants. We only take the supplies that we need and plunder for our soldiers, but we do not let them massacre the population as they did in Antioch."

"A noble request," one of the men replied. "We should have no problem granting it if we are able to breach the walls and take the city with your information. But I suggest you tell us quickly, and it had better be good, or both of you will face discipline for leaving camp without permission."

Rodrigo and Geoffrey agreed, and the four men gathered around the table with the map of the city after clearing away the garbage and plates of food to get a better look. Girard, however, refused to be a part of the conversation and relaxed upon a couch as he continued to drink.

Using the map as a reference, Rodrigo and Geoffrey pointed out that the walls on the opposite side of the city were very lightly defended, and the defensive mounds of earth on that side were large enough to hide a small force of men. They also pointed out that in front of the city, there was a gap between two of the mounds large enough for a siege tower to pass through with no ditch behind it. The gap was only protected with sharpened stakes, which could be removed or cut down.

Rodrigo then laid out a strategy that would enable the Crusaders to exploit the weaknesses. They could assault the walls at the front of the city with a siege tower, which would likely draw the inexperienced defenders away from other, already lightly guarded areas of the city. A small force, hidden behind the mounds under cover of darkness, could then scale the walls at the opposite side the city. Once inside, they could open the gates and allow a larger force hidden nearby to enter. The city defenses would likely collapse after facing an assault on two sides, with one already being inside the city, Rodrigo concluded.

"I like this plan," said one of the commanders, smiling and nodding in approval. The other man beside him also nodded. "It greatly increases our chances of taking the city and is far better than any other plan that has been proposed." He glanced toward Girard, who had not moved from the couch. "I am Gaston, and this is William. We are Barons from Lorraine and Burgundy, and that is Baron Girard of Auvergne. Tell us your names, and let us talk further details of this plan over some food and wine."

The five men began to formulate a strategy, and the lamps on the table had begun to flicker for lack of oil when the group finished their plan to take the city. Rodrigo and Geoffrey would be part of the group led by Gaston that would scale the walls on the south side of the city. William would lead the assault from the north with a siege tower. Much to his dismay, Girard and his men would be hidden in the wooded area outside the western gate and would wait for the gate to be opened.

Finally, some progress toward our goal, Rodrigo thought as he and Geoffrey made their way back through camp late that night. *Trusting our instincts and taking matters into our own hands turned out much better than I had anticipated.*

The next morning, the Crusaders went into the wooded areas north of their camp to begin cutting down trees and harvesting timber for the construction of a siege tower. Highly motivated from finally receiving some direction after days of inactivity, the men worked nonstop on the construction of the siege tower until it was complete.

✠

The air was cold and damp and the skies were still dark in the early morning hours of December 11, when the assault on Ma'arra was about to begin. Using the darkness as cover, Gaston led a group of fifty men to the base of the defensive mounds on the southern walls while a larger force of eight hundred men lay hidden in the forest outside the western gate. At the same time, on the other side of the city, men were working to remove the stakes that blocked the path of the newly constructed siege tower. The tower creaked and swayed as it slowly made its way down the road leading to the front of the city, pulled by mules and pushed by men from behind.

Dawn had finally broken, and as it began to brighten the night sky, it revealed an imposing sight for the city defenders. A twenty-five-foot-tall siege tower was moving toward them down the road, and the troubling sight of a newly exposed gap between two defensive mounds set off an immediate alarm among the city defenders.

"Listen. Do you hear that?" Gaston whispered to Rodrigo as they crouched behind the dirt mounds. They could hear the faint ringing of bells from guard towers in other parts of the city as they crouched quietly and listened. "The assault with the siege tower at the front of the city has begun. Now, let's see if your assumption about the defenders was correct." Rodrigo knew the success of the strategy for scaling the walls and opening the gates heavily depended upon most of the guards abandoning their posts to aid in the defense against the siege tower.

Gaston and Rodrigo crept to the top of the mound to peek at the wall. At first, the guards did not move, but as the incessant ringing of bells from the other towers continued, they began arguing with raised voices. One by one, they began to move off the walls, and soon there were only a few guards left. Rodrigo said nothing but turned to Gaston with a smile of content.

"You were right," Gaston conceded as they crept back down to the ground. "We will split up. Take twenty-five men around the mound and scale the wall on the right side of the tower, and I will go around this side and scale the wall to the left," he said, pointing to the wall. "Once we are on top, we will meet in the middle." Rodrigo nodded, and the orders were given for the group to split up.

Back down at the base of the mound, Rodrigo, along with Geoffrey and twenty-five men, crept around the right side and waited for Gaston's signal to begin the assault. "Get ready," Rodrigo said to Geoffrey and the other men around him.

"Now!" he yelled as he watched Gaston and his men begin their scramble over the opposite side of the mound. Rodrigo and the others did the same and then jumped down into the ditch just behind the defensive mounds. The ditch was only about five feet deep, and fortunately for the Crusaders, the bottom was muddy and damp but did not contain any sharpened stakes. Moving quickly, they helped each other up and out of the ditch as they gathered at the bottom of the walls. A loud bell could be heard in the guard tower above them as the Crusaders launched their grappling hooks from below.

In moments, several Crusaders were scaling the walls on both sides of the guard tower. The three panicked guards above them ceased sounding the alarm and scrambled to stop the Crusaders, but it was too late. Cresting the top of the wall and drawing his sword off his back, Rodrigo countered the spear thrust of the guard who rushed at him, cutting the head off of the spear. Dropping the useless weapon, the guard began to draw an axe from his side when Rodrigo struck back, killing the guard with a downward slash that bit from his neck to his sternum. The other two guards were dead within moments, and the men regrouped at the guard tower in the middle of the wall. The southern walls were now in control of the Crusaders.

"We need to move quickly! Girard is waiting for us outside the western gate!" Gaston yelled as he motioned the others to follow.

Rodrigo and the rest of the men began to move swiftly over the walls as they headed toward the western gates of the city.

They encountered only light resistance along the way. Rodrigo's predictions had been accurate, as most of the guards had abandoned their posts and moved to the front of the city. As the Crusaders moved over the walls, black smoke could be seen rising to the north. Another short skirmish ensued with the guards in the tower of the western wall, which quickly fell to the Crusaders.

Rodrigo, Geoffrey, and several other men climbed down into the city interior to open the gate below. Above them, Gaston threw the tower flag over the edge of the wall, signaling Girard and his men. With a triumphant roar, eight hundred Crusaders led by Girard burst out of surrounding forest and began rushing toward the western gate. Rodrigo and the others were still struggling to open the reinforced gates when Gaston climbed down into the city interior and approached them.

"Rodrigo!" Gaston called out. Rodrigo ran over to Gaston as the others continued to work on opening the gate. "The smoke rising to the north can only mean one thing," Gaston said with concern in his voice. "The defenders are trying to set fire to the tower. Stay here with ten of my men and open the gates for Girard. I will take the rest and go to assist William. Once Girard and his men are inside the city, then you can move north as per our plans. We must ensure that William and his men break through before the tower is consumed by flames."

"Yes, my lord," Rodrigo answered. Gaston turned to give the orders to his men and then began to head north. Rodrigo returned to Geoffrey and the other men just as they finished removing the last of the timbers that reinforced the gates. The gates swung open, and waiting on the other side was Girard, who strode through the gates into the city like a conquering hero. He was surrounded by his men, who were cheering and yelling with excitement as they flooded into the city around him. *He acts as though he single-handedly captured the entire city while Gaston and William are still fighting for control to the north,* Rodrigo thought as he approached Girard. "My lord, Gaston has already left to assist William. Perhaps we should leave some men here to secure the gate before moving north," he suggested as Girard's men continued to rush in around them.

Girard stopped abruptly and turned to Rodrigo, staring at him with contempt. "Do not give me advice on what I should do!" he snapped in reply. "You have no authority here, and I do not care to listen to any more of your counsel."

Rodrigo was taken back by the response but was able to maintain his composure. "My lord, it was simply a suggestion to make sure that a way into the city remains open," he said as Geoffrey came up to join them.

Girard remained silent for a moment as he looked at his men, who stood by and eagerly awaited his orders. Rodrigo noticed the faces of the men around him, and a feeling of dread began to grow. He could see the manic look in their eyes from adrenaline-fueled excitement and an eagerness to engage the enemy. He had seen the same look on the faces of the soldiers at the massacre of Antioch.

At last, Girard turned to Rodrigo and Geoffrey. "I will admit that your plan has gotten us into the city, but I am no fool," he said with disdain. "I know that both of you conspired with Gaston and William to take all the credit for capturing the city while leaving me out." His voice began to rise. "If the four of you want all the glory for capturing the city, so be it! I will take the best plunder for myself, and the rest of you can fight over the scraps!" he said with a sneer. A sickening feeling came over Rodrigo as he realized that Girard had just used them to get into the city so he could enrich himself with loot and plunder.

Turning his back on Rodrigo and Geoffrey, Girard addressed the eight hundred Crusaders awaiting his commands. "The city is ours to loot!" he yelled, and he was answered by the raucous cheering of the soldiers. "I will allow you to keep whatever you can carry, but you will bring the rest back here to me!"

Rodrigo felt his blood beginning to boil as he walked toward Girard. "What are you doing? Gaston and William are still engaged in battle and await the arrival of your men!" Rodrigo yelled in frustration, pointing to the north. "Your accusations are false! We seek no glory for taking the city. We only asked that you spare the inhabitants!"

Girard did not immediately respond. Instead, he motioned for two of his men to come and stand by his side.

"I made no such agreement," Girard replied. Turning back to face his men, he raised his voice and addressed them. "Go now, men! Loot everything you can, and spare no one! No prisoners shall be taken this day, and no quarter shall be given to our enemies!" he yelled. Like a pack of ravenous hounds released from their master's grasp, the soldiers began to swarm into the city streets with a hunger for plunder and a thirst for blood.

Rodrigo watched helplessly as the soldiers dispersed into the streets and began smashing their way into houses and buildings, followed by the familiar screams of terror emanating from within. All the feelings of horror and anguish he had felt at Antioch came rushing back to him. "You murderous dog!" Rodrigo yelled at Girard. His temper now at its peak, he began to move toward Girard and raised his sword as the two soldiers stepped forward to block Rodrigo's advance.

"Take one more step," Girard said from behind his guards, "and I will have you arrested and imprisoned for threatening a superior officer."

Rodrigo nearly shook with rage, and his thoughts raced as he stared at Girard. *Even if I were to subdue or kill him, would that change anything? No. I would be sacrificing my life, my mission, and everything I have out of anger and hatred for this man.* Rodrigo lowered his sword as he clenched his teeth in the bitter realization that he was powerless to do anything. *I thought I could prevent another massacre. I have failed. I was a fool to place my trust in such a man!*

Rodrigo felt Geoffrey's hand on his arm. "Let it go, brother," Geoffrey said. "There is nothing more we can do." At Geoffrey's words, the red haze of anger that clouded Rodrigo's vision began to part.

Rodrigo looked down in anguish and frustration as they turned and walked away. Though he felt sick to his stomach, he knew

Geoffrey was correct and there was nothing they could do to change what was already happening.

"Let's go and assist Gaston and William. When the battle is over, we can tell them what has occurred here and let them decide what to do," Geoffrey suggested as they reached the gate. Gathering Gaston's men who were still waiting for them, Rodrigo and Geoffrey began to head north through the city.

3 2

THE WICKED FEAST

The city of Ma'arra had fallen to the Crusaders, and its citizens were helpless to resist the bloody wrath of the victorious. William and Gaston had successfully broken through the defenses to the north, but lost control of their men soon after due to the weakness of their authority and leadership. Their men rushed into the city and, ignoring the orders to spare the civilians, joined in the ruthless slaughter and looting that were already taking place. The pillaging of the city and butchering of innocent civilians was even greater than what had taken place at Antioch. The uncontrolled release of the soldiers' repressed energy created an orgy of violence and murder that wreaked utter devastation within the city.

Rodrigo and Geoffrey had gone outside the city walls soon after William and Gaston had lost control of their men. Refusing to be part of the destruction and violence taking place within, they waited until early morning the following day to enter. The appalling aftermath of the slaughter was unlike anything Rodrigo had ever seen before. Dead bodies of the civilians—men, women, and children alike— littered the streets at every turn, and every building was ransacked.

The streets were awash with blood, as many of the corpses had been dragged outside their residences and heaped into piles like refuse. Clouds of flies swarmed around the piles, and the stench of death was overpowering throughout the city. Revulsion mixed with anger and outrage gripped Rodrigo as they walked the streets and surveyed the destruction. The disturbing images they witnessed haunted Rodrigo, and he began to see the faces of the dead in his sleep in the nights that followed.

When order and control were finally restored by the commanders, Gaston and William severely chastised Girard for his rogue behavior and selfish abandonment of their plan. Unwilling to accept any responsibility for losing control of their own men, the two blamed Girard for everything and confiscated the plunder he sought to keep for himself as punishment for his actions.

In an attempt to further punish Girard, Gaston and William had tasked him and his men with clearing the city of the dead and burying the corpses in the ditches outside the city walls. However, because he was resentful of his fellow commanders' actions against him, Girard's efforts in completing the task were minimal, and it was mostly left undone. Five days after the fall of Ma'arra, piles of dead bodies still lay inside the city walls, and the ditches outside were full of corpses and could hold no more. The nauseating smell of rotting flesh began to permeate large areas of the city. To make matters even worse, the city's granaries and storehouses were discovered to be mostly empty. The Crusaders were ultimately denied what they had come for, and the food and supplies they had brought with them had been completely exhausted.

Rodrigo and Geoffrey had taken up quarters along with the other men in a building near the center of the city. They sat in their cots late that morning, and neither of them had eaten anything in two days due to the extreme shortage of rations. A somber, listless mood had come over Rodrigo in the days since witnessing the devastation. Guilt consumed his thoughts. *Had we not gone to our commanders with our strategy, this horror might have been prevented. How could I have placed my trust in such weak and incompetent men?*

Rodrigo was leaning back against the wall, staring blankly into space, when Geoffrey voiced his frustrations out loud. "I do not know which is worse, the gnawing hunger in my belly or the sickening smell of death that blankets the city. Together they are enough to drive one mad," he said with disgust as he covered his nose and mouth with his hand. "The entire city has been looted and destroyed, and there is nothing else here for us. Why do we not go back to Antioch? Why do we linger in this place, surrounded by death and facing starvation?"

"I asked Gaston that same question when I saw him yesterday," Rodrigo said, breaking his long silence. "I suggested that we leave Girard and his men here to finish the job while the rest of us go back to Antioch, since we are out of food and supplies anyway."

"Those are my thoughts exactly," Geoffrey said.

"Gaston told me that his orders were to stay here and secure the city until the leaders were able to make the journey or send envoys to decide what to do with it," Rodrigo answered as he continued to stare into space.

"What?" Geoffrey exclaimed. "That is foolishness! Everyone knows there is no communication between our leaders in Antioch. Waiting for them to arrive could take weeks or even months! Who knows how long?" He raised his arms in frustration.

Rodrigo sighed and slowly shook his head. "As I said before, these commanders are worthless. They only know how to follow orders and cannot think for themselves."

Geoffrey's brow furrowed. "Then perhaps we must do the thinking for them, like the last time we sat idly for days. At least we know they will listen to us. Why don't we have a look around and see if we can think of a way to convince them to return to Antioch?"

Rodrigo finally sat up, and his mood began to change at the prospect of doing something to alleviate their desperate situation. "Perhaps you are right. There must be something we can do to convince them. Let's go to their camp and discuss some ideas along the way. At least we will be away from the stench of the city."

Rodrigo and Geoffrey left the makeshift barracks and walked toward the city gates. Gaston and William had set up quarters outside the city to be away from the stench that filled the streets. As Rodrigo and Geoffrey neared the gates, the putrid stench began to disappear, and both began to breathe in more freely and deeply once clear of the foul, fetid air.

A strange new scent had arisen to take its place, however—the scent of roasting meat wafted through the air as they walked. The rumbling and complaining of their empty stomachs had become incessant, and the unexpected savory smell captivated their senses. Thoughts of tearing into a succulent piece of roasted meat caused their mouths to water as they unconsciously quickened their pace.

"Do you smell that?" asked Geoffrey.

"Yes. My first thought was that they had started burning the bodies, but it doesn't smell like charred flesh," said Rodrigo, raising his head and sniffing the air. "Maybe they found an animal to butcher?" His eyes widened at the thought. "Let's go and find out." They turned onto another street and cut through an alley, and the smell grew stronger as they drew closer to the source.

"That definitely smells like roasting meat. Perhaps they have some to spare," said Geoffrey, smiling in anticipation.

As they approached the end of the alley, a soldier came out of a side doorway from a building ahead of them, carrying something with both arms that was covered by a cloth. The man was hunched over as if to conceal whatever he was carrying and was moving furtively. This struck both men as odd, since all the looting had been done in the open. Rodrigo's eyes narrowed as they watched the man hurry away. *What is he doing? Perhaps he has discovered a hidden stash of loot. But why is he being so secretive about it?*

The soldier was walking away from them toward others gathered at the base of the city wall. Smoke was coming from some fires at the center of the gatherings. When they passed by the building that the soldier had come from, both Rodrigo and Geoffrey had to cover their noses and mouths, as the stench of death was overpowering and both nearly gagged from the smell.

They hurried into an open area between the buildings and the city wall where the men had gathered around the fires. They could see the soldier who had left the building sit down among them.

"Something is not right here, brother," Rodrigo said, wincing from the stench as he took his hand away from his mouth. "I want to see what that soldier was doing inside of this building, and perhaps you can find out what is happening over there." He pointed to the men gathered by the fires. "I will meet with you when I am finished." Geoffrey nodded, still covering his mouth.

Rodrigo turned and walked back to the building as Geoffrey approached the men. Rodrigo drew a cloth from his belt and covered his nose and mouth as he reached the doorway. With one hand holding the cloth in place, he pushed the doorway open with the other and entered.

He instantly recoiled in revulsion as he witnessed the macabre scene within. Strewn throughout the front of the building were the rotting corpses of men, women, and children. The bloated corpses were in various states of decay and lay among broken pieces of furniture. He grimaced in disgust, but although he felt sickened by what he saw, he knew that many buildings within the city contained similar horrors, so he felt compelled to explore further. *Why was that soldier in here? What was he after, and what was he carrying?*

Rodrigo's eyes were watering from the putrid stench as he walked through a hallway and into a large room. There, on a long table in the middle of the room, he beheld an abomination. Two of the corpses had been laid on the table, stripped of their clothing, and were lying facedown. Large chunks of flesh had been carved from their buttocks and thighs, and lying on the table next to the corpses was a butcher's knife. Strips of cloth like the one the soldier had been carrying were on the table next to the bodies.

The blood was pounding in Rodrigo's ears, and his vision began to blur as he felt himself overcome with nausea at the nightmarish scene around him. Turning, he quickly walked back outside. Coughing violently, he stumbled across the alley and leaned against the stone wall opposite the building. He leaned over to vomit, but nothing came out, as his stomach was empty. The bitter taste of bile and stomach acid filled his mouth as he spat and wiped the tears from his eyes with the cloth.

The revulsion he felt gave way to outrage as he left the alley and walked toward the fires, mentally preparing himself for what he was sure to find. As he drew closer, he could hear conversation among the men and saw Geoffrey standing outside the group. One of the men near Geoffrey handed him a piece of meat that had been roasted on a stick. Rodrigo's eyes widened with alarm at the sudden realization of what was about to occur. "Geoffrey, stop! *Stop!*" he shouted as he began running and waving his arm to grab Geoffrey's attention.

Geoffrey turned to look at Rodrigo and lowered the stick he had been handed just as Rodrigo reached the group. "What is it? What's wrong?" Geoffrey asked.

"Do not take part in this wicked feast!" Rodrigo yelled, interrupting the conversations around the fires. "The meat they consume has been harvested from the Saracen dead!"

Geoffrey dropped the meat upon the ground and stood in stunned silence, sickened and horrified at what Rodrigo had revealed to him. Rodrigo looked around at the groups of soldiers. Some had stopped eating and looked down at the ground as they hung their heads and averted their eyes. Others turned to him with angry scowls, and still others ignored him completely as they continued to hungrily bite into the bits of roasted flesh upon the sticks.

"Have you all gone mad?" Rodrigo asked loudly as he and Geoffrey stepped back from the group. "Since when do Christians eat the flesh of men for want of food?"

One of the men, angered by Rodrigo's words, put down his stick and stood up. "Who are you to judge us!" he yelled. "We have not eaten in days! We starve in this city while our leaders do nothing!"

"None of us has eaten in days!" Rodrigo responded angrily. "But eating the flesh of men is a mortal sin! Do you not fear for your immortal souls?"

Another man stood up from the fire to answer Rodrigo. "Little Peter has told us that the Saracens are not men! He has told us that they are soulless animals meant to be butchered! It is not a sin to eat the flesh of an animal!" he yelled in defiance, and many around him murmured their agreement and nodded their heads.

Rodrigo said nothing, but studied the faces of the men who were looking at him. *These men are starving and desperate, but only the blasphemous teachings of Peter the Hermit could lead them to justify a mortal sin.* He could see the conviction in the eyes of the men around him. All conversations had ceased, and most of the men were staring at Rodrigo to see what would happen next, although some continued to ignore him and eat their meal.

Without saying anything, Rodrigo entered the circle of men and grabbed a large branch that was sticking out of the fire and still smoldering on one end. *It is obvious that my words will have no effect on these men. Perhaps something stronger is needed.* He turned and walked away from the group back toward the buildings, still holding the branch, and was quickly followed by Geoffrey. "Thank God, brother! You came just in time," Geoffrey said, catching up to Rodrigo. "They would not answer my questions about where they got their supply of meat. I was suspicious when they handed me some, but I am so hungry that when I saw and smelled the roasted meat, I no longer cared and nearly ate some!"

"Even here, the poisonous tongue of Peter the Hermit continues to corrupt men's souls, leading them to commit the vilest of blasphemies," Rodrigo muttered in disgust as he walked with a purpose toward the building.

"What are you going to do with that?" asked Geoffrey, pointing to the branch.

Rodrigo remained silent until they reached the building. "Here, hold this," he said, handing Geoffrey the branch, which was now alight at one end. "But do not come inside."

Covering his mouth again with the cloth, Rodrigo entered the building. He emerged a few minutes later, carrying the end of a large sack in one hand while covering his mouth with the cloth in the other. He dropped his cloth as he took the torch from Geoffrey, and kicking open the door, he threw it inside. There was an instant blaze from within the building as the torch landed on the floor amidst broken vessels of oil. Geoffrey again followed Rodrigo as he strode back toward the group.

Smoke was now billowing from the windows and the door of the building, and many of the men stood and stared in shock at

Rodrigo's return. "What have you done?" one of them angrily demanded.

"Here!" Rodrigo yelled to the men, flinging the sack toward the group. The untied sack opened as it flew and landed in the middle of the group by the fire. Two rotting human heads rolled out as the men standing near them recoiled at the sight, and all the men abruptly stopped eating. "Here are the animals that you feast upon!" he yelled. "No, do not stop!" he shouted as he walked among the groups. "For this is the choice you all have made! May God have mercy on your souls for what you have done!" Saying no more, Rodrigo turned and walked away, followed by Geoffrey as he headed back toward the center of the city.

"Where are we going?" Geoffrey asked. "I thought we were to talk to Gaston and William. We should tell them what we have seen here. Perhaps this will convince them to return to Antioch."

Rodrigo stopped walking and stared at the ground for a moment. *Our current situation is the result of the last time we visited William and Gaston with our concerns. I have had enough of their incompetence, and it is likely they would try to cover this up to avoid any embarrassment anyway.* "I do not believe that going to them will do any good," Rodrigo said as they watched some soldiers run by them carrying buckets of water. "I have lost all faith in their leadership. I think we should go to Antioch and inform Count Raymond of what is taking place here."

"You think we should tell Count Raymond about this?" Geoffrey asked, frowning with skepticism. "How is it even possible to travel to Antioch to tell him? It is a three-day journey, and we have no food or supplies. And what makes you think Count Raymond would even do anything about this?"

Rodrigo nodded as he listened to Geoffrey. "All are valid points, brother, but let us examine the choices we are now faced with. One choice is to stay here and continue to starve in a city filled with rotting corpses where men have resorted to cannibalism while our incompetent leaders do nothing. Or we can again leave camp without permission, return to Antioch, and inform Count Raymond of our desperate situation and trust in God that something will happen," he said as Geoffrey stood in silence, thinking about the choices that lay before them.

Still frowning, Geoffrey spoke at last. "I suppose returning to Antioch makes more sense, but I do not think we could make the journey without food or supplies," he said, folding his arms.

"That is true, but if we use the last of our coin to buy enough food for one day, Antioch is only a one-day journey by horse, and I know where Girard keeps his mounts," Rodrigo said with a slight grin.

"You plan on stealing Girard's horses?" Geoffrey asked, his eyes widening at the suggestion.

"I realize this plan is not without risk and possible consequences," Rodrigo admitted. "So, I can do this alone, if you prefer not to be involved."

Geoffrey breathed out a long sigh and slid his hand across his face. "Your plan is completely mad, brother. However, being in this place has already driven me to near madness and staying here any longer surely will. Why not?" he declared, unfolding and raising his arms.

Rodrigo grinned broadly as he as patted Geoffrey on the shoulder. "No person in their right mind would ever choose to stay here if given a choice," he said with a laugh. "Come, let's gather our belongings and begin looking for food to buy wherever we can. This evening we can pay a visit to Girard and relieve him of his mounts," he said as they began walking toward the center of the city.

ON TO JERUSALEM

A solitary figure knelt in silent prayer before the figure of Christ at the front of the sanctuary in the Church of Saint Peter. The rays of sunlight, made visible by the dust in the air, created a radiant glow about the figure as they shone down through the windows of the church. His brow was knitted tightly, and the burden of leadership had felt very heavy of late. *Forgive us, Father, for our quarrels and inability to unite under one cause. None of us wish to abandon Jerusalem to the Saracens; however, pride and stubbornness prevent us from coming together and moving forward. Grant me the wisdom, oh Lord, to know what to do.*

The silence was broken by a servant, who approached the figure from behind. "My lord, two knights have just arrived from Ma'arra who identified themselves as Sir Rodrigo and Sir Geoffrey. They claim to have urgent news that they must deliver to you personally."

Count Raymond remained silent for a moment as he bowed his head and made the sign of the cross before standing up. *It is curious that these two men would be delivering a message from Ma'arra. Perhaps there is a reason why their leaders chose to use them instead of their personal messengers.* "I know these men. Escort them to my chambers and tell them I will meet with them there," he said as he walked to a door in the back of the sanctuary.

The priests' chambers at the back of the church had become Count Raymond's personal study in the months following Adhemar's death. With the death of his close friend and spiritual advisor, Raymond had been reluctant to appoint anyone to fill the position and had begun to spend most of his time in solitude, praying for God's guidance and a solution to the stalemate that had paralyzed the Crusader army and seemed unlikely to end.

A knock came at the chamber door. "Enter," Raymond commanded. His servant entered, followed by Rodrigo and Geoffrey.

They walked to the end of the table, and Rodrigo spoke. "My lord, thank you for receiving us."

Raymond noted that their appearance had changed considerably since their last meeting. Both men appeared exhausted and much leaner, with hollow, sunken expressions upon their faces. *They certainly do not look well.* "Sir Rodrigo, Sir Geoffrey, please sit down," Raymond said with a smile. "You look a bit *weary* from your journey. Can I offer you some food and wine?"

Both men's expressions brightened at the offer, but Rodrigo glanced at Geoffrey for a moment before speaking. "We would gladly accept your offer of food and wine, my lord, but we would not feel right enjoying a meal while we bring news of our fellow Crusaders starving in Ma'arra."

"Starving?" Raymond asked with raised eyebrows. *Why was there no mention of this in the last report?* "The last news I received from the leaders at Ma'arra was that of a triumphant victory. There was no word of being short on food and supplies. Did something happen to the storehouses within the city?"

"No, my lord," said Geoffrey, speaking up. "The granaries and storehouses were discovered to be nearly empty after we took the city. What little they contained was only able to sustain the men for a few days afterward."

Raymond sat forward and rested his chin on one fist as his brow began to crease. *Why was this not mentioned earlier? Perhaps we made a mistake in allowing these young nobles to lead on their own.* "I see. So, the men are starving and are in desperate need of food."

"That is not the only problem, my lord," Rodrigo said. "The city reeks with the foul stench of thousands of Saracen dead. When the city fell, the men rushed in and began looting and massacring the population, and now none of the commanders want to take responsibility for disposing of the corpses."

"That is disgraceful," Raymond said with disgust. "They dishonor the dead and themselves." *Only the most incapable leaders would allow such a thing to happen. Indeed, it was a mistake.*

"It gets worse, my lord," said Geoffrey, pausing for a moment as he and Rodrigo looked at each other. "Some of the men have resorted to cannibalism for want of food. Rodrigo and I came upon a group in the city who were feasting upon the flesh of the dead Saracens."

"What?" Raymond exclaimed as he sat up. "What kind of lawlessness and sacrilege is being allowed to take place there?"

"It is true, my lord," said Rodrigo. "I do not believe the commanders were aware of such actions, but I believe they would not wish to report them either. If word got out, these problems and others would reflect poorly upon their leadership and control of the city."

Raymond sat back in his chair as he studied Rodrigo and Geoffrey for a moment. *Now I understand why they are here instead of the commanders' personal messengers.* "I would assume, then, that you either lied to your leaders about your need to return to Antioch or left camp without their permission. Is that correct?" Raymond asked.

"You are correct, my lord. We did not come by order of the commanders. We left the city on our own without their knowledge," Geoffrey admitted, lowering his eyes.

Raymond did not immediately respond to their admission of guilt but took a moment to reflect upon the situation. *Adhemar had warned me of the tendency of these men to flout his authority and act according to their own will. If he were here, I am sure he would want them punished. However, the leaders in Ma'arra have obviously failed by allowing the conditions to deteriorate so rapidly.* "I understand why you thought it necessary to bring this to my attention," Raymond said at last. "But do you feel this was a wise decision? You two risk much by your actions."

"Yes, we do, my lord," Rodrigo said, looking directly at Count Raymond. "If we stood by and did nothing, then many more men would be subjected to starvation, more atrocities would be committed, and eventually our commanders would be forced to send word when the men began to revolt. We know we disobeyed orders by leaving camp and coming here, but we felt we had no choice but to bring you this information."

Raymond nodded slowly as he listened to Rodrigo's explanation. "I will investigate these issues that you have brought to my attention, but leaving your camp without permission cannot be overlooked. You will return to your barracks here in the city and await my decision on what will be done."

"Yes, my lord," they answered as they got up from the table and were escorted out by a servant.

Raymond sat for a time at the table as he thought about the meeting and contemplated his next move. *How terrible the conditions at Ma'arra have become. The leaders there must be held to account. Perhaps the men's suffering has not been in vain, however. Some good may yet come of this deplorable situation if I can use this information to break the stalemate.* As he rose from the table and exited the chamber, a sense of grim determination came over Raymond. He finally knew what to do.

✠

The news of the starving Crusaders at Ma'arra being forced to live in a city filled with rotting corpses, and the resulting atrocity of cannibalism that had taken place, quickly spread throughout Antioch. The growing frustration of the Crusaders in Antioch at the prolonged inaction of the leaders had been slowly building and was now at its peak. The news was like a spark that set ablaze piles of tinder that had been steadily growing for months. The soldiers, tired of being confined to the barracks, began openly defying orders by marching through the streets and surrounded the buildings occupied by their leaders, threatening to destroy the city if immediate actions were not taken.

Faced with riots and the prospect of losing control of their men, which would ultimately cost them their mission to take Jerusalem, the Crusader leaders, led by Count Raymond, held an emergency meeting. The next day, food and supplies were sent south to Ma'arra, and plans were made to exit the city.

Two weeks later, on January 13, 1099, Count Raymond, along with the rest of the Crusader leaders, Count Robert, Duke Godfrey, Duke Robert, and Tancred, gathered their remaining men, around nine thousand Crusaders, and finally headed south to Jerusalem. Prince Bohemond refused to join them and stayed behind with all his men, thus founding the second Crusader state, the Principality of Antioch. The first Crusader state, the County of Edessa, had been previously established by Count Baldwin.

REVELATIONS BY THE FIRE

The Crusader detachment at Ma'arra had rejoined with the main army on their journey south, and together their combined force numbered around twelve thousand men. Although they only numbered about one-fifth of their original strength and size, the morale of the soldiers was high, for at last they were moving forward toward their final objective: to liberate the holy city of Jerusalem from the hands of Saracens and place it back under Christian control.

The months slowly trudged by as the Crusader army marched south along the coastline. Surprisingly, they met no resistance traveling through the Turkish villages and near the larger cities on their journey. Not only were the cities and villages absent hostilities, but many offered to pay tribute or outfit the Crusaders with food and supplies when they passed through, making the journey much less difficult than expected.

The reasons for this were unclear. Word of the massacres that had taken place during the sieges of Antioch and Ma'arra may have traveled south, and the villages and cities may have wished to avoid the same fate. Another rumor that began to circulate was that the Islamic caliphate in Egypt known as the Fatimids were expanding their control out of North Africa and had captured Jerusalem from the Turks. If the rumor was true, then perhaps the Turkish villages and cities simply wanted the Crusader army to hasten their march south into Fatimid territory.

It was April when the Crusader army reached and set up camp outside the ancient city of Tyre. Although Count Raymond had been able to use the information brought by Rodrigo and Geoffrey to break the stalemate between the leaders, he could not completely overlook their punishment for disobeying orders. Deciding to follow in Adhemar's footsteps, he had them relegated to guard duty and menial camp duties for the time being.

✠

The campfire flickered under the gentle ocean breeze to the rhythmic pulsing of the waves breaking on the seashore in the distance. The fire crackled as the breeze sent tiny embers floating into the air and shadows from the firelight danced upon the ground. Sitting on stumps and leaning against their spears, Rodrigo and Geoffrey sat in quiet contemplation as they gazed into the light of the flames that evening.

At last, Rodrigo broke the silence as he looked at the silhouette of the city of Tyre against the night sky. "This city has a lot of history. I remember my uncle telling me of a famous siege that took place here by Alexander the Great."

"What happened?" asked Geoffrey, looking up from the fire.

"Part of the city used to be situated on an island just off this coastline," Rodrigo said, pointing to the sea. "Its high walls and strategic position were thought to have made it impregnable against an attack by land. So confident of this was the king of Tyre that he refused to surrender to Alexander. He killed the envoys Alexander sent to the city and threw their bodies off the walls."

"Yes, that does sound *extremely* confident," Geoffrey said with a slight grin. "What was Alexander's response?"

"He built a massive land bridge using timbers and rocks that extended all the way to the island," Rodrigo answered, sweeping his hand across the horizon from the land to the sea. "He was able to move his siege equipment, weapons of war, and all his men across the land bridge and captured the city. Such was Alexander's ingenuity, creativity, and determination that he was able to achieve this legendary feat."

"That is impressive. I imagine the king of Tyre immediately regretted his decision," Geoffrey said with a smirk. "What happened then?"

"The king and the entire population of thirty thousand people were massacred, crucified, or sold into slavery, and the city was destroyed," Rodrigo answered, staring contemplatively into the fire. The flickering light from the flames reflected in his eyes, bringing back scenes of the horrific massacres at Antioch and Ma'arra. Rodrigo squeezed his eyes shut for a moment and let the haunting images fade before opening them again. "I wonder, brother, will we be recorded in history as the celebrated liberators of the Holy Land from the Saracens? Or will we be known throughout the ages for brutally massacring thousands of innocent civilians in pursuit of our goal?"

Geoffrey pondered Rodrigo's question in silence for a moment. "I do not know, brother. We have discussed that the loss of innocent life is an inevitable reality of war, but I suppose the extent of that loss is often determined by the leaders in those conflicts. How history will treat us, then, largely depends on them. Do you agree?"

"I agree," Rodrigo said as he poked the fire with the end of his spear, stirring the embers. "And it is the loss of innocent life and our leaders' failure to stop it that has caused me to question everything that we are doing in the Holy Land." He withdrew his spear. "Years ago, I met a traveler named Marcellinus. His travels had taken him all over the world, including to Jerusalem, where he lived and worked for a few years. He told me that he did not believe the Pope's proclamation and his reasons for wanting to invade the Holy Land and recapture Jerusalem. Marcellinus said they were naught but lies."

"And did you believe him?" Geoffrey asked, raising his eyebrows.

"I did not want to at first," Rodrigo said, staring into the fire. "But I made up my mind to discover the truth for myself. Now I can see that all the things Marcellinus told me have proven to be true. According to the Pope, we are liberating the Holy Land and Jerusalem from Saracen oppression and atrocities toward the Christians living here. Yet where is the evidence of that? We have seen none. We know that Christians were living together with Saracens in Antioch, and no doubt it is the same way in Jerusalem. Where is the oppression? Who are committing the atrocities?" asked Rodrigo, looking up at Geoffrey.

Geoffrey thought for a moment. "We are."

"Correct. We are the ones that have committed atrocities and massacred tens of thousands of innocents in the name of the Pope and the holy Catholic Church—all of it for reasons that have proven to be untrue. Therein lies the irony of our situation. We have journeyed to the Holy Land and perpetrated the very acts that we have come all this way to stop. To make it even worse, evil men like Peter the Hermit are allowed to spread poisonous lies, and the Church will do nothing to stop it!" Rodrigo said, raising his voice in disgust. "It is for all these reasons that I feel I can no longer be a part of it."

"What? How can you say that?" Geoffrey asked. There was surprise and concern in his voice as he stared at Rodrigo. "So, you are choosing to reject your faith just as Richard has done?"

"No, not like Richard," Rodrigo answered, looking at the ground and shaking his head. "I will always have faith in God, brother, and he will always be at the center of everything I do and everything I am." He looked back up. "But I will no longer allow myself to be led by the Pope or the Roman Catholic Church."

Neither man spoke for a time, but the frown of concern on Geoffrey's face began to disappear. "I understand your decision, brother. I do," he said at last. "However, I cannot let go of my Catholic faith as easily as you. I am committed to my faith and my oath to the Pope to capture Jerusalem and seek to recover any holy relics within the city."

"I understand and respect your decision as well," Rodrigo said, nodding. "As for me, I no longer care whether we capture Jerusalem or not. However, I will fulfill my duty to Count Raymond as a loyal knight employed in his service until the final outcome. And if Jerusalem falls, then I will fulfill my oath to secure any holy relics that may be found there. I believe we must do everything in our power to keep them from the hands of evil men like Peter the Hermit who would only use them to increase their power and influence."

"Peter the Hermit," Geoffrey said with disdain. "At least his plan to become Count Raymond's spiritual advisor is not quite working out the way he intended." He stood up and stretched his limbs, then walked to a pile of wood nearby and began picking out pieces to put on the dying fire.

"Fortunately, that is true," said Rodrigo, poking the firewood again with his spear. "With the way Peter Bartholomew has been touting his discovery of the Holy Lance and his close relationship with Count Raymond, he seems a more likely choice. Although Count Raymond appears to be in no hurry to fill the position," he said with a grin. *I do not believe that Count Raymond thinks either man is fit to take Adhemar's place.*

"It will be interesting to see where this rivalry leads, anyway," said Geoffrey as he added more wood to the fire.

✠

The moon made its journey across the sky and slowly succumbed to the light of dawn upon its arrival in the east. With its arrival came the soldiers to relieve Rodrigo and Geoffrey as they retreated to their tent to get a few hours of sleep before starting their day. It seemed to Rodrigo that he had barely closed his eyes when he felt a hand upon his shoulder, shaking him and rousing him from his slumber.

"Rodrigo, wake up!" Geoffrey said with urgency in his voice.

"What? What is it?" asked Rodrigo, blinking his eyes and still half asleep.

"You are going to want to see this, brother," said Geoffrey excitedly. His eyes were wide, and he was moving quickly about the tent in eagerness and anticipation.

245

"See what?" Rodrigo asked, sitting up and rubbing his eyes.

"Come with me, and I will show you!" Geoffrey said as he turned and walked out of the tent.

What has gotten Geoffrey so excited as to disregard sleep? Rodrigo thought as he quickly dressed and put on his boots. Exiting the tent, he shielded his eyes from the sun, which was now high in the sky. Squinting, he walked to where Geoffrey was waiting. "Now, tell me what is going on so that I may weigh its importance against the comfort of my cot. Sleep is a valuable thing, you know, especially when you do not have enough of it," he said as he stretched and yawned.

"Trust me brother, you will not be disappointed. Just follow me, and I will explain when we get there. We do not want to miss this," Geoffrey said. Rodrigo followed as he began to walk through the camp, headed toward the sea.

Just outside the main camp was a path that led them down to a rocky area where many Crusaders were gathering. Beyond the rocks was a broad, sandy area a short distance away from the sea. Rodrigo and Geoffrey made their way through the crowd to stand on the edge of the rocks, overlooking the sandy area. A huge crowd had gathered and formed a circle around the sand, and many stood on the rocks above to watch. In the middle of the circle, men were stacking two large piles of wood and straw, side by side, nearing seven feet in height.

Rodrigo looked down on the strange spectacle from their vantage point and finally turned to Geoffrey to speak. "So tell me, what is going on here?"

"Do you remember when we were talking last night about the rivalry between Peter the Hermit and Father Bartholomew?" Geoffrey asked.

"Yes," Rodrigo said. "What of it?"

"Last night, here in camp, while we were on guard duty, I was told that they got into a loud argument in front of a large group of soldiers," said Geoffrey. "Peter the Hermit publicly decried the Holy Lance as a false relic and accused Father Bartholomew of planting it himself. When Father Bartholomew defended his discovery and the legitimacy of the Holy Lance, Peter the Hermit challenged him to prove its authenticity and his faith in its powers."

"Prove it how?" Rodrigo asked, looking down at the scene below.

"In an Ordeal by Fire."

"What?" Rodrigo exclaimed, eyes wide.

"Peter the Hermit challenged him to undergo an Ordeal by Fire to prove his faith in the Holy Lance, and Peter Bartholomew accepted," said Geoffrey.

An Ordeal by Fire was a trial in which the accused would walk a certain distance and subject themselves to grave injury or even death from fire, coals, or red-hot irons. Lack of injury would denote intervention by God, thus proving the accused's innocence, or in Peter Bartholomew's case, the authenticity of the Holy Lance.

Rodrigo stood silent, frowning as he thought. *Why would Father Bartholomew agree to such madness? Can he not see that he is walking right into a trap that Peter the Hermit has set for him?* Rodrigo noticed one of the men by the piles of wood who stood out from the rest. He was giving orders and directing the others where to place the wood and straw.

Geoffrey also noticed him and leaned over to Rodrigo as they watched the men stack the wood. "Look at the man giving orders. Is that Richard?"

"It is," Rodrigo said with folded arms as he watched the men work. Rodrigo was too far away to hear what was being said, but from Richard's body language, it was clear that he was in charge. Rodrigo's eyes narrowed as he watched Richard order the men to stack the wood even higher.

When they were finished, they began to pack straw into the gaps of wood. *The piles are stacked so closely together that there is scarcely enough room to walk through. Clearly, they want to make sure that Father Bartholomew will fail.* Rodrigo grimaced and shook his head as he then watched Richard order his men to throw pitch onto the stacks of wood to make them burn even hotter. *Unless there is truly a miraculous intervention, he will die if he attempts this ordeal.*

Scanning the sandy area below them, Rodrigo saw Peter Bartholomew suddenly emerge at one end of the crowd. He was wearing his priest's robes and walked forward and knelt on the sand, lowering his head and folding his hands in prayer. Rodrigo recalled how nervous Peter Bartholomew had been during the discovery of the Holy Lance, but this morning he seemed calm and stoic, ready to face what lay ahead. On either side of him stood his deacons.

Peter the Hermit stood nearby, his arms folded across his chest, staring with a scowl at the kneeling Peter Bartholomew. Several soldiers stood next to him, including Richard, who was holding a torch.

The crowd near Peter Bartholomew parted, and Count Raymond emerged, carrying a small wooden box and followed by his guards and servants. Count Raymond walked until he was in front of Peter Bartholomew and stopped. Peter Bartholomew was helped to his feet by his deacons as Count Raymond began to speak to him.

Rodrigo strained to hear what was being said, but he was too far away. Peter the Hermit then gave a nod to Richard, who walked toward the huge piles of wood and straw. Richard lit the first pile of wood and then the next before slowly backing away and returning to Peter the Hermit's side.

Count Raymond opened the box, and Peter Bartholomew withdrew the Holy Lance. He raised it above him and looked to the heavens as he prayed aloud, but Rodrigo could hear nothing above the crashing waves in the distance, the murmur of voices around him, and the crackling of the raging bonfires in the middle of the crowd.

Peter Bartholomew lowered his hands and clutched the Holy Lance to his breast and began his slow walk toward the bonfires. Some of those in the crowd near the fires had to back away and keep their distance due to the extreme heat. Peter Bartholomew lowered his head as he neared the bonfires but kept the same pace as he proceeded forward into the roaring flames.

Rodrigo watched the surreal scene intently as Peter Bartholomew entered the blazing inferno and his figure completely disappeared within the flames. A tense and prolonged silence followed. Then, audible gasps were heard from the men around Rodrigo as Peter

Bartholomew suddenly reappeared on the other side, staggering slightly with his head down, but still standing and moving forward beyond the flames. The top and back of his head were black and smoking, and his hair was completely singed away. His robes were also blackened and on fire in some places, and smoke trailed from him as he staggered toward the deacons waiting on the other side. Finally, he reached them, still clutching the relic, and fell to his knees as they quickly moved to help him.

"He did it! He survived the Ordeal!" a soldier standing next to Rodrigo exclaimed.

"That remains to be seen," Rodrigo said skeptically. Peter Bartholomew, appearing unable to rise of his own accord, was helped by his deacons, who placed his arms over their shoulders as they stood and began moving through the crowd. The Holy Lance was placed back into the box by another deacon, who followed the others as they carried Peter Bartholomew back toward camp.

"He is gravely wounded by the flames. It will indeed be a miracle if he is able to recover," Rodrigo said, continuing to watch until Peter Bartholomew was out of sight.

Rodrigo and Geoffrey stood silently for a time until the flames of the bonfires began to die down and the crowds began to disperse. "So much for Peter the Hermit's competition?" Geoffrey said at last.

"Indeed, brother," Rodrigo replied. "This was a calculated move. At least now we know the lengths that snake is prepared to go to get what he wants. We must be as wary of him as we would a poisonous adder, slithering among the rocks upon which we tread."

JERUSALEM AT LAST!

The Crusader army continued its journey south along the coast, stopping two weeks later for a period of three days to mourn the passing of Peter Bartholomew, who finally succumbed to his wounds sustained in the Ordeal by Fire. He was given a grand funeral by Count Raymond that was attended by all the leaders, save for Peter the Hermit, who was nowhere to be seen.

Along with Peter Bartholomew's passing, the Holy Lance and his vision of Saint Andrew were largely discredited and fell into obscurity. The sudden vacancy in the religious leadership left the door open for Peter the Hermit, who seized upon the opportunity to gather up more followers. Although he lacked popularity and influence among the Crusader leaders, Peter the Hermit's followers among the Crusader knights and warriors seemed to increase daily, as did the frequency of his sermons and teachings.

Late in May, the Crusader army finally reached the port city of Jaffa, where the road to Jerusalem turned east through the desert. The weather was growing increasingly hotter as summer approached, and the rumors that Jerusalem was now under control of the Fatimid Caliphate were confirmed to be true. In addition, new rumors were being circulated that a giant Fatimid army was being assembled in Egypt to stop the Crusaders from retaking Jerusalem.

The many weeks of travel with relative ease were over. The road eastward to Jerusalem had quickly become barren and inhospitable. To make matters worse, the scout reports told of abandoned villages, empty granaries, and wells that were either filled in or poisoned, reminiscent of the tactics used when they had crossed the Anatolian peninsula. Cattle had also been driven away or slaughtered and left to rot in the sun. Even the few trees along the road had been cut down, depriving the army of any firewood or timber for siege equipment. It was clear that the Fatimids were anticipating their arrival and were making the Crusaders' journey through the desert as difficult as possible.

Motivated by the closeness to their long-awaited goal, the Crusader army pressed doggedly on under the difficult conditions and the blazing heat of the summer sun. The long columns of soldiers and wagons stretched down the barren road as they marched, far into the distance, until they disappeared into the arid desert.

Finally, on June 7, 1099, with food and supplies running dangerously low and nearly out of fresh water, the Crusaders were given their first glimpse of the holy city of Jerusalem. The road crested along a high precipice before descending onto lower ground, and there on the horizon, like a mirage rising from the heat of the desert floor, the ancient and holy city of Jerusalem lay before them at last. It had been nearly two years since they had left Constantinople on a perilous uphill journey fraught with constant battles, hardships, disease, starvation, and desertions.

Many of the Crusaders fell to their knees, wept with joy, and gave thanks to God at the sight of its broad walls and magnificent towers, as well as the Church of the Holy Sepulcher and the golden Dome of the Rock, which glittered under the sun. Rodrigo stood silent as he surveyed the city below and wiped the sweat from his brow. Although he was relieved to have reached their goal at last after their long and difficult journey, his feelings were much different than he had once anticipated. He did not share the same overwhelming sense of joy as the other Crusaders. Instead, he saw a city where Jews, Saracens, and Christians lived together in peace and were now in the shadow of an invading army that sought to take the city by force. As he stood, the memory of looking down into the slumbering city of Antioch after they had scaled the walls flashed in his mind.

The Crusader leaders decided to set camp that night along the broad precipice to give all the men the chance to renew their spirits and reignite their motivation at the sight of the magnificent city. A special Mass was held that evening in the camp to give thanks to God for allowing them to reach their goal and to ask for his aid and protection in taking the city. Two of the Crusaders were absent from the Mass taking place, however, and stood at the precipice, looking out at Jerusalem.

Rodrigo and Geoffrey marveled at the city, which lay before them like a jewel resting beneath the moonlit desert sky. "So, what do you think the chances are that our leaders will be able to capture the city?" Geoffrey asked.

Rodrigo smiled faintly as he continued to study the city and its surroundings. "The view of the city from up here does offer a strategic vantage point," he mused. "Right now, I believe we are at a considerable disadvantage. It is far too big for us to surround, and we have no siege equipment. We are short on water and supplies, and most likely the Fatimids are gathering their forces in Egypt to march against us. It is the same situation we faced when we first besieged Antioch, although now, we only have a quarter of the men we had then and almost no cavalry."

"Perhaps we should not have skipped Mass and should be praying for a miracle right now?" Geoffrey asked with a laugh.

"I think our leaders are going to need one, brother. We are not in a good position to take the city," Rodrigo said solemnly. "I want to show you something." He pointed to a section of Jerusalem. "Do you see that building with the golden dome on the north side of the city?"

"Yes," Geoffrey said, looking to where Rodrigo was pointing.

"That is where the Temple Mount is located," Rodrigo said. "That was the foundation of the temple built by King Solomon in ancient times, long before Christ. I was able to study some old maps of Jerusalem that I found in a library in Toulouse when we were there. I am glad that I did."

"Yes, that was a good idea," Geoffrey said. "If we make it inside the city, we will need to know where we are going."

"Now, look at the building to the right of the golden dome. Do you remember the location of the holy relics that Adhemar revealed to us when he first spoke to us about our mission?" Rodrigo asked.

"Yes. He told us that they were being kept in a mosque somewhere near the Temple Mount," said Geoffrey.

"That is correct. I believe that building to the right of the golden dome is the al-Aqsa Mosque that Adhemar spoke of. It is the only building large enough to be a mosque in that area of the Temple Mount. If our leaders somehow manage to take the city, that is where we must go," said Rodrigo.

"So, do you have any idea how they might achieve that feat?" asked Geoffrey.

"None," Rodrigo said with a laugh. "If it is truly God's will, then it will be done, although I have no idea how." Although it seemed as though the odds of taking Jerusalem were slim, an unusual sense of calm had come over Rodrigo. Leaving the fate of the city completely in God's hands and being indifferent to the outcome felt much better than the normal stress that would accompany such a situation. As the two sat down upon the precipice, the stars came out and filled the evening sky above the city as they continued to engage in light-hearted conversation and laughter well into the night.

36

THE FIRST ASSAULT

The Crusader leaders held a meeting at the edge of the precipice the following day and used their vantage point above Jerusalem to devise plans to lay siege, knowing they could not surround the entire city. It was decided that Count Raymond and his men would set up camp outside the southern walls of the city, while Duke Godfrey and the Normans would set up a separate camp to the north. Although most of the city would not be blocked by the siege, having two separate camps would allow them to assault the city from two different points simultaneously.

As the Crusader army descended off the precipice onto the plains around Jerusalem, they encountered a strange sight. They began to pass long lines of civilians, numbering in the thousands, traveling away from the city. They had with them all their belongings on pack mules and wooden carts in long caravans on the side of the road. Upon investigation, it was discovered that Jerusalem's Fatimid governor, Iftikhar al-Dawla, had ordered that all Christians be removed from the city when he received word of the Crusaders' arrival.

There was probably more than one reason for this. It may have been that al-Dawla feared acts of treachery by the Christians, or he may have wanted to conserve food and supplies. Another possibility was that it was a request by the Christians themselves, who feared persecution during the siege. Whatever the reason, they were now leaving the city and had been left to fend for themselves. Rodrigo stared at the faces of the Christian civilians as they passed each other, one group marching away from the city while the other marched toward it. *I am glad that they will be safe, at least, if the city falls. However, if that happens, now that the Christians are gone, I fear our leaders will be much less inclined to spare the local populace. I wish they had expelled all the civilians, not just the Christians.* Although the Christians remained silent as they passed, it was clear from the many forlorn faces and angry looks that they were unhappy with the arrival of the Crusaders and with being forced to leave their homes. By midday, the Crusader army arrived at their respective positions around the city and began to set up their camps.

Three days after setting up camp, the leaders ordered the men to prepare for an assault on the city. It was their desire to capitalize on the general euphoria and high morale of the men after having finally reached their goal. However, the walls of Jerusalem were exceedingly high and broad, nearing forty feet in height, and their plan to create scaling ladders by foraging timber around the city came up woefully short. From the materials on hand, only a single ladder was produced that could reach the top of the wall and sustain the weight of multiple soldiers. The lack of siege equipment did not dampen the Crusaders' morale, however, and having been bolstered by the zealous preaching of Peter the Hermit, they were more than willing to move forward with the assault.

"This is utter foolishness," Rodrigo muttered to Geoffrey as he watched the scene with his arms folded across his chest. *How can our leaders believe that assaulting the city with a single ladder will be successful?* The Crusaders had lined up in battle formations at the edge of the city. Count Raymond was at the center of the line along with Peter the Hermit, who had blessed the scaling ladder with holy water and was now giving a motivational speech to the soldiers before they began their assault.

"Harken to me, all ye followers of Christ our Lord! Years of toil, strife, and sacrifice have brought us to this very moment where God shall at last grant us a final victory over the Saracen invaders!" Peter yelled to the cheers of those around him. Standing on a stool so he could be seen and heard, he continued. "The Christian inhabitants have safely been released, and now the only occupants are the Saracen vermin and the Jews, the killers of Christ, who committed the act in this very city! We, the faithful followers of Christ, shall reclaim the city for the Pope and the holy Catholic Church, its rightful rulers!" The cheers of those around him continued as a knight stepped forward out of the ranks to stand by Peter. "This brave knight beside me, Sir Rainbold, has volunteered to lead the assault on the walls and shall be the first to claim the city in the name of Christ our Lord and the one true God! *Deus vult!* God wills it!" he yelled as the ladder was brought to the front of the line and the Crusaders began cheering and chanting, "*Deus vult! Deus vult!*"

Rodrigo and Geoffrey watched a small group of Crusaders begin their advance as those around them yelled encouragement and cheered them on. Rodrigo remained silent and glanced at Peter the Hermit out of the corner of his eye. *It is obvious that the men in Count Raymond's army have completely fallen under the spell of this madman. Has Peter the Hermit grown so powerful that he is able to bend Count Raymond to his will as well? Surely, Count Raymond knows that lives will needlessly be thrown away with this foolish assault!*

Twenty Crusaders on either side of the ladder held their shields high for protection as they carried it toward the wall while arrows and rocks began to rain down upon them. Behind them, the chants of "*Deus vult!*" continued as the Crusaders weathered the intense bombardment and finally reached the wall. Only a few had fallen along the way and were dragged back to the safety of the lines. The tough and determined group of Crusaders managed to raise the ladder while working together to shield each other from the deadly downpour. Once the ladder had been set, the cheers of the Crusader army grew even louder, and those below the ladder struggled to hold it in place so others could begin the climb.

Sir Rainbold was the first to ascend, and he held his shield above him, now filled with arrows, climbing the ladder as quickly as he could. The cheers from the Crusaders had reached a crescendo as he reached the top of the ladder just below the battlements. Grasping the top of the ladder with his shield hand, he drew his sword and prepared to climb over the battlements onto the wall. The Fatimid warriors were waiting for him, however, and a pair of poleaxes swung down at him from both sides as he reached the top. The heavy poleaxes sliced cleanly through armor, flesh, and bone, severing his sword arm at the elbow and his shield arm at the shoulder, sending both arms along with his sword and shield down to the ground. Sir Rainbold toppled backward and landed forty feet below, breaking his neck instantly.

The cheering of the Crusaders feebly died away as they witnessed the fate of Sir Rainbold, but Peter the Hermit shouted at those around him to continue their chanting and encouragement. More groups of Crusaders began to rush forward to replenish the steadily depleting numbers of the men trying to assault the wall. Many were shot down by arrows, crushed by rocks, or met similar fates at the top of the scaling ladder. *Thank God we are not part of the assault groups today,* Rodrigo thought as he watched the scene in grim silence. *I feel pity for these men, but perhaps this is what it will take to break the spell of Peter the Hermit and their trust in him.*

"How long is Count Raymond going to let this go on?" Rodrigo growled in disgust to Geoffrey as they watched several valiant yet futile attempts to assault the wall and observed the resultant carnage. At last, a trumpet sounded, signaling the retreat. The Crusader army broke their formations, withdrew from the wall, and walked back to camp in utter defeat and humiliation, listening to the taunts and cheering of the Fatimid warriors on the walls above.

GIFTS FROM THE SEA

A somber feeling lay over the entire camp that evening, and the exultant mood of the Crusader army had ended abruptly with the deaths of Sir Rainbold and the Crusaders who had given their lives assaulting the wall that day. The funeral rites for those who died were short and informal and were performed by some of Count Raymond's priests, but Peter the Hermit was nowhere to be seen. The next morning, Geoffrey and Rodrigo awoke from their slumber and began to prepare for their daily camp duties.

"I hope Count Raymond now realizes that placing his trust in Peter the Hermit will only lead us down the road of destruction, like it did the People's Army," Rodrigo said as he and Geoffrey left their tent.

"I agree. Count Raymond seems to be a sensible leader, although I fear at times, he opens himself to the influence of others, as he did with Adhemar," Geoffrey said. "I am going to the supply wagons this morning to help distribute the camp's daily rations. I am curious to see how much is left."

"Yet another obstacle we must overcome if we are to have any chance in taking the city," Rodrigo said. "I will volunteer to go with the foraging party to see what else we can gather from around the camp."

Later that afternoon, encouraging news arrived in camp from the port city of Jaffa that ships carrying food, supplies, and building materials for siege equipment had arrived. When the Crusaders had first arrived in Jaffa, before turning eastward toward Jerusalem, the leaders had drawn upon their experience from the siege at Antioch and dispatched ships to Italy with orders to bring back supplies and building materials. Wisely, the leaders had also used their wealth to purchase enough horses and pack animals to retrieve the supplies once they arrived. Rodrigo and Geoffrey volunteered to join a group of a hundred men that was assembled that evening to retrieve the cargo as quickly as possible.

Fatimid horse archers were constantly harassing any Crusaders moving around Jerusalem. The city gates on the east and west had been left unblocked, and the Fatimids were free to send small groups of cavalry to harass and engage any Crusaders that left the safety of the camps. The group chosen to go to Jaffa was composed mainly of knights due to their skill on horseback in combat. However, they were ordered not to engage the Fatimids and to head directly to Jaffa under cover of darkness. Once the supplies and building materials were secured, they were to protect the shipment at all cost. That night, the group rode out of camp in secrecy under the moonlit sky.

They were able to reach the precipice overlooking the city without incident and were well on their way to Jaffa, which would take them two days traveling on horseback. The return journey would be much longer and more dangerous, as they had to bring several large carts full of supplies and building materials back to Jerusalem. The group rode until dawn and then stopped to rest and eat. Makeshift shelters were set up to provide shade against the heat of the noonday sun. Rodrigo and Geoffrey used their lances to hold up some hides and cloth to create a barrier against the sun, and they relaxed in the shade it provided after the long night's ride.

Geoffrey lay on the ground with his hands behind his head as he glanced over at Rodrigo, who was sitting up and staring at the ground. "You should relax and get some rest; we still have a full night's ride ahead of us," he said as Rodrigo sat in silence. "What has you so troubled?"

Rodrigo stared out at the road. "Peter the Hermit's influence in our army has grown to a point where the men are willing to recklessly follow his lead without rational thought behind their actions. Our leaders, though prone to making mistakes, are not fools. I do not believe any of them would have allowed the last assault to take place if it were not for Peter the Hermit's insistence with all of the men enthusiastically behind him."

Geoffrey slowly nodded. "That is likely true. I know you were hoping that the failure of the assault would lessen his popularity and influence with the men. Do you not believe that is happening?"

"It may for a time," Rodrigo said. "But it always seems that the moment I begin to think his power and influence are diminishing, he will manipulate the circumstances and turn everything back in his favor." Rodrigo picked up a rock from the ground and began turning it over in his hand. "He is a clever one, I will give him that."

"So, what do you think can be done about it?" Geoffrey asked.

"I do not know, brother," Rodrigo said. "My fear is that with the arrival of supplies and building materials for siege equipment, our chances of taking Jerusalem will grow considerably. That means that the chances of a bloody massacre and the possibility of Peter the Hermit acquiring the holy relics increase as well." He threw the rock out into the desert.

"What if we were to bring our concerns to Count Raymond?" Geoffrey asked.

"I thought about that," Rodrigo said. "Count Raymond will likely order his men to spare the civilians, as he did at Antioch. However, he holds no control over the rest of the army, and with the considerable sway Peter the Hermit has over his men, they may not follow orders anyway. Also, I do not believe that Count Raymond views Peter the Hermit as anything more than an overzealous priest, so there would be no reason to stand in the way of him going after the holy relics."

Both men sat in silent contemplation for a while. At last, Geoffrey spoke. "What if we sought help from one of the other leaders?"

"Why would any of them listen to us or help us?" Rodrigo asked skeptically. "We are not familiar with any of them."

"We are familiar with one," Geoffrey said.

"Who?"

"Lord Tancred," Geoffrey replied. "I believe he would remember us from our meeting in the tower at Antioch and the assistance you gave him with the messenger that night. He is a brave warrior with many men, and I know he has no love for Peter the Hermit, especially after he caught him deserting camp. If we went to Tancred and told him about our mission and our concerns for the civilians, perhaps he would listen and help us."

"All of that is true," Rodrigo admitted. His frown faded, and there was a renewed enthusiasm in his voice. "That is an excellent suggestion. I had not thought of him." He sat up straight. "That is what we must do, then, when we get back to Jerusalem. We must figure out a way to get to Duke Godfrey's camp and speak to Tancred to see if we can enlist his help."

"That sounds like a plan, but let's not steal any horses or sneak out of camp this time," Geoffrey said with a smirk.

"Agreed, brother. Agreed," Rodrigo replied with a laugh.

✠

The blazing sun began its descent on the horizon, and the group resumed their journey through the desert by the light of the moon. They finally reached Jaffa the next morning, exhausted from the long night's ride. The cool breeze of the Mediterranean was a welcome relief compared to the hot and arid desert lands they had been traveling through. The group was allowed to eat, rest, and recover while the expedition's leader, Sir John, attended to business before they made their way down to the harbor in the afternoon. He did not want to waste any time in the city and was determined to stay focused on their mission.

"Look! There they are!" one of the Crusaders riding next to Rodrigo and Geoffrey called out as they followed the road that led down to the city harbor. Framed against the blue waters of the

Mediterranean, they could see six Genoese galleys waiting for them at the docks, loaded down with supplies and building materials. Many of the Crusaders began cheering at the sight of the bountiful gifts that had arrived from the sea.

Though they were weary after their long journey from Jerusalem, their mood began to transform into one of hope and enthusiasm as they came closer to the ships. Everyone in the group knew that obtaining the supplies and materials was vital to the success of their goal. Once they arrived at the docks, the men immediately began working to unload the cargo onto the wagons that Sir John had acquired in the city.

Late that afternoon, as the Crusaders worked diligently to unload the cargo, a curious sight came across the horizon. Rodrigo stopped working for a moment and stared out to sea. He could see the sails of several ships coming into view as many more began to dot the blue horizon. He used his hand to shield his eyes from the sun and squinted to make out the symbol on the sails, but they were still too far away. *The ships do not look European. Could this be a Turkish or Fatimid fleet?*

The Crusaders continued to work the rest of the afternoon with growing unease as the looming presence of the unknown fleet of ships grew larger. By early evening, when the Crusaders had completed their work for the day, the sails of the Fatimid Caliphate could clearly be seen from the harbor. The entire harbor was now effectively blockaded by the fleet, and no more ships could leave or enter without passing through them.

Rodrigo and Geoffrey mounted up with the rest of the group to return to the city for the night. "Thank God, the supplies and building materials arrived just in time," said Geoffrey as he grasped his reins.

"Yes, I agree. One day later, and we may not have received them," said Rodrigo, glancing back out at the ships.

"I feel badly, though, for the captain and the sailors that came all the way from Italy to deliver this cargo," Geoffrey said. "I am sure they have been well paid, but now they cannot leave and return to

Europe. They will be stranded here in Jaffa for who knows how long."

"That is true," Rodrigo said, nodding. He thought about what Geoffrey had said as the group began moving back up the road toward the city.

✠

The next morning, the group returned to the harbor to unload the last of the materials before returning to Jerusalem. Rodrigo stopped for a moment as he and Geoffrey unloaded some timber onto one of the carts. He leaned against the cart, looking at all the materials and supplies they had gathered so far, and then looked back out at the galleys as Geoffrey's words replayed in his mind. *They will be stranded here for who knows how long.*

"What is it?" asked Geoffrey as he looked at Rodrigo, who had a far-off look in his eyes as he stared at the galleys. "What are you thinking about?"

"Something you said yesterday made me think of a lesson my uncle taught me when I was young," Rodrigo said. "He taught me that victory often depends on the effective and efficient use of one's resources."

"I am sure we will put all these resources to good use," Geoffrey said with a smile. "I do not see your point."

"The ships!" Rodrigo exclaimed. "We have acquired enough building materials for one siege tower, but I am sure there is more than enough wood in these ships to build another one, thereby doubling our chances of success."

"That is an interesting idea, but do you really think the Genoese sailors would agree to dismantle their own ships to provide us with more building materials?" Geoffrey asked with a furrowed brow.

"Under normal circumstances, no, but like you said yesterday, they are stranded here indefinitely," Rodrigo replied. "They cannot sail from the harbor, for if they try and are caught by the Fatimids, they will likely be put to death for aiding us. If they try to escape by traveling inland, they will be forced to abandon their ships. Perhaps, if our leaders would be willing to compensate them for providing us with the extra materials, they could escape and recover the cost of their galleys at the same time."

Geoffrey nodded. "You are right, that would benefit everyone," he said. "Let's finish unloading the cargo and then go and speak to Sir John and see what he thinks about it."

Later that afternoon, Rodrigo and Geoffrey sought out Sir John. The idea was well received, and the three men met that evening with the leader of the Genoese sailors, Captain Embriaco. A price was negotiated for the merchant galleys, and the following day, both groups immediately set upon the task of dismantling the ships and harvesting the extra wood for building materials.

3 8

A CURIOUS SPECTACLE

The Genoese sailors and Crusaders worked together tirelessly for two weeks to complete the arduous task of dragging the galleys onto dry land, dismantling them, and harvesting the wood and materials. Although it would cost them extra time, the additional building materials for a second siege tower were worth delaying their return. A small group of ten men was sent back to the Crusader camp to inform the leaders of the reason for the delay. At the end of the two weeks, the work was done, and the group began their journey back to Jerusalem. The pace of travel was much slower, however, and the long train of wagons hauling wood and materials extended far down the road.

"How long do you think it will take us to get back?" asked Geoffrey as he and Rodrigo rode alongside the slow-moving caravan.

"At this pace? Maybe five days," Rodrigo answered.

"Do you have any ideas yet on how to get to Duke Godfrey's camp to enlist Tancred's aid?" asked Geoffrey.

"None," Rodrigo said. "I guess we will have five days to think about it and come up with a plan."

Slowly the Crusaders, accompanied by the Genoese sailors, made their way back through the inhospitable desert toward Jerusalem. The group traveled mostly in the evenings and at night to avoid the heat of the desert sun and to conserve water, sleeping in the early morning and resting during the day. Finally, just over three weeks after they had left Jerusalem, they reached the precipice overlooking the city. As they traveled along the road by the edge of the precipice, they beheld a curious spectacle taking place below them. Unsure what to make of it, Rodrigo, Geoffrey and many of the other men rode to the edge to take a better look.

"What in God's name are they doing down there?" Rodrigo asked Geoffrey as they stared at the bewildering sight. Far below them, they could see long lines of Crusaders marching around the massive walls of the city. From their vantage point, the Crusaders looked like ants encircling a building.

"Perhaps our leaders are reenacting Joshua's march around the walls of Jericho, hoping they will crumble after seven days," Geoffrey joked. "It is impossible to tell what they are doing from up here."

Rodrigo continued to stare. *This is definitely not a strategic or military tactic, and that tells me that our leaders are not the ones behind this.* "Let's get these supplies to the camp and find out what is going on," he said as they turned their mounts back to the road.

The group began its descent toward Jerusalem, splitting up as they neared the city, with half of the supplies moving toward Duke Godfrey's camp to the north and the other half toward Count Raymond's camp. As they neared the camps, they began to pass long lines of marching Crusaders, who shouted praises to God at the sight of the wagons full of supplies. The men were unarmed and dressed in plain clothes, and priests were leading various sections of the lines, reading aloud from the Bible as they marched. Even stranger still, all of the men were marching barefoot upon the hard, rocky ground. *There is only one person that could provoke our army into this kind of behavior,* Rodrigo thought as he stared at the men.

Rodrigo and Geoffrey rode ahead of the group as they approached Count Raymond's camp. The camp appeared mostly empty, save for the guards posted around the camp at various intervals. They dismounted near a group of guards. "We are with the group that just returned from Jaffa," Rodrigo called out to one of them. "What is going on here? Why are all the men marching barefoot around the city?" He pointed to the long lines of men marching in the distance.

"Four days ago, Little Peter of Amiens told of a powerful vision in which he was visited by the spirit of Bishop Adhemar," the guard said. "In his vision, Bishop Adhemar admonished our leaders for their pride and lack of faith, and said that was the reason that our first attempt to assault the city failed. Bishop Adhemar then revealed to Little Peter that if our entire army demonstrated humility and faith in God and performed a penance by fasting for three days and marching around the city barefoot, Jerusalem would fall soon after."

Rodrigo said nothing as he shook his head with disgust. *As I suspected, Peter the Hermit is manipulating the situation once again. He disavows any responsibility for the failure of the first assault and used his knowledge of the coming building materials to lend credibility to his lies.*

"Will anything happen after the march?" Geoffrey asked the guard.

"After the march, we will break the fast with a meal here in camp. Later this evening, we are to gather on the Mount of Olives, where Little Peter will preach a sermon," said the guard. "God willing, the city will soon be ours."

"Thank you for this information," Geoffrey said as he and Rodrigo turned from the guards and returned to their horses.

Rodrigo and Geoffrey rejoined the wagons to help bring them into camp and organize the supplies and building materials. Later that afternoon, they relinquished their mounts and headed back to their tent as the Crusaders began slowly trickling back into camp from their long barefoot march around the city. It was obvious that many were exhausted from the long, hot march and the lack of energy from three days of fasting. Yet when they arrived in camp, most were ecstatic to see the newly arrived food, supplies, and building materials and continued to praise God and give thanks.

The morale in camp was high that afternoon, yet for some, the mood was vastly different. A brooding frown was etched on

Rodrigo's face as he looked into the eyes and smiling faces of the men returning to camp. A gnawing feeling of frustration was growing in his belly as he and Geoffrey made their way back to their tent. He felt an overwhelming urge to stop and yell at the men for their foolishness in believing Peter the Hermit's lies. He clenched his jaw as he fought the urge and averted his eyes to the ground as he quickened his pace.

When they reached the tent, Rodrigo dropped his weapons and belongings on the floor as the words nearly burst from his mouth. "I cannot believe what is happening!" he said aloud, raising his hands in frustration. "Our entire army believes this absurd lie by Peter the Hermit and is willing to do his bidding without question!"

"He had a vision of Bishop Adhemar scolding our leaders and blamed the failure of the first assault on them," Geoffrey said with smirk as he placed his sword and belongings under his cot. "You have to admit, that is a pretty bold lie. I just find it hard to believe that our leaders allowed it."

Rodrigo sat down on his cot with an exasperated sigh. "I am sure they allowed it for the same reason they proclaimed the discovery of the Holy Lance—to boost the morale of the army." He hunched over with his forearms on his knees, staring at the floor. "They want to use Peter the Hermit's vision to raise the morale of the men, but they do not seem to understand that he is undermining their authority and setting himself up as the spiritual leader. Now he has the entire army doing his bidding."

"Are you not looking forward to attending his sermon on the Mount of Olives?" Geoffrey asked sarcastically as he lay down on his cot and folded his arms behind his head.

"Of course he chose the Mount of Olives to preach his sermon. By doing so, he wishes to emulate Christ our Lord. It is pure blasphemy!" Rodrigo said angrily.

Geoffrey stared at the roof of the tent for a moment before speaking. "Do you think Tancred will be at the Mount of Olives, or will he stay in Duke Godfrey's camp?"

"That is a good question," Rodrigo said as he thought for a moment. "My guess is the leaders will skip the sermon and stay in camp to devise plans to build the siege equipment and assault the city." He sat up. "If we go to the Mount of Olives this evening with the others, I doubt anyone will even notice if we leave and go to Duke Godfrey's camp." A faint smile began to appear on the corner of his mouth. "It looks like Peter the Hermit provided us an easy way to get to get there. I only hope that we can persuade Tancred to help us."

39

TRUST IN A GOOD MAN

The sun was beginning its retreat down into the hills west of Jerusalem, casting its light upon the holy and revered Mount of Olives where Peter the Hermit was preparing to give his sermon. The ancient olive trees dotted the gently sloping hillside, which created a natural amphitheater where Jesus of Nazareth had once preached to the masses. Below the Mount of Olives lay the Garden of Gethsemane, where Jesus prayed with his disciples and was arrested the night before his crucifixion.

After partaking in the meal to break the fast, Rodrigo and Geoffrey, along with the rest of the Crusaders, began to exit the camp and head toward the Mount of Olives, passing the garden along the way. A wooden platform had been constructed near the top of the hill so that Peter the Hermit could be seen and heard by all those below him. The safety of the soldiers attending the special Mass was a priority as thousands gathered to hear the sermon. Guards were positioned around the Mount of Olives, while mounted soldiers patrolled near the unblocked gates to protect against any Fatimid warriors who might venture out to attack or harass the Crusaders.

The soft glow of the evening twilight had settled upon the hills and the Mount of Olives as Peter the Hermit ascended the platform and prepared to address the masses. In one hand, he held a wooden cross, and in the other he carried a Bible. A hushed silence came over the crowd as Peter stood on the pulpit, a lone figure standing above thousands of onlookers who covered the hillside around him. He remained silent at first, stalking the pulpit and casting a malevolent gaze upon the masses below. Torches were placed on the platform behind him, casting his looming shadow across the hillside.

"Harken to me, all ye faithful warriors of almighty God!" he shouted, breaking the silence. "Upon this hillside—indeed, upon this very spot—our Lord Jesus Christ, King of Kings, Lord of Hosts, preached his divine message to his faithful followers. So it was in ancient times, and so it shall be this very night!" At the bottom of the hill near the edge of the crowd, two men began to walk away from the masses while those around them remained transfixed on the sermon being preached from above.

Rodrigo glanced back and could see Peter the Hermit continue his sermon from afar as they neared Duke Godfrey's camp. *Thank God we do not have to listen to any more of that poisonous filth!*

Peter the Hermit remained true to form during his sermon that evening. There were moments of shouting and wild gesticulation, and others where the masses had to strain to hear him. Rodrigo knew Peter the Hermit's well-practiced technique would weave a hypnotic spell upon the hearts and minds of the thousands of Crusaders attending that evening. The Jewish and Saracen inhabitants of the city would undoubtedly be transformed into vermin and insects to be destroyed by those who operated as the righteous instruments of God.

Once they arrived in Duke Godfrey's camp, Rodrigo and Geoffrey inquired and were told where Tancred and his men were located. It was not long before they reached his section of the camp.

"Halt," said a guard outside a large tent as they approached. "State your business."

"We are knights from Count Raymond's army, and we have urgent news for Lord Tancred," said Rodrigo.

"What urgent news?" asked the guard with narrowing eyes.

"We are only allowed to deliver the news to Lord Tancred

himself," Rodrigo answered. "Please inform him that Sir Rodrigo and Sir Geoffrey, the knights he met in the guard tower in Antioch, must speak to him regarding matters of the utmost importance. I am sorry I cannot tell you more, but this news must be revealed to him alone."

The guard hesitated for a moment, then turned and entered the large tent. "I guess we will soon find out if you were correct about the impression we made on him in Antioch," Rodrigo whispered to Geoffrey as they waited.

Soon the guard returned, and Rodrigo and Geoffrey were escorted into the tent. Rodrigo noted the surroundings as they entered. Though large and spacious, the interior was absent the luxuries and accommodations of the other nobles' tents that he had been in. With only simple furnishings adorning the inside along with weapons and other supplies, it truly was a soldier's tent. Seated at a table within was Tancred, who rose to greet them. "Sir Rodrigo, Sir Geoffrey, come in! It has been quite some time. It is good to see you again," he said with a smile.

"Thank you for receiving us, Lord Tancred," said Rodrigo, breathing a small sigh of relief. "In truth, we were unsure that you would even remember who we were."

"Indeed, I well recall the evening we spent together in the tower before meeting with Firouz's messenger. My uncle also informed me that you performed bravely in the mission to open the gate on the night that Antioch was taken. Please, sit," Tancred said, motioning to the seats in front of them at the table. "So, what is this *news of utmost importance* that you wish to share with me?" he asked with a grin.

"My lord," Geoffrey began as they sat down. "We came here this evening hoping that we could enlist your help with a secret mission sanctioned by Pope Urban himself." Tancred listened in silence as Geoffrey explained their mission.

"So, why do you come to me for help?" Tancred asked after Geoffrey had finished.

"With Bishop Adhemar gone and no one else to help us, our mission now lies in jeopardy," Rodrigo replied. "We had to make a choice of continuing the mission by ourselves or turning to someone we trust for help."

"And what makes you think you can trust me?" asked Tancred bluntly, staring at Rodrigo. "Why not take this to someone more familiar to you, like Count Raymond?"

"We thought about trying to enlist the help of Count Raymond, but we truly believe that because of his ties to our rival in this mission, he was not the right person to talk to," Rodrigo said. "Forgive me, Lord Tancred, but to be honest, we are not entirely certain we can trust you. However, we do believe you to be a good man and a brave warrior. As you are the only other Crusader leader that is familiar to us, we thought we would take a chance in appealing to you for help."

Tancred stared at the two in silence for a moment, scanning their faces for a sign of their intentions. "Why does your mission now lie in jeopardy?" he asked.

"There are others that know about the Pope's mission," said Geoffrey. "One of the knights originally assigned to this quest has enlisted the help of Peter the Hermit, who has a great many men at his disposal. Now they both seek to acquire the holy relics. Knowing these men, we can only presume that they seek the relics not for the Pope, but for their own personal status and power. This is why we seek your aid."

Tancred studied their faces again for a moment before speaking. "Now I understand why you came to me for help. It is widely known that I despise Little Peter the loud-mouthed priest. He is a deserter and a coward, and I have never liked him. If he, too, seeks these holy relics, it can only be for selfish reasons. Therefore, I will agree to help you insomuch as I can. However, taking the city will not be easy, and everything depends on completing this difficult task."

"Thank you, Lord Tancred," said Rodrigo. "Your help means much to us. If this mission is successful, you may take all the honor and credit, for we seek none. We only want to ensure these items are safely delivered to the Pope and kept out of the hands of evil men who seek them only for power and personal glory." Rodrigo paused for a moment. "We have one other request, my lord," he said, glancing at Geoffrey. "If the city falls, we ask that the Temple Mount be preserved as a place of sanctuary and refuge for the city's inhabitants to avoid the slaughter and destruction that occurred at Antioch."

Tancred reflected for a moment on Rodrigo's request. "I can have my men secure the area of the Temple Mount once we arrive and not allow it to be looted or sacked. The city's inhabitants will be safe if they go there," he said, looking at both men. "However, should I fall during the assault of the city, as there is always that chance, then I can guarantee nothing, and you will again be on your own."

"We understand. Thank you, my lord," said Rodrigo. Outwardly, Rodrigo maintained his calm composure, but inwardly, he breathed a long sigh of relief.

Tancred sat back in his chair as he continued. "Once the siege towers are constructed, the day before we begin the next assault, I will summon both of you from Count Raymond's camp, and you will stay here with my men. If we are to carry out this plan, you will need to be with me when we breach the walls and enter the city." He paused for a moment before speaking again. "I think it best if our plans are kept secret from Count Raymond, since Little Peter is close to him. If Raymond happens to inquire about the summons, I will simply tell him I wish to discuss a personal matter with both of you, and you will return when we are finished. I am sure he will be too busy with planning and preparation to notice if you do not return. Do you agree with this plan?"

"Yes, my lord. We agree," Rodrigo said. Geoffrey nodded. "Thank you again for everything." They rose from the table.

As they walked back through camp, Geoffrey began to speak. "Truth be told, brother, that went much better than I anticipated," he said. "But do you think Tancred will follow through on his word if we take the city? Or perhaps he will bend to the will of his men or lose control if they get caught up in the looting?"

Rodrigo thought for a moment. "I believe Tancred is a man of his word and is wise enough to see Peter the Hermit for what he is. He is a strong leader, so I am sure that his men will obey his commands and that we can place our trust in him."

Later that evening, Peter the Hermit's fiery sermon had come to an end, and thousands of Crusaders began to descend the Mount of Olives by the light of the full moon, which had risen from the hills to guide their way. Rodrigo and Geoffrey walked with the long lines of Crusaders returning from the Mount of Olives as they made their way back to Count Raymond's camp. The night passed quietly, and once they arrived, they returned to their tent for some rest.

40

THE SECOND ASSAULT

On the morning of July 13, horns blared from within the city, cries and warning bells could be heard from the towers, and frantic activity atop the city walls signaled the beginning of the second Crusader assault on Jerusalem. Two massive, sixty-foot-tall siege towers began to inch their way forward out of the Crusader camps. The twin juggernauts of wood and iron crept sluggishly toward the walls on opposite sides of the city like lumbering giants, burdened by their own weight. Horses whinnied and snorted as they strained to pull the ropes attached to the towers, and the Crusaders behind yelled and grunted with exertion as they pushed with all their might.

The wooden wheels of the tower creaked under the strain of the weight as though they might break at any moment, and the tower slowly rocked from side to side as it moved over the ground. The ground between the camp and the walls of Jerusalem had been leveled and cleared of rocks and debris, but such was the height and weight of the massive towers that any movement, even on level ground, was difficult. If the tower toppled or the wheels broke, it would be disastrous for the Crusaders.

The whole of the Crusader army watched with tense anticipation on both sides of the city as the towers drew ever nearer. Rodrigo and Geoffrey had been summoned by Tancred the night before and had awakened that morning with a renewed spirit and energy. As an outlet for that energy, both men had volunteered to help move the towers toward the city walls. Although it was a difficult and somewhat dangerous task, they would only help to move the tower to the walls and then return and wait for Tancred's orders. Both men strained with effort as they pushed the giant tower down the path. "Get ready!" Rodrigo yelled to Geoffrey and those around them as he glanced up at the city walls from behind the tower. "We are coming into range of the archers!"

Just as Rodrigo spoke, the whistling of hundreds of arrows began to fill the air around the towers, and the metal tips bit into the wooden towers with a thud, accompanied by cries from some of the men around them as the arrows found their mark. Shields were raised along with handheld wooden barriers to protect the men and horses as they continued to move forward amidst the deadly rain of arrows.

Soon after, the first trails of smoke from lighted arrows could be seen arcing off the top of the walls. The horses whinnied with panic as the lighted arrows struck the wooden barriers and the ground around them, creating a layer of smoke that began to blind and choke those pushing the tower. Rodrigo coughed and his eyes began to water and sting from the smoke, but he continued to push with all his strength.

Fortunately, the Crusaders had prepared for such tactics and had covered the tower with hides that had been soaked in water overnight. Men with buckets of water ran from behind the tower to throw on any shields or barriers that had been set alight. Horses that were struck down by arrows were cut loose and dragged to the side, while the wounded men were carried back to the safety of the battle lines. Time seemed to stand still as the towers inched ever closer to the walls, and the Crusaders bravely pressed forward against the endless barrage of arrows and stones from above. It felt like they had been pushing the tower for hours when Rodrigo glanced up and realized they had reached the base of the wall.

A triumphant cheer erupted from the battle lines as Duke Godfrey's siege tower finally ground to a halt in front of the northern wall of the city. The few horses that were left were freed and allowed to gallop to safety, and men began to climb onto the lower level of the tower.

The gigantic tower had six levels, each ten feet in height and large enough to accommodate about twenty men. Ladders were constructed inside the tower to ascend the various levels, and a drawbridge on the sixth level could be lowered to allow men to storm onto the top of the walls. The very top of the tower had a platform that was created as an overwatch, enabling archers to attack the enemy and defend those crossing the drawbridge. Rodrigo and Geoffrey left the tower and returned to Tancred and his men, helping to carry and drag the wounded with them along the way.

A few ladders had been constructed from the spare wood and building materials, but the Crusaders knew that the key to victory lay in the success of the siege towers, and nearly every piece of wood they had had gone into their construction. A steady stream of men from the Crusader battle lines was fed into the tower as they began their climb to the top. Once the levels were filled with men and the archers were in place, firing back at those on the walls, the drawbridge on top was opened. The heavy drawbridge crashed down directly onto the battlements, crushing a few of the Fatimid bowmen who had failed to move out of the way in time. With a furious battle cry, the Crusaders rushed across the drawbridge onto the walls and began to engage the enemy.

The battle for control of the city walls was fierce and violent. Both siege towers had successfully reached the walls, and the Crusaders were now launching their assault from both sides of the city. Men were continuously fed into the tower in a steady stream that went up the tower and poured out the top onto the walls, like water being pumped on a fire that would not be extinguished.

Rodrigo and Geoffrey watched with Tancred and his men from the battle lines in tense anticipation as the battle for control of the walls raged on. The Crusaders fought valiantly and were making steady progress as sections of the wall fell to their advance. If the

Crusaders were able to break into the guard towers on the walls and gain control, they would have access to the streets below. Rodrigo watched as the Crusaders closed in on one of the towers. He glanced over at Tancred, who had his sword drawn and appeared ready to give the order to his men to move to the siege tower.

The orders never came. Rodrigo watched as the Fatimid warriors rallied and began to push the Crusaders back from the tower, slowly and steadily, until it was no longer in danger. Many times throughout the day, just when it seemed like the Crusaders were gaining the upper hand and were beginning to overwhelm the Fatimid defenders, they were pushed back at the last moment, and the tide of battle would begin to swing the opposite way. A back-and-forth battle on both sides of the city raged all morning and well into the afternoon.

The Fatimids had put up a rugged defense, and both sides had accrued significant losses. Had the battle continued into the evening, the Crusaders might well have been victorious, but a critical weakness within the towers themselves prevented it. The soaked hides and leathers covering the towers had dried out in the hot afternoon sun, and the Fatimids had not let up on the tactic of shooting lighted arrows into the towers.

This became increasingly effective as the day wore on, and the flames became more and more difficult to put out. By late afternoon, the tower had caught on fire in several places, and smoke now filled the levels, causing the Crusaders within to gasp and choke as the smoke filled their lungs while they waited to ascend the levels. With the risk of the entire siege tower going up in flames, Duke Godfrey finally called for a withdrawal, and the trumpets blared, signaling the end of the assault.

The Crusaders used their horses to pull the smoking siege tower, now riddled with arrows, back to camp while listening to the taunts and cheering of the Fatimid defenders upon the walls. Losses on both sides were substantial, and the Crusader dead and wounded were brought back into the camps. Soon, many tents were overflowing with the wounded. Rodrigo and Geoffrey helped transport the wounded back to camp while priests were busy giving last rites to the dying.

✠

The starry twilight of the desert sky brought a tranquility that stood in stark contrast to the violent and bloody chaos that had reigned that afternoon. The mood in camp that evening was one of frustration at having come so close to victory only to have been denied over and over. Morale was still high, however, and the Crusaders worked diligently into the night repairing the fire- and smoke-damaged siege towers to prepare for another assault in the morning.

Rodrigo decided to take a walk by himself after the evening meal. He wanted to be alone with his thoughts and clear his head after a day filled with emotional highs and lows and transporting wounded and dying men. He walked along the edge of the camp, looking at the walls of Jerusalem, and could see the many torches and lamps being lit as dusk approached. In a part of the camp not far away, he could hear the pounding of hammers on wood and metal as the men worked to repair the tower. *The siege tower took a lot of damage today. If we are not able to break through by early afternoon tomorrow, it may not last the entire day. How many men did we lose today, and how many more will die tomorrow? And what will happen if we do break through? If Tancred falls in battle or we are unable to reach the Temple Mount, what will happen to the civilians?*

He walked until he reached the edge of camp and stopped and stared at the walls that stretched to the north, which quickly faded away into the darkness. The waning moon and cloud cover made it difficult to see into the distance. He could see that the walls north of the camp were lower, however, and the torches and lamps were scarce compared to those where the assault had taken place. Rodrigo's thoughts began to drift back in time to all the battles they had fought over the years, all the way back to the beginning. His eyes widened as a strategy suddenly came to him, one that could greatly increase their chances of taking the walls on their next assault.

While his first inclination was to bring the strategy to the leaders, he hesitated for a moment as a myriad of mixed thoughts and emotions flooded his mind. He felt excited at the prospect of using a new strategy to take the walls after having spent an entire day frustratedly watching men lose their lives. However, the thought of what had happened when he and Geoffrey brought a strategy to the leaders at Ma'arra caused him to hesitate. The painful memories of the bloody massacre that had occurred because of those actions, and the terrible feelings of guilt afterward, gave him pause.

He began to pace back and forth. *This strategy may save the lives of many of our men and allow us into the city, but at what cost? How many more innocent lives will be put at risk if it works? No, it is better for me to remain silent and allow God's will to determine what happens tomorrow.*

He stopped pacing and looked to the heavens in silent prayer. *Lord God, please help me to . . .*

As he looked up, the silhouette of the Mount of Olives against the darkening sky caught his attention and diverted his thoughts. *What will happen if Count Raymond is able to break through into the city tomorrow, and we do not? Peter the Hermit and his horde will slaughter the civilians as they move through the city and will begin to search for the relics once they reach the Temple Mount. No! I must do everything in my power to prevent that from happening.* Rodrigo set his jaw with determination as he began his march back through camp.

41

REVISITING AN OLD STRATEGY

R odrigo and Geoffrey entered the tent and saw Tancred sitting at a table along with a few of his men, who stopped their conversation when the two approached.

"Thank you for seeing us, my lord," said Rodrigo.

"Have a seat," Tancred replied. "If you are concerned about Count Raymond missing your presence in his camp, he has not even bothered to send inquiry about the summons. No doubt he is too preoccupied with his siege tower and Little Peter's counsel to care," he said sarcastically as Rodrigo and Geoffrey sat down at the table.

"Thank you for letting us know, my lord, but that is not the reason for our visit," Rodrigo replied. "We came to talk to you about an idea for a strategy that may greatly increase our chances of taking the city walls tomorrow. It is one that has worked in the past, and I believe it could work again now."

"An idea for a strategy?" asked Tancred with raised eyebrows. His men at the table looked on with interest. "Please continue. We would be happy to hear about anything that may increase our chances of taking the city tomorrow."

Tancred and the others sat quietly as Rodrigo began to recount the strategy that had allowed them to win Count Raymond's tournament. Tancred nodded slowly. "A sound strategy then, but how do you propose that we hide a sixty-foot-tall siege tower inside a tent?" he asked. A low rumble of laughter erupted from some of the men seated near him.

"Not necessarily in a tent, my lord, but through deception and misdirection," Rodrigo replied.

"And how would that be accomplished?" asked Tancred as the laughter died down.

"There is a waning moon and cloud cover tonight, so it will be dark—too dark to see beyond the camps from the walls of the city," Rodrigo continued. "There is an area of the city, farther north of camp, where the wall becomes lower and is less well defended. If we can move the tower to that section of the city tonight without the Fatimids knowing, then we will have a much better chance of successfully assaulting the wall tomorrow morning while they work to adjust their defenses."

"Too dark to see, yes, but the Fatimids have ears, do they not?" asked Tancred, drawing a bit more laughter from those around him. "How do you propose to move such a massive object in silence?"

"With misdirection, my lord. We can launch an assault of the wall tonight with whatever ladders we have left. The attack will last just long enough for us to move the siege tower into its new position. We could also increase the deception by having woodworkers hammer on wood and steel in the camp during the night to make the Fatimids believe that is where the tower is being repaired," said Rodrigo. "No strategy is infallible, my lord, but just as it worked years ago in Toulouse, I believe it can work again and may just offer us the advantage that we so badly need."

Tancred sat silently for a moment with his elbows on the table and his hands folded together, supporting his chin. At last, he spoke. "It sounds like a viable strategy to me, but I do not know if Duke Godfrey will feel the same way. He will do what he wishes with his siege tower. However, I will arrange a meeting this evening and request that you speak to him on my behalf. Return to your quarters, and you will be summoned if he accepts the request."

✠

Later that evening, Rodrigo and Geoffrey were summoned to Duke Godfrey's tent and waited outside to see him.

"What is taking so long? We are wasting valuable time," Rodrigo muttered to Geoffrey as he shifted anxiously. *If this strategy is to work, then there is little time to waste!*

"Patience, brother," said Geoffrey. "All you can do is present your plan, and the rest is up to him."

"Duke Godfrey will see you now," said the guard, appearing at last.

Rodrigo and Geoffrey were escorted into the large tent. It was well lit with lamps, and several people were standing about a large table with wine and food. The tent was much larger than Tancred's and better furnished, but not nearly as comfortable as Count Raymond's or opulent as Bishop Adhemar's. A man at the head of the table addressed them as they entered. "Sir Rodrigo and . . . Sir Geoffrey . . . come forward," he commanded. "What word do you bring on behalf of Tancred?"

"Thank you for receiving us, Duke Godfrey," Rodrigo said as they approached. He opened his mouth to speak when he was suddenly interrupted by one of the men in the tent.

"Sir Rodrigo and Sir Geoffrey!" the man shouted as he stepped forward. A snarl of contempt masked his face, and his voice was filled with condescension. Walking to the table and standing beside Duke Godfrey was Baron Gaston from the siege at Ma'arra. "The horse thieves and the deserters!" he said loudly, so that everyone in the tent could hear.

"You know these men?" asked Godfrey with raised eyebrows.

"I do," Gaston said as he stared at Rodrigo and Geoffrey. His lips curled into a sneer as he explained. "They stole horses from my camp in Ma'arra and fled to Antioch. Such cowardly actions amount to thievery and desertion, for which they have yet to answer." His sneer twisted into a contemptuous grin as all eyes turned to Rodrigo and Geoffrey and whispering could be heard among the men.

The unexpected interruption caught Rodrigo completely off

guard, and he stood dumbfounded for a moment, not knowing how to respond. He could see Gaston arrogantly staring at him from Duke Godfrey's side with a smirk of satisfaction. Rodrigo's initial shock subsided, and his fists began to tighten at the memory of Gaston's incompetent leadership and the horrors at Ma'arra. He finally found his tongue as he returned Gaston's stare and angrily growled his response. "*You* would accuse *us* . . ." he began, pointing his finger at Gaston.

Without warning, Geoffrey stepped in front of Rodrigo and cut him off as he began to speak. "It is true, my lord, what Baron Gaston has said!" Geoffrey loudly proclaimed to all in the tent. Rodrigo lowered his hand and stayed silent as Geoffrey continued.

"We took some horses that did not belong to us and left camp at Ma'arra without permission," he calmly admitted to all those in the tent. His confident and unabashed admission had captured the group's attention, and the whispering ceased as they began to listen.

"We did it for reasons we felt were just, although Gaston may not agree," Geoffrey continued. "It is not true, however, that we have yet to answer for our actions. We confessed our deeds immediately to Count Raymond upon arrival in Antioch, and he listened to our reasons and gave us our punishment as he thought fit. However, despite all of this, we remain in good standing and retain his trust and confidence, as well as Lord Tancred's—else why would be here this night regarding important matters on his behalf?" Geoffrey's calm and confident demeanor shifted the focus in the room from a near heated exchange between Rodrigo and Gaston to one where everyone was listening to what he had to say.

"Go on," said Godfrey. The rest remained silent.

"I tell all of this to you, my lord, truthfully and without excuses, my right hand before God," Geoffrey stated, raising his right hand. "I would only ask that Gaston do the same."

"What do you mean?" asked Godfrey as all eyes in the room shifted to Gaston.

"Baron Gaston," Geoffrey said with a raised voice. "Did you, or did you not, use the plan that Rodrigo and I presented to you that allowed you to take the city of Ma'arra?" He stared at Gaston. "I ask that you speak truthfully, before all of us, with your right hand to God as I have done."

The tent went silent as everyone listened and waited for Gaston to answer. His arrogant smirk had faded into a frown of irritation as he stared at the ground.

"Well, Gaston?" asked Godfrey impatiently. "Let us have your answer and get on with it!"

"We did," he begrudgingly replied.

Duke Godfrey nodded with a smile of approval as he looked at Geoffrey and then around at the others in the tent. "Well then, let us sit, all of us, and we will hear what news they bring to us from Tancred," Godfrey said. Everyone in the tent sat down and listened as Rodrigo laid out the strategy before them.

"I like this plan, but if it is to work, then we must move on it quickly," Godfrey said after Rodrigo had finished. "Gaston, where are we with the repairs to the tower?"

"They are nearly complete, my lord," Gaston said.

"Is it possible to move the tower over the ground behind the camp to this section of the city wall?" Godfrey asked, pointing to an area on a map lying on the table.

"I believe it is, my lord," Gaston replied.

"What do the rest of you think of this plan?" Godfrey asked, raising his voice over the other men in the room, who had begun talking among themselves. "Speak up and make yourselves useful! Let's take a vote and decide, for if we are to act on this plan, we must do so quickly!"

Everyone in the room, including Gaston, voted unanimously to put the plan into action.

Duke Godfrey gave orders to his men to begin preparations before returning to Rodrigo and Geoffrey, who were still seated at the table. He stood over them as he spoke. "You may return to Tancred and inform him that we agree to this plan. If it is successful, then it is likely we shall be the first into Jerusalem ahead of Count Raymond! I am well aware of his ambitions regarding the city. If *we* are the first to breach the walls, however, then I shall have a more legitimate claim to be the ruler of Jerusalem!" he said with a broad smile, putting his hands on Rodrigo and Geoffrey's shoulders. "Rest assured, if that happens," he continued, leaning down between them and lowering his voice, "Tancred and the both of you will not be forgotten. Go now and tell him to prepare."

✠

That night, Rodrigo lay awake in his cot until the early morning, feeling conflicted as he thought about all that occurred and what lay ahead. He felt extremely grateful to Geoffrey for saving what could have been a disastrous meeting, but it was Duke Godfrey's final comments before leaving that had left him with feelings of unease. It seemed as though his efforts were once again helping to further the greed and ambitions of their leaders, and he began to question whether he had made the right decision.

Rodrigo shut his eyes and covered them with his hand. He tried to take solace knowing that he had made his decision in an effort to protect innocent lives and thwart the ambitions of an evil man. There was no doubt as to what would happen if Count Raymond's tower successfully breached the city defenses and theirs did not. However, if the strategy proved successful and Duke Godfrey broke through into the city, how could Rodrigo be certain that their plan with Tancred would even work and prevent another massacre? The truth was that there was no certainty, and he agonized over the thought of what might happen again due to his actions.

He suddenly felt a slight nudge at the side of his cot. He removed his hand and opened his eyes to see Geoffrey standing over him. "Tancred has just given the orders to prepare, brother. We must get ready," he said as he turned and walked back to his cot. Rodrigo slowly sat up and rubbed his eyes, then shook his head. *It is too late for regrets. I must push such thoughts from my mind.* Reaching under his cot, he grabbed his armor and his sword and began to prepare for what was to come.

42

THE THIRD ASSAULT

As dawn broke on the morning of July 14, 1099, the exhausted Fatimid guards atop the towers and walls of Jerusalem were roused from their brief slumber by the sounds of the Crusader siege tower, once again lumbering toward them to begin the day's assault. They were stunned, however, to see that the tower was no longer in front of them, but farther north, moving toward a section of the wall that was much lower and thus harder to defend. Cries and shouts of alarm filled the air along the city walls, and the Fatimids scrambled to shift their defenses to the north as the giant siege tower moved ever closer.

The strategy had been a success. The assault with ladders the previous night had distracted the Fatimid guards, who had failed to notice the movement of the tower from behind the camp toward the city walls farther to the north. The ease with which they were able to repel the assault that night also lulled them into a false sense of security, allowing them to drop their guard for a moment as most of them slept, exhausted from a full day and night of defending the walls against constant attacks. The blaring horns and the shouting of warriors startled many of the guards from their brief slumber, and they began to move quickly in an adrenaline-fueled panic as they raced to defend the northern wall.

It was not long before both siege towers had reached the walls, and the third assault on Jerusalem was about to begin. Duke Godfrey's tower was now higher than the wall being defended, which gave the archers on top of the tower a better vantage point as they shot down at the Fatimid warriors. The Crusaders charging onto the wall also had an advantage, as the bridge was angled slightly downward, allowing them momentum as they rushed out of the tower.

Rodrigo and Geoffrey stood at the front of the battle lines with Tancred and his men, watching in tense silence and waiting as the men on the ground began to enter the bottom of the siege tower. The Fatimids continued to defend with lighted arrows, but with much less volume than the previous day, as they were still scrambling to shift their defenses. A great cheer erupted from the Crusaders as the drawbridge fell and the first Crusaders rushed out of the siege tower to engage the Fatimid warriors on the walls.

Rodrigo glanced at Tancred at the front of the line. He stood out from the rest of his soldiers because of his height and his blue tunic with a red cross. His also carried a blue shield with a white griffon. Tancred would be leading the charge into battle, and Rodrigo knew that for their plan to work, he would need to make sure that Tancred survived the assault. Rodrigo gripped his shield and sword tightly. *If he falls, then everything I tried to do will have been in vain.*

The fierce and bloody fighting continued as the morning hours passed and the sun grew higher in the sky. The heat of the day also began to rise, and beads of sweat ran down Rodrigo's face as they watched the back-and-forth battle for control of the walls. All of Tancred's men waited in tense anticipation for the moment he would give the orders to charge into the tower. The numbers of dead and wounded were beginning to mount as men were continually being brought back into camp.

The battle raged on as the sun reached its zenith and then began its descent in the west. The Crusaders were losing many men, but they had twice as many as the Fatimid defenders, and the fresh troops that were constantly fed into the towers began to finally shift the tide against the exhausted Fatimid warriors. The order to enter the tower could come at any time as Rodrigo watched and waited.

Just like the previous day, however, the afternoon sun beat down relentlessly, drying out the hides and leathers that protected the towers. Soon the flames from the lighted arrows began to take hold and needed to be extinguished, lest the fire consume the tower and those inside.

As Rodrigo watched, he began to hear raised voices of concern from the men around him, and someone in the ranks yelled, "Look!" Men were pointing to the south, where billows of black smoke began to appear above the city. A swiftly moving rider from Count Raymond's camp approached their lines. Word quickly spread that Count Raymond's siege tower had caught fire and was now burning out of control. The faces of the men on the ground around Rodrigo had fallen from hope and anticipation to fear and apprehension as the dire news spread throughout the ranks.

A giant plume of black smoke rose into the sky above the city, and smoke from the many small fires on Duke Godfrey's tower continued to grow as men frantically tried to put them out, but to no avail. Once again, it seemed as though the Crusaders would be standing on the cusp of victory, only to be denied. Hopelessness began to pervade the ranks, and they watched with consternation as their final chance to reclaim Jerusalem slowly slipped from their grasp.

A lone figure stepped forward to the front of the battle lines and turned to address the men behind him. "Brave knights and warriors, listen to me!" Tancred shouted. "Our time has come! Count Raymond's siege tower is finished, and ours will not last the day! We either take Jerusalem now, or we watch our final chance go up in flames! I would rather die fighting than leave Jerusalem in the hands of the Saracens! We have come too far to abandon our goal! Have faith and we shall not be denied! If you believe that God is with us, then prepare to follow me!" he yelled as he raised his sword to the cheering of his warriors. Rodrigo raised his sword and cheered along with the others, and he knew the time had come. A mixture of fear and excitement fueled his emotions. The fear was not for himself, however, but for what could happen if they made it into the city but Tancred did not survive. One of Tancred's warriors left the ranks and ran to the tower to order the soldiers to clear out and make way for their charge.

The warrior ran down to the tower and gave the order, and men began to climb out of the lower level. The word quickly spread up the tower as the men began climbing down the ladders and moving onto the ground. The fighting continued at the top of the tower as the black smoke began to creep into the interior levels from the areas outside that were on fire. Once the last of the men had cleared out of the bottom of the tower, Tancred let out a fearsome war cry and rushed forward, followed by Rodrigo and Geoffrey and all his men as they peeled away from the battle lines, yelling as they ran.

The entire army of Crusaders behind them erupted in shouting and cheering when they saw what was happening. The feelings of hopelessness and desperation were immediately dispelled, replaced with a renewed hope at the sight of the sudden charge. The Crusaders yelled fanatically and watched with wide eyes as Tancred, one of their fiercest and most respected leaders, led the final charge against the enemy. Ultimate victory or death and defeat hung in the balance at that moment.

The Crusaders standing at the base of the tower cheered as they held their shields aloft to protect themselves and those coming from the rain of arrows. Tancred was the first into the base of the tower, with Rodrigo and Geoffrey close by his side. Rodrigo coughed as they began to ascend the ladders through clouds of smoke that burned his lungs and stung his eyes. The drawbridge at the top of the tower had been closed to prevent the Fatimids from entering as they reached the smoke-filled top level.

The Fatimids had watched the scene unfold from above in bewilderment as the warrior in blue led hundreds of Crusaders charging across the ground and into the tower, backed by the raucous cheering of those behind them. They stood with fearful anticipation, staring at the closed drawbridge with smoke seeping from the cracks, for what lay in wait behind it. Nearly blinded by smoke and holding his breath, Tancred slashed the ropes holding the drawbridge shut with his sword, causing it to fall with a heavy thud onto the battlements.

The Fatimids watched as the drawbridge fell, and the blue warrior suddenly burst out of the smoke with a ferocious battle cry, like a demon conjured from a sorcerer's spell. He was running toward them, followed by others who let out terrifying shouts and had a look of madness in their eyes. Rodrigo followed Tancred as they leaped off the drawbridge and onto the walkway, striking down at the Fatimid defenders.

The Crusaders had the initial advantage coming off the drawbridge, as they were attacking from above, and Rodrigo caught a Fatimid warrior squarely in the chest with his boot as he leaped, knocking him backward into those behind him. Geoffrey followed closely behind, and without losing their momentum, they began hacking and slashing with their swords, cutting down the Fatimid warriors as they struggled to regain their balance.

Other Crusaders were pouring out of the smoke-filled siege tower and onto the walkway around them. Tancred fought like a cornered lion, almost reckless in his attack, as he swung his sword in a sweeping, downward arc, striking at anyone who stood in front of him. Rodrigo and Geoffrey protected Tancred's flanks with their shields as he carved a path toward the guard tower and struck down any defenders who moved in from the sides to try to stop him. Rodrigo moved as quickly as he could to keep up with Tancred, deflecting constant spear thrusts and saber slashes as they moved.

The narrow walkway was only about eight feet wide and was nearly impassable when crowded, a key tactic that had allowed the Fatimids to keep the Crusaders from advancing too far along the wall. So strong was Tancred's charge, however, that the tactic failed to halt his relentless drive toward the tower. In order to make room for their advance, Rodrigo began using his shield to push the Fatimid warriors over the sides of the walkway whenever he could. Yelling on both sides filled Rodrigo's ears as he moved forward, stepping over the bodies of the dead and wounded defenders that Tancred left in his path. The Crusaders moving behind them finished off the wounded as they kept pressing ever forward.

At last, they reached the tower door, having killed all the Fatimid defenders that stood in their way. Moving to the side, Tancred called forward two of his men, who began smashing the locked door with heavy axe blows. Tancred kicked open the splintered door and rushed inside, followed quickly by Rodrigo and Geoffrey.

Behind them, Crusaders continued to flood onto the wall and had nearly gained access to the tower on the opposite side as well. Although the siege tower had caught fire in several places, the flames had not yet reached the inside, and the Crusaders continued to use it as more and more moved onto the wall. The ladders were also being utilized, and a steady stream of Crusaders climbed unopposed onto different sections of the wall. The tide of battle had fully turned in favor of the Crusaders. The Fatimid warriors had put up a valiant defense, but now fatigued and demoralized by Tancred's ferocious assault, they began to give up more and more ground to the Crusaders, who continued to push them back down through the lower levels of the guard tower.

When Tancred and his men had killed all the defenders inside the tower, they at last had access to the streets below. The door of the tower burst open, and Tancred rushed out with Rodrigo and Geoffrey right behind him. He was the first Crusader to finally step foot inside Jerusalem. Fatimid warriors were waiting for them, but the city streets were broad, and they were unable to encircle the Crusaders as Tancred's men continued to pour out of the tower and engage the defenders in open combat.

Rodrigo stayed by Tancred's side and fought the Fatimid warriors as they came. He parried the saber thrust of the first warrior while blocking the slash of another with his shield. Striking back with his sword, he caught the first warrior's hand with his blade, severing his fingers and causing him to drop his weapon as he yelled in pain. The second warrior came at him again, this time striking low at Rodrigo's legs. Again, Rodrigo blocked his slash by lowering his shield and simultaneously swung over the top with his sword, striking the second warrior in the neck. The blow bit deeply, killing him instantly as he dropped to his knees, blood spraying from the fatal wound. The Fatimids continued to fight bravely in the streets, but their attacks were lessening, and some began to lose heart and flee. Rodrigo could clearly see fear and distress in the faces of the Fatimid warriors as they fought. *They must sense the end is near. If the gates are opened, the city will fall!*

Saber slashes whistled by his head and recoiled off his shield as Rodrigo continued to fight, always keeping Tancred in the corner of his eye. Soon the Fatimid warriors in the streets began to thin, and Rodrigo, Geoffrey, and Tancred rested for a moment from the battle as Tancred's men held the arriving Fatimid warriors at bay.

The muscles in Rodrigo's arms were burning, and the clothes beneath his armor were drenched with sweat. He was breathing heavily and could feel the weight of the mail armor on his chest as he and Geoffrey took a moment to regroup with Tancred. "We must get to the gate!" Tancred said between breaths. "There will be more coming! This way, follow me!" he yelled to all his men around him.

Leading the charge once again, Tancred ran down the street with Rodrigo, Geoffrey, and all his men following him. When they reached the gate on the northern wall of Jerusalem, a bloody skirmish ensued, but the Fatimid warriors were quickly overcome by the Crusaders who were already inside the city. Rodrigo knew that soon the gates would be opened and thousands of Crusaders would swarm into Jerusalem.

His strategy had been successful, and he was relieved that he, Tancred, and Geoffrey had survived the assault. The feelings of relief were short-lived, however, and began to change to apprehension as the Crusaders worked to open the gates. The critical second part of Rodrigo's plan was about to begin, and they would need to move quickly to secure the Temple Mount. He knew the Crusaders outside would show no mercy to the inhabitants of the city. He watched as the gates swung wide and the Crusaders entered Jerusalem, shouting at the top of their lungs, having reached their goal at last. It was clear that the yelling, frenzied mob was intoxicated with euphoria and consumed by a ravenous hunger for the blood of the city's inhabitants, having drunk from the poisonous cup of Peter the Hermit.

Rodrigo's heart sank at the all too familiar scene as the Crusaders flooded into the city. A desperate feeling began to grow inside him, and he knew the indiscriminate slaughter of tens of thousands of innocent men, women, and children, both Jews and Saracens, was about to begin.

43

SORROW AT AL-AQSA

T he last light of day surrendered to dusk as the sun sank down and died upon the jagged peaks of the western horizon. Its final rays cast a lurid glow upon a blood-red sky that mirrored the streets of Jerusalem below. Screams of terror, the wailing of the dying, and unheeded cries for mercy echoed throughout the city. The horrific massacre would continue well into the evening hours until the very streets ran red with the blood of innocent civilians.

After the gates had been opened and Tancred had time to gather his men, he and Rodrigo and Geoffrey, along with two hundred of his men, began to make their way through the city toward the Temple Mount. Duke Godfrey and the other leaders had allowed their men to rush into the city uncontrolled, and Rodrigo could hear and see the looting and pillaging taking place all around him as they moved through the city streets.

Rodrigo clenched his teeth in anguish and frustration as they ran by groups of marauding Crusaders who were smashing open the doors of houses and buildings and rushing inside. The scenes of the slaughter at Antioch and Ma'arra flooded back into his memory, and with them came the terrible feelings of guilt as the screams of the civilians rang out all around him. *Where is the Temple Mount? We must be getting close.*

They encountered a few small units of Fatimid warriors along the way, who briefly held up their advance before quickly falling to Tancred's men. At last, they came to a large wall with a gated entrance within the city itself. Rodrigo's heart leaped as they approached the gate. "We are here! This is the Temple Mount!" The gates were open and undefended, and Tancred, Rodrigo, and Geoffrey went inside, followed by Tancred's men.

They walked into a large inner courtyard, and Rodrigo could see hundreds of civilians who had already fled to the area in the wake of the slaughter. They were now seeking refuge inside two large buildings within the Temple Mount. The huge inner court was broad and flat and completely made of stone, and in front of them was the Islamic shrine known as the Dome of the Rock. The golden dome atop the building was unmistakable and could be seen for miles outside the city. Several hundred feet to the southwest, many people were fleeing to a large building with huge stone archways lining its front.

"There! That must be the al-Aqsa Mosque," Rodrigo said as they stopped and looked around the open court. The throngs of people at the Temple Mount began to panic at the sight of the newly arrived Crusaders and were moving frantically as they crowded the entrances to the two buildings, trying to get inside.

Tancred was looking around, studying their surroundings, when Rodrigo turned to him. "The civilians here are clearly seeking refuge, my lord. We must protect them." He could feel his heart beating rapidly as he waited for Tancred's reply. *Geoffrey and I have done everything we can to keep him alive up to this point. Surely now he will keep his word.*

"Yes, it appears that way," Tancred replied. "I do not see any Fatimid warriors here, only civilians." He continued to scan the area. "Wait for me here. I will speak to my men." Rodrigo and Geoffrey stood by and waited while Tancred gathered and gave orders to his men. He gave them instructions to guard the entrance and interior of the Temple Mount, allowing any civilians to come inside but to keep anyone else out, including other Crusaders. Rodrigo listened as Tancred also gave orders to leave the Temple Mount as a place of refuge and not to harm the civilians or loot and plunder any of the buildings inside.

Rodrigo hung his head and breathed a long sigh of relief. He felt sickened by what he knew was taking place outside the walls of the Temple Mount, but allowed himself some comfort in knowing that the inhabitants now had a place of refuge as he watched more civilians arrive through the gates. After giving his orders to his men, Tancred returned to Rodrigo and Geoffrey.

"Thank you, my lord, for honoring our agreement," Rodrigo said humbly as Tancred approached. "Now we may begin our search for any holy relics that may be kept inside the mosque."

The al-Aqsa Mosque was a massive structure with towering archways that lined the front of the building. The beautiful and ornate archways were nearly forty feet in height, with tall windows in the walls above them that had intricately carved wooden coverings. On top of the building was a stone terrace, and in the middle of the roof was a dome with the symbol of the crescent moon above it. Beneath the stone arches in front of the mosque was a long, covered walkway that stretched along the length of the building. Torches and lamps on the walls illuminated the walkway, and civilians continued to crowd into two massive wooden doors that were open at the front of the building.

As they neared the stone archways and the entrance to the mosque, Rodrigo turned to Tancred. "Before we begin our search, my lord, let me speak to the people at the entrance and inside the building to let them know that they are safe, and we are not going to harm them. Perhaps I can find someone inside that can help us in our search for the relics."

"That sounds like a good way to proceed," Tancred replied. "We will wait for you here while you speak to them." Rodrigo began walking toward the entrance to the mosque.

"Wait a moment! I will go with you," Geoffrey said as he left Tancred to join Rodrigo.

The two began to walk toward the entrance, when suddenly a

voice cried out in the Temple court behind them. "Lord Tancred! Lord Tancred!" someone yelled in the distance. Turning to see who it was, Rodrigo could see a soldier running toward them from the entrance of the Temple Mount. As the soldier drew closer, Rodrigo could see a look of desperation in the man's face, and the feelings of relief and comfort he had felt moments ago began to disappear.

The soldier was out of breath when he stopped in front of Tancred. "Slow down and catch your breath," Tancred told the soldier, whose chest was heaving in near exhaustion. "Then tell us what news you bring." Rodrigo and Geoffrey walked closer and stood by, listening intently as they waited to hear what the soldier had to say.

The soldier was still breathing heavily when he stood up straight and began to speak. "My lord, Count Raymond has requested immediate assistance from any available Crusader leaders," he said between breaths. "He is currently battling the personal guard of al-Dawla just south of here. Al-Dawla and his men have managed to fortify several buildings and are putting up fierce resistance. Other lords have already released most of their men inside the city. You are the only one I have found who still has his men with him and under control."

Tancred looked at Rodrigo and Geoffrey for a moment as he thought about what to do. "I must go," he said at last.

Rodrigo looked back at Tancred in silence as he felt his heart sinking, then let his gaze fall to the ground. The feelings of relief had now given way to helplessness, and he knew there was nothing he could do. The fateful words of Marcellinus echoed in his mind: *Trust in God, not in man*. He stared at the ground in bitter realization.

"My lord," said Geoffrey, stepping forward, "surely Duke Godfrey and the other nobles will be able to gather enough men to assist Count Raymond. What about our mission here, and the civilians you agreed to protect?" He motioned to the mosque ahead of them and the people crowding into the entrance.

Tancred looked at the mosque, then back out toward the city. "You will have to continue your mission without me," he said flatly. "I will leave some of my men here to guard the gates, and I will return when I am able. Count Raymond is an important leader in our army, and I simply cannot ignore his request for assistance in his time of need. The city will not be ours until al-Dawla is killed or captured. Forgive me, but I must leave you now." Tancred abruptly turned away from Rodrigo and Geoffrey and began to hurry back toward the gates of the Temple Mount, followed by the soldier.

Geoffrey turned to Rodrigo for an answer, but was met with stoic silence, and together they watched Tancred hurry away, calling most of his men to follow him as he left. Rodrigo knew that Tancred had no choice and was simply following the orders of his superior as any good soldier would do. With a heavy heart, Rodrigo knew that it was his own decisions that had led them to this moment, and he would have to bear the pain and anguish of the consequences of those decisions. A few of Tancred's men lingered momentarily at the gates after he left, then quickly departed to follow him as Rodrigo watched and shook his head. *I knew that Tancred's men would not stand by idly and guard this place while the rest leave to engage in battle.*

"We are on own now, brother. Other soldiers will soon be coming, and this place is no longer safe for the civilians," Rodrigo said with a worried frown. "We must get all the civilians that are here inside these two buildings and tell them to bar the doors and allow no one else inside. Let's start with those at the Dome of the Rock, and then we will return to the mosque." They began hurrying toward the building.

Just as they were approaching the crowd at the entrance to the Dome of the Rock, they saw several soldiers enter the Temple Mount through the gates not far away. The soldiers were carrying heavy bags of loot, which they set upon the ground as they stopped and began to look around the temple court. "Quickly, get inside!" Rodrigo yelled in Arabic to all those at the entrance. Few heeded his commands, however, and many were watching as a small group of civilians arrived and came through the gate where the soldiers were standing.

The soldiers immediately began to rip the belongings out of the hands of the civilians, and one of the soldiers violently struck a man who tried to protest, causing him to fall to the ground. Another soldier at the front of the group appeared to be giving orders, and the others grabbed the rest of the civilians, women and children among them, and threw them on the ground along with the man.

The crowd outside the Dome of the Rock went silent for a moment as they watched and waited to see what would happen next. Rodrigo's eyes went wide as the soldiers drew their weapons and stood above the civilians, who begged for mercy. The brutal murder he had witnessed Antioch was suddenly being replayed before him. "Stop! These people are innocent civilians!" he cried out in desperation.

His cries fell on deaf ears. The soldiers' weapons rose and fell as they butchered the civilians, while those still outside the Dome of the Rock screamed in terror as they watched the gruesome spectacle. Rodrigo's heart was racing, and he knew if the civilians did not get inside quickly and barricade the entrance, they would soon meet the same fate.

"Get inside, now!" Rodrigo yelled to those outside the Dome of the Rock. "Barricade the doors and let no one inside!" *If they can hold out until Tancred returns, they may still have a chance.* Panic and confusion began to take hold outside the building as many dropped their belongings and pushed and shoved to get inside the packed entrance.

Rodrigo and Geoffrey could see more Crusaders coming in through the gates, which only added to the panic outside the building. Many of the Crusaders were beginning to move toward them, and Rodrigo knew that time was running out. "We must get back to the mosque and get everyone inside before it is too late!" he yelled to Geoffrey as they turned and ran back toward al-Aqsa.

"Get inside! Get inside the building!" Rodrigo yelled to those still outside as they reached the crowd outside the mosque and began to wave everyone inside. "Leave your belongings! Soldiers are coming!" Panic had set in as the civilians rushed into the crowded building. Screams of terror could be heard a short distance away as the Crusaders reached the Dome of the Rock.

"We need to shut and barricade the doors!" Rodrigo yelled to some of the men by the entrance who were helping to move everyone inside. A large group of Crusaders were now moving across the open court and were closing in on them as the last of the civilians entered.

Rodrigo and Geoffrey followed them in, and they began to push the large doors shut when a familiar voice called out to them and sent a chill down Rodrigo's spine. "Rodrigo! Geoffrey!" Rodrigo quickly glanced back out the doors and saw Richard coming toward them, followed by several men. Just behind Richard, riding a pale horse, was Peter the Hermit.

"Quickly!" Rodrigo shouted as he and Geoffrey, along with several civilians, pushed the heavy doors closed. The sound of hurried footsteps could be heard on the walkway in front of them. "Find something to barricade the doors!" Rodrigo yelled to those inside as he, Geoffrey, and several men held them shut. Suddenly, the doors began to crack open by the force of many hands pushing from the outside. Rodrigo put his shoulder into the door and pushed as hard as he could.

He heard Richard's voice outside, commanding his men. "Open the door!"

The civilians inside were struggling to drag some heavy furniture to the front of the mosque to barricade the door, but it was too late. Rodrigo could feel his feet sliding backward on the smooth stone floor as he and the others strained with all their might to keep the doors closed. The doors flew open, sending both Rodrigo and Geoffrey reeling backward into the crowd of people inside the mosque. Recovering their balance and drawing their swords as they stepped forward, they could see Richard standing outside the doorway, surrounded by dozens of men. Just beyond them, Peter the Hermit watched as he looked down from his mount. "Bring them outside!" Peter commanded.

Richard stood and stared from the entrance as his men rushed into the mosque around him and surrounded Rodrigo and Geoffrey. The hundreds of onlookers inside the mosque watched and trembled with fear at the sight of the Crusaders with their swords and axes, bloodstained tunics, and grim, hollow expressions. "Drop your swords," Richard commanded. "You cannot win."

Rodrigo's eyes narrowed and he clenched his teeth as he quickly looked around and weighed his options. If they choose to fight, they might be able to hold out for a time and kill some of Richard's men, but eventually they would fall, and all would be lost. In that moment, Rodrigo realized that the holy relics, and even his own life, meant nothing to him. All that mattered were the lives of his friend and the hundreds of innocent civilians who had sought refuge in the mosque. "I will lay down my sword, and you may do with me as you wish! I only ask that you allow Geoffrey to go free and spare the lives of the civilians here inside the mosque," he said aloud, keeping a firm grip on the hilt of his sword.

Richard sneered in contempt at Rodrigo's offer as he looked around the interior. "You would lay down your life . . . for them?" he asked, pointing his sword at the men and women behind them in the mosque.

"I will lay down my sword as well!" yelled Geoffrey. "Just spare the civilians!"

"There will be no bargain!" Peter the Hermit shouted from outside. "Bring them to me, now!"

Steel flashed inside the mosque as Peter the Hermit's men fell upon Rodrigo and Geoffrey from all sides. Rodrigo swung his sword with both hands, slicing through the neck of the first attacker and out the other side into the arm of the next. The nearly decapitated man was dead before he hit the ground. Rodrigo stepped out the way and used his foot to drive the next attacker back. He swung his sword again, lopping off another man's forearm as he came at him with an axe. Rodrigo and Geoffrey fought back to back, holding the attackers at bay for a few moments as they fought bravely for their lives and the lives of the civilians, but Richard's men were too many.

One of the wounded soldiers on the floor managed to grab one of Rodrigo's legs, restricting his movement. Rodrigo pulled his leg free of the man's grasp as two others grabbed his arms. Rodrigo twisted and struggled to break free, but it was no use, and he was dragged to the ground as the soldiers began to pummel him into submission with their fists and the heels of their boots. Geoffrey had also succumbed to the attackers and was similarly beaten and subdued.

"Enough!" Richard commanded. "Take them outside."

Rodrigo and Geoffrey were roughly hauled up from the floor by their arms and dragged outside. The light of dusk was now gone, and the torches and lamps illuminated the area outside the mosque as Rodrigo and Geoffrey were dropped in front of Peter the Hermit, who looked down at them from his steed. "Bind their hands," he commanded. The men around them forced their arms behind their backs and bound them with cords, leaving them facedown. Rodrigo strained to look up and watched as some of the men helped Peter the Hermit off his mount.

Once they were on the ground, Peter walked past them into the entrance of the mosque before turning to speak to his men outside. "'Before him, all will be gathered, and he will separate them, one from another, as a shepherd separates the sheep from the goats,'" he began, as if preaching a sermon to his men. "'He will set the sheep on his right, and the goats on the left. Those on the right shall inherit God's kingdom, while those on the left shall be cast into the eternal fire.' These men are goats and have aligned themselves with these filthy Saracens and those rejected by God!" Peter yelled, pointing with his left hand down at Rodrigo and Geoffrey. Looking around at his men, he continued. "All of you are at God's right hand, and together we shall inherit God's kingdom. Now, let us go forth and cleanse this unholy place of the evil that resides within and continue the Pope's holy mission."

"Those people are innocent, you murderous coward!" Rodrigo yelled, lying on his side. "You—" His words were cut short as one of the soldiers' boots connected with his jaw. Rodrigo winced as pain shot down his jaw and into his neck. He listened to the footsteps of the men going inside and the screams of terror that began to emanate from within. He felt hands grab his arms and force him up to his knees. Blood dripped from the corner of his mouth and from a dozen wounds on his body. He looked over at Geoffrey, who was also forced up to his knees. The doors to the mosque snapped shut, muting the terrible sounds coming from inside. In front of the doors stood Richard, who looked down at them with disdain.

"I warned you to abandon this quest, Rodrigo. But you would

not listen," Richard said. "You stubbornly persisted, and now look where it has gotten you. I told you, the stubborn man will someday be crushed and never recover."

"What do you want us to do with them?" asked the soldier standing beside Geoffrey.

Richard stared at Rodrigo and Geoffrey with cold, dead eyes. "Take them away from here and kill them. Leave their bodies in the streets, and then return to guard these doors and let no one inside. After we finish cleansing this place of the Saracen filth, Father Peter and I have important work to do and will not wish to be disturbed." He opened the door to enter the mosque.

"Richard, let us go! You have what you came for!" Geoffrey shouted. "You were once our brother!"

Richard paused for a moment at the door and turned to look back. "Sir Geoffrey of Charney and Sir Rodrigo of Castile . . . you were *never* my brothers," he said as he entered the mosque and shut the door behind him.

"Get up!" one of the soldiers ordered as he hauled Rodrigo up by his arm. The other removed a torch from the wall and then walked back to Geoffrey and pulled him up to his feet.

The four marched down the walkway as the flickering torchlight cast long shadows in the arches of the corridor. When they reached the end, they turned and walked across the open court toward the gates of the Temple Mount. Rodrigo could see light coming from the wide-open doors of the Dome of the Rock as they walked past, and the bodies of civilians strewn about the ground in front of the entrance.

They exited the gates of the Temple Mount and walked into the streets. Rodrigo felt the soldier's boot on the back of his legs, once again forcing him to his knees. The other did the same to Geoffrey. The area was dark, save for the light of the torch. "Let's kill them here. I do not want to miss out on the looting of these buildings," said the soldier holding Geoffrey. Placing the torch on the ground, he unsheathed a dagger and held it to Geoffrey's neck as he stood behind him and pulled back on his hair. "Do not bother begging for your life," he scoffed. "It will not do you any good."

"I will not beg for my life," Geoffrey growled in anger. "You piece of . . ." His voice was cut short as the sharp dagger slid across his throat, blood gushing from the wound as he fell forward, facedown onto the ground.

"No!" Rodrigo yelled, staring helplessly as he watched Geoffrey fall to the ground. Pain and sorrow gripped him as he squeezed his eyes shut, lowering his head as the terrible image seared into his brain. The soldier standing behind Rodrigo tightened his grip on his hair and jerked his head back up as he held the edge of his sword to his neck. Rodrigo's eyes cracked open as he saw Geoffrey's life slowly spilling out into a widening pool on the ground around him. Sorrow, guilt, and anger washed over him as a myriad of fleeting memories began to flash through his mind, from the death of his father until the present moment.

The soldier laughed as he held the bloody dagger and looked down at Geoffrey. "You were saying?" he said in a mocking tone. Turning to the other, he spoke again. "Well, what are you waiting for? Get on with it!"

Rodrigo closed his eyes and turned his face to the heavens. He breathed out a long sigh, releasing all the negative thoughts and emotions from within. He freely exposed his neck as he looked up and said a final, silent prayer. *Please forgive me, Lord. Forgive my mistakes and my failures, which have cost so many lives and allowed evil men to prevail. Please, Lord God, forgive me and receive me into your kingdom.*

"Don't have the stomach for it, eh?" said the soldier who was standing over Geoffrey. "Well, move out of the way, then. I will do it." He walked over and stood in front of Rodrigo, placing the dagger on his neck. "Just hold him still."

Rodrigo felt the dagger pressing against his neck and the beginning of the pull as a spray of blood covered his face. The blood, however, was not his own. Rodrigo opened his eyes in shock to see the soldier in front of him drop the dagger and stagger backward, holding his neck as blood poured between his fingers. Sinking down to the ground, the man coughed and squirmed as he tried to breathe, gagging on his own blood. Rodrigo then felt tugging on the cords that bound his hands. He was being cut free.

Though stunned by the unexpected turn of events, Rodrigo was beyond caring for his own life, and as soon as his hands were cut free, he got up and walked over to Geoffrey's still body and knelt beside him, turning him over and holding his head in his hands. No breath escaped Geoffrey's lips, and his lifeless eyes stared unblinking into the night sky. Rodrigo's eyes welled up with tears as he shut them tightly.

"You are Sir Rodrigo of Castile?" the soldier asked.

Rodrigo opened his eyes but said nothing. He looked down and placed his hand over Geoffrey's eyes and closed them. "I am," he answered at last, continuing to hold Geoffrey's head without looking at the man.

"You do not know me, but you once saved my life. While crossing the Taurus Mountains, I lost my footing and went over the side of a cliff. I nearly died that day, but you risked your life to save me. I could not take the life of a man who saved my own. My debt has been repaid," he said, sheathing his sword. "You are free to go. I will not stand in your way." The man then turned and walked away into the darkness, leaving Rodrigo kneeling beside Geoffrey in the torchlight, which flickered as it lay on the ground.

"I know now, brother, what I must do," Rodrigo said as he gently laid Geoffrey's head upon the ground. As he withdrew his hand from Geoffrey's neck, his finger caught and pulled the chain of Geoffrey's necklace, exposing the golden cross, which glinted off the torchlight in the dark. Rodrigo removed the bloodstained necklace and placed it around his own neck.

"Farewell, brother. We will meet again in the kingdom of heaven," he said as he stood up. Rodrigo retrieved the sword from the dead soldier and headed back through the gates of the Temple Mount.

44

ROMANS 12:19

Gone were the feelings of pain, guilt, and sorrow, and in their place arose a singular, intense focus that drove Rodrigo as he moved through the darkness toward the al-Aqsa Mosque. When he neared the entrance, the door suddenly opened, and he quickly moved into the shadows behind the pillars. Several of Peter the Hermit's men came out and began arguing among themselves outside the entrance as Rodrigo listened.

"He told us to stay here after we finished. We need to follow his orders!" one of the men said.

"Who knows how long they will be down there?" another argued. "They might be down there all night, hoarding the best plunder for themselves! Stay if you want. I am not going to wait around for them!" He turned and walked away into the darkness, heading toward the Dome of the Rock. The rest of the group quickly followed him, leaving the door to the mosque cracked open. When the sounds of their footsteps could no longer be heard, Rodrigo quietly crept forward out of the shadows and slipped inside the open door.

The interior of the mosque had become a grisly nightmare. Blood and the bodies of the Saracen dead were everywhere. Moving quickly, he stepped over the bodies and walked past huge columns and decorative archways that led toward a shrine at the far end. In the middle of the mosque, a large tapestry had been torn down and placed on the floor. On it was a hoard of plunder that had been looted from the building. Though the interior was illuminated by lamps, much of it remained dark and shadowed, allowing him to go unnoticed as he strode down the center of the mosque toward two soldiers standing near a doorway by the shrine, engaged in conversation.

Like a predator ambushing its prey, death leaped upon the soldiers before they knew what had happened. One lay facedown on the ground, blood gushing from a severed neck, as the other soldier lay on his back and breathed his last, staring up at Rodrigo, who now stood over him. Rodrigo walked to the door by the shrine and opened it, revealing a curved stone stairway descending downward.

Slowly, he walked down the curved stairway into the darkness, placing one hand against the wall to keep his bearings while keeping a firm grip on his sword with the other. The wall of the staircase was rough to the touch like the wall of a cave, and the stairs appeared to be carved out of the ground. Farther down the staircase, he could see a glow of light at the bottom. When Rodrigo reached the bottom of the stairs, he emerged into a cavern illuminated by several lamps. The cavern appeared to be another shrine, and there was an altar in one corner and a rug for praying, in the style of the Saracens.

Lying on the floor in the middle of the cavern were the bodies of two Saracen men. The hands of the men were bound behind their backs, and their throats had been slit. Rodrigo noticed that bruises covered the men's faces. *It seems these men were taken here and beaten before they were executed. Perhaps they were forced to divulge information.* He began to search the cavern, and in one corner he found tools and pickaxes with fresh piles of dirt nearby. Rodrigo grabbed one of the lamps and ventured farther into the corner of the cavern by the excavation. A small crevice had been exposed there, just wide enough for a man to fit through.

Rodrigo squeezed through the crevice and emerged into an open area. He held the lamp up high, revealing a massive chamber that seemed to be carved out of solid stone. The walls and ceiling of the square chamber were smooth and level and at least thirty feet in diameter. *What is this place?* Rodrigo wondered as he walked through the chamber. *It would have taken decades to carve this chamber out of solid rock.* The chamber was empty except for a pit in one section of the floor that had recently been exposed. Tools for excavation had been left on top of the piles of rock fragments surrounding the hole. Rodrigo held his lamp above the pit, revealing a ladder descending into the darkness below.

Rodrigo climbed down the long ladder and looked around when he reached the bottom. He could see a tunnel that stretched forward until it disappeared into the inky blackness. Rodrigo followed the tunnel, advancing farther and farther into the belly of the Temple Mount. What ancient secrets lay hidden there, he did not know, nor did he care. He had a different mission now, and that was all that mattered to him as he continued to move forward without fear or hesitation. The tunnel continued for quite some time, and Rodrigo noticed that the timbers that formed the structure of the tunnel were extremely old and rotten and looked as though they might collapse at any moment.

At last, the tunnel came to an end, and he could see an opening ahead. Rodrigo stepped through the opening into a large cavern. The broad cavern was man-made, and its walls and ceiling were rough and lined with a wooden framework like the tunnels behind him. In the middle of the cavern was single large timber that jutted up from the ground to the ceiling, supporting the entire framework. There were two tunnel openings within the cavern that appeared to have been recently excavated by the telltale tools that lined the walls near the openings. Rodrigo suddenly stopped and listened. He could hear voices coming from one of the tunnels. He placed the lamp upon the cavern floor, readied his sword, and waited.

The voices were growing louder as they approached, and soon he could see the wavering light from a lamp that someone was carrying down the tunnel, guiding their way. "We will need to bring more men when we return for the rest . . ." said one of the voices in the tunnel. Rodrigo gripped his sword tightly and his eyes narrowed as he recognized the voice of Peter the Hermit.

"We will need at least five, and I will have to choose them carefully," the other man said. Rodrigo clenched his teeth at the sound of Richard's voice as he waited in silence.

Two figures emerged from the tunnel into the cavern where Rodrigo was waiting on the opposite side, blocking the exit. Richard was first, holding a lamp and guiding their way, followed by Peter the Hermit, who was carrying a small sack. Both men immediately halted in their tracks and stared with wide eyes, dumbstruck at the menacing sight of the bloodied revenant standing before them whom they had believed was but a corpse on the streets of Jerusalem.

Recovering his composure after the initial shock, Richard quickly narrowed his eyes, and a scowl came over his face as he stepped forward into the cavern and drew his sword. "Rodrigo!" he shouted with a snarl. "You are a harder man to kill than I first believed!" He placed the lamp on the floor. "No matter. From what I can see, you appear to be half dead already. I will be glad to finish the job myself."

Peter the Hermit cowered fearfully behind Richard with wide eyes. His face had grown pale, as if it was Death's messenger who waited for him across the cavern. "Kill him! Kill him quickly!" Peter shouted, his voice trembling with fear.

Rodrigo stood up straight and walked toward the two with a seething intensity in his eyes. "Drop your sword, Richard," he ordered, holding his sword in front of him with both hands. "You cannot win."

A scornful laugh erupted from Richard as he began to circle the cavern while Peter the Hermit followed behind him. "I cannot win? Look at you!" Richard said loudly with a sneer. "You are bleeding from a dozen wounds, you have been severely beaten, and you look as though you can barely stand! You always were arrogant, Rodrigo, even now, facing death."

"I do not speak with arrogance, Richard, nor do I believe I can defeat you on my own," Rodrigo said as he maintained his guard and began circling away from Richard.

"Then who else is with you?" asked Richard, staring at Rodrigo. "Where is Geoffrey? If he is not by your side, then it can only mean one thing—that he is dead, and you are all alone," he said scornfully.

"Geoffrey is gone, and his blood is stained upon your hands. But you are wrong, for I am not alone!" Rodrigo answered. "The Lord God is on my side, and he is here, all around us," he said, looking about the cavern as if sensing the presence of the Holy Spirit. "He spared me this night from your murderous hand and brought me here to face you." He looked back at Richard.

Richard slowly nodded as he stopped in his tracks. "You have been extremely fortunate tonight, Rodrigo, but your good fortune is about to end, and you will soon join Geoffrey."

"I do not fear death. I welcome it," Rodrigo replied as he stopped, his eyes locked with Richard's. "For when it comes, I will enter God's kingdom. But you . . . you will *not*. Where you are going, there is only sadness and sorrow. When you die, you will be trapped in a place of eternal torment where there is only weeping and a gnashing of teeth, forever!"

"Kill him! Kill him!" Peter the Hermit shrieked as he cowered behind Richard.

With a furious roar, Richard suddenly lunged at Rodrigo, who parried the heavy blow as the clash of steel echoed throughout the underground chamber. The sounds of metal on metal were deafening as Richard continued his ferocious attack, and Rodrigo had to use every bit of his strength to defend against it.

"You are weakening, Rodrigo!" yelled Richard, momentarily pausing his attack.

Without warning, Rodrigo charged back at Richard, slashing at him with his sword, trying to mount a desperate offense with his ebbing strength, but to no avail. Richard easily parried the blows as he moved backward and countered the attack by slashing downward. The tip of his sword caught Rodrigo's forehead, slicing it open as it traveled downward across his right eye. A searing pain broke his concentration and momentarily blinded Rodrigo as he stumbled backward and came to a stop when his back hit the timber in the middle of the cavern. A deep rumbling echoed throughout the cavern and the tunnels when he struck the timber, and a small shower of dust and rock particles fell from the ceiling.

Rodrigo held his sword in one hand between himself and Richard as he placed his other hand over the wound across his face. He could no longer see out of his right eye, and blood from his forehead dripped between his fingers and down his forearm. His labored breaths came through clenched teeth, but he kept his back against the pillar as he stood his ground.

"You are finished, Rodrigo!" yelled Richard as he moved forward and swung his sword with both hands in a deadly blow aimed at Rodrigo's head. Rodrigo could see the flashing arc of the blade out the corner of his left eye. With no strength left to parry the attack, he bent his knees and lowered his head to dodge the blade as it sliced through the air. His footing gave way as he shifted his weight, causing him to fall to the ground, and Richard's sword missed its mark and bit deeply into the timber above Rodrigo.

The timber quivered under the heavy blow, and a loud noise like a thunderclap came from the ceiling above Richard's head. Richard looked up just as a heavy stone broke loose from the ceiling of the cavern and fell, striking him between the eyes, crushing his skull. Richard's lifeless body crumpled to the floor instantly, while the bloody boulder rolled away, revealing the mortal wound. Across the cavern, Peter the Hermit stood frozen with fear at what he had witnessed.

Dirt and dust particles continued to shower from the ceiling as Rodrigo used his sword as a crutch to help him get to his feet. Rodrigo mustered all of his strength and began to walk toward Peter the Hermit, dragging his sword behind him. As Rodrigo came closer, Peter's eyes grew even larger, and he shook with near panic as he threw the bag he was carrying at Rodrigo's feet. "Take it! Take it! There is much, much more! It is yours—just spare my life, I beg you!" he cried out in desperation.

"Do not mistake me for one of your men," Rodrigo said as he walked past the sack, keeping his one good eye focused on the cowering creature in front of him. "I care not for gold, nor treasure, nor any holy relics that may be here in this place." He stopped and stood over Peter the Hermit, who cringed in his presence.

"What is it . . . that you want then?" Peter asked with a trembling voice. "Anything. Anything! Whatever you want, just spare my life, I beg you."

"I seek only the will of God, that justice may be done in his name, and that wrong be made right," Rodrigo answered, staring down at the pathetic creature before him.

"Please, please do not kill me," Peter the Hermit begged, falling on his knees with his hands clasped together. "Wait, wait!" he said loudly. "You told me once that it is not your place to make final judgment upon me." He looked up at Rodrigo with watery eyes and lips quivering with fear.

Rodrigo stood in solemn silence for a moment before speaking. "You are right. It is not my place to judge you or anyone else, for only God can be our judge." He looked down at Peter. "This night, I have come to realize all the mistakes that I have made on this journey. Many times, I chose to take matters into my own hands, abandoning my trust in God and placing it in the hands of men. To my shame and dishonor, these choices resulted in the loss of thousands of innocent lives and the death of a brother." He paused for a moment. "Now I can clearly see that both of us are responsible for all of this pain and suffering. While you poisoned the hearts of men with your words, through my choices and actions, I helped bring those same men into the cities where innocents were slaughtered. We are both guilty of these crimes, and God shall be our judge." He cast his sword aside, sending it clattering across the cavern floor.

Reaching down to the excavation tools leaning against the wall beside the cowering figure, Rodrigo grabbed the handle of a large sledgehammer. Turning around, he dragged the heavy hammer toward the timber in the middle of the room. Peter the Hermit stared as Rodrigo stood before the timber and hefted the sledgehammer into the air.

"What . . . what are you doing?" Peter the Hermit cried out as he stared at Rodrigo.

Rodrigo looked at the timber with a renewed determination as he began to speak. "Any holy relics in this place belong to God, and God alone. Here they shall stay, along with you and I, forever." *Strengthen me one more time, oh Lord, that your will may be done.*

Straining with effort, Rodrigo swung the heavy hammer and struck the rotting timber, opening a large crack in its side. The entire cavern seemed to reverberate from the blow as rocks and dirt began to rain down amidst the groaning of the timbers throughout the chamber.

"Father Peter! Sir Richard! Are you there?" a voice called out in the tunnel at the far end of the cavern. Many voices and the sound of footsteps could be heard approaching them.

"I am here! I am here!" Peter the Hermit cried out. "Come quickly, before it is too late!" he shouted with panic-fueled desperation.

Rodrigo looked at Peter the Hermit with his one good eye as he lifted the hammer again with the last of his strength for one final swing. *"Deus vult!* God's will be done!"

Rodrigo swung the hammer with all his might just as several of Peter the Hermit's men entered the cavern. The rotting timber exploded under the impact, and with a thunderous roar, the roof of the cavern and the tunnels collapsed, and the weight of the earth came crashing down upon them.

45

DEEP IN THE REALM OF
THE DEAD

"Rodrigo! Rodrigo!" a voice called to him from above. "Come here, lad. It is time for your lesson."

The young boy ran into the castle from the courtyard and went up the stairs and down the hallway into his uncle's study. Rays of sunlight shone down from the windows above as his uncle waited for him at a table in the middle of the large room. The table was surrounded by shelves full of books and scrolls that chronicled the campaigns and strategies of the greatest generals in the battles of antiquity. Climbing onto a stool, the boy looked up at his uncle with a smile, eager for the day's lesson.

"What were you doing out there in the courtyard?" his uncle asked him as he looked down at the young Rodrigo.

"Practicing with my wooden sword," Rodrigo answered with a smile.

"Ahh . . . good boy, always practicing," his uncle replied, patting him on the head. "But you are eight years old now. It is time to start practicing with a *real* sword. The added weight will increase your strength." He made a fist and pointing to his forearm.

"Really, Uncle? Can I use your sword?" Rodrigo asked, beaming with excitement.

His uncle laughed. "No, no, lad. I will get you one you can use. In time, you will be able to use one like mine," he said as he opened a book on the table. "Let us begin our lesson for today. We have been studying the personal qualities of the great generals in history. Do you recall the qualities that we spoke about?"

"Yes, Uncle," Rodrigo replied. "We talked about courage, integrity, wisdom, and discipline."

"Good. Besides those important qualities, there is another one that all the great leaders and generals shared. The quality they shared was tenacity and perseverance in the face of difficulty—never giving up, even when things were at their darkest. All of them faced times in their lives when all seemed lost, yet they persevered and went on to great victories and accomplishments. I too have experienced great trials in my life, even exile by the king, but I never gave up, and neither should you." He smiled as he looked into Rodrigo's eyes.

Rodrigo listened intently, staring up at his uncle as he thought about what he had said.

"Remember, no matter what situation you find yourself in, be strong in your faith, never lose hope, and always give thanks to God," his uncle said, placing his hand on Rodrigo's head. "I am gone now, Rodrigo, but do not give up. One journey is over, but a new one is about to begin. Trust in the Lord, and he will guide your way." His uncle's voice seemed to fade away as he spoke.

"You are gone now? I do not understand. What journey, Uncle?" Rodrigo asked as he looked up at his uncle, puzzled by his words. He could no longer see his uncle's face, and the rays of sunlight in the study suddenly grew dim. The books and shelves around him began to blur, and then everything went black.

Rodrigo inhaled suddenly and opened his eye, but saw nothing except the darkness that surrounded him. He had been dreaming and had awakened inside a pitch-black tomb, deep beneath the earth in the realm of the dead. He put his hand to his forehead but could not see his hand before his face. The blood on his forehead was dry and crusted, and he could not open his right eye. His throat was dry and parched, and his entire body ached. He did not know how long he had lain unconscious.

He began to feel about him gingerly, trying to understand why he was still alive and had not been crushed when the cavern collapsed. Next to his shoulder, he felt the base of the timber he had struck that had caused the collapse. It extended up a few feet above him, and resting on top, he felt the elongated shape of a large boulder. As much as he could surmise, the base of the timber had prevented the boulder from crushing him and created a shield from the rest of the falling earth and debris. Slowly, he began moving his limbs, and although he was battered and bruised, he did not seem to have any grievous injuries or broken bones.

He felt around the small pocket of space he was in, but he appeared to be trapped and could not find a way out. There was one small opening near the ground, wide enough to reach through with his arm into another open space, but far too small for the rest of his body. He pushed against the stones and broken timbers around him with all his strength, but none would move. A moment of despair overtook him as he lay back down on the ground and breathed in the heavy, fetid air.

Why, Lord, have you spared me from the falling rocks, only to leave me trapped in the darkness, deep in the belly of the earth, to suffer a lingering death? he lamented. As he shifted his weight to the side, he felt something jab into his ribs. He grasped the object, which appeared to be part of the handle from the sledgehammer that must have broken during the collapse. The broken handle was a few feet long, but jagged at one end. *If I cannot move the stones around me, then perhaps I can dig into the ground and widen the opening large enough to move through.*

With renewed hope, Rodrigo turned over, clutching the broken handle in both hands, and began clawing and scratching into the earth below the small opening. The ground beneath him was hard and compact, but it was not solid stone and could be moved. Slowly and steadily, he began digging into the ground and widening the opening. His efforts were slow and laborious, as he had to constantly scoop and remove the earth after digging for a while. After digging for a long time, his muscles were burning, and his limbs began to cramp from exhaustion.

His progress was extremely slow, and he no longer had the strength to dig continuously. He lay on his back to rest and felt like giving up, but the words of his uncle came floating back to him. *I never gave up, and neither should you.* Rodrigo recalled the many times his uncle had faced overwhelming odds in battle only to emerge the victor. He thought about his own battles against seemingly impossible odds and the victorious outcomes. The thoughts renewed his strength and determination, and he began to dig again.

At last, the opening became wide enough for his entire body, and with effort, he managed to squeeze himself through. He had moved into another pocket of space, a bit larger than the last, and after searching, he found other openings and rocks that could be moved. The wooden framework in the cavern seemed to have prevented it from filling in completely, leaving open pockets of space within the collapsed cavern. Wherever he could create an opening by moving the rocks, he would continue forward, until at last he crawled into an open space large enough to stand.

As he searched the space for another opening, he felt something on the ground under his foot. He knelt down to examine the object and realized he had found the sack that Peter the Hermit had been carrying. He opened the sack and reached inside, to see if there was anything that could be useful to him. The small sack was mostly full of coins, which he discarded and left on the ground, but then he felt some other small objects, one of which made his heart leap. He pulled a finger-sized piece of stone from the sack and held it in his hand as he put the sack back on the ground.

He recalled the lamp that Richard had been carrying, and realized that what he held might be a piece of flint they had used to light the lamp. He removed his belt, and using the square metal edge of the belt buckle, he struck the stone, which immediately created sparks that illuminated the space for a brief second. He felt a great relief in being able to see his surroundings, even if only for an instant, and silently gave thanks to God for the blessing. He struck the stone several more times, and each time would look around quickly to see if there was anything else in the space around him.

Although he found nothing else on the ground, he spotted another opening large enough to move through after clearing away some rubble and debris. *The sack was lying near the tunnel opening that Richard and Peter emerged from. I must be getting close!* He put the flint and belt buckle back in the sack and began to work on one of the openings. When it was large enough to move through, he retrieved the sack and the broken handle and crawled through to the other side. Once through, he soon realized he was in a much larger space that was clear of rubble. He removed the flint and buckle from the sack and struck the flint to illuminate his surroundings. The flash of light revealed that he had finally made it to one of the tunnels and was at last free of the cavern. He fell to his knees and breathed a long sigh of relief. *Thank you, Lord, for delivering me from that tomb and leading me to this tunnel.*

An idea suddenly came to him, and he tore off a piece of his tunic and wrapped it around the broken handle, creating a crude torch. Using the flint and steel, he showered the frayed cloth with sparks until it began to smolder and finally caught fire. He replaced the items in the sack and stood up, holding the torch high. The flames of the torch flickered slightly, signaling the movement of air in the tunnel and a possible opening ahead. Picking up the sack and holding the torch before him to guide his way, Rodrigo began to walk down the tunnel. The flames of the torch did not last long, and when it went out, he would walk in the dark for a time before stopping to relight the torch.

Rodrigo continued to walk for what seemed like hours, tearing off bits of his tunic for the torch as he went, but less and less often to conserve what he had. Rodrigo was relieved that the tunnel did not dead end, nor did it seem affected by the cave-in. His tunic was nearly gone when at last he came to a stone staircase leading upward. He followed the steps until it leveled off, revealing a ladder going up. Looking up the ladder, Rodrigo breathed a sigh of relief and thanked God when he saw the twinkling of stars above through an opening. He climbed the ladder out of the pit and emerged into the stone structure of an ancient building surrounded by barren desert. Its crumbling façade lay cracked and exposed, staring into the sky.

Rodrigo turned and looked behind him. He could see the walls of Jerusalem in the distance. He had traveled far outside the city through an underground passageway, perhaps an escape tunnel used in ancient times. Rodrigo looked up at the stars in the peaceful night sky and pondered the choices before him. He could make his way back to Jerusalem, back to the slaughter and carnage that he had left behind, or he could walk farther into the barren desert, away from what he was sure to find and into the unknown. Again, his uncle's words came floating back to him: *One journey is over, and a new one is about to begin. Trust in the Lord, and he will guide your way.*

Rodrigo made his decision and began his new journey into the vast and barren desert ahead of him. Jerusalem grew smaller and smaller in the distance until it finally faded from sight. Rodrigo continued to walk, trudging slowly along the hills of the wide-open desert, a lone figure framed against the night sky. Rodrigo walked until he could walk no more. A new dawn had finally broken on the horizon, filling the sky with brilliant red and golden hues as it chased away the night. Rodrigo's throat felt as dry as the desert around him, and he was overcome with dizziness as he sank to his knees. His vision blurred, and he could no longer see where he was going. He saw figures floating in the air in front of him, and he seemed to be hallucinating. Then everything went dark, and he collapsed upon the ground.

46

A NEW JOURNEY

Rodrigo awoke to the sound of birds singing outside a window above the bed on which he lay. He reached up and touched a cloth bandage that covered his forehead and his right eye. He was in a room, on a bed, but he did not know where he was or how he had come to be there. He slowly moved his feet off the side of the bed and sat up. Many bandages covered the wounds over his body, and beside the bed on a small table was a bowl of water and a stone drinking cup. Rodrigo took the cup and dipped it into the bowl and drank his fill. The room was simple, and beside the small table there was a chair. Someone had been watching over him.

Leaning over to the window, just above the bed, Rodrigo peeked out. The lush green trees and plants outside seemed to be teeming with life. He turned when the door to the room creaked open to reveal an older woman, who stopped and stared at him for a moment, seemingly surprised to see him awake. She was dressed in a simple blue robe and wore a shawl on her head. She had a kind face and said something in a language he did not understand as she walked over to him.

"Do you speak Arabic or Frankish?" Rodrigo asked her in both languages as she came closer.

"I grew up in Jerusalem," she answered in Arabic, "so I speak Arabic as well as Aramaic. My name is Rebecca, and I have been taking care of you and tending to your wounds." She smiled as she sat down in the chair beside the bed. "Many did not think you were going to survive after we found you, but you are both young and strong, and I knew you would recover."

"Where am I, and how did I come to be here?" Rodrigo asked, looking about the room.

"We found you nearly two days ago, wandering alone in the desert, a half day's travel from Jerusalem. You had lost a lot of blood from your wounds, and you were delirious from lack of water. Had we not found you when we did, you surely would have died," she said as she looked at the bandages covering his face and his wounds.

"Who are you?" Rodrigo asked.

"We are a mixed band of Christian and Jewish refugees from Jerusalem. We have settled here on the banks of the Jordan River, for now," she said, glancing out the window above the bed.

"Thank you, Rebecca," Rodrigo replied humbly. "I am deeply in your debt. My name is Rodrigo. I am a knight and was part of the Crusader army."

"Your name is Rodrigo?" Rebecca asked with a smile as her eyes widened. "The young woman was correct after all." She paused, looking down for a moment in near disbelief. "When we found you, you were near death," she continued. "Several in our group wanted to leave you to die once they realized who you were from your armor. But there was a young Armenian woman from Antioch with us, who said she recognized you and knew who you were. She said that you had protected her and several others in a church while the city was being looted and plundered. She was the one who insisted that we take you with us and nurse you back to health."

Rodrigo sat speechless.

"It is mysterious, the people that God brings into our lives and how he works at times, is it not?" Rebecca asked.

Rodrigo remained silent for a few moments as he reflected deeply on what she had said. *Three times now, the Lord has allowed me to live when clearly I should have died.* "Indeed . . . it is," he said at last, nodding and looking back up at Rebecca. "The young Armenian woman from Antioch, is she still here? I would like to speak to her again and thank her for saving my life."

"No," Rebecca said, shaking her head. "She and some others have traveled on to Jericho. They hope to return to Jerusalem when it is safe to do so. We may also return when it is safe, but that remains to be seen. What about you? Will you return to Jerusalem and rejoin your army there?" she asked.

"My time as a Crusader is over," Rodrigo answered, looking down in contemplation. "I have begun a new journey. Once I am able and have the means, I will make my way back to my home in Europe."

"I see," Rebecca replied. "We have plenty of food we can give you to aid you in your journey, but not much else, I am afraid. Perhaps some of the coins you were carrying could help you purchase what you need."

"What do you mean?" Rodrigo asked.

"You do not remember?" she asked with a grin. "When we found you, you were carrying a sack that contained some items along with a few coins. It was not much, but enough to pay for your passage back to Europe, perhaps. It is underneath the bed, next to your armor and other belongings." She moved her chair back from the bed.

Rodrigo leaned over, reached under the bed, and pulled out the sack he had found in the tunnel beneath the Temple Mount. He opened it and reached in, pulling out some coins along with the piece of flint and his belt buckle." *God will provide,* he thought with a smile as he placed the items back into the sack and set it on the floor.

"I have kept all your belongings in my care until now. I hope it will help you on your journey home," Rebecca said with a smile.

"I do not know . . . how to thank you," Rodrigo stammered, at a loss for words.

"You do not have to thank me," Rebecca replied. "God brings people into our lives as part of his plan. We only need to respond when he does, and not question why."

"Yes," Rodrigo humbly agreed. "You are right."

"I will go now and let you rest," said Rebecca, rising from the chair. "In a while I will bring you some food. You will need to eat to regain your strength."

Rebecca walked to the door, leaving Rodrigo as he sat on the edge of the bed. "Oh yes, and do not forget the cup."

"The cup?" Rodrigo asked, confused. "What cup?"

"The drinking cup by the bed. I have been using it to give you water the past two days. The cup was in the sack also, so it belongs to you," Rebecca said as she turned and walked out the door.

Rodrigo reached over and picked up the drinking cup beside the bowl of water on the table. He turned it over in his hand as he looked at it. The small stone cup was dark red with lighter bands of color running through it, and it fit comfortably in the palm of his hand. It was highly polished and carved from a single piece of stone. The cup was simple, yet beautiful in appearance. Rodrigo stared at the cup in his hand with awe and wonder. *Could it be?*

EPILOGUE

Father Gregory walked briskly down the brightly lit and exquisitely ornate halls of the Lateran Basilica in Rome on his way to see Pope Paschal II. The news of the Crusader victory at Jerusalem was all over Europe and was widely celebrated as a triumph of the Catholic Church and its leaders. Though many of the senior clergy expressed horror at the brutal massacre of the population that had taken place after its capture, the bloody aftermath was but a footnote as the Christian world rejoiced that Jerusalem was now back under its control.

For the Saracens in the Holy Land, however, the brutality of the First Crusade would galvanize the many different factions into a unified force. The unintended consequence would trigger decades of holy war between the Saracens and Christians, and the latter would struggle to maintain a precarious grasp on Outremer, the name given to their lands beyond the sea. Pope Urban II, the man who had set all the events into motion, was not able to enjoy the fruits of his labors, however. He had passed away two weeks before the news of the Crusaders' victory at Jerusalem had reached the Lateran Basilica.

Father Gregory knocked at the door of Pope Paschal's chambers. "Yes, come in," a voice uttered from within.

Father Gregory opened the door and entered the Pope's chambers, carrying a sack. "I am sorry to disturb you, Your Holiness," he said meekly, bowing his head in deference.

"Yes? What is it?" the Pope asked, peering up from his desk.

"A knight recently came to the palace bearing this, Your Holiness," Father Gregory said, holding up the sack and placing it on the Pope's desk in front of him. "He said he had traveled here from Jerusalem and claimed to have been a member of something called the 'Knights of the Crucem Auream.' He gave a detailed account of his time in the Holy Land with the late Bishop Adhemar of Le Puy, so I believe he is telling the truth. He left this and said it belongs to you, Your Holiness." He bowed again before stepping back from the desk.

The Pope said nothing but grasped the end of the sack and turned it over, spilling the contents onto his desk. He stared at what he saw for a moment before turning to look up at Father Gregory with a frown of confusion and displeasure. There on his desk lay five necklaces with crosses made of gold.

✠

Rodrigo grasped the large iron ring attached to the double doors at the entrance of the building. He lifted it and let it fall with a thud as he stood at the door and waited. A few moments passed, and then one of the large wooden doors creaked open to reveal a young woman who peered at him from inside.

She was dressed in the black robes of a nun and wore a wooden cross about her neck. "Yes? Can I help you?" she asked. She stared at him for a moment, and there seemed to be a faint glow of recognition in her eyes, but the crease in her brow told him that she was not sure where it came from.

"Do you not recognize me, Sister Mary?" Rodrigo asked with a slight grin in the corner of his mouth. "Have I changed so much? Or perhaps it was simply too long ago?"

"You know my name," she answered with a smile. "You must have been here before. What is your name, sir?"

"My name is Sir Rodrigo Santos of Castile. Many years ago, I became lost on my way to Toulouse when I found this place. May I come in?" he asked.

"Yes, please come in," she said as she opened the door wide and stepped out of the way. "Please forgive me. Although you look familiar, I cannot recall your previous visit." He entered the monastery, and she closed the door behind him. "Will you be staying long? Can I offer you some food and water?" she asked.

"Please," Rodrigo said as he looked around. "I only wish to rest a short while as I journey back to my home in Castile."

Sister Mary turned and left, so he walked farther inward while he waited. The monastery of San Juan de la Peña had not changed since his last visit. The beautiful exterior of the buildings, carefully constructed to blend with the rocky cliffs, and the clean and spacious yet humble interior of the monastery had made a deep impression on him. *It is so different from the ostentatious palace of the Pope in Rome, the grandeur of the Hagia Sophia . . . or even the late Bishop Adhemar's tent,* he thought with a grin. *I truly feel at peace here and can feel God's presence in this place.* He walked to the front of the sanctuary, past the wooden pews and pulpit to a cross hanging on the wall and knelt before it in silent prayer. *Thank you, Lord, for bringing me safely back to this place and allowing me to complete my journey.*

He stood up and turned around to see Sister Mary waiting for him at the back of the sanctuary. "I have prepared some food and water for you. Please, follow me," she said.

She led Rodrigo to a small room near the back of the sanctuary. He entered the room and sat down at the table, which had a plate of food and some drinking water prepared for him. The simple room was the same as it was when he had first stayed there after discovering the monastery. "I have some other things I must do, but I will return to check on you when I am finished. There is a bucket of water and a cloth by the mattress if you wish to clean yourself," she said as she pointed to the bucket in the corner of the room.

"Thank you, Sister Mary. Your hospitality is greatly appreciated," Rodrigo said as Mary left the room and closed the door behind her. Rodrigo bowed his head in silent prayer before he broke the bread and began to eat. As he ate his meal, his thoughts began to drift backward to the conversation he'd had in the room with Marcellinus. Vividly, he recalled their heated debate that night and his struggle to believe that the Pope would lie to the masses. He remembered the fateful words Marcellinus had said as he left the room: *Place your trust in God and not in man. Men are fallible and may lead you astray, but God will always guide you and lead you to truth and salvation.* Rodrigo paused for a moment as he reflected again on what Marcellinus had said. *How true those words of wisdom proved to be.*

Rodrigo finished his meal and got up from the table. He moved his chair across the room and set it down in front of the bucket of water and grabbed the cloth to clean the dust of travel from his arms and face. He splashed the cool water onto his face and arms and used the cloth to clean himself. As he wrung the damp cloth back into the bucket, he looked down and noticed his reflection in the water. He ran his fingers down the long scar on his forehead and across his right eye as he stared at his reflection. He realized how far he had come since that night and how different he was at that moment.

A knock came at the door, followed by Sister Mary's voice. "May I come in?" she asked.

"Yes, please," Rodrigo replied. "I am finished with my meal."

The door to the room opened, and Mary came in holding something in her arms wrapped in a cloth. "I have prepared some food for you to take with you on your journey home. I will give it to you when you are ready to leave. Do you need anything else?" she asked.

"No, thank you," Rodrigo replied, looking up from his chair. "I will finish washing and then take my leave." Mary smiled and turned to exit the room when Rodrigo thought of something and suddenly spoke up. "Sister Mary, a man named Marcellinus was also here when I first stayed at the monastery. Do you remember him, and has he ever been back?" Rodrigo asked.

Sister Mary turned around, and her eyes and expression suddenly brightened at the mention of Marcellinus's name. "Yes, I remember now!" she exclaimed, her face beaming with a smile.

"When you first came here, he left you a horse and supplies to take with you on your journey to Toulouse."

"Yes, that is correct," Rodrigo replied, returning her smile. "The man, Marcellinus, has he returned to the monastery since then?"

"Yes, he has," she said, nodding. "Marcellinus has been back to the monastery several times over the years. He travels often and widely, as you may recall, and will rest here when he journeys through this part of Europe."

"I see," said Rodrigo. "Should he pass this way again, I would like to leave him a message and some coin, if I may, to repay him for the kindness that he showed to me many years ago."

"Of course. What message do you wish to leave for him?" Mary asked.

Rodrigo looked down for a moment and then looked up with a smile. "Please tell Marcellinus that Sir Rodrigo has returned from his journey to the Holy Land and has found what he was looking for. I would also like to extend an invitation for him to come and visit me in my homeland of Castile, where we may trade tales of our journeys and adventures."

"Oh, you have returned from the Holy Land?" Sister Mary exclaimed, her eyes widening with interest. "The news is all over Europe that Jerusalem has been reclaimed for the Christians. You must have quite a tale to tell."

"Yes, I do," Rodrigo replied. "Although I have been back in Europe for several months now. I traveled through the Italian Peninsula and visited Rome, and then I spent some time visiting an old friend of mine in Aquitaine before coming here. We spent time in the Holy Land together, and he is busy chronicling the adventures that we had." He smiled as he thought about his visit with Jean. "I was still in Aquitaine when I received word of my uncle's passing, so I am finally going home to pay my respects to the great man who raised me from the time I was a boy."

"What will you do then?" Mary asked.

"I don't know," Rodrigo said as he pondered her question. "Perhaps I will purchase some land and start a family. I believe my time as a soldier and a wandering knight has come to an end."

Mary smiled and nodded. "I will see you out when you leave," she said as she turned and walked out the door. When he was finished, Rodrigo got up and walked into the sanctuary, where Mary was waiting for him with the bundle of food.

"Thank you, Sister," said Rodrigo as he took the bundle from her. "Before I go, I would like to give something to this monastery to show my appreciation for the kindness and generosity that it has shown me and all who enter this place." He reached into a small pouch on his belt and withdrew the stone cup.

Mary took the polished stone cup from Rodrigo and turned it over in her hands. She smiled broadly at the gesture, and her eyes gleamed with delight as she admired the cup. "It is beautiful!" she exclaimed. "Thank you, and this is exactly what we need. The cup we used for the sacrament broke not long ago, so we have been using an old wooden one. This cup will be perfect! Where did it come from?" she asked, still staring at it.

"It came from Jerusalem," Rodrigo answered.

"Jerusalem?" she asked with wide eyes. "Well, perhaps this is the very cup that Christ used during the Last Supper," she said with a smile.

"Perhaps it is," said Rodrigo, returning her smile as he walked to the door of the monastery. "God be with you," he said. Then, turning, he walked through the door and exited the monastery.

"God be with you as well on your journey home!" she called out as she watched him from the doorway.

Rodrigo mounted his horse and filled his lungs with the crisp mountain air. He took one final glance back at Mary standing at the front of the monastery, then spurred his horse down the pathway as he headed home.

THE END

LEADERS OF THE FIRST CRUSADE

PRINCE BOHEMOND
OF TARANTO

COUNT RAYMOND
OF TOULOUSE

TANCRED OF HAUTEVILLE

BISHOP ADHEMAR
OF LE PUY

DUKE GODFREY
OF BOUILLON

BALDWIN OF
BOULOGNE

DUKE ROBERT
OF NORMANDY

COUNT ROBERT
OF FLANDERS

EMPEROR ALEXIOS I
KOMNENOS

PETER THE HERMIT

COUNT HUGH
OF VERMANDOIS

COUNT STEPHEN
OF BLOIS

TIMELINE OF THE FIRST CRUSADE

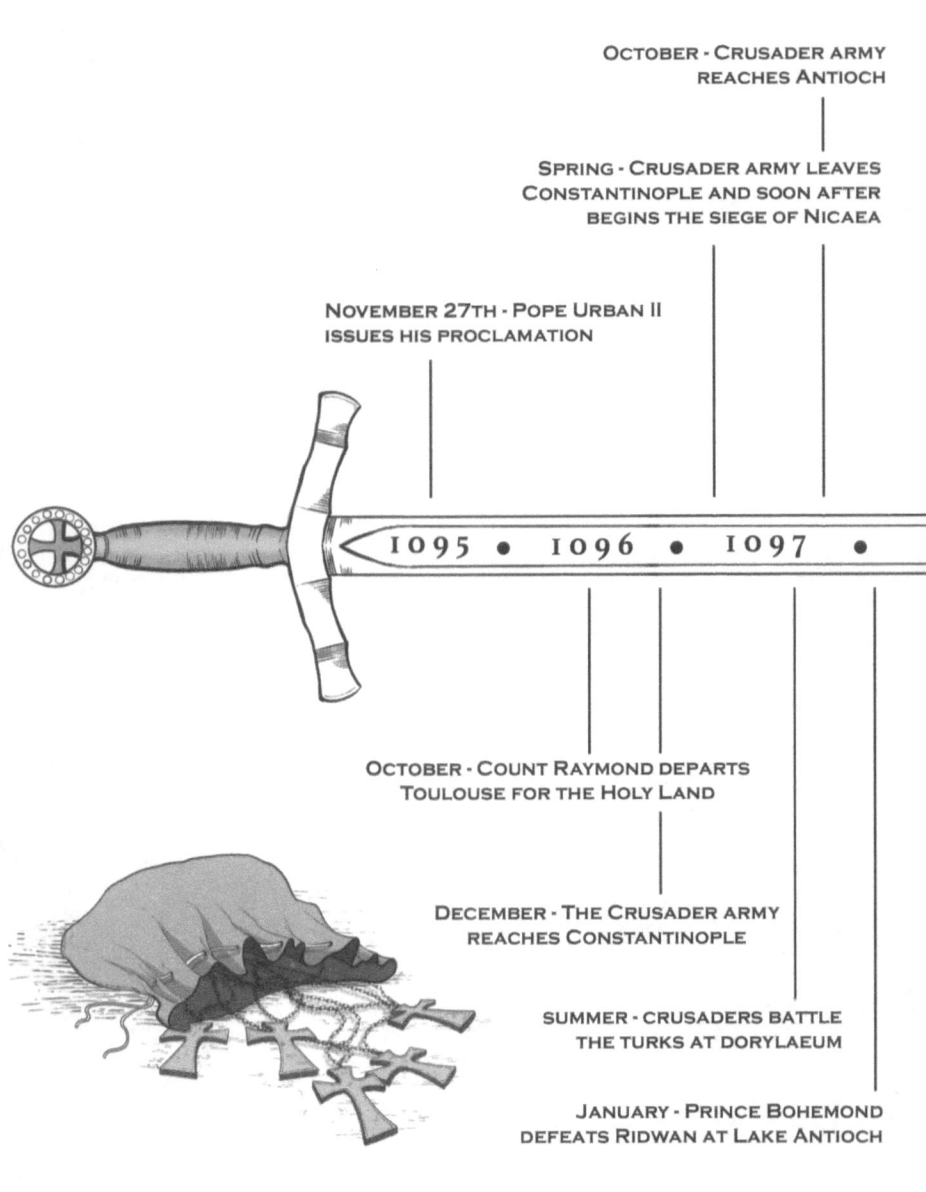

OCTOBER · CRUSADER ARMY
REACHES ANTIOCH

SPRING · CRUSADER ARMY LEAVES
CONSTANTINOPLE AND SOON AFTER
BEGINS THE SIEGE OF NICAEA

NOVEMBER 27TH · POPE URBAN II
ISSUES HIS PROCLAMATION

1095 • 1096 • 1097 •

OCTOBER · COUNT RAYMOND DEPARTS
TOULOUSE FOR THE HOLY LAND

DECEMBER · THE CRUSADER ARMY
REACHES CONSTANTINOPLE

SUMMER · CRUSADERS BATTLE
THE TURKS AT DORYLAEUM

JANUARY · PRINCE BOHEMOND
DEFEATS RIDWAN AT LAKE ANTIOCH

JUNE 17TH · GEONESE SAILORS ARRIVE
IN JAFFA BRINGING SUPPLIES AND TIMBER
FOR SIEGE TOWERS

DECEMBER 11TH · MA'ARRA FALLS
TO THE CRUSADERS

JUNE 7TH · CRUSADERS FINALLY REACH
JERUSALEM

JUNE 28TH · THE CRUSADERS DEFEAT
KERBOGAH'S ARMY

1098   •   1099

JANUARY 13TH · CRUSADER ARMY DEPARTS
ANTIOCH FOR JERUSALEM

JULY 15TH · JERUSALEM FALLS TO THE
CRUSADERS AND IS ONCE AGAIN IN
CHRISTIAN HANDS

JUNE 2ND · ANTIOCH FALLS TO THE
CRUSANDERS

APRIL 20TH · PETER BARTHOLOMEW DIES
FROM WOUNDS SUSTAINED IN THE ORDEAL
BY FIRE

AUTHOR'S NOTE AND ACKNOWLEDGEMENTS

March 2003. I was part of the US Army 3rd Infantry Division, camped out for weeks in the Kuwaiti desert along the border of Iraq. It was there that the story of *Deus Vult, A Tale of the First Crusade*, first entered my imagination. While biding our time in that vast, desert wasteland, something unusual happened.

I was staring into that endless, desolate horizon one evening, allowing my thoughts to wander, when I began to envision a medieval knight, trudging alone through the desert under the light of the full moon. The vision itself seemed entirely random, yet I felt compelled to know more. When I asked myself why he was there, and what was he looking for, the story began to take shape in my mind.

During the time I spent in Iraq after the war, the beginning and ending of the story became clear, and the plot began to take shape, but I was still unsure of the exact context and setting in which it should be told. It was not until 2008, after returning from my second tour of duty in Afghanistan, that I finally had my answer. I had regaled a friend with my vision for the tale and told him that I was contemplating using the Crusades as the setting for the story. Upon hearing this, my friend advised me that it would be best if I based it on a historical account of the Crusades and avoid something completely fictional.

Although I've always loved studying history, especially historical battles, I assumed that research on the Crusades for the story's setting was going to be a bit dry and tedious. In retrospect, I could not have been more wrong. The First Crusade has been one of the most fascinating adventures I have ever encountered. Full of epic battles, magnificent triumphs, horrible atrocities, and larger-than-life characters, it proved to be the ideal setting for the story that I wanted to write for so long.

The framework of the story that I created in my mind fit perfectly within the setting of the historical events of the First Crusade. I had found the piece of the puzzle that finally completed the picture. The story, once entwined within the historical context, metamorphosized into something larger, broader, and more complex, yet still retained the soul of the original tale, which is one man's search for truth and trust in God.

Although my main character and his journey are fictional, I did my best to stay true to the historical timeline of events along with those leaders who took part in the First Crusade. I sincerely hope that you enjoyed the tale as much as I enjoyed researching and writing it, as you followed the Crusaders on their incredible journey to the Holy Land to reclaim the city of Jerusalem.

Finally, I would like to thank all those who helped me to realize my long-awaited goal of bringing this tale to light: Aaron Redfern, the editor, for all his work and help revising the novel. Nic Ferrari, for his fantastic illustrations on the cover and interior. Cathy Helms, the graphic designer, for all her help in formatting the novel, finalizing the cover jacket and guiding me through the process. Thank you all very much.

James Lopez

www.ingramcontent.com/pod-product-compliance
Lightning Source LLC
Chambersburg PA
CBHW020328180626
46812CB00001B/97